MURDER

IS NO

LAUGHING MATTER

A Maisy Malone Mystery

Starring

Roscoe Arbuckle & Minta Durfee

LARRY NAMES

EAGAN HILL PUBLISHING

USA

To the Memory of Beloved Brother

Gerald Wayne Names
(1943-2015)

Whose Greatness in Life
Can Best Be Measured
by the Success of His Children

An eerie hiss and a sudden rush of cold air in her face stirred Mary Sullivan from her peaceful slumber at the plush Hotel Alexandria an hour before dawn on the third Tuesday of March. She opened her eyes, blinked them twice, and saw her sickly younger sister Marjorie floating beside her bed. Absolute darkness surrounded them, making the younger sibling appear to be glowing and translucent. Seeing her sister in this manner startled the older girl.

Marjorie giggled. "There's no need to react this way, Mare. I was in your dream, and now I'm here beside you."

Mary heard herself speaking softly. "Yes, Marjie, I know. I saw you. Why are you out of bed so early? It's still dark outside."

"It's not dark where I am, Mare."

"Where are you?"

"Tell Ma I tried to wake her, too." Marjorie turned and looked over her right shoulder. She turned back to her sister. "There's Pa. He wants me to go with him, but I can't. Not yet. Not until the truth is known."

Mary sat up in her bed and watched Marjorie fade into the dark. Then more cold air filled the room.

A flash of memory of the dream she had been having before her sister's appearance struck Mary. In it, she saw a shadow standing beside Marjorie as she lay asleep in her bed in the adjoining room. Then that unnatural hissing awakened her. She gave it a thought. It sounded like someone exhaling a deep breath. The sigh of death!

In the next instant, Mary threw back the blanket, sprang from the bed, and raced across the room to the closed door to Marjorie's room. She grabbed the knob, turned it, pulled hard, but the door would not open. Fearing the worst, she beat on the door with both fists as she bawled. "Marjie, wake up! Wake up, Marjie!" Tears erupted from her eyes.

Cordelia Sullivan heard her firstborn's cries from her room that adjoined Marjorie's on the other side. Her maternal instincts instantly launched her into action. Off went the blanket. Bare feet to the floor. Across the room to the other door to Marjorie's room. The knob turned, but the door would not open. Her Irish brogue cried out. "Marjorie? Are you all right, Darlin'?" She paused, hoping for an answer. "Marjorie?" Still no sounds from her daughter's room; only the muffled pounding on the door to her oldest daughter's room and Mary's frantic cries. "Blessed Mary, Mother of God, please don't take my child. Please! Not yet! Not now, dear Lord! Oh, please!" She drooped to her knees, now leaning against the door and crying copious tears.

Mary Sullivan threw herself against the door separating her room from her sister's. Nothing happened. She tried a second time with the same result. Then a third, and finally the jamb holding the lock broke, giving Mary access to her sister's room.

Immediately, Mary went to Marjorie's side. She gasped because her sister did not appear to be breathing. "Marjie! Wake up, Marjie!" She shook her sibling's left shoulder. No reaction. "Oh, Marjie, please wake up. Please." Mary tears flowed all the more. "Oh, Marjie." She wept more until she recognized her mother was beyond the other door, also weeping. "Oh, Ma!" She went to the door, unlocked it, and opened it. Her mother was sitting on the floor. "Oh, Ma!" Mary fell on her knees and embraced her mother. "Oh, Ma! Marjie's gone."

Other guests on the same floor of the Alexandria were awakened by the disturbance in the three adjoining rooms occupied by Mrs. Sullivan and her two daughters. Several of them stepped into the hall, each of them in pajamas covered by a bathrobe or housecoat. They whispered to their neighbors, all of them curious about the sickly young woman in suite 510. A few stayed in their rooms and called the front desk to report the commotion; a few demanded someone do something about it immediately.

Within five minutes, the hotel's general manager, Mr. Samuel J. Whitmore, formerly of West Virginia, was called in his residence and informed of the turmoil on the fifth floor.

"I'm sorry to disturb you, Mr. Whitmore."

Whitmore's Tidewater accent was still very evident. "That's quite all right, Gladys. Is there a problem?"

"Yes, sir, there is, on the fifth floor."

"Which suite is it?"

"Five-ten, sir. The one with the sick girl from Seattle."

"Yes, I remember Miss Sullivan and her mother and sister. Call Dr. Newmark and Mrs. Reikel immediately. And tell them it's urgent."

Whitmore wasted no time dressing, simply donning a maroon bathrobe over his sky-blue pajamas and sliding his feet into black felt slippers. He gave his hair a quick brushing, then hurried to the elevator, pushed the call button, then waited impatiently for the car to arrive, which it did a minute later.

The elevator door opened to reveal the night operator, a swarthy middle-aged man with coal black hair in the same style of uniform worn by the hotel's bellboys.

Whitmore entered the car in three quick steps. "Take me up to five, José. And don't stop for anyone."

"Yes, sir, Mr. Whitmore." The elevator operator closed the door and put the lift into motion. In less than a minute, he stopped the car on the fifth floor and opened the door for Whitmore.

"Good work, José. Now go back down to the third floor and wait for Dr. Newmark and Mrs. Reikel. They should be waiting for you."

"Yes, sir, Mr. Whitmore."

The hotel general manager exited the elevator to a sight he feared: guests milling about in the hall, all muttering and whispering to each other about what might be happening in suite 510. As he weaved his way through them, he nodded politely and held up his hands to urge them to step back and let him pass. He spoke to them in a confident voice. "I don't know any more than all of you. So, please let me by."

All complied, although some grudgingly.

Whitmore arrived at suite 510. He knocked on the door.

Still quite distraught, Mary spoke softly to her mother. "I'll get it, Ma. It's probably someone wanting to know what's going on here."

Mrs. Sullivan held out her right hand toward her daughter. "Tell them to call for a doctor, Mary. She might not be gone. She could still be alive. We can't know for certain, can we?"

"Yes, Ma, I'll call for a doctor, but let me answer the door first."

"Yes, you answer the door, Mary. I'll stay right here."

Mary left her mother in the doorway between Marjorie's room and her mother's. She went to the door, unlocked it, and opened it, expecting to see the night manager but surprise held her tongue when the visitor turned out to be someone else.

"Miss Sullivan, I'm Samuel Whitmore, the hotel's general manager.

I understand there might be something wrong in this room. This is your sister's room, isn't it?"

"Yes, sir, it is."

"Is she all right? I've ordered our desk clerk to call Dr. Newmark and his nurse, just in case she needs medical assistance."

"I can't be certain, Mr. Whitmore. I'm not a doctor or a nurse, but I do believe my sister Marjorie has passed over to the other side."

Whitmore stiffened. "I'm so sorry to hear that, Miss Sullivan." He looked past Mary. "Is your mother awake?"

"Yes, sir, she is."

"May I come inside?"

Mary stepped away from the doorway.

The hotel general manager entered the room and immediately saw Cordelia Sullivan sitting on the floor in the doorway to her room. He went to her and knelt in front of her. "Mrs. Sullivan, I'm Samuel Whitmore, general manager of the hotel. I'm very sorry about your daughter, Mrs. Sullivan. Just in case she hasn't really passed over, I've had my desk clerk call for Dr. Newmark to examine her. He should be here very soon."

"It's too late, Mr. Whitmore. My Marjorie is gone, passed over to the other side to be with her father." She crossed herself. "May he rest in peace as well." She crossed herself again. "I don't know what I'll be doing now. It's only Mary and me now."

"Don't worry yourself about the hotel bill, Mrs. Sullivan. I'll see that it's taken off the books. Stay here at the Alexandria as long as you need to tend to any personal business regarding your daughter."

"Thank you, Mr. Whitmore. That's very kind of you."

"Would you like me to assist you to your feet, Mrs. Sullivan?"

"Yes, sir. That's so gracious of you."

Whitmore moved behind the mother and put his hands under her armpits. He lifted as she pushed herself upward with her legs.

Now on her feet, she faced him. "I would like to see my Marjie now, if you don't mind, Mr. Whitmore."

"Certainly, Mrs. Sullivan. Allow me to assist you." He put his left arm around her shoulders and held her right forearm gently with his right hand.

The lady wobbled as she walked to her daughter's bed.

More controlled than her mother, Mary moved deliberately to her sister's bedside to join her mother there.

Tears rippled down Mrs. Sullivan's cheeks again. "Oh, my darlin'

Marjorie." She burst out crying again and buried her face in the general manager's chest.

Mary put her right arm around her mother's waist and grasped her left arm with her left hand. Her tears were less copious as she laid her head on Cordelia's left shoulder.

A new round of subdued chatter came from the hall. Then a man with a commanding German accent silenced most of it. "Let me pass. I'm Dr. Newmark. There's a seriously ill girl in there. So, let me pass."

Two women followed the physician. Mrs. Anna Reikel, a part-time nurse for the hotel, and Elisabet Reikel, a part-time chambermaid and novice nurse being trained by Mrs. Reikel, her aunt by marriage.

Wearing a gray overcoat and carrying his black medical bag, Dr. Newmark burst into the room with his nurse and her understudy directly behind him. "Where is she? Where is my patient?"

Whitmore, Mary, and Mrs. Sullivan shifted their eyes to the doctor and his nurse. Words eluded them.

Newmark went to the other side of the bed. He took one quick look at Marjorie, placed his valise on the bed, opened it, withdrew his stethoscope, inserted the earpieces into his ears, took hold of the single resonator, and placed it on the young woman's chest in the vicinity of her heart. A few seconds, seeming to be minutes, ticked by. In another instant, he released the acoustic medical device, placed his hands on her chest, and pushed as hard as he could several times. Then he repeated his initial examination with the stethoscope. More drawn-out seconds dragged by. Hearing nothing again, he straightened, took hold of the blanket's edge with both hands and pulled it gently over Marjorie's ashen face.

The doctor turned to the deceased's mother. "I'm sorry, Cordelia. There is nothing I can do. Marjorie is gone."

Mother and daughter erupted into tears once more as they held each other, their heads over the other's right shoulder.

Just then, Mrs. Reikel, the hotel nurse, stepped up to the bed. She took one look at Cordelia and Mary and realized what had happened. She moved quickly to comfort them.

Newmark and Whitmore stepped back from the bed. Both shook their heads slowly. Neither could do anything more to console the two women.

Detective Sergeant James Edward Browning came into work that same morning still depressed and saddened over the murder of his good friend and fellow lawman, federal undercover detective Thomas White. Word had it that White was shot and clubbed to death early Sunday morning in Little Tokio by members of the *Kumiyaei*, a Japanese criminal organization similar to the Italian Black Hand. White had infiltrated the gang and found plenty of evidence on some of its members, enough to send some of them to prison. Being Japanese on his mother's side, he felt it was his duty to ferret out these criminals for the good of the decent law-abiding Japanese in Los Angeles. Now he was dead.

Browning greeted his fellow officers with nods and waves of his hands but not with many words as he passed through the station to find a seat for the morning briefing. Before entering the room, his partner Bill Ingram stopped him.

"Captain Murray wants to see us in his office right way, Ed."

"Really? What's up, Bill?"

"Beats me. George Willett told me to find you and get up there as soon as you came in."

"And he didn't say anything about why the captain wants to see us in office first thing this morning?"

Ingram shook his head. "Not a word. I pressed him, and all he had to say was, 'I don't know nothing, Bill. Just that he wants to see the two of you in his office right away.' That's it. Now you know as much as I do."

"Okay then. I suppose we best be getting up there."

The two detectives entered the outer office of Captain Alexander W. Murray, captain of LAPD detectives. They were greeted by Jim Crehan, a Canadian immigrant and rookie officer temporarily serving as Murray's receptionist. He smiled at them. "Good morning, detectives.

The captain said for both of you to go right in as soon as you arrived."

Ingram hesitated. "You first, Ed."

"Why should I go first?"

"You make a better impression than I do. If it's bad news, then the captain won't bark so loud if you go first."

Browning nodded. "Good point." He led the way into Murray's office.

The captain was seated behind his desk when the two detectives entered his office. He looked up at them, his expression dark and a bit foreboding. "Sit down, detectives."

Browning and Ingram sat in the two straight-back chairs facing the captain's desk.

Murray put away the paperwork he had been going over. Then he folded his hands in front of him and rested his forearms on the desk. "I've got a special assignment for you two today."

Being the senior man, Browning spoke for both men. "A special assignment, sir?"

"Yes. There's been another death at the Hotel Alexandria just this morning, and I want the two of you go over there and speak to the hotel's general manager Sam Whitmore and the attending doctor. His name is Newmark. He pronounced a young woman dead in her bed at five-thirty this morning. Apparently, she came here from Seattle for her health. Her mother and older sister came with her. This is pretty much routine stuff, but we have to be on the record that we at least looked into it. Just interview Whitmore, the doctor, the mother, and the sister. Take Nellie Sharpe with you so she can take notes. The young woman who died apparently passed in her sleep from whatever it was that made her and her mother and sister come down here. These people have money, which is why they're staying at the Alexandria. Just so you know, this is coming from the chief. He'd go over personally, and so would I, but both of us have too much on our plates this morning. And just so you know, the chief ordered me to put the two of you on this detail. It's what you get for the way you handled the Quinn murder case last month."

Browning and Ingram glanced sideways at each other for a whole second before returning their focus on the captain again.

"Any questions, gentlemen?"

Both detectives shook their heads and spoke simultaneously. "No, sir. No questions."

"Good. When you're done at the hotel, report back here. The

chief wants to know right away if there's any reason to suspect foul play with this young woman's death. Now get out of here. I've got more important things to do."

Browning and Ingram left without saying another word. They kept their silence all the way to the stairway, then down to the first floor, where they stopped and faced each other.

Ingram started their undertone conversation. "Why do you think the captain is mad at me? I had nothing to do with the Quinn case."

"I don't think that has anything to do with it, Bill."

"Then tell me why he picked us for this dog and pony show."

"It's my guess he picked us because Tom White was our friend."

"I don't get it, Ed. I thought it was all hands-on deck to catch Tom's killers."

Browning nodded in agreement. "It is, but maybe the captain figures it would be better for us if we had a little diversion from all that. I'm still grieving over Tom's death. We all are. Nealy is just as upset as I am. She spent most of yesterday with Tom's widow. Poor Lillian, she doesn't know whether to cry or scream, she hurts so bad."

"That makes sense, Ed. The part about this assignment being a diversion, I mean. I'll believe that if you do."

"It's what I want to believe, Bill. So, let's get our butts over to the Alexandria and do our jobs."

The Alexandria was the classiest hotel in all of Los Angeles and possibly west of the Mississippi River as well. It opened on Lincoln's birthday in 1906 on the southwest corner of South Spring and West 5th Streets, the first five-star luxury hotel in the city. In a mere seven years, it had already hosted several notable persons; among them President William Howard Taft who gave a speech to a ballroom full of local dignitaries. Architect John B. Parkinson designed the initial structure to be a ten-story upscale hotel. Five years later a twelve-story addition was built on the south side of the original building.

Browning, Ingram, and police stenographer Nellie Sharpe decided to walk the four city blocks from the Central Police Station to the Hotel Alexandria.

"Say, Ed, how long have you and Nealy been living here in Los Angeles?"

"Seven years. Why?"

"Just wondering. I haven't been here that long, so I've never been in the Alexandria before. Have you?"

Browning chuckled. "Never stepped foot in there. Don't think I can afford it. Too rich for my tastes from what I hear. Not that I wouldn't like to take Nealy there sometime, it's just too fancy and too costly from what I hear. Someone told me they charge fifteen cents for a bottle of Coca-Cola."

"Then this will be a first for both of us. Do you think they might have a policeman's discount in their restaurant?"

"Which one?"

Ingram's feet stuttered a step. "Do you mean it's got more than one restaurant?"

"I've been told it's got at least three."

"Three? This I got to see."

Nellie Sharpe walked behind the two detectives. "One of them is a ballroom where they hold special events."

Ingram looked over his shoulder. "How do you know this? Have you been there?"

"I wish. One of the girls in the office told me about it. I also heard a lot of motion picture people dine there in the evening, especially on Saturdays."

As they crossed Spring Street, Browning exerted his leadership. "There it is, so let's remember we're going in there on police business, not as tourists from out of town."

Ingram acquiesced. "Of course, Ed, but let's not forget to ask about a policeman's discount."

Nellie spoke again. "Is he always like this, Ed?"

"Not always. Just when he's hungry. Skip breakfast again, Bill?"

"How'd you figure that out?"

"I'm a detective, Bill. It's my job to know these things."

They entered the hotel through the Fifth Street entrance. Five feet inside they halted to admire the lavish lobby, finished in Italian and Egyptian marbles, with ceilings in tones of ivory, gold, and green, while twelve stately pillars in polished brown marble rose from the mosaic floor.

Ingram made the first remark. "Will you get a load of this place? Is everything in here made out of marble?"

Browning answered him. "Looks like it, doesn't it?"

Staring at the giant columns that lined both sides of the lobby, Miss Sharpe had her say. "Looks like a palace, doesn't it?"

Ingram gazed downward. "Look at that floor, will you? Pure white tile and … what are those? Flying carpets?"

Nellie knew the answer. "No, they're Persian rugs."

Bill stared at her. "Persian rugs? How do you know this stuff, Sharpy?"

"Magazines and catalogs and the occasional illustrated book. I read a lot."

Browning smiled at Ingram. "Nealy does the same thing." He looked straight ahead. "There's the front desk. Let's go to work." He moved two steps before Ingram and the stenographer followed him.

The thirtyish desk clerk forced his face to appear amiable. "Good morning, folks. May I help you?"

Browning displayed his badge that was pinned to the inside of his lapel. "I'm Detective Sergeant Ed Browning, and this is my partner and our stenographer. We understand there was a death in this hotel earlier this morning. Is that right?"

The clerk lowered his voice and spoke with less exuberance in an obvious educated Texas accent. "Yes, Detective, you are quite correct."

"We'd like to speak about it with whoever is in charge here. I believe his name is Whitmore. Is he around?"

"Yes, sir. You are quite correct. His name is Mr. Whitmore. If you'll wait right here, I'll ring his office and tell him you would like to speak with him." The clerk picked up a telephone from beneath the counter. He thumbed the switch hook twice, then waited for a response. "Loretta? Mr. Lewis here. Please connect me to Mr. Whitmore's office." He paused to hear her polite response. Then another few seconds passed until the hotel's manager answered. "Mr. Whitmore? Preston Lewis here. There are two police detectives and a lady here to speak to you about the unfortunate incident earlier this morning." He paused to listen to Whitmore talk. Then, "Yes, I'll do that right away, sir. I'll have a bellboy show them the way to your office, sir." He replaced the telephone on the shelf beneath the counter. "Mr. Whitmore will speak to you in his office, Detective. I'll have a bellboy show you the way." He banged a bell on the counter, and almost by magic, a teenager in uniform appeared at the desk. "Freddie, please show these folks to Mr. Whitmore's office."

"Yes, sir, Mr. Lewis." He turned to Browning. "If you'll please come with me, folks." Freddie led his charges to Whitmore's office up on the Mezzanine level of the hotel.

As soon as the detectives and Miss Sharpe walked out of sight, Mr. Lewis placed another telephone call. "Hello, this is Mr. Lewis at the front desk. Mr. Whitmore would like Dr. Newmark to come to his office immediately. The police are here, and he would like the doctor to speak with them about the death of Miss Sullivan this morning." The desk clerk paused. Then, "Very good. I'll inform Mr. Whitmore that the doctor will come to Mr. Whitmore's office as soon as he is finished with the patient in his examining room."

Freddie the bellboy knocked on the general manager's office door, then waited to be summoned.

"Come in."

Freddie opened the door just enough for him to poke his head inside. "The police are here to speak with you, Mr. Whitmore."

"Show them in, Freddie."

The bellhop opened the door wider, then stepped aside to allow Miss Sharpe to enter ahead of the two detectives.

Whitmore stood up from his office chair as a courtesy to the lady. As soon as all three visitors were standing in front of his desk, the general manager looked past them at his employee. "Thank you, Freddie. That will be all. You may return to your duties now. Please close the door behind you."

The bellboy nodded, then executed Whitmore's orders.

"Good morning, officers, miss. I am Samuel J. Whitmore, general manager of the Alexandria. Forgive me for only having two chairs for guests in my office. I can have another brought in immediately, if you wish."

Browning smiled at Whitmore, recognizing the voice of a fellow Southerner. He replied in his own Georgia accent. "That's quite all right, Mr. Whitmore. My partner won't mind standing, will you, Bill?"

"I'm good, Ed."

"Mr. Whitmore, I am Detective Sergeant Edward Browning. This gentleman with me is my partner Detective Sergeant Bill Ingram. And this young lady is one of our police stenographers Miss Nellie Sharpe. She's here to record our conversation for our superiors in the police department."

The general manager smiled with all the cavalier heritage he had known since infancy. "My pleasure to meet you gentlemen and you Miss Sharpe. Won't you please be seated?"

Nellie sat first. "Thank you, sir." She removed her notepad and a pencil from her purse.

Browning took the other chair.

Ingram remained in place.

Whitmore started the serious conversation. "I assume you are here in regards to the most sad parting of Miss Marjorie Sullivan earlier this morning."

"Yes, sir, that's quite correct."

"Where would you like me to begin, Detective Browning?"

"Perhaps with some background on the deceased woman and her family. Our understanding is they came here to Los Angeles for the young lady's health."

"Yes, that's quite correct, Detective. Mrs. Sullivan and daughters checked into the Alexandria just two weeks ago. March fifth, I believe. I can have the desk clerk verify the exact date, if you wish."

"We can ask Mr. Lewis about that when we go downstairs again."

"Certainly. I'll give the word to all our employees to give you their complete co-operation, sir."

"Thank you, Mr. Whitmore. That's much appreciated, sir, and quite refreshing, too. Most of our investigations meet with resistance by those we question."

"I assure you, Detective, that you won't find that here at the Hotel Alexandria. Our employees are trained to give our guests and visitors every possible courtesy while they are here on the premises. If any one of them gives you the slightest hesitation to answer your questions, please make their behavior known to me and I will deal with that person with the utmost haste."

"Thank you, Mr. Whitmore."

Someone knocked on the door.

"Ah, that is most likely Dr. Newmark, our house physician. I sent for him the moment I was informed that you detectives were here in the building." He looked past the visitors. "Come in!"

Browning, Ingram, and Sharpe turned their faces to the door. It opened, revealing the presence of the good doctor.

"I came as fast as I could, Sam. Are these people the police?"

"Yes, they are, Philip. Allow me to introduce them." The general manager started with Nellie. "This young lady is Miss Sharpe. She is a police stenographer. She's here to take notes on our conversations with these gentlemen." He extended his left hand toward Browning. "This gentleman is Detective Sergeant Edward Browning. And standing with you is Detective Sergeant Bill Ingram."

"How do you do, miss, detectives?"

Noting the physician spoke with a slight German accent, Browning spoke for his associates. "Pleased to meet you, sir."

Whitmore spoke. "Dr. Newmark pronounced Miss Sullivan deceased, Detective Browning."

"Yes, I came as quickly as I could. I was much too late to save her. She had been dead for at least twenty or thirty minutes."

"I understand she was ill already when she and her mother and sister arrived here in Los Angeles. Is that true, Doctor?"

"Yes, it is. She was suffering from heart failure, and she died from it when it was induced by phthisis."

Browning's face scrunched up. "*This-iz*, Doctor? I'm not familiar with that ailment."

"Phthisis is pulmonary tuberculosis, Detective Browning." The physician assumed a professorial manner. "There is no cure for it with modern medicine, but some patients do manage to overcome it with rest and lots of sunshine. It was Mrs. Sullivan's hope that her daughter's health would improve here in Los Angeles over time by her exposure to our warmer, dryer weather. Sadly, they came here too late for Miss Sullivan to benefit from our climate."

"I see."

Newmark turned the table on Browning. "Tell me, Detective, why is the police department interested in this death when there were no policeman coming here to ask about the other two deaths we had here recently at the Alexandria?"

"Other two deaths, Doctor? We only know of this one. But you say there were two others recently?"

Whitmore answered for the doctor. "Yes, that is correct, sir. Mrs. America L. Lee, an eccentric and very wealthy club woman here in Los Angeles, and Mr. George W. Clarke, vice-president of the Homer Laughlin China Pottery Company of East Liverpool, Ohio. Mrs. Lee died of heart failure, while Mr. Clarke died from a cerebral hemorrhage. Like Miss Sullivan, Mr. Clarke had come to Los Angeles for his health. Unlike Miss Sullivan, Mrs. Lee and Mr. Clarke were quite advanced in age, both over sixty years."

"That's probably why our department failed to express any interest in their deaths. Typical natural causes for people their age."

Newmark picked up the conversation again. "Miss Sullivan, on the other hand, Detective, although being quite young, she did have a previous illness that caused her health to slowly deteriorate gradually since childhood. Mrs. Sullivan, Marjorie's mother, told me her daughter had contracted a case of scarlet fever as a child that resulted in the gradual deterioration of her heart."

Browning nodded. "Now, Doctor, you said Miss Sullivan died from an attack of this disease called phthisis."

"Yes, that's correct, Detective. It's a slow ailment that gradually fills the lungs with fluid, which then causes the weakened heart to give out from an inability to beat due to the pressure from the fluid buildup in the lungs. I'm certain the coroner will agree with my diagnosis, sir."

"Where is the body now?"

Whitmore interjected an answer. "Two gentlemen from the Bresee mortuary will be coming for it quite soon, I expect. In the meantime, Miss Sullivan's remains stay in her bed."

"We would like to see the body, if we may, Mr. Whitmore. And speak to the mother and sister as well."

"Certainly, Detective Browning. I will take you up there myself."

Newmark asked a final question. "Are you through with me, Detective? I have patients waiting for me in my office."

"Yes, Doctor, for the moment. If we need to speak to you any further, we'll call on you in your office. It's on the ground floor, isn't it?"

"Yes, sir, it is."

"Good day then."

Newmark bowed slightly, turned around, opened the door, and left the office.

Whitmore remained seated for the moment. "Detectives, I should tell you that it has been my experience in the hotel business that deaths, accidents, other unusual events in the hotel … come in cycles of three." He made a slight chuckle. "This is not a superstition, as some might expect. No, sir. The course of events has proven over and over again to be a psychological fact. When I was notified of Miss Sullivan's passing, all of the suspense I had been feeling after the deaths of Mrs. Lee and Mr. Clarke came to an immediate end." A sigh of relief issued through his lips. "I must tell you folks that I was able to relax and cease the worry over who would be the third to die in this cycle of three. In a place this large, where nearly every day our guest list numbers more than a thousand persons of all ages, which is not to mention the hundreds of employees we have here, there is always the certainty of the appearance of death, and I have gotten entirely over the dread fear that hotel men in the past have shown when anything of this sort comes up. It is a statistical impossibility for a hotel to avoid such things, and the traveling public no more thinks of death, ghosts, and other phenomena of this character in a superstitious light." Grinning,

Whitmore slapped his desk with the palm of his hand. "With that said, shall we go up to the fifth floor and call on the deceased young woman's family members?" He rose from his chair.

Browning, Ingram, and Miss Sharpe remained silent all the way to Mrs. Sullivan's suite on the fifth floor. Not so Whitmore. To Ingram's delight, the general manager invited the three of them to remain in the hotel for lunch, at the hotel's expense, of course.

The lead detective pulled out his pocket watch to check the time. "It's only eighteen minutes after nine. I'm certain we can wrap this up in the next hour or so, Mr. Whitmore. So, we probably won't be here for lunch."

"We start serving lunch at eleven o'clock, Detective Browning. Why don't you take a tour of the hotel to fill the time? You've seen the lobby. Wait until you see our dining rooms and ballrooms. We have a few suites that are unoccupied. I think you will find them charming."

Ingram begged like a child wanting ice cream. "Come on, Ed. Let's hang around for the tour and then lunch. Be a sport for once."

Browning looked at the stenographer. "What do you say, Nellie? Shall we accept Mr. Whitmore's invitation?"

"I'd like to take the tour, Ed. And lunch here would certainly be better than any of the restaurants near the station. So, I say yes."

Browning faced the man in charge. "We accept, Mr. Whitmore."

"Delightful, Detective, delightful! When you finish talking with Mrs. Sullivan and her daughter Mary, please come back to my office and I'll have one of our people show you folks around the Alexandria. I'm certain you will enjoy the tour and lunch in whichever restaurant you choose."

When they arrived at suite 510, the general manager knocked on the door. Nearly a minute passed before it opened a quarter of the way.

Mary Sullivan held the doorknob. "Mr. Whitmore."

"I'm sorry to trouble you and your mother, Miss Sullivan, but these folks with me are from the police department. They have come talk to you and your mother about Miss Marjorie. Would this be a good time for you'all?"

"Certainly, Mr. Whitmore." Mary opened the door wider as she stepped back and to the side. "Please come in."

Mrs. Sullivan sat primly on the settee with her legs crossed at her ankles, her knees pointed sideways, and her hands clasped on her lap. Crying over her daughter's death had made her eyes red and her complexion sallow. She tried to smile, but the hurt in her heart simply would not allow it.

Whitmore cleared his throat. "Madam, these folks are from the Los Angeles Police Department. Allow me to introduce them." He did so, one-by-one. They dipped their heads politely when their names were spoken by the hotel general manager. Then he revealed their purpose for being there. "They wish to express their condolences, and then they would like to speak to you'all about your daughter's passing."

Mrs. Sullivan looked directly at Browning. "There's no need for you to console me, Detective. No words can ease my pain for now. So, let's get on with your real purpose in being here."

"Yes, madam, we completely understand your position. So, I'll get to the point of us being here."

Right then, Mary Sullivan sat down beside her mother. "I assume you will have some questions for me as well Detective. Am I correct in feeling so?"

"Yes, Miss Sullivan."

Mrs. Sullivan looked at Nellie Sharpe. "My dear, why don't you sit in the armchair? I think you will find it much more convenient for you to record our conversation."

"Thank you, Mrs. Sullivan." The stenographer took the mother's advice and seated herself in the armchair that matched the shape and the upholstery of the settee.

Mrs. Sullivan gestured to Browning by extending her right-hand palm up and fingers together. "Please begin, Detective."

"Thank you, madam. It's the department's policy to ascertain the cause of each death in our city. If your daughter had passed away in her own home, we would accept the judgement of the attending physician or the coroner's verdict without question. We have already spoken with Dr. Newmark and received his decision on your daughter's cause of death, but we haven't heard the coroner's verdict yet. We assume he will examine her at the mortuary. Until then, we have to ask you some questions about your daughter's illness."

"Didn't you ask Dr. Newmark about her illness?"

"No, we didn't. We only asked him about the cause of her death. We felt it would be more appropriate to ask you those questions because you have known her since birth."

"Yes, of course. Please continue then."

"How long has your daughter been ill, Mrs. Sullivan?"

"Since she was a child. She contracted scarlet fever when she was five years old. At first, we were uncertain what her illness was. We thought it might be nothing more than a cold, but then the symptoms for scarlet fever began appearing. Our doctor back in New York treated her with the latest methods and medications. Her father and I thought we might lose her then, but she gradually improved and recovered from the fever. However, she suffered some heart damage just like Beth in Louisa May Alcott's novel *Little Women*. She would catch a mild cold, and her breathing would become very labored. Then our doctor back in New York suggested we move out to Seattle because the winters were milder. She seemed to get better in Seattle, but this winter she took a turn for the worse. Our doctor there in Seattle suggested that we move to a drier climate, so we came down here. We've been here for the past two weeks. Marjorie seemed to be getting better under Dr. Newmark's care. When we went to bed last night, she was feeling the best she has felt since she was a little girl. I went to bed thinking we might move down here permanently. But that's all gone now. We'll be taking her home to Seattle once the mortician here is done with her."

"Which of you found your daughter this morning?"

Mary didn't hesitate. "I did. A strange noise awakened me, and then the most peculiar thing happened before my very eyes. I saw my sister Marjie dressed in her confirmation dress standing by my bed. She said she tried to wake Ma, but when she couldn't, she came to me to say she had been in my dream. I said I knew that because I had seen her there. Then I asked her why she was out of bed so early because it was still dark outside. Then she said it wasn't dark where she was. I asked her where she was, but she didn't say. She only said for me to tell Ma she tried to wake her. Then she looked over her shoulder and said Pa was waiting for her to go with him, but she said she couldn't go with him until the truth is known. Then she faded out of sight and was gone. Then I recalled the dream I'd just had, and it shook me."

Deeply absorbed by Mary's story, Browning leaned forward and fixed his eyes on her eyes. "What was it that shook you, Miss Sullivan?"

"I saw a shadow standing beside Marjie as she lay in her bed fast asleep. Then I heard a hissing noise … like a train engine blowing out steam but not as loud. That's when I got out of my bed and went to see if Marjie was all right, only to find the door between our rooms was locked."

Mrs. Sullivan interjected a corroborating statement. "The door between my room and Marjie's was also locked."

"Did either of you lock your door to Miss Marjorie's room before retiring last night?"

Mary shook her head. "I know I didn't lock mine, but I can't say whether Marjie locked it."

The mother spoke. "I never lock the door to Marjie's room."

"Did she usually lock the door when she retired for the night?"

Mary twisted her head slightly to the left and glared at Browning. "What are you trying to say, Detective Browning? That my dear sister locked the door to do ... to do what, sir?"

Cordelia Sullivan gasped and covered her mouth for a second with the fingers of her right hand. Then her face reddened with anger. "Are you implying my daughter did some sort of harm to herself?"

Browning shook his head. "No, Mrs. Sullivan, I'm not implying anything. I need to get all the facts. I'm just doing my job."

"And your job is to insinuate that my daughter took her own life?"

"No, Mrs. Sullivan. I'm just trying to get all the facts here." He focused on Mary again. "I'll ask you again, Miss Sullivan. Did your sister ... or you ... usually lock the door when you retired for the night?"

"I can't say whether Marjie ever did, Detective Browning, but I know for certain that I never did in the entire time we've been staying in this hotel."

Mrs. Sullivan rose to her feet. "Detective Browning, I believe we are finished with you people. Please leave now."

"I'm sorry if I've upset you and your daughter, Mrs. Sullivan."

"I don't care a tinker's damn for your apology, Detective. Now please leave." She aimed a scowl at the hotel's boss. "Mr. Whitmore, would you kindly escort these people out of my suite immediately?"

"Yes, madam. Of course." He waved his right hand at the door. "If you would please."

Nellie Sharpe stood up from the chair she had been occupying and walked to the door. Browning and Ingram followed her. Ingram turned the doorknob and opened the door for his associates. They exited, and he followed them into the hall.

Whitmore came out next, closing the door behind him. "I'm sorry about all that, Detective. I had no idea they would react in such an unpleasant manner."

"It's all right, Mr. Whitmore. I've been treated much worse than that in my career as an officer of the law. How about you, Bill? Have you been treated worse?"

Ingram nodded. "Oh, yeah."

"And you, Nellie?"

"Only by my own mother."

Browning faced the hotel's general manager with a slight smile. "A prerequisite for being a police detective, Mr. Whitmore, is to have a skin as tough as an alligator's hide. If you don't, you'll never get the truth out of a suspect."

Whitmore winced. "You don't suspect Mrs. Sullivan of having done something terrible to her own daughter, do you, sir?"

"What's that line from Shakespeare's *Hamlet*, Mr. Whitmore? 'The lady doth protest too much, methinks.' Or something like that." The lead detective shrugged. "I'm just doing my job, Mr. Whitmore. Just doing my job."

Despite disappointed protests by his partner Bill Ingram and police stenographer Nellie Sharpe, Ed Browning decided to forego a tour of the Hotel Alexandria and the free lunch offered by general manager Sam Whitmore. "We're going back to the station to report to Captain Murray just like he ordered us to do."

Ingram groused. "Do we have to, Ed? I mean, we might never get another chance to get a free lunch at a place as swanky as this joint."

Nellie piled on her support. "He's right, Ed. This may be the only chance we'll ever get to eat here."

"If you two will quit whining and get your feet moving toward the door, I'll make you this deal. I'll bring you here for lunch one day next week or the week after for sure. Fair enough?"

Nellie looked at Ingram. He nodded at her, then she turned back to Browning. "Only if you bring Nealy with us. I want someone I can have a little girl talk with, while you two are babbling on about the next boxing match or some other sports thing."

Browning laughed. "You've got a deal, Nellie. I'll bring Nealy. For now, let's get out of here."

As soon as the trio exited the Alexandria and were headed back to Central Police Station, Ingram elbowed his partner gently. "Okay, Ed, what's the real deal about us leaving here without taking the tour and getting a free lunch?"

"Ever been down to the harbor at San Pedro on a really hot summer day, Bill."

"I did once. Since then, I try to stay away from there when the weather's sweltering. Why do you ask that?"

"Why do you stay away on a scorching summer day?"

"Because the harbor stinks to high heaven."

"And why does it stink to high heaven?"

Nellie took a quick step forward to get between the two detectives. "I know what you're getting at, Ed. The harbor smells bad because of all the dead fish floating on the water."

"Right you are, Miss Sharpe. And back there in the Alexandria …" He paused.

Together, Nellie and Bill grinned and chimed. "You … smelled something fishy."

Browning chuckled. "You two catch on quick."

When the detectives and stenographer arrived back at the station, they went straight to Captain Murray's office on the second floor, where the captain's assistant Jim Crehan greeted them. "The captain didn't expect you back so soon, Sergeant Browning. He's got Detective Sergeant John Fitzgerald in his office right now. Apparently, he's being honored again for capturing an armed pickpocket last week."

Ingram nodded. "He should be. First, that big Irishman, and Jim Hosick and Sam Browne save all our tails back in November when they wrestled that maniac with the dynamite tied to him to the ground and kept him from blowing up the whole station, and now he takes down a pickpocket carrying a loaded thirty-eight revolver. The man's a real hero in my book. He looks danger straight in the eye, then risks his own life to save others."

"You'd do the same, Bill, if you were in his shoes at times like those."

"I wouldn't be so sure about that, Ed. I'm pretty much a coward at the sight of a gun."

Browning chuckled. "Well, we'll see about that, if a circumstance of do-or-die ever arises for the two of us. My gut tells me you'll hold your ground."

"You think too highly of me, Ed."

Browning patted his partner on his back. "I know a brave man when I see one, old pal."

Just then, the door to Captain Murray's office opened wide, and big Jack Fitzgerald joined them. "Say, boys. We missed you at the morning briefing. Captain said you two were on a special assignment."

Ingram nodded. "That's right, Jack. There was another death at the Hotel Alexandria early this morning, so the captain sent us over to see if there was anything … unusual … about it."

"And did you find anything unusual there?"

Ingram started to answer. "Ed seems to—" A nudge from Browning's hip stopped his partner from saying anything more.

Browning smiled at Fitzgerald. "A young woman died of natural causes. Nothing out of the ordinary, Jack. Nothing like you usually deal with. By the way, congratulations on corralling that pickpocket the other day."

"Thank you, Ed. It wasn't anything you boys wouldn't have done under the same circumstances."

"You're too modest, Jack."

"Me? Modest? You're too kind, Ed. Well, I've got to be going. Duty calls, you know."

"Don't we."

Fitzgerald left the office.

Crehan spoke up. "The captain will see you now, Sergeant."

Browning waved Nellie Sharpe to go in ahead of Ingram and him.

Murray rose from his desk upon seeing Nellie. "I'm glad you came with them, Miss Sharpe. Just in case we need to verify anything, I'm sure you'll have it down in your notes. Please sit down."

"Thank you, Captain." She sat.

"You, too, Ed. Bill, why don't you grab that chair by the wall over there and sit with Miss Sharpe and Ed?"

"Yes, sir." Ingram did as Murray said.

"Now tell me, Ed. How did your investigation go? Pretty routine, I should think, right?"

"Well, Captain, there was more to it than I expected."

Murray jerked back in his padded office chair. "More than you expected? How so?"

"Well, Captain, we interviewed the hotel's general manager first. Mr. Samuel Whitmore, that's his name. He was more than gracious and quite helpful at first."

"At first?"

"Yes, sir. He offered to give us the run of the place and even escorted us up to the suite where the young woman died early this morning. But before that, he called in the doctor who declared the girl to have died from phthisis."

"What was that you just said?"

"Phthisis. It's a Greek word for pulmonary tuberculosis, a disease where the lungs fill up with fluid and pressure the heart so much that it can't beat right and eventually causes death."

"Yes, I've heard of that, but I've never heard it called ... what was it you called it?"

"Phthisis. It's spelled p-h-t-h-i-s-i-s. But it's pronounced *this-is*."

"Okay, go on."

"The doctor's name was Newmark. From the sound of him, I'd say he came to America from Germany. Not that that means anything. We all have ancestors who came from somewhere else, don't we?"

"Go on."

"Well, Captain, Dr. Newmark told us how the young woman and her mother and sister came down here from Seattle because of her poor health. Her doctor up there said the drier climate of Los Angeles would be better for her. The mother said her daughter seemed to be getting better under Dr. Newmark's care, but she still died in the night. Then the sister told us that she heard a strange noise in the night and got up to check on her sister. However, the door between their rooms was locked. When I asked if the door being locked was something the dead girl usually did at night, the sister became quite offended and so did the mother. Then the mother told us to leave. So, we did."

"Were you implying that the dead girl took her own life?"

"It was a possibility, Captain."

"Well, you can scratch that idea right now. Just a half hour ago, the chief called down to me and told me an investigation into the young lady's death was unnecessary. Assistant Coroner Seager went over to Bresee's mortuary and examined the corpse, and he came up with the same diagnosis as Dr. Newmark did. The young woman died from heart failure caused by pulmonary tuberculosis. So, Ed, this case is closed. Miss Sharpe, write up your notes right away and see that two copies are sent to my office as soon as you're finished." He focused on Browning. "Good work, Ed. Now you and Bill take the rest of the day off. Go have lunch at the Alexandria, if you like. That general manager at the Alexandria called the chief and said the hotel would pick up the bill, if the three of you and anybody else you wish to bring along want to go there for lunch today or tomorrow. So, the three of you can take tomorrow off and go have lunch at the Alexandria on the hotel's dime."

Browning forced a smile. "Thank you, Captain. I'll bring my wife along and maybe a friend or two, if you don't mind."

"Certainly, Ed. You do that. Same for you, Bill. And you, too, Miss Sharpe."

Ingram and Nellie smiled and nodded. "Thank you, Captain."

"Now, if you don't mind, I have other work to do."

Without another word, the investigating team left the room, then straight through the outer officer and out to the hall. Halfway down the stairway Browning sniffed the air. "Smell that?"

Ingram sniffed. "Sure do."

Nellie spoke for the two men. "All the way from San Pedro."

By the end of the day, Assistant County Coroner Howard Seager had officially declared Marjorie Sullivan's demise to be by natural causes. Only three problems with his findings: Detective Sergeant Ed Browning, Detective Sergeant Bill Ingram, and stenographer Nellie Sharpe. They had no contrary proof; just Browning's hunch, which Ingram and Sharpe shared.

Over supper that evening, Browning told his wife all about it. "I'm telling you, Darling, that young woman didn't die from heart failure brought on by … phthisis. I don't care what that German doctor says or what the coroner's office findings are. I think someone murdered her. And for all I know that same someone may have killed those other two people who died in that hotel earlier this month. You better believe I'll be looking into their deaths starting first thing in the morning. And I don't care what that Tidewater twit hotel general manager Samuel J. Whitmore says about death, accidents, or any other unusual events happening in cycles of three. When Bill and Nellie Sharpe and I talked about it back at the station, we agreed that the way he joked about these so-called cycles of three was rather disturbing. Bill called it right on the money. He said, 'Murder is no laughing matter.' That's hitting the nail right on the head."

"But, Dear, didn't you say Captain Murray closed the door on any further investigating of this case?"

Browning frowned. "Yes, he did."

"Then why go on about it, if the case is closed?"

The detective slumped. "The mother said her daughter was getting better. She said Marjorie was feeling the best she had since coming down here to Los Angeles. What if she was getting better, Nealy? What if she was getting better and some monster took her life in the middle of the night?"

Nealy reached across the table and squeezed her husband's hand with all her heart. "Oh, Edward."

"That young woman deserves justice, Nealy."

"Of course, she does, Dearest."

Browning squeezed his wife's hand. "I don't know how I'm going to get it for her." His head drooped to his chest. "You know, maybe I'm feeling this way about Marjorie Sullivan because we all lost a good friend in Tom White." He paused. "His funeral is Friday." He focused on Nealy's caring eyes. "You don't have to go, if you don't want to, Darling."

"Of course, I'll go. I'm your wife, remember?"

He perked up with a smile. "Yes, I remember you're my wife, which is why we're going out to lunch tomorrow. Captain Murray gave Bill and me and Nellie Sharpe a reward for checking into Marjorie Sullivan's death. He said the chief got a call from the general manager of the Alexandria offering the three of us and whoever we wanted to bring along to have lunch at the hotel. Are you up for that, Darling?"

"That will be wonderful, Dear."

Browning frowned again. "Yes, it will be, if I can keep my mind off Tom's funeral and the passing of that poor girl. I just know someone murdered her in the night, but who and how? I'm really at a loss, Nealy." He squeezed her hand once more. "I'm just not sure what I can do about it."

She pulled on his hand. "I've got an idea. If you and Bill can't investigate her death rightfully anymore, perhaps … you *know* … someone … who can."

A bit perplexed he leaned away from her. "What are you talking about? Someone who can inves—" He paused in mid-word. "Wait a minute. You're not …"

"Yes, I am. Why don't you call her right now?"

"But I thought she was making a movie in Venice this week."

"She was, but she said she'd only be there until today. She might be home by now. So, why don't you call her apartment at the Roosevelt and find out? If she's not there, then try calling Mabel. She should know if Maisy is home yet." She paused. "What have you got to lose, Edward?"

Browning snapped his fingers. "Just my job, if the chief ever finds out I asked Maisy Malone to investigate this girl's death after the chief closed the case."

Maisy Malone arrived home after dark that evening. She was more than exhausted after three days of shooting with a new director who was totally unfamiliar with her and the rest of the Keystone Studio actors. The experience dragged everything out of her. For the first time in the six months she had been employed at Mack Sennett's funnies factory she really understood that making a comedy—even a short one like *Cohen's Outing*—was a lot of work. For the first time, she understood the work Mabel Normand and all the actors and actresses at Keystone put into their films. Such appreciation left an indelible mark on her work ethic.

Then the telephone on her coffee table jangled, making her feel a bit worse. She debated silently whether to answer it or ignore it and drop face down on her bed and fall into a deep sleep.

"Answer it, Malone. Whoever it is will only call back later and wake you, if you don't. Then you'll really be irritated with yourself ... and the caller."

She pulled off her coat and dropped it on the sofa. In the next instant, she snatched her hat from her head and gave it a fling at the coat. Bull's-eye! A kick with the left foot and the shoe tumbled into the air higher than her head, then off with the right shoe before the left one hit the floor. A smile induced by the memory of when she tried out as a chorus girl made her feel a little better. "I still got it." She grabbed the stick of the telephone, brought it to her face with the transmitter up to her lips, then lifted the receiver close to her head.

"This better be important, whoever you are."

The caller chuckled on the other end. "Maisy, it's Ed Browning."

Her mood brightened. "Oh, hello, Eddie. What prompts you to call? Nelly finally wise up and kick your tail to the curb?"

"No, not yet Malone. She's still got just enough pity left in her heart to keep me around a while longer."

"Well, handsome, if she ever does throw you out, you can always bunk here."

"I don't think I'll ever get that desperate, Maise."

Maisy giggled. "She's close by, isn't she?"

"Right beside me ... as always."

"Lucky girl."

Nealy laughed. "Don't I know it, Maisy."

"So, what prompted you to call, Eddie? Got another murder you need my help with?"

"I swear, Malone. You are psychic. That's exactly why I called."

Maisy stiffened. "You're kidding, right?"

"Not this time, lady."

She flopped onto the sofa. "I still don't believe you, Eddie." She took a second to consider that he might be telling her the truth. Then a new thought struck her. "You're not talking about that fellow who was murdered over the weekend, are you?"

"No, not Tom White's murder. We're pretty sure we know who killed Tom. We just don't have enough evidence yet to make an arrest. No, not Tom's murder. I'm talking about the death of a young woman in her hotel room early this morning. Assistant Coroner Howard Seager has already determined her death was by natural causes. Her doctor said the same thing."

"And you suspect she was murdered?"

"It's more like a hunch on my part, Maise, but I'm not the only one who thinks the coroner's office could be wrong again. So do my partner Bill Ingram and Nellie Sharpe who was along with Bill and me when we interviewed the doctor on the case, the hotel's general manager, and the dead woman's mother and sister. We got the feeling that at least one of the four of them was holding back on something. The hotel's general manager, a fellow by the name of Samuel J. Whitmore, he even wrote off her death as the third one in a cycle of three."

Maisy leaned forward; her interest intrigued now. "A cycle of three? I've heard about that superstition. Bad things allegedly come in threes, especially death."

"That's what Whitmore said."

"So, you're telling me there were two other deaths in this same hotel recently?"

"Yes, a woman and a man. I checked on them in the newspapers. A woman named America L. Lee succumbed to heart failure in her hotel suite on March second, and a man named George W. Clarke died from a stroke in his room the next night. The lady was sixty-two, and the man was fifty-six. The hotel's general manager described them as being quite elderly."

"Fifty-six doesn't sound all that *elderly* to me."

"And neither does sixty-three to me."

Maisy wanted another clarification. "And you say all three of these people died in the middle of the night?"

"That's correct."

"That does sound suspicious." She paused for another thought. "And you say the assistant coroner declared all three deaths were from natural causes?"

"Right again, Maise."

"That does sound a little suspicious to me, too. But why aren't you and Bill digging further into this latest death?"

Browning heaved a long sigh before responding. "Captain Murray told us the chief said the case was closed when we reported back to him this morning."

"Did you tell him about your hunch that this girl was murdered?"

Browning's tone turned sour. "When the captain tells us a case is closed, then it's closed and that's that. And that's why I'm calling you. I'd like you to investigate it for us. Do you think you might be interested in doing that for me? Or at least, doing it for young Marjorie Sullivan?"

"Who's that?"

"The girl who died last night."

Maisy nodded to herself before answering his question. "I don't know, Eddie. It looks like I might be getting more roles at the studio now, so I might not have the time to do any sleuthing. Let me sleep on it, and I'll get back to you tomorrow. Okay?"

"Tomorrow would be good, but just one more little detail I left out."

"What's that?"

"The captain told us the chief had already closed the case ... *before* ... we got back to the station with our report."

"That sounds very suspicious to me, Eddie."

"That's what Bill and Nellie and I said. So, how about you joining us for lunch tomorrow and we can talk some more about it?"

"Lunch? Where at?"

"At the Hotel Alexandria."

Maisy perked up. "Really? Who's buying?"

"The hotel."

"The hotel? Now isn't that interesting."

The smile on Browning's face could be imagined over the phone. "Isn't it?"

"It sure is, Eddie. Just tell me the time, and I'll be there." Another idea popped into her tired brain. "Can I bring Mabel?"

"Be my guest. Bring anybody you want. The hotel's paying for it."

A tinge of joy raised Maisy's spirits. "Okay, where do we meet and at what time?"

Mabel Normand answered the telephone in her apartment at the

28

Ingraham Hotel. Annoyance tainted her greeting. "Hello."

"Mabes, it's me."

Mabel felt a little lilt in her mood. "Are you home?"

"Yes, the shoot in Venice went well. In three days, I was in front of the camera for a whole two hours. The rest of the time I sat around in my bathing suit with a beach towel over my shoulders. When the film is cut and spliced, I'll probably be in it for a whole half a minute, if that long. It's a good thing Vince DeDonatis was there the whole time."

"Why's that?"

"He protected me from all the beach wolves who kept coming around me when I was wearing nothing but my swimsuit. He even pulled his gun once to chase off some fellow with a foreign accent. A teenage boy kept doing stunts in front of me when I was on camera. At first, I didn't recognize him. Then he told me he's an extra at the studio. His name is Harold Lloyd. To get rid of him, I told him I'd put in a good word for him with Mack, if he'd leave me alone."

"Was he cute?"

"I'm not like you, Mabes. I don't judge men by their looks. I'm more like Minta who fell for Roscoe because of his smile and the twinkle in his eyes."

Mabel sighed. "Is this why you called me? To gripe about finally getting a decent role in a film?"

"No, I called you to ask you if you can get away from the studio tomorrow to have lunch with the Brownings and me."

"Eddie and Nealy?"

"The same. And Nellie Sharpe and Eddie's partner Bill Ingram."

"What's the catch, Malone?"

Maisy sweetened her tone on purpose. "No catch. Just lunch …" She added a touch of seduction to her voice. "… at the Hotel … Alexandria."

"Who's buying? It better not be me, Malone."

Still trying to sound innocent, Maisy put a little more sugar in her voice. "No, not you. The hotel management. It seems Bill and Eddie and Nellie made a favorable impression on the general manager there, and this is his way of thanking them. Eddie said his captain said they could bring a few guests along if they wanted to. That would be you and me, Mabes."

"I still smell a rat, Malone. What's the real reason you want me to come along?"

Maisy's pitch dropped two octaves. "Okay, if you must know the real reason, Eddie and Bill were sent to look into the death of a young woman at the Alexandria early this morning. A doctor and the assistant coroner declared her death to be by natural causes, but Eddie suspects she might have been murdered."

Mabel groused. "So, why don't *they* investigate her death, if Eddie thinks she was murdered? Why involve us?"

"Same old reason. The chief said the case was closed."

"Okay, it was closed. So what?"

"The chief closed the case *before* Eddie and Bill made their report to their captain."

Mabel was taken aback. "Wow! That does sound suspicious."

"Then you'll come with me?"

"Sorry, Maise, I can't. I promised Nappy I wouldn't ask for any more time off for a while. I don't see how I can convince him to let me off again since I made him that promise only last week when you wanted me to go to Venice with you on Saturday morning."

"Oh, yeah, now I remember."

Mabel snapped her fingers. "I've got an idea. Why don't you ask Minta to go with you tomorrow?"

"Minta has a contract, Mabes. How is she going to get away for lunch with me?"

"Same way you are. You call in sick."

Maisy wasted no time calling Roscoe Arbuckle's residence to ask his wife Minta Durfee to join her for lunch the next day at the Hotel Alexandria.

"Hello, Roscoe. It's Maisy Malone calling."

"Oh, hello, Maisy. How was the shoot in Venice?"

"It was great for Alice. She didn't have much to do except get lots of sunshine between the few scenes she was in. Charlie did most of the directing, while Mr. Lucas did most of the learning about directing a farcical comedy. The kid was a kid, but he played his part quite well, I thought."

"How about you, Maisy? How did you do?"

"I sat around a lot and soaked up a lot of sun. I could have used your help, Roscoe."

"And how's that?"

"Every man in Venice had to be on that beach all three days. If not for Vince DeDonatis, I might be in jail for murdering at least five of them who kept trying to do a lot more than strike up a casual conversation with me."

"That's too bad, Maisy."

"Thank you, Roscoe." She took a breath. "I called because I want to speak with Minta about having lunch with me and a few other folks tomorrow at the Hotel Alexandria. Is she there?"

"Yes, she is." He brought the mouthpiece close to his chest and called out for his wife. "Minta dear, you're wanted on the telephone. It's Maisy Malone calling. She wants you to go to lunch with her at the Hotel Alexandria. Tomorrow."

Maisy still heard him. It brought a smile to her face.

Minta responded. "I'll be right there, Babe."

Roscoe returned the mouthpiece to his face. "She's coming, Maisy."

"Thank you, Roscoe."

"Here she is."

He handed the telephone to his wife but remained very close by.

"Hello, Maisy. How are you?"

"Browner than I was."

Minta giggled. "Get lots of sunshine over in Venice, did you?"

"Too much, I'm afraid. If I went home to the Choctaw Nation right now, I might be mistaken for a half-blood."

"A half-what?"

"A half-blood. A half-Choctaw half-white. A half-blood."

"Oh, I see now."

"The Choctaw Nation is full of half-bloods, quarter-bloods, and mixed-bloods. That's anybody who is less than a quarter-blood."

"Okay, that clears that up." She took a breath. "Roscoe says you want me to go to lunch with you at the Hotel Alexandria tomorrow. Is that right?"

"Yes, it is, Minta."

"Well, I'd love to go, but we have work at the studio tomorrow. So, I don't see how I can go with you, especially since this is my first week there as an extra."

"All you have to do is call in sick in the morning. That's what I'm going to do."

"Gee, Maisy, I don't know …"

"Minta, you've got nothing to worry about as far as working at Keystone is concerned. Your husband is Roscoe Arbuckle, and excuse the expression, he carries a lot of weight around there already. You can pretty much do whatever it is you want. Mack won't fire you. And besides your big lug working there, we both have a friend in Mack's sweetie. She's got him on such a short leash, he'll do just about anything she wants him to do. How do you think I've kept my job all this time?"

"But why are you asking *me* to go to lunch with you?"

"Okay, Minta, I'll be perfectly honest with you. I'm going there to meet Ed Browning, his partner Bill Ingram, and police stenographer Nellie Sharpe, another friend of mine. They want me to look into the death of a young woman who died at the Alexandria early yesterday morning. They suspect she might have been murdered, but they can't investigate any further because the chief of police closed the case."

"So, you want me to work with you on this case?"

Maisy put a touch of authority in her voice. "Yes, I do."

"But I thought Mabel Normand has been your partner in these murder investigations?"

"She has, but she can't work with me this time. She promised Mack she wouldn't take any more time off to go sleuthing with me."

"Okay, but how are you going to get the time away from the studio to go sleuthing?"

"Well, I'm going to call in sick, too."

"Oh, Maisy, I'm sorry, but I can't lie like that. You'll have to get someone else to work with you this time."

"Look, Minta, Mabel suggested I get you to work with me on this case. I can understand you wanting to be honest, so I think I've got another plan. Are you interested?"

"Yes, I'm interested. Spill."

"I'll just tell Milo that you and I are taking an early lunch away from the studio and we might be back a little late. I'll tell him exactly why, and he'll cover for us."

"Cover for us? That sounds like he'll be lying for us. I can't abide by any lying, Maisy."

Maisy sighed. "Okay, I used the wrong word there. Milo won't be covering for us. If anybody asks about us, he'll simply tell them I asked for the time away from the studio for the two of us and he gave us permission. How's that work for you?"

"Can I go with you to speak to Milo?"

Maisy choked on a laugh. "I wasn't going to ask you to go with me, but after you pressed me to be honest, I can only say, sure, please come with me to talk to Milo."

"Can Roscoe come to?"

Maisy sighed. "Why not? The hotel is picking up the check, so all the better."

"Oh, I didn't mean to imply that I was asking if Roscoe can come to lunch with us. I only meant if it was okay for him to go with us when we speak to Milo. After all, with my big guy along, who can say no to us?"

A burst of laughter erupted from Maisy. "Oh, you're going to be a great partner on this case, Minta."

"And Roscoe, too?"

"How can I say no to you, Minta?"

Roscoe interjected his own observation. "I know exactly how you feel, Maisy. She kept needling me until I agreed on one knee *to ask her to marry me.*"

"I can believe that Roscoe. I really can."

Maisy made one more telephone call that night before retiring after a long day. She called Johnny Fowler, the taxi driver who was becoming more and more like her chauffeur since they met six weeks earlier.

"Can you come to the studio tomorrow morning at eleven-thirty?"

The Texas transplant drawled with pure delight. "Sure, Maisy. No problem. Will it be just you or will there be more than you?"

"Roscoe Arbuckle and his wife Minta Durfee will be with me."

"Where we going this time?"

"Lunch at the Hotel Alexandria. You're invited to join us, Johnny. The hotel is picking up the check."

"Let me guess. We're starting another investigation into a murder, right?"

"Maybe two or three murders. We won't really know for certain until we talk to Detective Browning and his partner."

"Count me in, Maisy. See you outside the studio gate tomorrow morning."

Maisy, Minta, and Roscoe went straight up the Tower
to speak with Milo before going to their assignments for
the day. They hoped to avoid being noticed, but they
failed.

Studio boss Mack Sennett saw them before they could climb
halfway up the first flight of stairs. "And where do you three think
you're going?"

A shudder ran down Maisy's spine as she froze in place, forcing
Minta and Roscoe to bump into each other. Maisy looked over her
shoulder at Sennett. "We're going up to see Milo for a second."

"And why are you doing that, pray tell?"

Her conscience was forced to tell the truth. "We've been invited to
lunch at the Hotel Alexandria, and we want to make certain Milo
knows we'll be off the lot for a while."

"Lunch at the Alexandria?" He paused. "And who invited you?"

"The Los Angeles Police Department."

Sennett sagged, knowing this conversation might be headed in a
direction he wanted to elude. He sighed. "Again, why, pray tell?"

Maisy felt the pain of being honest and simultaneously bathed in
the exultation of being candid. "Detective Ed Browning wants to talk
to us about a possible murder case."

Sennett frowned. "Is Mabel part of this?"

"Oh, no, Mack. She said she promised you she wouldn't take any
more time away from the studio to go sleuthing with me without your
permission."

Sennett squinted at Maisy. "Why am I getting a premonition that
you're sticking your nose into another murder?"

Roscoe held up his right index finger. "A possible murder, Mack.
The police don't know for certain yet if it was murder or just a death by
natural causes."

The studio head let his head droop to the left. "*Et tu, Brute?*"

Arbuckle's forehead wrinkled up. "I don't understand, Mack. I don't eat whatever you just said."

Sennett looked at Maisy with total disbelief. "Is this a joke?"

"No, Mack, it's not. Murder is no laughing matter."

Sennett sighed again. "I mean, what the big guy said."

"Oh, that." She turned to Roscoe. "*Et tu, Brute* is a line from *Julius Caesar,* the play by William Shakespeare. Brutus and some other Roman senators are stabbing Caesar to death when he says this to Brutus, a young friend of his. *Et tu, Brute.* It means, 'And you, Brutus.' It's Latin, Roscoe."

Arbuckle shook his head. "Now I wish I'd spent more time in school."

Sennett's head bobbled involuntarily. "Okay, okay. Go up and tell Milo I said you could have the time away from here." He held up his right index finger and shook it at Maisy. "But make certain you're back here no later than one-thirty. You got that, Miss Malone. One-thirty."

Maisy smiled down at Sennett, then blew him a kiss. "It's no wonder she loves you. You're the best, Mack."

"Beat it, Malone. The rest of us have got movies to make. Or did you forget that's what we do around here?"

Maisy giggled, then turned and jogged up the stairs with the Arbuckles right behind her.

Milo Cole had been romantically captivated by Maisy since the day she stepped off the Santa Fe Railroad's *California Limited* at the La Grande Depot in Los Angeles at 7:26 a.m. Thursday, September 26, 1912. As she casually disembarked from the coach, she caught a shoe heel on the top step, stumbled, and lurched forward directly into his arms. He caught her with all the strength and grace of a muscular trapeze aerialist swinging to-and-fro high above the sawdust-covered circus floor. The collision had no effect on the navy-blue chapeau crowning her naturally wavy auburn coiffure. She made no effort to remove herself from his strong but gentle hold, clutching her tight against his chest until her amber-flecked, whiskey-brown eyes met his roguish blues. He held her for a moment that he wished could be an eternity.

With a devilish grin, he spoke in Ivy League English. "I had hoped you would be glad to see me, Miss Malone, but this is much more than I expected."

She remained in his arms. "Well, I'm not exactly in the habit of throwing myself at men." The slightest hint of a Southern drawl lilted

Maisy's voice. "But all things considered, I could get used to it."

"Could you now?"

"You could stick around and find out."

"I just might do that."

"Fair enough then."

He tipped his black Bowler at her. "Milo Cole ... at your service. Mr. Sennett sent me to meet you and see that you get to the right hotel and then to the studio. He actually lives there, you know."

"No, I didn't know."

The alluring scent of her French perfume paralyzed Cole for an infinity of six seconds, until he replied slowly. "Well, he does." Then he realized he still embraced her. "I suppose you want me to let you go now."

Maisy smiled quite precociously. "For now, but who can say about later?"

Cole grinned to one side of his face with eyebrows raised. "You don't say?" Then he withdrew his arms from around her.

And that was the last time he had held her anywhere except in his dreams. Sure, there had been the occasional dinner date, but every one of them had been with at least one other couple. She had taken his arm whenever he escorted her when they went out somewhere, but she never let him hold her hand. And when those evenings came to their ends, she allowed him to walk her to her hotel door, but not once did she ask him to accompany her upstairs to her apartment. However, she did kiss him—on his left cheek, always—at the end of nearly every night out, but never in the company of others.

Still, Milo continued to daydream about ...

"Milo!"

The sound of Maisy's voice gave him a flash of hope. Then he saw Minta and Roscoe entering the office behind the girl who had stolen his heart that morning almost six months earlier. The moment was lost for him.

"Something I can do for you folks?"

Having become a close friend with Mabel Normand, the girl from the streets of Brooklyn, Maisy Malone, the girl from Oklahoma, had taken on some of the star actress's mannerisms and attitudes. The most primary one being Mabel's aggressiveness. "We only wanted to let you know that the three of us will be leaving the lot at eleven-thirty for lunch at the Alexandria, and we'll be back here by one-thirty."

"Does Mr. Sennett know about this?"

"Yes, we cleared it with him already."

Milo shifted his view to Arbuckle who nodded at him.

Minta made it unanimous. "That's right, Milo. Mr. Sennett made it clear that we must be back by one-thirty."

"Gee, Maisy, how did you swing lunch at the Alexandria? That's pretty swanky, isn't it?"

"We're meeting Eddie and Nealy Browning there. Eddie did his captain a favor, and in return his captain told him the hotel would pick up the check, if he and any of his associates would wish to dine at the hotel. Eddie wants to talk to us about a young woman who died yesterday under suspicious circumstances at the Alexandria."

"Oh, so you're getting involved in another murder case. Is that it?"

Roscoe spoke up. "Possible murder case."

Milo paled and sounded a bit perturbed. "Okay, so why wasn't I invited? I've helped you in all your previous sleuthing cases. Roscoe's only been on one."

Arbuckle nodded. "He's right, Maisy. Why should I get invited? I've only worked with you on one case, and I didn't do all that much except bop one guy on his head and scare the starch out of another."

Before Minta could throw in her opinion, Maisy shook her head. "Okay, okay. You're invited, too, Milo. Be out front by eleven-thirty. Johnny Fowler is picking us up then. We'll squeeze you in somehow."

"I'm not so sure I want to go, if you have to squeeze me in."

Roscoe turned more serious. "Milo can go in my place, Maisy. Like I said—"

Minta had the solution. "We're all going. I can sit on Babe's lap, if I have to. It's not that far to downtown from here." She cuddled up against her husband. "You won't mind, will you, Babe?"

Twisting himself into a corkscrew, Arbuckle blushed. "Aw, gee, Sweetie."

Johnny Fowler had his Studebaker Six parked and waiting on Alvarado Street just three car lengths up from the Keystone Studio entrance a good five minutes ahead of the appointed time Maisy had requested. He knew the actress well enough to understand how punctual she was and how she expected others to be as equally prompt. There was that about her and the fact that she and Mabel Normand always tipped him more than all of his other riders.

When she called him the night before at his home at 1704 Trinity, Maisy told Fowler she would only have the Arbuckles riding with her to the Hotel Alexandria for lunch. Seeing Milo Cole exiting the Keystone lot right beside Maisy caught the cabbie off his guard. Before this moment, he had surmised they were all merely going to dine at the city's fanciest hotel. Now he realized they might be meeting with Detective Browning and his wife to discuss a new murder case. For him, this meant more money and more excitement in his life. He might even get to use his six-shooter this time. With a thrill rippling down his spine, he started the taxi and drove it up to the studio gate.

Fowler leaned toward the open front passenger seat window with a big Texas grin. "Need a ride, folks?"

Maisy grinned back at him and naturally slipped into her country girl accent. "Sure do, cowboy."

"Where you headed, ma'am?"

"Got us a roundup down to the Hotel Alexandria. Think you can fit the lot of us in your fancy automobile?"

"Sure can, ma'am. Hop in!"

Milo shook his head, then looked at the Arbuckles. "One is from Oklahoma, and the other is from Texas. Can you tell the difference?"

Maisy looked over her shoulder. "I heard that, Milo. Why don't you crawl into the back seat and park yourself in the middle? Minta, you take one side, and I'll take the other. Roscoe, you get in front with Johnny."

Everyone followed her orders, and a minute later they were all in the right places.

Roscoe thought he would join the fun. He nudged Fowler with his left elbow. "Okay, pard. Let's head 'em up and move 'em out. My belly's hankerin' for some decent grub. So, let's get on up to that chuck wagon and hope they're spoonin' out more than bacon and beans."

Fowler chuckled. "Where'd you learn to talk like that, Roscoe?"

Arbuckle blushed. "Oh, you know. Working in show business, you hear people talk and you pick up things here and there. I hardly find any use for it now that I'm making movies."

Minta chastised the men in front. "Hey, you two! Will you quit your yammering and concentrate on the road. I'd like to get to that hotel in once piece, you know."

Johnny squeezed the steering wheel. "Yes, ma'am. We're off and running."

The Alexandria's lobby awed the five first-time visitors to the hotel. Minta Durfee expressed their initial feelings perfectly as they took in the luxury of the decor. "Will you get a load of this place?"

Maisy followed up with an observation of her own. "I've been in some swanky places in London and Paris and New York and Chicago, but none of them can hold a candle to this palace."

Roscoe let his appetite speak for him. "Looking at this ... *mansion* ... makes me wonder how great the food is here."

Milo's awe sounded more practical. "Do they sell postcards here? I want to send some to the family back in Connecticut. They'll never believe I ate here."

Fowler gaped at the marble columns. "I went to the Texas State Capitol in Austin once and thought it was something special. But this place? *Go-o-l-l-l-l-y!*"

The Brownings, Bill Ingram, and Nellie Sharpe had been sitting in armchairs across from the front desk for only a few minutes before their friends from the Keystone Studio arrived. They rose in near unison and walked calmly toward the newcomers.

Ed Browning spoke first. "Rather magnificent, isn't it?"

Maisy responded. "You got that right." She shifted her view to the detective. "Been waiting long?"

Nealy Browning answered for her husband. "No, not long at all, Maisy. Edward figured it would take you twenty to twenty-five minutes get here from Edendale. So, we arrived at ten-to-noon. I can't believe we're getting together again so soon after this past Sunday. One case after another, right?"

Browning smiled. "Now you know how Bill and I do our jobs. Right, Bill?"

"That's right, Ed. Same old grind patrolling the streets looking for lawbreakers. But not this time. Today we got the day off, and we get to dine in the lap of luxury instead of choking down a tuna salad sandwich in a greasy coffee shop on the east side of downtown."

Milo wedged his way into the conversation. "And the hotel is picking up the check, right?"

Browning nodded. "Yes, it is. To confirm everything, this morning I called the hotel to get a table reserved for us. The clerk at the front desk connected me to Mr. Whitmore the general manager here, and he said the hotel would be picking up the check ... even after I told him there would be seven of us having lunch here today."

Maisy interrupted. "But there's nine—"

"Will you let me finish, *Miss* Malone?"

Maisy threw up her hands in surrender. "Go ahead."

"Thank you." He cleared his throat. "Mr. Whitmore said it made no difference how many people would be in our party; the hotel was still picking up the check."

Ingram chuckled. "Ed almost invited half the department to join us here."

Nealy giggled. "I stopped him by telling him, if he did that, then he'd have to invite their wives as well."

Everybody laughed.

"I did invite one more person to join us."

Maisy asked the question. "Really? Who?"

"Walt Ballard. He kept his word not to go public with anything about the Nettie Soards case until we had the killer in custody. So, I got to thinking he just might be useful on this one as well."

A big smile brightened Maisy's face. "Good thinking, Eddie. We just might need someone to dig into the old newspaper files, right?"

Browning chuckled. "I knew I couldn't fool you, Maisy."

Just then, Sam Whitmore walked up to the group. "Well, Detective Browning, I see you'all have arrived. Or will there be more coming?"

"Yes, sir. Just one, but he may be little late."

"Should we wait for him?"

"No, I don't think so. I told our friend to go to the front desk and someone there would direct him to where we are dining."

"Very good, Detective. I will pass that word along."

"Thank you, Mr. Whitmore."

Whitmore nodded. "I have taken the liberty of setting up a long table in one of our banquet rooms on the second floor. I thought you'all might appreciate some privacy that way."

"That's very thoughtful of you, Mr. Whitmore. Thank you."

Whitmore nodded. "You are quite welcome, sir." He paused. "If I may, Detective, would you mind introducing me to your entourage? I already know Detective Ingram and Miss Sharpe from your gracious visit yesterday."

"Oh, yes, of course. How rude of me not to introduce them immediately, sir!"

"Not at all, sir."

"This is my wife, Nealy."

"Charmed, I'm sure, Mrs. Browning."

She smiled and held out her hand to Whitmore. "Edward told me you were a real southern gentleman, sir."

He squeezed her hand. "Why, thank you, ma'am." He smiled very politely at her. "I do believe I hear the voice of a real southern lady, Mrs. Browning."

"You are too kind, sir."

"Not at all, ma'am." He turned to Minta. "And who is this dear lady, Detective?"

"I'd like you to meet Mrs. Roscoe Arbuckle."

Whitmore looked from Minta to Roscoe and back again. He held out his hand to her. "I recognize your husband, Mrs. Arbuckle, having seen him on the stage several times since living here in Los Angeles. But I had no idea he was married to such an attractive lady."

Minta blushed and extended her own hand to him. "You flatter me, sir." When he accepted it and bowed politely, she giggled slightly. "You can call me Minta."

Roscoe spoke up. "My wife goes by her stage name, Mr. Whitmore. Minta Durfee."

"Yes, of course. Pardon me, Miss Durfee." The general manager turned to the last woman in the group. "And this young lady is?"

Before Browning could say her name, Maisy spoke for herself. "I am Maisy Malone, Mr. Whitmore. I'm an actress for the Keystone Film Company in Edendale."

Whitmore extended his hand. "How do you do, Miss Malone?"

She made no motion to shake his hand. Instead, she waved hers toward Milo. "And this handsome gentleman is Mr. Milo Cole, my escort and the top assistant to Mr. Mack Sennett, head of the studio."

Milo stepped forward and gripped the hotel chief's hand firmly. "How do you do, Mr. Whitmore?"

"How nice to meet you, sir? Welcome to the Alexandria."

"The pleasure is all mine, Mr. Whitmore."

Maisy then motioned to Johnny Fowler. "And this is my personal bodyguard and driver, Mr. Whitmore. He goes where I go."

Understanding her cue, Johnny maintained an austere aspect as he gave the man a barely noticeable nod.

Whitmore turned back to Browning. "Well, ladies and gentlemen, if you'all will please follow me, I will show you to the banquet room where you will be dining with us today."

Instead of crowding into an elevator car, Whitmore led them to the curved stairway to the second floor. "Mr. Joseph Reikel, our assistant manager in charge of our food services, will be your maître d'. He's been with us since the day we opened in oh-six. He's originally from Austria, but he's been here in the United States for twenty years now. I assure you'all that he and his waiters will provide you'all with the best the Alexandria has to offer. There he is now." He indicated with his hand a most debonair gentleman standing at the top of the stairway fourteen more steps away. When he attained the second floor, Whitmore stepped up to his subordinate. "Mr. Reikel, this is your party for lunch." He waved toward Maisy. "I believe you should direct yourself to this young lady." He smiled salaciously at her. "I do believe that she is in charge here."

"Yes, sir, Mr. Whitmore."

"Enjoy your lunch, Miss Malone." He turned to Browning. "You, also, Detective." He bowed slightly to the other three women. "Ladies, enjoy." He nodded to the men but said nothing more as he began his descent down the stairway.

As soon as all nine guests assembled at the top of the stairs, Reikel faced Maisy. "If you would follow me, please?"

Maisy responded in German. "*Vielen Dank, Herr Reikel.*" ("Much thanks, Mr. Reikel.)

The culinary manager showed some surprise to Maisy. "*Du sprichst Deutsch, Fräulein Malone?*" ("You speak German, Miss Malone?")

She smiled at him. "*Ein bisschen, mein Herr.*" ("A little, sir.)

"*Ihr Akzent ist ziemlich gut. Sie müssen sehr oft Deutsch sprechen.*" ("Your accent is quite good. You must speak German very often.")

"*Nicht so oft, wie ich möchte, Herr Reikel.*" (Not as often as I would like, Mr. Reikel.")

"*Ich würde gerne mehr mit Ihnen sprechen, Fräulein Malone, aber das Wichtigste zuerst. Ich stehe Ihnen zur Verfügung.*" ("I would like to speak with you more, Miss Malone, but first things first. I am at your service.")

"Thank you, Mr. Reikel."

Reikel led the group to a door marked with the words: Banquet Room Apollo. "Here we are, ladies and gentlemen." He opened the door for them, then stepped aside.

The group filed into a space that was divided in half by a gold and ivory curtain that accented the walls of the same color scheme. A snow-white tablecloth covered a single 12-foot-long table that was set with all the appropriate china dishes, sterling silver flatware, and crystal glasses. The chairs—three to each side and one on each end—were padded with red velvet cushions and backs.

Four uniformed waiters stood rigidly between the table and the side wall, each looking more like a man in the military than of a server.

The maître d' counted the chairs and then the number of guests. "I see we are one setting short, Miss Malone. We will correct that mistake immediately."

"Actually, Mr. Reikel, we are two settings short. We have another member of our party who should be along shortly."

"Yes, of course." Reikel clapped his hands at his waiters. "Two more chairs and two more place settings." The trio of servers vanished through the curtain. "Would you care to be seated now, Miss Malone?"

"Yes, Mr. Reikel, we would. My friends and I have much to talk about." She turned to Fowler. "Johnny, would you mind standing for the moment?"

"Sure thing, Miss Malone. I'll just ..." Seeing one waiter return through the curtain carrying two additional chairs cut him short.

Reikel pointed at his man. "Put them down there, Mr. Merry. I will rearrange this side, and you take the other."

The other two waiters returned, each carrying an identical place setting: china dishes and sterling silver flatware in one hand and crystal glasses in the other. Deftly each man placed them on the table, then set them in the same arrangement as their predecessors in front of the two new chairs. Then quietly without being told to do so, they rearranged the initial place settings to align with the rearrangement of the chairs.

Surprise sparkled on all the faces of the diners, but only Maisy spoke for them. "I am quite impressed by the efficiency of you and your waiters, Mr. Reikel."

"Mr. Merry, Mr. Ingles, and Mr. Wilson have been with me ever since we worked together at the Van Nuys Hotel, Miss Malone. I trained them myself. They are the best here at the Alexandria."

Maisy looked around at the others. "Well, folks, let's be seated."

The men, being gentlemen, waited for Reikel and his staff to seat the ladies before they sat down. Maisy at one end, Browning at the other. Milo sat to Maisy's right with Johnny to her left. The Arbuckles sat opposite each other; Roscoe to Cole's right and Minta to Fowler's left. Nealy sat to her husband's left with Ingram opposite her. Nellie sat beside Ingram, leaving the empty chair for Walt Ballard across from her.

In the next instant, Reikel presented Maisy with a single-page menu with the words printed in black, blue, and red on a stiff, creamy white parchment. Mr. Merry gave one to Browning, while Wilson and Ingles walked behind the other diners on opposite sides of the table and in opposite directions, distributing menus to them.

"Would you care to order now, Miss Malone? Or do you wish to wait while we serve you ice water?"

"Yes, go ahead and serve the water." She glanced around at her friends. "Everyone okay with that?" Seeing no dissents among them, she turned back to the maître d'. "We'll be ready to order in a minute, Mr. Reikel. I'll start." She opened her luncheon menu and immediately felt a burst of *déjà vu*, as if she had seen it before. Then a memory sent a shiver down her spine. The hotel's menu was a near replica of the luncheon menu she had seen during her brief time on *R.M.S. Titanic* the year before. The only differences between them being the White Star Line flag and emblem on *Titanic's* and the hotel's name, address, and a picture of the hostelry on the Alexandria's. The list of dishes were slightly different, and their printed order varied only slightly. "There's so much to choose from, Mr. Reikel. I'm not sure which to pick." She paused for a second before making her choices. "So, how about a bowl of Cockie-Leekie for starters? Then …" She heard whispering among the others. "Then for the main course, I'll have Chicken á la Maryland with dumplings. And for dessert, I'll have Apple Meringue."

Surprise struck Reikel. "Very good, Miss Malone."

Nealy leaned close to her husband. "Do you know what she just ordered, Dear?"

Maisy heard her. "Chicken soup with leeks, chicken breast covered in a crème sauce, bananas, and dumplings, and apple pie." She glanced up at the head waiter again. "I stowed away on the *Titanic* for a day and a night before they caught me and put me ashore in France. I saw and heard a lot in the short time I was onboard. I even managed to purloin a few souvenirs. One of them was a stack of first-class menus. And this one here is very much like one I have stored away in my sea trunk. I must have looked at them a hundred times on my crossing home last year." She focused on her friends at the other end of the table. "If you have any questions about the food, I'm certain these gentlemen can answer them for you."

Reikel smiled at Maisy. "*Jetzt kann ich verstehen, warum Sie für diese netten Leute verantwortlich sind, Fräulein Malone.*" (Now I can understand why you are responsible for these nice people, Miss Malone.")

Maisy smiled back at him. "*Danke, mein Herr.*" ("Thank you, sir.") Then she pointed to the menu. "I see you have replaced *From the Grill* and *Buffet* with *Á La Carte*. Can we order from there as well?"

"Yes, you may, Miss Malone."

"Did you hear that, folks? You can order anything you want under *Á La Carte*." Seeing she had instigated a round of chatter, she looked back at Reikel. "Better give us a few minutes."

"As you wish, Miss Malone."

The banquet room door opened, and Walt Ballard entered the hall. He gave everyone a wave of his right hand. "Have I missed anything?"

Browning answered for all but Maisy. "Just Maisy showing off her foreign languages skills."

Ballard stopped beside her chair. "How many languages can you speak, Maisy?"

"I can speak nearly all of them, but I only know enough words and phrases in the ones I do know to keep me out of trouble when I'm around people from that country." She turned to the maître d'. "Mr. Reikel, this gentleman is Mr. Walt Ballard, a friend of ours from *The Times*. He's here to do a story about the hospitality of Hotel Alexandria and its courtesy to the law enforcement community here in Los Angeles."

Reikel focused on Ballard. "Welcome to the Hotel Alexandria, sir. Please allow me to show you to your seat."

The reporter's first thought was rather sarcastic, but he restrained from airing it. Instead, he remembered his manners in the presence of ladies. "How kind of you, Mr. Reikel!" He sat down, picked up the menu on his plate, and gave it a quick perusal.

After seating Ballard, Reikel focused on Browning. "Now who is also ready to order?"

The detective from Georgia made his request. "I'll have the corned beef, vegetables, and dumplings. And for dessert, I'll have that apple pie that Maisy ordered."

One by one, Reikel heard their orders, while his waiters wrote them down on a notepad. Since Ballard had arrived last, the maître d' came to him last. "And for you, sir?"

"I think I'll try this Galantine of Chicken. I don't know what it is, but it sounds interesting."

Reikel took the menu from the reporter. "Allow me, Mr. Ballard. Galantine of Chicken is a log of various meats and vegetables baked in the skin of a chicken, then cooled overnight and served in thin slices with a vegetable of your choice and creamed potato slices."

"Sounds good. I'll have peas with mine."

"Very good, sir." The head waiter motioned to his three waiters, and the four of them vanished behind the gold and ivory curtain.

Maisy tapped Fowler on his right forearm. "Johnny, would you mind taking a look behind that curtain? I don't want anybody hanging around back there eavesdropping on us."

The taxi driver *cum* bodyguard nodded, slid his chair away from the table, and went to the curtain where the waiters had gone. Slowly, he pulled the drape aside, peeked behind it, then turned back to Maisy. "Nothing back here but two swinging doors that probably go to the kitchen."

"Thank you, Johnny." She waved him back to his seat, then looked down the length of the table. "Okay, let's get down to business, starting with you, Eddie."

"Okay." He made a quick scan of everyone seated there. "I'm sure you all know why we're here. A young woman died in this hotel early yesterday morning. The hotel's doctor determined she died of natural causes. Assistant County Coroner Howard Seager agreed with the hotel doctor. Natural causes. Bill and I think differently. Why do we think so? Call it a hunch on my part. Call it instinct. The hotel's physician, Dr. Newmark, when we talked to him, he seemed to be too eager to say her death was caused by an ailment called phthisis. That's an ancient Greek word for pulmonary pneumonia. The ailment builds up fluid in the lungs until the heart can't beat from the pressure and the patient dies from heart failure.

"Then we spoke with the young woman's mother, Mrs. Cordelia Sullivan, and the victim's older sister, Miss Mary Sullivan. By the way, the young lady who passed away was twenty-year-old Miss Marjorie Sullivan. Mrs. Sullivan gave us more details about her daughter's health than Dr. Newmark did. Marjorie had been sick since childhood. She contracted scarlet fever and never fully recovered from the scars it left on her lungs. The Sullivans came out west from New York on the advice of their physician back there. They moved to Seattle where they retained a new physician who advised them to bring Marjorie down here to Los Angeles where the climate is warmer and drier.

"That was two weeks ago. Since then, according to the hotel doctor and Mrs. Sullivan and Mary Sullivan, Marjorie's health seemed to be improving right up to the night before she died. Although both the mother and the sister seemed to be quite distraught, they reacted a bit too defensive when I asked Mary if Marjorie had ever locked the doors to her room before that night. The mother asked directly if I was insinuating her daughter had taken her own life. I told her I was only doing my job. She then told the general manager to throw us out of her suite. We left without any further questions of Mrs. Sullivan and her daughter Mary."

"Then we returned to the station to report to Captain Murray. We had barely started to tell him how things went at the Alexandria when he told us the case was closed by order of Chief Sebastian. We thought that was a bit curious because he was the one who ordered the investigation in the first place.

"The topper of all this was …" Browning ceased talking at the sight of Maître d' Reikel and his four waiters returning with serving trays with bowls of soup for those diners who had ordered them. "I'll go on with this after we're served."

Reikel smiled with courtesy. "Please, sir, do not let us interrupt your conversation."

Browning smiled back at the head waiter. "You're not interrupting. We were just talking about the loss of one of our detectives a few days ago. Tomorrow is his funeral, and we were wondering if our friends from the Keystone Film Company would be attending the services."

"Oh, yes, Detective, I read about it in *The Times*. So very sad. He was a good man, I understand."

"One of the best."

"Well, please go on. We will be back in ten minutes with your entrées. Until then …" He bowed and backed away from the table to the exit from the banquet room to the kitchen.

Browning watched Reikel and his servers depart. "Since I didn't order soup with my meal, I'll go on with what I was saying while the rest of you enjoy your first course.

"As I started to say, the topper to our visit here to the Alexandria was our interview with Mr. Whitmore. Without us asking, he said it was his experience in the hotel business that deaths, accidents, and other unusual events in a hotel … come in cycles of three. He made a big deal of it not being a superstition. He said the course of events have proven over and over again to be a psychological fact. Then he said the strangest thing of all. He said when he was notified of Miss Sullivan's passing, all of the suspense he had been feeling since the deaths of two other hotel guests, a woman named Mrs. Lee and a gentleman by the name of Mr. Clarke, both of them having died a couple of weeks earlier. He heaved a huge sigh of relief, chuckled, and ran his hand over this head. Then he said he was able to relax now and cease worrying about who the next person would be to die in the hotel and complete the cycle of three. He followed that with the excuse that nearly every day the hotel's guest list would number over a thousand people of all ages. He added to that the hundreds of employees they have here. He said having that many people in the hotel at any one time was almost a guarantee that one of them would die here. He capped it off by saying he had gotten entirely over the dread fear that hotel men in the past have shown when anything of this sort comes up. It is a statistical impossibility for a hotel to avoid such things, and the traveling public no more thinks of death, ghosts, and other phenomena of this character in a superstitious light."

Walt Ballard spoke up. "We ran that story this very morning in *The Times*. I read it at the station. Yesterday morning when I saw you and Bill leave the station with Miss Sharpe, I wondered what was up then. So, you boys think this young woman might have been murdered?"

"It's all rather curious, don't you think, Walt?"

"Yes, I do."

Maisy finished her Cockie-Leekie. "I'm really glad you agree, Walt, because we need your help with this case."

"You do?"

Browning confirmed Maisy's declaration. "Yes, we do, Walt."

"Okay. So, what do you expect me to do?"

Maisy answered him. "We expect you to be our decoy."

"Your decoy?"

Browning added part two to their reason for wanting the reporter on the team. "And we need you to dig into the morgue for us."

"The morgue?"

Maisy grinned. "At *The Times*, Walt."

"That's a relief. So, what will I be looking for?"

Before either Browning or Maisy could answer, Reikel and his waiters returned with everyone's main dish.

Maisy expressed her delight at seeing the Chicken á la Maryland. *"Oh je, Herr Reikel! Es sieht so prächtig aus! Ich kann es kaum erwarten, es zu probieren."* ("Oh, my, Herr Reikel! It looks so sumptuous! I can hardly wait to taste it.")

"Ich hoffe, es gefällt Ihnen, Fräulein Malone. Bon appetit!" ("I hope you enjoy it, Miss Malone. Bon appétit!")

"Merci, Monsieur." ("Thank you, sir.")

Surprise stunned Reikel. *"Vous parlez aussi Français?"* ("You speak French, too?")

"Un peu plus que je ne parle allemand." ("A little more than German.")

"I will have to watch what I say around you, Miss Malone." He laughed. "I'm afraid anything I say might cause me trouble."

"*Wie ich um Sie herum, Herr Reikel.*" ("As will I around you, Mr. Reikel.") And she laughed with him.

Reikel bowed to Maisy, then clapped his hands to signal his men to leave the room. And they did.

As soon as the waiters went through the kitchen doors, Maisy took charge again. "As we were saying, Walt, we want you to look for any stories about deaths in hotels here in the Los Angeles area. We want to find out if this is the first time three people have died in one hotel in a short period of time or has it happened in the past. If it has happened before, then we need to look for any connection to the people who are working or living at the Alexandria now."

Ballard nodded. "I get it. Yes, great idea. But I don't think I can do it alone. I'll need help from somebody else at the paper. Got any ideas how I get some?"

"Sure. Tell them the truth. Tell anyone you ask to help you that you're looking for any other examples of a cycle of three deaths or accidents in a hotel because you want to see if there's any validity to Whitmore's belief in cycles of three. I should think you will get all sorts of help if you tell them that you're looking to do a story on cycles of three. If you find any—or you don't find any—deaths or accidents or fires or whatever in a cycle of three, either way you've got a story. One that supports Whitmore's belief in cycles of three or one that disproves his theory of cycles of three. You win either way, right?"

A big grin spread over Ballard's face. "Sure, I get it. I'm a winner either way."

Maisy focused on police stenographer Nellie Sharpe. "I've got a job for you, too, Nellie. I'd like you to go through any records at the police station to see if anyone working here at the Alexandria has ever been in trouble with the law here in Los Angeles."

"How do I justify doing that, Maisy?"

"If anyone asks you why you're doing it, tell them the truth."

"And what would that truth be?"

"The truth is you're simply curious if there's anything to this cycle of three superstitions that Whitmore spoke about in the newspapers. And just like Walt at *The Times*, that might get you some help from other people at the police department. Or from someone married to someone at the police department." She looked at Nealy Browning and smiled.

Nealy smiled with excitement. "And how would I justify doing such a thing, Maisy Malone?"

"Tell them the truth. You're just as curious about cycles of three as Nellie is. And you are, aren't you?"

The detective's wife laughed. "Miss Malone, you are so very, very clever. How ever did you get that way?"

"From being raised on a farm and wondering which came first, the chicken or the egg, Mrs. Browning."

Everyone laughed.

Maisy smiled. "I don't know everything, but I do know all of us had better eat some of this delicious looking food in front of us before Mr. Reikel and his waiters come back and ask us if we're ready for dessert and coffee."

Everyone followed Maisy's advice and began eating their entrées. Then to a man and each woman they all remarked on the wonderful taste of their food.

After swallowing a second bite of his veal and ham pie, Roscoe remarked about the flavor of the dish. "This is so scrumptious, Maisy. I almost wish you had another murder to investigate so we could eat here again." He dug into the pie with the determination of a ravenous beast.

"Murder is no laughing matter, Roscoe."

The room fell silent.

Arbuckle stopped his fork halfway to his mouth. "I'm so sorry, my friends. I didn't mean to be so insensitive."

Browning spoke for everyone. "We all know you meant nothing by it, Roscoe. I might have said the same thing if my mouth hadn't been full of this wonderful, corned beef."

Milo supported the detective. "Me, too, Roscoe. My salmon kept me from making a fool of myself." Then he realized what he had just said. "Not that you—"

Maisy patted Cole's arm. "Why don't you quit while you're behind, Milo dear?"

"Yes, I suppose I should."

Minta had to speak next. "Now you know why my big lug gave up the stage and took a job in silent pictures."

Everyone laughed, then resumed concentrating on their meals.

After finishing their desserts and the waiters filled their coffee cups for the last time, Maisy resumed telling the group what their assignments would be in this investigation started by Detectives Ed Browning and Bill Ingram. "Now, where was I? Oh, yes, I remember. I was giving out jobs to all of you, and I left off with Nealy." She focused on Browning. "Eddie, Bill, you two got roped into this investigation by your Captain Murray and Chief Sebastian. It's my thought that they expected the two of you to go through the motions of a police investigation at this hotel and report back to them that there was no reason to believe any foul play was involved in the death of Marjorie Sullivan, that she passed away in her sleep due to natural causes, and that's that. But Chief Sebastian called off the investigation before you could tell Captain Murray you suspected there was foul play involved in her death. Am I right?"

Browning answered her. "Yes, you are, Maisy. And it's because the Chief closed the case before, we could make a full report that we came to the conclusion that there's something fishy going on here."

"I'll bet you think someone higher up in the city government called Chief Sebastian and told him to call off the investigation."

Both detectives nodded at her, but only Browning replied. "That's exactly right, Maisy."

"And I'll bet you think someone at this hotel called that higherup first and asked that the investigation be called off."

The two men nodded again, but this time Ingram spoke for them. "You're so right, Maisy, and that's why Ed called you to pick up where we left off."

"Well, Bill, you and Eddie aren't through with this investigation. Not by a longshot. I'd like you two to do what you do best."

The eyebrows on both men jumped up, but only Browning spoke. "And what is it that we do best, Miss Malone?"

She smiled. "You snoop."

Everybody laughed.

Everyone except Browning and Ingram. The former retorted. "That's not what I'd call it."

Nealy Browning stopped laughing, but her smile remained. "Oh, my dear Edward. You tell me all the time how you and Bill snooped around some place looking for evidence of someone breaking the law in this alley or on that corner or in such-and-such a business or house."

"But I don't call it snooping."

"Well, Edward, what else would you call it?"

The other eight people in the room chuckled, snickered, simply let out a loud guffaw.

Red-faced from embarrassment, Browning was at a loss for words.

Not Ingram. "She's right, Ed. Admit it. We're both just a couple of snoops."

Maisy came to Browning's rescue. "And it's because you're really good at snooping that I would like the two of you to look into the deaths of Mrs. America L. Lee and Mr. George W. Clarke. You might start with the undertakers who handled their funerals as well as the mortuary handling Miss Sullivan's body before it's shipped to Seattle."

Browning turned to his partner. "Didn't I tell you she was sharp as a tack?"

Ingram looked back at Maisy. "Then what do we do?"

"Look up the coroner's investigation and then talk to their doctors and family members, if they had any."

"Why would we do that?"

"Because I think both of them were said to have died in their sleep just like Marjorie Sullivan supposedly did. I want to know for certain that they did."

Browning nodded. "I get it. If all three of them died in their sleep, then that's probably more than a coincidence. Right?"

Maisy nodded. "That's right. Probably ... a lot more ... than ... a coincidence. More than likely, all three were murdered, and if all three were murdered, then it's most likely the same person murdered all of them ... in the same way." She glanced around the table. "And that's why Roscoe, Minta, Milo, Johnny, and I have to get chummy with as many of the employees ... and residents ... and guests of this hotel as we can."

Minta queried. "And residents and guests, too?"

"Yes, and residents and guests, too. Any one of the employees or residents or even a guest could be the killer. So, we talk to as many of them as we can and see how much gossip about the three deaths we can pick up. Then we get together and compare notes so we can start ruling out suspects."

Milo's mouth twitched. "That's a lot of people, Maisy. Didn't Ed say there are more than a thousand people here in the hotel on any given day? When are we going to find the time to do all that? We've all got jobs."

"Not on Saturday afternoons and all-day Sundays and weekday evenings." She smiled coyly and flashed her eyelashes at him. "And you can work with me, if you want to, Milo."

He was hooked, and everyone else knew it, especially Maisy who had been catching him and throwing him back time after time since the day they met at the train station six months ago.

Walt Ballard could hardly wait to get back to his desk at *The Times* building on the northeast corner of 1ˢᵗ Street and Broadway. On any other day, he would have walked the five blocks to the newspaper, but he was in a real hurry this time. So, he jumped on the first Red Car he saw and was delivered to his destination in less than ten minutes. He raced upstairs, passing several co-workers along the way. Then one of them caught his eye as he reached the second floor. He stopped to talk to her.

Nearing fifty years old, tall, lithe, and authoritative, Grace Collins was a freelance writer who wrote opinionated and humorous essays for magazines and newspapers under the byline of Lillian Collins, her middle name. Her husband Lew worked as a real estate broker, and their son Herbie was a student in his first year of college.

"Mrs. Collins, how are you today?"

"Why, Mr. Ballard, I'm just fine, thank you. And how are you?"

"I'm absolutely great, Mrs. Collins." He took one step closer to her. "Say, do you have a moment to spare? I'd like to talk to you about a project I've just been offered."

Her piercing gray eyes attempted to read into his expression. "A project that you've just been offered?"

"Yes. But you see, I can't do it alone."

"And you want me to help you with it?"

Ballard broke out big grin. "You know, the second I saw you just now, I knew you were the right person for me to recruit for this project I just accepted over lunch."

"Your flattery will not do, Mr. Ballard. Please get to the point."

"Okay, I will." He moved a half-step closer to her and lowered his voice. "Did you see that piece in this morning's paper on page eight in part two? The one headlined '*Mystic Death Cycle of Three Complete*' about the death of that young woman at the Hotel Alexandria?"

Mrs. Collins stiffened. "As a matter of fact, I did read it. Rubbish, if you ask me. That man Whitmore is a superstitious buffoon to talk about such nonsense as death, accidents, and other odd events coming in cycles of three. Pure poppycock!"

"Then you read it, I see."

"Initially, it turned my stomach. But then I realized those were my creative juices churning away inside me, and now I am thinking about giving some serious consideration to writing a column about events such as death coming in cycles of three."

Ballard's excitement erupted inside him to the point where he nearly reached out and embraced the lady, but he restrained himself and lowered his voice a few more decibels. "That's just wonderful, Mrs. Collins! That's exactly what I plan to do with this new project I've been offered. And now I'm —"

She interrupted him. "And now you want me to help you with it." She shook her head. "I think not, Mr. Ballard." She moved toward the stairs.

He moved agilely to intercept her before she could take the first step down to the first floor. "Don't say no yet. You haven't heard the whole deal."

She withdrew her foot from taking the step down the stairs. "And how could there be more to *the whole deal*, Mr. Ballard?"

The reporter leaned as close to her as he could and still maintain the necessary propriety of conversing in a public place. He tilted his head to the left to whisper in her left ear. "The *more* to the whole deal, Mrs. Collins, is ... mur ... der."

Her eyes widened with shock and fear, and her body stiffened to the point of becoming statuesque. For several seconds, catatonia held her mind and muscles in total rigidity. She didn't even breathe.

Ballard leaned a little closer. "Mrs. Collins? Did you hear me?"

The sound of his voice and the feel of his hot, moist breath on her ear and cheek melted the hyperarousal that had been holding her captive for the several seconds that had the feel of a lifetime.

"Mrs. Collins?"

She leaned an inch closer to him. With a dry mouth and lips, she whispered back. "Did you say murder, Mr. Ballard?"

"Yes, I did."

Her muscles and mind relaxed as the fear she had experienced began to dissipate. She stepped back and faced him, her expression as stiff as that of a clergyman at a funeral, her eyes as empty as those of the deceased. "I think I would like to go someplace more private and discuss this further with you, Mr. Ballard. As soon as I turn in my column for tomorrow's paper."

Sergeant George Willett sat at his desk discussing an early morning arrest with Patrolman Dick Lansing when he noticed Nealy Browning and Nellie Sharpe enter Central Police Station shortly after one o'clock that afternoon. Thinking their appearance together at the station to be odd, he waved a hand at Lansing. "Hold that thought, Dick, and give me a moment while I speak to the ladies who just walked in."

"Sure, Sarge." The young patrolman turned to see who Willett meant but did not recognize either of the women.

Willett broke out his most congenial smile. "Mrs. Browning, what a pleasant surprise to see you here!"

Both ladies stopped and turned to face Willett. Nellie's face took on a blank expression, while Nealy smiled back at him. "Oh, hello, Sergeant Willett. How are you today?"

"I'm fine, ma'am." His next thought was to ask her why she had come into the station, but he held his tongue when he saw her husband and Bill Ingram enter the building close behind the two women.

Nealy tilted her head a bit to the right as she increased the breadth of her smile. "I'm glad to hear it, Sergeant."

"Is there anything I can do for you, Mrs. Browning?"

"No, Sergeant, I don't believe so."

Ed Browning interjected himself into the conversation. "I'm sorry, George. I was going to tell you myself about why my wife is here. She and Nellie are going to do some research for me and Bill."

"Research, Ed? Research on what?"

"Did you see that piece in *The Times* yesterday where the general manager at the Alexandria spoke about bad things happening in cycles of three?"

"I don't read *The Times*, Ed. I read the *Evening Express* from the front-page headlines to the department store advertisements on the back page. Not every word, mind you. But I do look them over for just about anything that catches my eye." He chuckled. "It's the policeman in me, Ed."

Browning politely smiled back. "Of course. I do the same thing."

"You were telling me why your missus is here with Miss Sharpe."

"Yes, I was. Well, as you know, Captain Murray sent Bill, Miss Sharpe, and me to the Hotel Alexandria to see if there was any reason to suspect foul play in the death of a young woman who died there in her sleep the other night. We followed orders and found no reason to suspect foul play. But we did think it was odd what Mr. Whitmore, the hotel's general manager, said about cycles of three. Do you know about cycles of three, George?"

"Sure. Who hasn't? It means bad things happen in threes. It's just common knowledge, Ed."

"Well, Bill and Nellie and I got to talking about it, and we wondered if there's any truth to it. So, we decided to see if bad things really do happen in threes by checking the records on murder cases here in Los Angeles. I told my wife about it, and she said she'd help Nellie look through the records for any proof of it."

"Sounds like a waste of time, Ed, but if the ladies want to do that for you and Bill, then they can be my guest." Willett held up his right index finger and shook it gently. "I'll tell you what, Ed." He lowered his hand and leaned forward a bit. "Patrolman Lansing here has wanted some time away from walking the streets in the dark, so how about I assign him to help the ladies?" He looked at the young officer. "What do you say to that, Dick? You can start right now, and I'll take you off night duty in the meantime. Okay?"

As soon as Willett said his name to Browning, Lansing's demeanor transformed from general curiosity to absolute pleasure. "Sure thing, Sarge. I'd be more than glad to help the ladies do their research."

Willett smiled. "There you go, Ed. If Lansing's not enough, I'll pull Officer Krebs away from street patrol to help out. How's that?"

"Can we afford to take two men away from patrolling, George?"

"You let me worry about that, Ed." He focused on Nealy. "Do you want Dick to start right now, Mrs. Browning?"

Nealy looked at Nellie. "What do you think?"

"I think we should take Officer Lansing with us right now."

Nealy turned back to Willett. "You heard her, Sergeant."

"Off with you, Dick, and mind your manners with Mrs. Browning and Miss Sharpe or you'll be back walking a beat before you know it."

"Yes, sir, Sarge."

Willett smiled once more at the two women. "Good luck with your research, ladies."

Both replied. "Thank you, Sergeant Willett."

The desk sergeant turned back to Browning. "Don't worry, Ed. I'll see to it that they're not bothered down there."

"Thanks, George. I'll rest easy knowing you're on the job. For now, Bill and I must go upstairs and see Captain Murray."

At the landing between the two flights of stairs, Ingram leaned toward his partner and spoke softly. "You know what, Ed? That Maisy Malone really knows her stuff. Telling George the truth was the right thing to do."

"Half the truth, Bill."

"Half?"

"We didn't tell him the part about us looking for any evidence of a murder."

Ingram chuckled. "Yes, you're right, Ed."

Browning waggled a finger at his partner. "Remember what you said, Bill. Murder is no laughing matter."

Johnny Fowler dropped Maisy, Milo, and the Arbuckles off at the front gate to Keystone Studio in plenty of time for them to get back to work. Milo returned to the office in the Tower. Maisy went back to the set of her movie, and Minta found a seat on the extras bench, and Roscoe met up with Mabel Normand just outside the set where their movie *For the Love of Mabel* was being filmed.

"How was lunch at the Alexandria, Roscoe?"

"Wonderful, Mabel. I've never been in a place like that before. And the food was even better."

"Really? What'd you have?"

"I started out with Consommé Fermier. Maisy explained it to me. That's French for farmer's soup. It's a vegetable broth that was so very delicious. I ate it with soda crackers. For the main course, I had veal and ham pie. It was slices of veal and ham stacked in layers inside the thinnest crust that was six inches wide. And for dessert, I had this apple pie that was called Apple Meringue. I only had one wedge of it, but I believe I could've eaten a whole pie, it was that good."

"That all sounds so delightful, Roscoe. So how did your meeting with Maisy and the two detectives go?"

"Swell! This time Minta and I get to do some real sleuthing instead of me just knocking some guy on the noggin. Maisy wants us to talk to as many hotel employees and residents as we can and see what kind of gossip is going around about the three deaths that have happened at the hotel so far this month."

"Does Maisy expect there will be more deaths at the Alexandria yet this month?"

Roscoe scrunched up his face with thought. "She didn't exactly say that, but she did kind of imply that there might be more." He paused a second as his face broke out with a boyish grin. "Can you imagine what that would mean?"

Mabel smiled and shook her head. "Yes, I do. Somebody will start seeing ghosts in the halls, and that'll send Maisy on the hunt for apparitions in the night. The Alexandria will become spook central."

Roscoe eyes beamed with delight. "Do you really think so? Gosh, wouldn't that be something?"

"Yes, wouldn't it?" She hooked her right arm around his left at the elbow. "Come on, big boy. Let's get your makeup on again and back into your costume. We've got a movie to finish. Ol' Pathé is already so irked about you leaving for lunch early and coming back a half hour late that he let the whole cast and crew break for lunch ten minutes early and return to the set a half hour later than usual."

After a quick visit to the makeup room and then wardrobe, Mabel led Roscoe to the main building where all the indoor filming stages were located. They stopped just outside the set where they were filming. "Whatever you do, Roscoe, don't mention a word about lunch with Maisy and the others. If Pathé hears you, he'll explode like a box of dynamite."

"Thanks for the warning, Mabel. Mum's the word."

The two stars walked onto the set and were instantly approached by Lehrman. "And how was your lunch at the Alexandria, Roscoe?" He actually smiled at them; a most uncommon occurrence when he was directing a film.

"It was great, Henry."

"Good for you. Now, I see you are back into costume, and you have your makeup on again. Also, very good. Now, can we get back to making this movie?"

Arbuckle nodded. "I'm ready to work, Mr. Director."

Mabel gave Lehrman a weak smile. "Me, too, Henry."

Lehrman glanced around the set at the other actors and crew. He clapped his hands. "Okay, everybody. Now we shoot the scene where Mack and Ford plot to keep Roscoe away from Mabel. Are you ready, gentlemen?"

Sennett and Sterling nodded and took their positions.

"Roll film! Action!"

The two actors went into motion, speaking to each other about their plan to foil Arbuckle's attempt to romance Mabel and making facial expressions to accentuate their speech.

Lehrman watched them closely. Satisfied with the scene, he called for the cameraman to stop cranking the camera. "Let's do it again, only this time you change places."

Sterling and Sennett followed the director's order and switched to the other man's spot. Face-to-face again, they chuckled and shook their heads.

Lehrman groused. "And what is this laughter about?"

Sennett answered for both actors. "It's a private joke, Henry." He looked back at Sterling. "Right, Ford?"

"Anything you say, Mack."

The director appeared quite unhappy, but he returned to business. "Good. Now we work. Roll film! Action!"

Although now in juxtaposition and showing their opposite profiles to the camera, both actors became serious and repeated their lines as before.

The director studied their expressions and movements very closely again before ordering the cameraman to halt the filming. "I can't tell which take I like better. We look at them in cutting room and decide then. Yes?"

Being the producer of the film as well as an actor in the movie, Sennett voiced his approval. "Good enough for me, Henry. How about you, Ford?"

"Sure. Let's look at it in the cutting room."

Lehrman nodded. "Good. Now we set up for Roscoe and Mabel in their scene together."

In a matter of minutes, the property master directed his crew of three muscular stagehands into action. In no time at all, they had the props removed from the room where Sennett and Sterling had been plotting to keep Roscoe from romancing Mabel. Minutes later, they had Mabel's parlor furnished and ready for filming where the bashful beau presents the lovely object of his sweet intentions with a bouquet of flowers in his first attempt to win her away from the stiff-necked suitor played by Sennett.

The director voiced his pleasure. "Very good job, Mr. Herman. And fast. That, too. Good job, boys." He turned to his two actors for this scene. "Mabel, you hear a knock at the door. You go to answer it. Roscoe, you are on the other side of the door. We shoot you knocking on the door outside later or maybe tomorrow. We see how this goes first. Now to your places please."

Mabel went to the armchair in the room, sat down, picked up the morning newspaper, and pretended to read it as she waited for the director to call for action.

Roscoe went around the set to the door, knocked on it as a signal for Mabel to move into action, then patiently waited for her to open the door.

"Very good, people. Roll film, Mr. Wright. Action!"

Mabel turned a page of the newspaper. She closed the newspaper and looked toward the door. She asked herself aloud. "Who can that be at the door?" She put the paper on the end table beside her chair, then stood up, walked to the door, and took the doorknob with her right hand. As in every such movie scene, the door opened away from the camera. She opened it wide enough for the camera to pick up three-quarters of Roscoe's body. He held the flowers in front of him. The script called for him to be bashful at this moment. He was anything but. Fact was, Roscoe had a big grin on his face.

Lehrman put his megaphone to his mouth. "Roscoe, what's wrong with you, my friend? You are supposed to be tongue-tied and shy in the presence of the young lady you so desire to court and eventually marry." When Arbuckle offered no response, the director lowered the megaphone and turned back to the cameraman. "Stop filming, Walter. We have a problem."

Mabel leaned closer to Arbuckle. "It's the lunch at the Alexandria isn't it, Roscoe?"

The big man shrugged. "You might say that Mabel ."

"I thought so."

"Actually, it's getting a bigger part in Maisy's new investigation. It's got me all tingly inside. I can't wait for today's filming to be over, so Minta and I can start questioning people like Maisy wants us to do."

"You're kidding, aren't you?"

Lehrman walked onto the scene but stopped halfway to where his two actors were conversing. He feigned not to be listening to them by scanning the script he held in his left hand and nodding at each page as he pretended to be reading it.

Seeing their director standing close by now, the comic turned quite serious and lowered his voice even more. "Oh, no, Mabel. Weren't you all excited the first time you went sleuthing with Maisy?"

She answered in one octave above a whisper. "Yes, but I didn't think it was going to turn into a career like it seems to have happened for Maisy. This is the fifth murder she's tried to solve in the sixth months she's been here. I'll bet there's not a single private detective in the whole county who's had that many cases to solve in the past year. Maybe even in the whole state. And she always picks the ones the police can't solve."

"That's why it's so exciting, Mabel. She can solve murders that stump the police. Even Eddie Browning thinks that's incredible."

"Yes, and she incenses the police chief and infuriates the county attorney at the same time because they're embarrassed that she makes all of them look bad in the process."

"Gee, I never thought of that."

Lehrman had heard enough to set him off. "Well, Mr. Arbuckle, you had better start thinking about that and about your job here. If you can't focus on your work, then you just might be out of job before you know it."

Mack Sennett sat in his chair close enough to overhear Lehrman but not in a proximity to Mabel and Roscoe to perceive their exchange. "Hey, Henry, what's going on there? Why are you barking at my stars?"

The director turned to face his boss. "They are talking about that crazy Maisy Malone and not concentrating on their work."

Sennett stood up from his seat and joined Lehrman in the middle of the set. He waggled the fingers of his left hand at Mabel and Roscoe. "Come here, you two."

The leading man and leading woman obeyed without hesitation.

As was his way in situations such as this, the producer smiled ever so sweetly at them. "Now tell me, what's this you're doing that's upset my director so much that he's raising his voice at you in anger?"

Arbuckle didn't have the experience with Sennett to answer him, but Mabel had enough for the whole crew. She leaned toward her more than close friend and took on her coquettish persona. "Oh, Nappy, you know how intensely sensitive Henry can be when he thinks things are not going his way. He's just overreacting to our little conversation about the lunch Roscoe and Minta had at the Alexandria this afternoon."

Lehrman exploded again. "Lunch at the Alexandria? That is *not* what I heard."

Sennett turned to his director. "Just calm down, Henry, and tell me what it was that you did hear that's got you so upset."

"They were talking about that snoopy girl, that Maisy Malone that Mabel insists you keep around here only because she and Mabel are so chummy-chummy."

Roscoe found the nerve to speak up. "That's not the whole truth,

Mr. Sennett. I was just telling Mabel how excited I am to be a part of Maisy's sleuthing group on the new murder she's helping the police with."

The studio head's attitude transformed at the words *new murder*. He clinched his jaw to keep himself from exploding. Then he snarled at Roscoe through gritted teeth. "Do you mean to tell me that lunch I let you and Minta and Milo and Maisy go to at the Alexandria was all about Maisy dragging the three of you into another murder investigation for the police?" Before Roscoe could answer, Mack turned on Mabel. "Are you in on this as well?"

Before Mabel could respond, Arbuckle nudged her aside and with wide eyes and arched eyebrows and spoke up for her. "Maisy made it clear that Mabel won't be part of this case, Mr. Sennett. She said Mabel had made you a promise of some kind that she'd stay out of Maisy's next murder investigation, so she asked Minta and me to be part of her sleuthing group."

"And you accepted?"

"Yes, sir, we did."

"And when do you plan on doing this sleuthing for Maisy? We work pretty long hours around here, you know."

"Maisy said we should only go sleuthing in evenings and Sundays, just so it wouldn't interfere with our work here at the studio."

Although seething inside, outwardly Sennett reversed his attitude in the next beat of his true heart, forcing his next words to flow from his mouth like a breath of spring air. "She really said that? Maisy, I mean."

"Yes, sir, she did."

The producer turned to Mabel. "Did you really say that to Maisy? About your promise, I mean."

The little girl in Mabel blinked away a pair of intentional tears and nodded at the man who could warm her heart with a smile and a tilt of his head. "Yes, Nappy, I did."

As much as he wanted to embrace Mabel right then in front of the whole cast and crew, Sennett pursed his lips and fought back his desire to shed a few of the tears stirring to rise from deep in his soul. He cared too much for Mabel to show his true affection for her, so to hide the emotion, he turned to his seemingly cold-hearted director. "There you go, Henry. Now can we get on with the business at hand?"

Cooled off now, Lehrman's voice softened considerably. "Sure, Boss." He turned to his two actors. "Back to your places?"

Playfully, Mabel pinched Lehrman's left cheek. "Anything you say, Henry."

As they returned to their places, Roscoe leaned close to Mabel. "You pinched his cheek."

"If you're jealous, I can always spank yours, you know."

Red-faced with discomfiture, Arbuckle moved away from her. "I don't think that will ever be necessary, Miss Normand. My cheeks belong to my Minta."

Mabel closed the gap between them, grabbed his right arm with both her hands, and looked up at his eyes with a sweet smile. "Lucky girl."

"No, Mabel. Lucky me."

Detectives Browning and Ingram were on their way out of Central Police Station when Desk Sergeant George Willett called out to the senior partner. "Hey, Ed. Telephone call for you. It's Walt Ballard from *The Times*. He's says it urgent."

Both men stopped in front of the door, exchanged inquiring looks, but said nothing to each other. Then Browning focused on Willett. "Urgent, you say?"

"That's right. He was real excited about something he wouldn't tell me about. He said it was for you or Bill. So, it must be important."

"Well, can you switch the call to the holding room phone? No sense in tying up yours."

"Sure thing, Ed."

The two detectives remained silent until they entered the holding room and found it vacant. They nodded at each other and went straight to wall telephone to wait for it to ring. As soon as it did, Browning took the receiver from the switch hook and put it to his left ear. "Hello, George. It's me."

"Okay, Ed. Here's Ballard."

After hearing two clicks, one signaling the change from Willett's desk telephone to the station operator and the other from the operator to Walt Ballard's telephone at *The Times*, Browning spoke into the receiver of the wall telephone. "Detective Browning here."

"Ed, it's Walt Ballard. There's no one here but me, so we can be free to talk."

"Same here, Walt. Are you calling to tell us you've already found something?"

"Yes, I've got the names and addresses of all three funeral homes that handled the bodies of the three dead people from the Alexandria."

"That's great, Walt. Bill and I were just leaving to go back on our beat. So, your timing is perfect."

"You might want to write these down, Ed."

"Of course." He turned to Ingram. "Write this down, Bill."

"Sure." Ingram took his pencil and notepad from the left inside pocket of his coat. "Ready."

"Go ahead, Walt, but go slow. Bill doesn't write too fast."

"Okay, here goes. The Sullivan girl is at the Bresee Brothers Funeral Home at eight-fifty-five South Figueroa." He paused. "Am I going too fast?"

Browning repeated the information for Ingram. "Bresee Brothers at eight-fifty-five South Figueroa. Got it?"

Ingram nodded. "Yes, got it."

Ballard heard the lawmen. "Okay, good. Next is George W. Clarke, age fifty-six, died March third, Pierce Brothers handled his funeral. They're at eight-ten South Flower."

"George W. Clarke age fifty-six, died March third, Pierce Brothers, eight-ten South Flower. Got it, Bill?"

"Yes, I got it all."

"Great, gentlemen. Now last but not least. Mrs. America L. Lee, age sixty-three, died March second, native of New Orleans, funeral was handled by Sutch's Funeral Parlor at eight-forty-two South Figueroa. The owner and undertaker is Wendall H. Sutch. Get all that?"

Ingram nodded at his partner.

Browning replied to Ballard. "Bill says he got it, Walt."

"Well, there's more, gents. The article about the deaths of Mrs. Lee and Mr. Clarke stated the *hotel's resident physician* who attended them and pronounced them dead and then said how they died was Dr. R.L. Cunningham, not Dr. Newmark as you were led to believe by Mr. Whitmore."

"Really?"

"Really. Cunningham said Mrs. Lee died from heart failure caused by what he suspected were complications from liver and kidney issues. Then he said Mr. Clarke died instantly from a stroke that was *probably* brought on by an apoplectic condition. Note the word *probably* there."

"Bill is underlining it already, Walt. In other words, this Dr. Cunningham wasn't certain what killed Mrs. Lee and Mr. Clarke."

"You catch on quick, Ed."

"I try." Browning paused. "Bill and I will have to check on this

Dr. Cunningham tomorrow and see what he has to say about all this."

Ingram shook his head. "We can't tomorrow, Ed. Tomorrow is Tom White's funeral."

A shadow fell over Browning's face. "Yes, of course. Well, then Saturday. We'll examine him then."

Ingram nodded.

"Anything else, Walt?"

Ballard sighed. "Well, that's all I've got for now."

"So, what was urgent about this, Walt?"

"I thought you two would like to see Miss Sullivan's corpse before she's put on the train for Seattle tonight."

"Good thinking, Walt. We certainly would like to have a look at her. I know Dr. Newmark and Assistant Coroner Seager saw her, but I'm not sure we can trust either of them. What do you think?"

"I don't know about the doctor, but I've interviewed Seager on more than one death since I've been working Central Station. He's almost as slick as his boss who really can't be trusted to tell the truth."

"Same here, Walt."

"Will you boys let me know right away if you find out anything really interesting at the funeral parlors?"

"Certainly, Walt. Right after we tell Maisy."

Ballard groaned. "Of course, Maisy. She should be told first, shouldn't she?"

"You know her well, Walt."

"That's what scares me about her, Ed. I think she can see right through me."

Browning chuckled. "I've got news for you, Walt. She sees right through *all of us*."

"Yeah, well, I'd better get back to digging through all those old papers. Talk to you later, Ed. Oh, and good luck with the undertakers. Something tells me you're going to need it."

"Thanks, Walt. We'll call you later with what we find out. Bye." He replaced the receiver on its hook and turned to Ingram. "Shall we go to work now?"

Ingram shriveled where he stood. "Aren't you just a little worried about what we'll find out?"

"Yes, I am, now that you mention it. How about you?"

Ingram shivered. "Me, too, Ed. Me, too."

Maisy sat impatiently in a folding chair on the set of her movie, *Cohen's Outing*, waiting and hoping for director Wilfred Lucas to call it the end of the day an hour or more early. No such luck. This man ruled his set with an iron fist inside a velvet glove, just like Pathé Lehrman. She twisted and fidgeted and quietly watched Alice Davenport, the film's leading lady, acting out the scene where she discovers her husband has slipped away to the beach with his conniving pal. Maisy's part in the production had been completed the day before at the beach in Venice, but Mr. Lucas required all his people to remain with the film crew until the last shot was taken. As he put it, "You might learn something about this business by sticking around." So, Maisy followed the director's orders and kept her seat and did nothing to annoy any of the other cast members not in the scene or the crew members watching and waiting for their orders to do the work they were hired to do.

Finally, at 4:30 on the dot, Lucas shouted cut, and everyone there, except him, heaved a sigh of relief. To the casual onlooker, seeing all the people on the set suddenly start chattering and going into motion might have seemed a bit surreal, but to these motion picture folk it was just another day of filming coming to an end.

The director raised his megaphone to his lips. "See you all first thing tomorrow morning for any final retakes, if we need to shoot any, that is."

One by one the cast members said their farewells for the night to Lucas and slowly melted away from the set, while the crew members stayed behind to restore order to the props and sweep the floors. The cameraman and his assistant broke down their equipment and took the film they had shot that day to the laboratory for developing. Being the man in charge of everything and everyone, Mr. Lucas stayed to the last, just in case anyone wanted to ask him a question or two and to make certain everyone had done his or her job that day.

Maisy stayed behind with the director.

When all was done and they were alone, Lucas smiled at her. "Is there something you need, Miss Malone?"

"Well, yes, there is, Mr. Lucas."

He lifted his right hand with the palm toward Maisy. "We're all alone now, Miss Malone, so you may address me as Will."

"Okay, Will."

"Would you mind if I call you Maisy?"

"No, of course not."

"So, Maisy, how may I accommodate you?"

His use of an eleven-letter word raised a warning flag in her mind that was followed by an imaginary nautical signalman sending her a semaphore message that advised her to put a little humor in their conversation. *"Well, Will,* ... I ... *was wondering* ... if you might be ... *willing* ... to see your ... *way* ... clear to letting me take tomorrow off since all my scenes were shot at the beach in Venice and there's nothing left for me to do in this movie."

The director's smile vanished. *"Maisy,* ... your ... *meager* ... attempt to ... *amuse* ... *me* ... or yourself, I find quite abhorrent." The smile returned. "But I wonder if you have a better reason for taking the day off. You are under contract here, are you not?"

"Yes, I am, but usually I'm only another extra around here. I'm pretty certain the only reason Mack put me in this movie is because he's got this fetish for women in bathing suits, and I fill one out fairly well. In other words, I make pretty good scenery in the background."

Lucas nodded. "I rather thought that myself, Maisy."

"So, Will, if you let me have tomorrow off, I can join the other extras and maybe pick up a fin for the day if another director needs to put someone like me into the background of his film."

"I see what you mean, Maisy. So, yes, you can take the day away from our set, if you like. But ..."

Maisy waited for the other shoe to fall. "But?"

"But ... I would rather you have you here on the set ... for three reasons. The first, of course, being we might need you for any retakes we might have to shoot. The second being, if we do have the need for retakes, before we use up the additional film, I would like to hear your thoughts about the originals. And third ... you probably don't know this ... Mack asked me to consider you for a new position at Keystone. He said you have a keen eye and a quick mind, and you might make a good director, if given the chance. But first, he wants to know what your directors think of you as an assistant director. And thus far, I'm of the opinion that you will make a good assistant director."

Maisy blushed. "Gee, Will, I have to admit I'm shocked and quite flattered at the same time. And I don't know what else to say."

"Well, do you still want to be elsewhere tomorrow?"

A joyous smile spread over Maisy's face. "Well, not now, Will. I only hope you'll keep me in mind for your next picture."

"You'll be at the top of my list, Maisy."

Maisy met up with Mabel and Milo at the foot of Mack's Tower. "You know, nearly all afternoon, all I've been able to think about is all that delicious food at the Alexandria." She grasped Milo's left arm at the elbow, leaned against his upper arm, rubbed her cheek on his shoulder, and cooed like a dove. "What do you say, handsome? Do you want to take me out to dinner at the Alexandria this evening?"

Mabel grabbed Milo's other arm in the same manner as Maisy had done with the left. She even rubbed her cheek on his shoulder and cooed just as sweetly as Maisy. "Say yes, handsome, and you can take both of us out to dinner at the Alexandria this evening."

Milo knew this game all too well. The resident "Bobbsey Twins" had played it on him quite often before this, but never had they pressed him to take them to a place as fancy as the Alexandria.

"I'd like to do nothing better, ladies, but I simply can't afford it."

Maisy flashed her eyelashes at him. "We won't eat too much, Milo honey. I promise."

"It's not your eating I can't afford. It's your drinking." He glanced at Mabel. "Especially yours, Miss Normand."

Mabel pouted. "Hey! I resemble that remark. I'd take offense, if it wasn't so very true." Suddenly, she leaned away from Cole and snapped her fingers. "Hey! I've got an idea, and here it comes now."

Walking toward them were Wilfred Lucas, Henry Lehrman, and the studio head. Sennett was talking, while his two directors listened: all three men totally unaware of the trio in front of them.

Mabel released Milo's arm. "You two wait here, while I go make a deal for our meal ticket." She separated herself from Cole and sashayed straight toward the triumvirate of directors.

Maisy giggled. "I don't think you'll have to pick up the check after all, handsome."

"One of these days, Maisy Malone, you two are going to get me fired from this place."

"Mack will never fire either one of us, Milo. Not as long as Mabel works here. She's the real attraction around here, you know."

"Yeah, I guess you're right."

"I know I'm right. Now watch the pretty lady in action."

Lehrman saw Mabel approaching them first. "Don't look now, Mack, but here comes trouble."

Sennett and Lucas shifted their gaze in the same direction. Mack felt a sudden desire to be elsewhere—and in a hurry. Will could only smile politely at the sight of Mabel sashaying toward them in a mildly provocative manner. Lucas didn't know her well enough to recognize this was her way of getting what she wanted from a man. But Sennett knew. All too well he knew, and more so, he knew that whatever it was she wanted, she wanted it from him.

One more labored step and Mack came to a dead stop. "Boys, you go on ahead. This is for me."

Lehrman stopped one pace past Sennett, while Lucas took two more steps before halting. Pathé continued to stare at Mabel as he spoke to Sennett. "Should we wait for you in the Tower, Mack?"

"Yes, do that. I'll be up as soon as I handle this, whatever *this* turns out to be."

As Mabel passed the two directors, Lehrman acknowledged her with a nod. "Mabel."

Lucas made the same gesture but recognized her differently. "Miss Normand."

Still focused on Sennett, Mabel greeted them with a single word of one syllable. "Gents." And kept on walking straight ahead.

The studio boss slowly shook his head as he watched Mabel sway her hips even more now that Lehrman and Lucas were out of sight. As she closed the distance between them to a mere two feet, Sennett groaned. "What is it you want now, Mabel?"

She took one more step, stopped, strapped her arms around his neck, smiled sweetly, sighed, and whispered ever so softly. "I want you, Nappy. I want you to take me, Maisy, and Milo to dinner at the Hotel Alexandria this evening."

"Is that all?"

"Yes, that's all."

Sennett lowered his voice to a whisper. "And what do I get in return, my little Miss Cutie Pie?"

"You get a night out with your number one attraction, Nappy."

The key man at Keystone sighed. "I've had a long day, so I guess

I'll have to settle for dinner with you."

"Me, Maisy, and Milo, Nappy dear."

"Oh, yeah, I forgot. All right. Dinner it is for the four of us at the Alexandria. Okay."

Mabel stood on her tippytoes and gave Mack a big wet kiss on each cheek. "Seven o'clock?"

"I can do seven. Do we meet there, or do I pick you up?"

"We meet there. In the lobby. Okay?"

"Okay. Now beat it."

Mabel gave him one more hug, then raced away to tell Maisy and Milo the good news.

Sennett watched her go and spoke to himself under his breath. "Heaven knows I love that girl, but she's going to be the ruin of me yet." He waggled his head. "And there's nothing I can do stop it."

Excited like a kid with an ice cream cone, Mabel rushed to give the good word to Maisy and Milo. "He'll meet us at the hotel at seven."

The two girls danced up and down together for a few seconds before Maisy stopped and turned to Milo. "That's perfect for me. How about you, handsome?"

"I'll be there."

The three of them headed toward the main gate to catch the next Red Car back to the city. Halfway there, Milo stopped and snapped his fingers. "I forgot to tell you, Maisy. Ed Browning called and wanted you to call him back as soon as you get home this evening. He said he's got some new information for you."

"Fine time to tell me that, Milo. Did he say anything other than it's new information?"

Cole shook his head. "Nope. Just that."

Maisy stared down at her feet for a few seconds before an idea came to her. "I got it. I'll call Johnny to pick me up and take me to the hotel. While we're inside dining with Mack, he can ask around to the other taxi drivers about Marjorie Sullivan's death and see if he can pick up anything. Then we can compare notes afterward. Okay?"

Mabel and Milo nodded their agreement.

"Good. Now let's catch that Red Car and get shed of this place until tomorrow."

As soon as she sat down in her apartment at the Roosevelt Hotel, Maisy called Ed Browning at his home. "Hello, Eddie. Milo said I was to call you because you had some new information for me."

"Yes, that's right, Maisy. Let me start from the beginning, right after Bill and I returned to the station from having lunch with you and the other folks.

"You were right about telling people the truth when they asked us what and why we're looking into the deaths of Marjorie Sullivan, Mrs. Lee, and Mr. Clarke. When Nealy went into the station with Nellie Sharpe, Sergeant Willett stopped them and asked them what they were doing there. Bill and I came in right after them, and we told George that Nealy was there to help Nellie dig through some of the old records for any deaths similar to Marjorie Sullivan's. I told George they were doing it for me because I was interested in seeing if there was anything to this cycle of three business that Mr. Whitmore had told us about. Just like you said, George thought that was interesting and he assigned an officer go help Nellie and Nealy with their research.

"Then we went up to Captain Murray's office to thank him for the wonderful lunch we had at the Alexandria. Just to cover our hind parts before the gossip machine got rolling about why we're checking the records for similar deaths to Miss Sullivan's, we told Captain Murray what we were doing and why. He told us not to waste too much time on it, and we told him about Nealy and Nellie checking the records for us. He approved their involvement as long as it didn't take Nellie away from her regular police work. I assured him she wouldn't let it get in the way of her job at the station."

"So how did Nealy and Nellie do today?"

"They didn't find anything yet, but I'm sure they will in time."

"So, what else happened this afternoon?"

"Lots." He cleared his throat. "On the way out to walk our beat, we received a telephone call from Walt Ballard. He told us he had already found the names of the mortuaries, their addresses, and the people to talk to at each one.

"The first thing that came to mind for us was the locations of the funeral homes. They were all within a block of each other. Sutch's Funeral Parlor and the Bresee Brothers mortuary are across the street from each other on South Figueroa, while the Pierce Brothers mortuary is a block over from them on South Flower. These are the closest funeral homes to the Alexandria in the entire city. What do you think of that?"

Maisy snickered. "Probably the exact same thing you are, Eddie. Someone at the Alexandria didn't want all three bodies going to the same mortuary be-e-cau-au-au-se ... ?"

"Because he didn't want the same mortician to examine all three of them?"

"Give that man a cigar! You're right on the nose, Eddie."

Browning took a deep breath before speaking again. "Then you think this proves somebody at the Alexandria was trying to hide something?"

"Absolutely. Your hunch was on point, Eddie. There is definitely something off with the deaths of these three people. Especially with the death of Marjorie Sullivan who was very young compared to the other two decedents."

"And Bill and I think we might know what it is."

Maisy's voice deepened. "Okay, I'm all ears."

"We talked to the undertaker at each mortuary who examined one of our decedents, but we didn't tell any of the three that we're looking into the other two deaths. We didn't want to say anything that might influence their answers to our questions."

"Makes sense. Go on."

"When we asked each of them if he found anything unusual about the body, each of them retrieved his book of autopsy notes and read us what he had learned. Mrs. Lee was examined by Mr. Wendall Sutch. He determined that she died from a *cessation of breathing*. When we asked him to explain that he said she simply quit breathing in the middle of the night and died. Now this is the strange part. Mr. Sutch said she may have died from something called *Pickwickian syndrome*. I didn't know what that was until he explained it to me. Do you know what *Pickwickian syndrome* is?"

"I've heard of it." She paused. "Let me think for a second." Maisy pursed her lips in thought. "Pickwick is the main character in Charles Dickens's *The Pickwick Papers*."

"The what?"

"*The Pickwick Papers*. That's a humorous novel by Charles Dickens. I read it while I was in England. If you want to know more about it, ask Nealy. She reads a lot, so I'll bet she can tell you all about it."

A touch annoyance slipped into Browning's voice. "Okay, I'll do that later, but how does this book fit into our case here and now?"

"Well, there's a character in the book named Joe who's very fat and who eats lots of food and suddenly falls asleep at any time and during any situation."

"That's kind of what Mr. Sutch told me. He said Mrs. Lee was obese and over sixty years old and had a diagnosed heart condition as well. He said these things together can cause a person to stop breathing when they are sleeping, and after five minutes or so without air, the brain begins to die. Then once the brain is dead, the body begins to die one organ at a time."

A tinge of conceit puffed up Maisy's voice. "That's *Pickwickian syndrome* all right. So, what about the man who died at the Alexandria?"

"Well, Mr. Clarke apparently had a stroke that probably shut off the blood to the part of his brain that regulates breathing. Therefore, Mr. Clarke eventually stopped beathing and died. He had come here from Ohio for his health, but we don't know what his condition was that caused him to remove himself here. Neither Mr. Whitmore nor Dr. Newmark mentioned it."

"Okay, what about Marjorie Sullivan? What did her undertaker say about her cause of death?"

"First, let me tell you what else Walt Ballard told me. It seems that Mrs. Lee and Mr. Clarke were both pronounced dead by the *house* … doctor, one Robert L. Cunningham. According to this doctor, Mrs. Lee's death was probably due from heart failure induced by trouble of the liver and kidneys. Then he said Mr. Clarke's death was caused by a stroke that was probably brought on by an apoplectic condition."

"Did he really say *probably* in both cases?"

"That's what Walt said the article said."

Maisy mused. "Hm-m! Sounds like this Dr. Cunningham was *probably* guessing their causes of death."

"My thought exactly."

"Is there more on those two earlier deaths, Eddie?"

Browning nodded. "Only this one thing. Mrs. Lee's body was supposedly taken by the undertakers from the Booth and Boylston funeral directors."

"Let me guess. Their mortuary is in the same neighborhood as the other three you mentioned."

"Close. Their place is three blocks south of the Pierce Brothers on Flower Street."

"So did these Booth and Boylston undertakers do an autopsy on Mrs. Lee?"

"Apparently not. Mr. Sutch said the Booth and Boylston people were too busy to handle Mrs. Lee's funeral, so they passed her over to him because he was available at the time."

"Okay, Eddie. So, what about Miss Sullivan now?"

"Right. Miss Sullivan. Her undertaker was Mr. Melvin Bresee. He showed us a note in his journal that we found to be very interesting. He wrote that Dr. Newmark had told him that Marjorie Sullivan had died from phthisis pressuring her heart to the point that it stopped beating, which then caused her breathing to stop and bringing on her demise."

"That sounds like a reasonable diagnosis."

"We thought so, too, until Mr. Bresee said he ran a tube down into her lungs to draw out some of the fluid that Dr. Newmark said was in them. He wrote in his journal that he could only extract a little more … than an ounce … of phlegm."

"An ounce? That doesn't sound like much."

Browning chuckled. "It's not. According to Mr. Bresee, an ounce shouldn't have put anywhere near enough pressure on her heart to make it stop beating, even though she was skinny as a toothpick. His words, not mine."

'So, Eddie, what are you thinking about all this information you and Bill dug up today?"

"I'm thinking my hunch is spot on, Maisy."

She giggled. "That's an English phrase. I've never heard you say it before now."

"What? Spot on?"

"Yes."

"Would you prefer me to say my hunch is on target?"

"That's what it means, Eddie. The center of a shooting target is a spot. That's why people say something hits the spot. They're referring to the spot on a shooting target."

"That's a bullseye, Maisy."

"It is here in America."

Browning shook his head. "I've got to get out more."

"Oh, shoot! That reminds me. I have to change clothes. Johnny will be here any minute to pick me up."

"Johnny? Johnny Fowler?"

"Yes. Johnny Fowler. He's driving me to the Alexandria for dinner with Mabel, Mack, and Milo. Johnny's going to hang around with the other taxi drivers who park around there to see if he can pick up any gossip about the cycle of three deaths at the hotel."

"Well, have a good time. If you or Johnny pick up anything while you're there, please call me right away, will you? No matter what time of the night it is. Okay?"

"Sure thing, Eddie. Now I need go. Good-bye."

Before he could bid her adieu, Browning heard the distinct click of her ending the call.

Nealy came into the room and sat down in the big armchair that her husband usually occupied. "So, what did Maisy think about all the information you and Bill learned today?"

"She agrees with my hunch about this case as much as I do now."

"That's good."

"By the way, Darling. Have you read a book by Charles Dickens called *The Pickwick Papers*?"

"Did Maisy tell you to ask me that?"

"Yes, she did."

"And it has something to do with the case, doesn't it?"

Browning shrugged. "Well, you know Maisy."

Nealy smiled, stood up walked over to him, sat down on his lap, and threw her arms around his neck. "Don't we both, Dear?"

Walt Ballard had already retired for the night when Ed Browning called him. He almost didn't answer. "This better be good or I'm hanging up."

"Walt, it's Ed Browning."

The reporter sat up straight in bed. "Ed, you talked to Maisy?"

"Yes, I did. I told her everything Bill and I learned this afternoon, starting with what you passed on to us."

"And what did she say about it?"

"Just as we suspected she would. This is sounding more and more like a murder case as we learn more and more about it."

"I agree totally, Ed. And wait until you hear what else Mrs. Collins and I pulled out of the morgue this afternoon."

"Mrs. Collins? Who's she?"

"Oh, didn't I tell you about her?"

Browning groaned. "No, Walt, you didn't."

"She's a freelance writer that we occasionally publish in *The Times*. Brilliant woman, good writer, and now an excellent partner in digging into the files with me."

"Okay, we've established her credentials. So, what else did you find this afternoon?"

Ballard paused intentionally for effect. "Mrs. Collins found two more suspicious hotel deaths."

"At the Alexandria?"

"No, not there, but still in the county. One happened at the

Travers Hotel here in Los Angeles the night before Mrs. Lee and Mr. Clarke died. The other happened last Thursday at the Butte Arms apartment building in Long Beach."

"And how did these people die?"

The reporter chortled. "I knew you'd ask that. The one on the second was a retired lawyer from Chicago named Claudius Peters. He attempted to commit suicide by hanging himself from his bedstead, but the chambermaid found him in time to get someone to call for an ambulance to take him to County Hospital, where he died on the morning of the second from a stroke. Here's the kicker about him. He left a suicide note, several letters to authorities to notify his friends and family members back in Illinois, and a will. It's the will that's odd. He left all his personal effects in his hotel room to the chambermaid."

Browning snorted. "That is odd."

"Makes you wonder what the chambermaid was doing for him besides cleaning his room."

The detective cleared his throat, ignoring the intent of Ballard's remark. "Do we have the name of the chambermaid?"

"No, not yet. I called the hotel and asked, but no one there seemed to know squat about her or this Mr. Peters and his death."

"Hold on, Walt. Let me get Nealy in here to write all this down. Then Bill and I will pay a little visit to the Travers on Saturday."

"Sure, Ed. I'll hold on."

Browning covered the mouthpiece with his right hand. "Nealy, would you come in here please? And bring a pencil and a notepad with you. I've got some important information from Walt Ballard I need to have written down."

His wife came into the room a few minutes later, pad and pencil in hand. She sat down on the sofa. "I'm ready."

Browning repeated the information about Peters to Nealy, then returned to speaking with Ballard. "Okay, I'm back, Walt. So, tell me about this death in Long Beach."

"This one is really fuzzy, Ed."

"Oh? How so?"

"Well, to start with, the cause of death is multiple choice."

"What's that you said? Multiple choice?"

Ballard chuckled. "That's what I said, Detective." He snickered. "Multiple … choice. For beginners, the dead man's name was either *Don-nel-son* or *Don-nal-son* or *Don-nald-son* with a D before the *son* part. You know how newspapers screw up the names of people."

"Yes, I do. So, go on."

"Well, anyway, the first story about this guy Donelson—I'm going with that spelling because he was from Sweden. The first article about him appeared in *The Long Beach Daily Telegram*. I called down there to find out what they had to say about him because we only printed a summation of what they printed."

"Yes, of course. Go on."

"Like I was saying, the Long Beach paper said Donelson's body was found by the manager on the evening of February twenty-seventh around eight-forty. He was slumped over a small gas range, but the gas wasn't on and there was no smell of gas in the room, so that ruled out the gas as a cause of death. The next day an autopsy was performed by a couple of doctors down there. They came to the conclusion that he either died from a stroke or he starved to death, or he starved himself to death because he was supposedly a little light between the ears. The Long Beach police held a quick investigation, and they reported other occupants of the building said Donelson had occasional visitors from Pasadena who might have been relatives. So far, nobody has come forward to claim the body or his possessions. Here's the kicker with that. He had bank deposit slips in his room that totaled nearly four thousand dollars."

"*Four thousand?*"

"I said nearly."

"What kind of work did this man do?"

"He was a ship carpenter."

"A ship carpenter doesn't make that kind of money in a year. He must have been saving up for a long time. Did the article state the name of the bank?"

"No, but the reporter at the *Daily Telegram* said it was the *Exchange National Bank* on the southeast corner of Pine and East First Street."

Browning held his breath for a second. "Long Beach. Hm-m. Bill and I can't go down there asking questions. Who do we know who can do that for us? Maisy can't go. She and the others from Keystone have to work during banking hours. So, who does that leave? Johnny Fowler, I suppose. But Long Beach is more than a spin around the block from here. So, would he, do it?"

"I've got the perfect person for you, Ed."

"Who? You?"

"Oh, heck no!"

"Then who?"

Ballard chortled. "Mrs. ... Grace ... Lilian ... Collins."

Johnny Fowler drove his Studebaker up to the main entrance of the Hotel Alexandria on Fifth Street, where a uniformed doorman hurried up to open the car door for the taxi's fare. Out stepped Maisy Malone dressed stylishly for the occasion in a floor-length sapphire blue satin dress with mink trim angling down the left side of the V-neckline that revealed both collarbones down to the point of her sternum. Her hair was highlighted by a feathery silver headpiece, and a gold chain and locket adorned her chest down to the mid-point of her breastbone.

The doorman offered her his arm. She accepted. He paraded her to the entrance where a second doorman greeted her with a friendly smile, a tip of his top hat, and a few words. "Good evening, Miss." He opened the door for her, and her escort led her into the lavish lobby and straight to her party of friends, which included a pair of surprises: the Arbuckles.

Sennett gleamed. "Look who's right on time for a change."

Maisy ignored him. "Hello, everybody." She focused on the one married couple in the group. "Roscoe, Minta, I didn't expect to see you folks here."

Roscoe broke out his usual smile. "Minta and I enjoyed lunch so much this afternoon that we decided to try the dinner menu this evening, but we didn't expect to see all of you here, too. Maisy, you look amazing in that dress."

"Thank you, Roscoe."

Minta leaned against her man. "If I'd known you and Mabel were going to be here and so fashionably dressed, I would have thrown on my evening gown as well."

Maisy patted Minta's forearm. "You look just fine, dear. Correct me, if I'm wrong, but isn't that a Belle Époque dress from Paris?"

"How did you know that?"

"I spent a little time in France a while back, and I made the rounds of all the dressmakers. I didn't buy anything, of course." She smiled at Sennett. "Vaudeville pay isn't nearly as good as movie money." She winked at the studio head, then looked back at Minta. "Besides, you look divine in that dress. Black and white checkered fabric surrounded by black muslin. She looks simply divine, doesn't she, Mabel?"

"Oh, yes, I agree totally. You look marvelous, Minta."

Minta waved off both women. "Not as divine as you, Mabel. What is that gown you're wearing? It looks fit for a princess."

Maisy intervened. "Please allow me, your highness. *The Duchess of Normand* has attired herself for a night out on the town in a devoré velvet evening dress trimmed with metallic lace made from Wedgewood blue velvet cut to a gold satin ground with the bodice and underskirt featuring metallic gold lace."

Mabel waggled her head. "Stop it, Malone. You're embarrassing me."

Sennett interjected his own opinion. "I don't think anybody could ever embarrass you, Duchess."

Minta sided with Maisy. "I still say you look gorgeous, Mabel."

"Thank you, Minta. What do you say we girls go inside and leave these clowns to fend for themselves?"

Sennett shot out his own rejoinder. "Go ahead, Mabel. You do that. The boys and I will dine by ourselves, and I'll only have to pick up the check for the three of us, instead of the three of us *and* the three of you." He turned to Roscoe and Milo. "Gentlemen, shall we?"

Before they could take a single step together, Mabel surrendered. "Okay, Nappy, you win. You can pay for all of us."

The studio head winced. "Somehow or another, I think I just got bamboozled."

Mabel took his arm with both her hands. "Oh, Nappy, you're such an easy mark." She winked at Maisy and Minta. Come on, girls. Let's go eat. The boss is buying."

Mabel and Mack led the way past the elevators to the corridor that went to the main restaurant. Roscoe and Minta came next, then Maisy and Milo. In a minute, they arrived at the restaurant entrance where they were met by the food service manager Joseph Reikel.

"Good evening, ladies and gentlemen. When I heard you had made a reservation for this evening, I told myself that I had to be here when you arrived so I could personally show you to your table." He eyed the studio boss. "I was told you would be bringing a party of four, Mr. Sennett. But I count six in your group."

"We ran into Mr. and Mrs. Arbuckle in the lobby, and I asked them to join us, Joe. I hope that's not a problem."

"For you, Mr. Sennett, there are no problems in my restaurant. I see we have a reservation for Mr. and Mrs. Arbuckle as well. Give us a moment, and my waiters will arrange two tables to accommodate all of you together."

"Thank you, Joe."

Maisy leaned close to Milo and whispered. "Mack and Joe sound like they know each other quite well."

Milo whispered back. "They should. I make a reservation for Mack to dine here with someone from the studio almost once a week ever since he and Mabel, Mr. Sterling, and Mr. Lehrman arrived here in Los Angeles last summer. Lots of movie people eat here on weekends."

"Really? So where have I been all this time?"

"I thought you knew, Maise."

"I guess I don't know as much about the people at the studio as I thought I did. Maybe I should spend more time with my friends and a little less time at the city library."

"I can fix that for you anytime you want."

"You can't afford to do that, Milo."

Cole shook his head. "You surprise me, Maise. As Mack's personal assistant and part-time actor, I'm paid two salaries. Eighteen a week for being an extra, whether I get on screen or not. And fifty a week to do everything Mack tells me to do."

"Well, Mr. Rockefeller, *how do you do?*"

"He also pays me for writing a script now and then."

Maisy pulled away from Cole. "You're joking?"

He shook his head. "Nope. No joke. He also pays me to be his assistant director on the films I write for him. What do you think of them apples, tootsie?"

She shivered intentionally. "I'm speechless."

"Here, I thought you knew all this."

"You, handsome, are a well-kept secret."

Joe Reikel received a signal from his waiters. He turned to Mack. "Your table is ready, Mr. Sennett. Please follow me."

In the next two minutes, the three couples were seated at their table and reading over their menus with delight. Like the lunch menus, these were knockoffs of *R.M.S. Titanic*'s first-class bill of fare.

A puzzled expression tweaked Minta's face. "There are no prices on my menu."

Mabel explained. "If you have to ask the price of something, dear, then you can't afford it. Besides, Mack is paying, so who cares what anything on here costs. Just order whatever you want. He can afford it." Sitting next to his place at the end of the table, she reached over and patted his left forearm. "Can't you, Nappy?"

Sennett leaned close to his star attraction. "Mabel, why don't you wait until we've finished our first bottle of wine before you start being rude to everybody?"

She leaned away from him. "Aw, you're no fun."

One-by-one, starting with Roscoe who sat at the opposite end of the table from Sennett, the group gave their orders to the waiters. Mack placed his last. "Let's start with a nice claret for those having beef and a bottle of Chardonnay for those having fish or foul. As for my repast, I would like to start with oysters, consommé, the salmon with the mousseline sauce and cucumbers. After that, I'd like the roast duckling with apple sauce, green peas, and creamed carrots. For dessert, bring me the Waldorf pudding. I haven't had that in a while." He returned the menu to the waiter. "And since I'm paying for this, I'd like a bottle of a fine rosé." He waved at the other diners. "Bring glasses for all."

Sennett waited for the wait staff to vanish. "Okay, everyone. Since I'm paying, there will be no shop talk this evening. We're here to enjoy the best dining experience in town. And if you want to chat, chat about anything except the movie business. For starters, I'd like to hear what Maisy has to say about this new murder case all of you are involved in with her. Maisy, the floor is all yours."

Surprise painted Maisy's face with mellow colors. "Mack, I'm shocked. Ever since we solved the murder of Masi Tanaka, you've shown very little interest in my sleuthing adventures."

"Adventures? Is that what you call them?"

"For lack of a better word, yes."

Sennett nodded. "Okay, I can live with that. I could live with that a lot better, if you would write me a script that has lots of laughs in it."

"I'd love to write you a script, Mack, but not about murder."

He appeared taken aback. "Why not about murder?"

Maisy's face turned grim. "Murder is no laughing matter, Mack."

A frown covered his aspect. "No, I guess it isn't. So, how about a script for me and Ford playing our versions of Sherlock Holmes? Can you whip up one like that?"

Although Maisy hesitated, Mabel jumped into the deep end. "Sure, we can, Nappy. Just give us a few days, and I'm certain Maise and I can come up with something funny for you."

Sennett twisted his lips in thought. "Hm-m. Malone and Normand collaborating. That just might work. Okay, girls. Go for it."

Mabel added a personal touch. "Only if I get to direct it and Maisy gets to be my assistant director."

"Now you're pushing it, Normand."

She leaned closer to him and lowered her voice. "That's the deal, Nappy, or we walk … both of us."

He looked her straight in the eye. "You're kidding."

She didn't budge.

He turned to Maisy. "She's kidding, right?"

Maisy shrugged. "It's her call, Mack."

The studio head slumped in his chair. "Why did I ever get into this business?"

The wine steward and a waiter brought them a bottle of rosé and glasses all around. He popped the cork and poured a tasting flight into Sennett's glass.

Mack lifted the glass, swished the wine for color and purity, sniffed it for aroma, then sipped it for taste. He paused to consider the results. Then he smiled at the steward. "Very good, my friend. You may pour." He held out his glass to receive his own portion, then waited for everyone at the table to receive theirs. As soon as all were served, he raised his glass. "A toast! To the launching of a new writing and directing team! May they be as good at creating innocent laughs as they are at snaring villainous killers!"

Mabel and Maisy waggled their brows at each other and added their elation to the moment. With glasses raised, all pronounced their agreement. "Here, here!" Then Sennett led them in their first taste of the evening.

Replacing his glass on the table, Mack returned his attention to Mabel's best friend. "Okay, Maisy. You were about to tell us how your new adventure into solving murders for the police is going."

"Well, there's not much to tell yet. We're still in the early stage of gathering information about the victim ... or victims. We're uncertain about who might have been murdered or even if they were murdered. So far, the evidence of foul play is rather scant. But we've made some definite headway into the investigation. Each bit of information and possible evidence is leading us closer to proving there has been at least one murder and now possibly as many as ... three ... or more."

Everyone gasped. Some mumbled a single word. "Three?"

Mabel said the number very distinctly. "*Three or more?*"

"Yes, and we're looking for any deaths in hotels in other cities here in the county. Who knows what we'll find outside of Los Angeles? Maybe nothing, maybe a lot. We'll know more in the next few days, I hope."

Milo had the first question. "We just started looking into one death this afternoon. How did you come up with three deaths now?"

"Walt Ballard, Ed Browning, Bill Ingram, Nealy Browning, and

Nellie Sharpe went right to work this afternoon. Walt found the stories about the first two deaths at the Alexandria this month. Some of the information in them didn't fit with the information in the article in yesterday's *Times*. Ed and Bill spoke with the undertakers who handled the bodies of the deceased. What they learned from them didn't tally with what was in the newspaper. They're sorting that out over the next few days.

"Nealy and Nellie haven't found anything yet, but I'm sure they will before too long. Johnny Fowler is outside right now talking to the other taxi drivers to see if they know anything about the people in this place. That leaves Roscoe and Minta."

Roscoe cleared his throat. "That's why we came here tonight, to see if we could pick up some gossip about the people here and what they might know about Miss Sullivan's death. So far, no luck."

"Well, there you have it, Mack. We're only beginning to dig into the deaths of the three people at this hotel. So far, it all looks fishy, as Ed put it."

Sennett saw the waiters coming with their appetizers. "Speaking of fishy, here come my oysters and salmon. Yours, too, Roscoe. You'll love the oysters and the salmon here. I love them so much I order them every time I come here." He waited for everyone to be served. "Anyone want to say grace?" No one responded. "I didn't think so. Dig in everybody. Food is always better when someone else is paying for it, isn't it, Mabel?"

"You got that right, Nappy."

When everyone finished their desserts, Joe Reikel returned to their table for the first time since seating the group. "I hope everyone enjoyed our cuisine here at the Alexandria."

Sennett spoke first. "Superb, Joe. Absolutely superb. Anyone think different? Roscoe?"

"It was all delicious, Mack. You were so right about the oysters and salmon. Best I've ever had."

"Glad you enjoyed them, Roscoe."

Reikel continued his usual attention to special patrons. "Is there anything else I can do for you and your party, Mr. Sennett?"

"No, Joe, I think we're good. But let me ask." He glanced around the table. "Anyone want anything else?" Seeing no takers, he looked at Reikel again. "Yep, we're good, Joe."

The food service manager looked at Maisy. "Miss Malone, I hope you enjoyed your dinner as much as you enjoyed your lunch today."

She smiled and decided to answer him in German. *"Es war alles sehr gut, mein Herr."* ("It was all very good, sir.")

Reikel clicked his heels and bowed. *"Vielen Dank, Fräulein Malone. Ich hoffe, Sie werden uns bald zu einer weiteren Mahlzeit begleiten."* ("Thank you, Miss Malone. I hope you will join us for another meal very soon.")

"Darauf kannst du dich verlassen, mein Herr." ("You can count on it, sir.")

"Very good, Miss Malone." He focused on Roscoe. "And you, Mr. Arbuckle and Mrs. Arbuckle, I certainly do hope we will be seeing more of you here at the Alexandria in the future."

Roscoe broke out his best smile. "You better believe it, Mr. Reikel. You keep serving food like this, and we just might become regulars here. Right, Dear?"

"Yes, that's right."

Reikel eyed Mabel. "And you, Miss Normand, it was a true delight to see you here again. You should persuade Mr. Sennett to bring you here more often."

Mabel smiled precociously. "If the boss would up my pay to what I'm really worth to the studio, he won't have to bring me here. I'll be bringing *him* here more often."

Sennett grinned at Reikel. "I just might do that, Joe. I'd eat here every night, if I could afford it, but I can't because I have to pay this lady more and more after every picture, she makes for us."

The studio's main star waved at the maître d'. "He won't admit it, Joe, but it's my pictures that keep the studio in business."

The Keystone boss glared at her with a very facetious smile. "You won't have to make so many pictures anymore, Miss Normand, now that we've hired Mr. Arbuckle here."

Mabel knew she had reached her limit with Sennett. "Do you mean I'll be getting more time off to myself?"

"Time off? Are you kidding? My cleaning lady needs an assistant, and I'm thinking you just might fill the bill."

The actress threw her napkin onto the table, but she said nothing. Instead, she had another idea for when the exact moment was right.

Sennett looked up at Reikel. "Send the check over to the studio, will you, Joe?"

"Certainly, Mr. Sennett."

Mack slid his chair away from the table and offered his left hand to Mabel. "Shall we go?"

She remained seated because *the moment* arrived sooner than she expected. "No, I don't think so. I think I'll go up to the ballroom with Maisy and Milo and see if I can find a partner who wants to dance with a has- been from Keystone."

His eyebrow rolled up. "Suit yourself, young lady. Just be on time for work tomorrow." He saluted the others. "See you all tomorrow." He turned away and headed for the corridor to the lobby. "See you next time, Joe."

As Mabel steamed, Maisy leaned across the table to her. "Did you really mean it about going up to the ballroom with Milo and me?"

"No, dammit! And he knows it." She slid her chair away from the table. "I'll see all of you at the studio ... tomorrow." She stomped her right foot and stormed off after Sennett.

Maisy glanced around at the Arbuckles and Milo. "Well, shall we go up to the ballroom and see who might be around who can share the latest gossip with us?" When the three of them remained still and not answering her, she sighed. "Don't worry about those two. They do that all the time. You'd think they were married or something."

Walt Ballard made an arrangement with Maisy to have Johnny Fowler drive Lilian Collins down to the Exchange National Bank in Long Beach Friday morning. Lilian had intended to take the Red Car to port city, but Johnny changed her mind when she emerged from her home at 1945 South Burlington.

"Mrs. Collins?"

She stopped a few feet from her front door and looked at Fowler leaning against the rear passenger door of his Studebaker. "I did not call for a taxi, young man."

"No, ma'am, I know you didn't. Walt Ballard sent me to drive you to Long Beach this morning."

"I'm taking the streetcar."

Johnny chuckled. "Mr. Ballard said you would be … a little … obtuse. I think that was the word he used. At least, Miss Malone said that was what he told her."

"Who is Miss Malone?"

"Miss Maisy Malone, Mrs. Collins."

"Oh, yes, now I recall that name. Mr. Ballard said she's something of an amateur sleuth and she investigates unsolved murders. And Mr. Ballard is working with her on one right now. Am I correct, young man?"

"My name is Johnny Fowler, Mrs. Collins. And yes, you are quite correct about Maisy. She said for me to pick you up here this morning and drive you to a bank down in Long Beach so you can ask someone there some important questions about some fellow who died a couple of weeks ago."

Lilian pursed her lips as she studied Fowler for a few seconds. "You seem to know a little something about the murder case Mr. Ballard asked me to help him with, so I believe I will trust you to drive me to Long Beach. Do you know the way, Mr. Fowler?"

"Yes, I do, ma'am." He stood up straight, turned, grabbed the door handle, and opened the door for her. "And you can call me Johnny. Mr. Fowler was my father."

During the drive to Long Beach, Johnny and Mrs. Collins became more acquainted with each other and with the investigation now absorbing their free time. Fowler hailed from Texas; she came from Illinois. Both were married. He had two young children; she had one teenage son in his freshman year of college. She had lived in Phoenix, Arizona where her son Herbert was born. Both had only been in Los Angeles for the past few years. He had known Maisy for a couple of months now; she was eager to meet the real-life female version of the fictional Sherlock Holmes.

They arrived at the Exchange National Bank at the southeast corner of East 1st and Pine Avenue exactly two minutes before ten.

"Are you always so punctual, Johnny?"

"I try to be. Get a fare late to where they want to go usually means no gratuity. Same with getting them there too early. The closer to the exact time they want to be there, the bigger the gratuity."

"You aren't expecting a gratuity from me, are you?"

Fowler chuckled. "Oh, no, ma'am. Maisy pays me quite well to drive her around. Whatever the normal charge would be, she tacks on ten percent for every hour I'm driving her around or driving someone she wants me to take somewhere, just like I'm doing with you. Since I've been driving for her, my wife's been able to buy better groceries for me and the little ones. We're saving up to buy a house, too."

"That's very commendable, Johnny." She looked at the entrance to the bank. "Right on time, Johnny. The bank is about to open. See? There's a gentleman at the door now."

"Let me open your door for you, Mrs. Collins."

"No, Johnny, you stay where you are. I have no wish to make any false impressions with the gentlemen of this bank. I will let myself out of your taxi. But thank you for your courtesy."

The middle-aged man unlocking the bank door saw Mrs. Collins exit the taxi, then he watched her approach the building. Not knowing her, his initial thought was she must be a new customer. He opened the door for her. "Good morning, madam. Welcome to the Exchange National Bank. Please come right in. I am William J. Gardiner, the first cashier. How may we help you today?"

A few feet inside now, Mrs. Collins scanned the premises quickly, then turned back to Gardiner just as he completed closing the door. "I believe you said you are the first cashier, sir. Am I correct?"

"Yes, madam, you are quite correct."

"Then can you direct me to someone with more authority than you have here, sir?"

Gardiner ignored her dismissal of him. "Certainly, madam. That would be Mr. McQuigg. May I tell him what your business is here?"

"Yes, you may. My name is Lilian Collins. I am a freelance writer for several newspapers and magazines in this county. I am working on a story about one of your deceased depositors."

Great concern dismayed the man as displayed by the sudden change in his skin tone from sallow to ashen. "One of our deceased depositors, you say?"

"Yes, you are quite correct."

"May I inquire as to this person's name?"

"You may, but I believe I will reserve that piece of information for Mr. McQuigg. You did say that was his name, did you not?"

"Yes, I did, madam. You said your name is … Lilian Collins?"

"Quite correct, Mr. Gardiner. Now, will you tell Mr. McQuigg I wish to speak with him?"

"Yes, madam. Please wait here. I won't be a moment." Gardiner left her standing in the lobby by herself for the moment as he disappeared through a doorway behind the cashiers' counter.

While Mrs. Collins waited, a gentleman came into the bank and went to the assistant cashier's window. Then another customer, also a man, entered the building and went straight to the customer's desk where he picked up a pen and a deposit slip and filled out the amount he was placing in his account. Then Gardiner returned to the lobby.

"Mr. McQuigg will see you now, madam. Would you please follow me to his office?"

"Certainly, sir."

Gardiner led her through the same doorway he had used and into a long hall with three doors on each side. He stopped at the first one on the left and opened the door. Poking his head inside the room, he announced Mrs. Collins to the gentleman inside. She walked past Gardiner into the office, noting the name on the door in gilded gold letters: M. V. McQuigg. And his titles: Vice-President and Private Home Loans Officer.

McQuigg stood straight and tall behind his desk. "Good morning, madam. I am Martin McQuigg." He motioned to a straight-back chair in front of his desk. "Do please sit down."

"Thank you, sir." She sat slowly and primly, placing her handbag on her lap as she did and holding it with both hands.

The banker sat down in his highbacked chair. "Mr. Gardiner tells me your name is Mrs. Lilian Collins, that you are a freelance writer for several reputable publications here in southern California, and that you are here to make inquiries about a depositor of this bank who is now deceased. Is that correct, madam?"

"Indeed, sir. You were properly informed. I am working with a reporter for *The Los Angeles Times* on a story about the death of a Mr. Charles J. Donelson a few weeks back. One of the stories we read in your newspaper here, *The Long Beach Daily Telegram*, revealed that the police found several bank deposit slips in his rooms at The Butte apartments that totaled nearly four thousand dollars."

"Oh, yes, I recall reading about that very same thing in *The Daily Telegram*. Tragic, very tragic. His death, I mean. Yes, Mr. Donelson was a depositor at this bank, Mrs. Collins. I never met the gentleman, but I am certain either Mr. Gardiner or Mr. Wallace the assistant cashier can tell you something about Mr. Donelson."

"That would be nice, Mr. McQuigg, but I am not so interested in Mr. Donelson as I am in his account at this bank."

"I am sorry, Mrs. Collins, but that would be privileged information that by law we are not permitted to reveal."

She smiled at him graciously. "Think me not a fool, Mr. McQuigg. I am very much aware of the laws concerning the confidentiality between lawyers, physicians, and bankers and their clients, patients, and depositors. I believe in the case of this institution the laws are called banker-client privilege."

"You are quite correct, Mrs. Collins."

"But I am also aware that these laws only apply to living persons, not deceased depositors. Am I correct about that, Mr. McQuigg."

The banker retained his stone face as he responded. "Once again, madam, you are quite correct. So please tell me what it is exactly that you wish to know about the account of the late Mr. Donelson and also explain to me why you are so interested in his business."

"Certainly, sir. I can see why you would desire to know why Mr. Ballard and I have an interest in this man's death. We believe there may have been foul play involved in his death."

Suddenly, McQuigg leaned forward in his chair and placed his arms on his desk. "Foul play? And what makes you think there was any foul play with his death? The police made no such assumption. Neither did the two physicians who had been caring for him prior to his demise. They made the final decision that Mr. Donelson died from a stroke."

"Yes, I know about that, sir. But I am still interested in his account with this bank. Can you tell me exactly how much money he has on deposit here?"

"Yes, certainly. He has no money on deposit in this institution."

The banker's reply completely caught Mrs. Collins off-guard. "Do mind repeating that, Mr. McQuigg?"

"Certainly. Mr. Donelson has no money on deposit in this bank at this time."

She winced. "I do not understand, sir. How can that be? *The Daily Telegram* stated—"

He interrupted her. "I am very much aware of the stories in the newspaper, Mrs. Collins. Yes, Mr. Donelson did make deposits in this bank that came near the total of four thousand dollars, but after his death, his account was closed by a relative of his through an attorney."

A bit speechless now Mrs. Collins paused to give this news some serious consideration. Realizing there was more to the death of Charles J. Donelson than previously suspected by Walt Ballard, she lifted her handbag a few inches. "Would you mind terribly if I take notes of our conversation, Mr. McQuigg?"

He gestured with his right hand. "Please do, Mrs. Collins. I see by the expression on your face that you believe Mr. Donelson's demise is not so simple as the police determined it to be."

"You are quite correct, sir."

"Well, madam, I can only reveal what I know about Mr. Donelson and his business with this bank. For anything more, I suggest you call on our police department and ask them what they know."

"Thank you for your recommendation, Mr. McQuigg. I will certainly do that as soon as we are finished here." She opened her purse and removed a pencil and a notepad. "Now I believe you said Mr. Donelson's account was closed by someone acting through an attorney. Is that correct, sir?"

"It is, madam." He raised his hand to stop her from asking her next question. "I know what you are thinking, Mrs. Collins. You're going to ask me for the names of the lawyer and his client. I can only tell you this much. The attorney's name is George L. Bachman, and his office is in the Long Beach Bank Building across the street. As for his client, he would not tell us that person's name."

"Then why did you let him close the account and withdraw the money in it?"

"We did not let him withdraw the money, Mrs. Collins. We are keeping the money in the bank until Mr. Bachman can provide us with proof that his client has a legal right to the money. Thus far, Mr. Bachman has failed to do so. You might say the ball is in his court for now."

"I take it that you have no idea who his client is."

McQuigg shook his head. "Not really. We believe Mr. Donelson has relatives living in or around Pasadena, but thus far, the police have not found anyone who claims to be Mr. Donelson's relative other than Mr. Bachman's client."

"You said his client was from Pasadena. How do you know this to be true?"

McQuigg raised his right hand to her. "I misspoke, Mrs. Collins. He did not say where his client resided. We are only *assuming* Mr. Bachman's client is from Pasadena. A bit of a faux pas on our part, I'm afraid."

"Excusable for sure, Mr. McQuigg." She cleared her throat. "So, when did Mr. Bachman first approach the bank about Mr. Donelson's account?"

"He came in here a week ago Tuesday and stated unequivocally that his client was the sole surviving relative of the deceased and that this person, whoever he or she may be, had every right to the funds in Mr. Donelson's account. Mr. Wiley, the bank's president, informed Mr. Bachman that, as soon as he had a statement signed by a judge of the local court ordering him to do so, then he would gladly turn over the funds from the account of the deceased. But until then, those funds would remain right here in this bank."

Lilian nodded. "I see. Has Mr. Bachman returned here since then with any proof or further demands on the bank to hand over the funds from Mr. Donelson's account?"

"No, he has not come in here since his only visit last Tuesday." He leaned forward on his desk. "Frankly, Mrs. Collins, I don't believe Mr. Bachman or his alleged client will ever come into this bank with the proper document ordering us to hand over Mr. Donelson's funds. It's my opinion that Mr. Bachman's client is not a relative of the deceased, and therefore, he or she is not legally entitled to the money."

Mrs. Collins returned her pencil and notepad to her purse. "I am in total agreement with you, Mr. McQuigg." She rose from the chair. "Thank you for your time and the information, sir. You have been very helpful. Good day."

McQuigg stood up. "You are quite welcome, Mrs. Collins. Please allow me to show you out."

"Thank you, sir, but that won't be necessary."

"Then good day, madam."

The first cashier saw Lilian coming from McQuigg's office. He smiled ever so politely at the gentleman depositor at his window. "Will you excuse me for a moment, Mr. Schmucker? I won't be but a minute, sir." Without waiting for a response, Gardiner left his post at the cashiers' counter and hurried out to the lobby to intercept the freelance writer. "Pardon me, Mrs. Collins."

She stopped abruptly. "Yes?"

He smiled with all due courtesy and spoke softly. "Did you get all the information you needed from Mr. McQuigg, madam?"

"Yes, I believe I did. Mr. McQuigg was quite helpful."

"Good. Allow me to escort you to the door."

"That will not be necessary, Mr. Gardiner."

His smile expanded, but his voice dropped another level. "But I must, Mrs. Collins. I believe I have something to share with you that Mr. McQuigg may not have told you."

Surprised, she allowed herself to smile back at him. "Why thank you, Mr. Gardiner. How thoughtful of you!"

He motioned to the bank entrance. She started in the direction, and he accompanied her a half-step behind. At the doorway, he opened it for her. "Is that your taxi out there, Mrs. Collins?"

"Yes, it is."

"Then allow me to assist you to it."

"Thank you again, Mr. Gardiner."

He permitted her to exit the bank ahead of him, then followed her to the Studebaker's rear passenger door. "I must hurry, Mrs. Collins, so allow me to be brief. Did Mr. McQuigg tell you about the woman who came into the bank last week and made several remarks about the death of Mr. Donelson?"

Although astonished, Lilian tried not to show it. She smiled. "No, he said nothing of the kind." She paused. "Should he have told me about this woman?"

"Yes, but *I* can't tell you about her right now. Could we meet for lunch, Mrs. Collins? So, I can tell you all about her?"

"Certainly, sir. Where?"

"Meet me at The Chicago. It's a block east at two-nineteen East Pine. I take lunch at twelve-thirty. Is that all right with you?"

"The Chicago … at twelve-thirty. My driver and I will be there."

Gardiner looked quizzical. "Your driver?"

"Yes, him." She pointed at Fowler sitting behind the steering wheel of his taxi.

The cashier smiled nervously. "Yes, of course. I will see you and your driver then." He turned and scampered back into the bank.

She watched him go. "Well, that was rude. He could have at least opened the door for me."

After informing Fowler of her intention to seek out lawyer Bachman, Mrs. Collins crossed the street to the Long Beach Bank Building. The National Bank of Long Beach occupied three-quarters of the first floor with its own entrance in the very middle of the Pine Avenue side of the structure, while a separate entry on the 1st Street side led to the four upper floors. Entering the latter, she looked for the wall directory of residents in the offices above and found it beside the elevator. With a quick perusal of the occupants, she spied the name she wanted: G. L. Bachman, Attorney-at-Law, Room 203. To be certain of the lawyer's name, profession, and room number, she opened her purse, took out her pad and pencil, and wrote the information at the bottom of the page where she had inscribed the notes from her interview with Mr. McQuigg. Being a very frugal person, Mrs. Collins forewent taking the elevator because it would require her paying the operator a gratuity; and instead, chose to climb the stairs to the second floor. The ascent did increase her breathing, but not so much that she had to rest a moment when completed. She looked at the number on the office door directly in front of her: 205. To its right, she read 207. She turned to the left, went several steps down the hall, and arrived at her intended destination, a door with a window of frosted glass and the name and profession of the occupant etched in gold letters. The notion of knocking quickly passed to be replaced by the thought that a lawyer would have an assistant or a secretary in a reception room to take telephone calls and to screen any visitors. She turned the doorknob and entered the office to find a young man of teen years sitting behind a double-drawer desk.

"Good morning, madam. May I help you?"

"I would like to speak with Mr. Bachman."

The youth smiled politely. "Yes, of course, madam. May I tell him your name and your purpose for wanting to see him?" He picked up a pencil and prepared to jot down the information he requested on a lined notepad.

"I am Mrs. Lilian Collins. I am a freelance writer for a number of newspapers and magazines in this county, and I am here to speak to Mr. Bachman about his representation of a client of his who has retained his services in the matter of the largesse left on deposit at the Exchange National Bank across the street."

When he finished making his notes, the clerk motioned to a vacant chair a few feet from the hallway door. "Please be seated, Mrs. Collins, and I will tell Mr. Bachman you are here." The young man rose from his swivel chair, went to the door leading to the inner office, opened it a third of the way, held it there as he poked his head inside, then spoke to his employer. "There's a Mrs. Collins here to see you, Mr. Bachman. She says she is a freelance writer and wishes to speak with you about the Donelson account in the bank across the street."

Unknown to the assistant, Mrs. Collins had remained standing and had taken two steps closer to him and the door to the inner office.

An elderly male voice responded to him. "Tell her I'm busy and to come back another day."

"Yes, sir."

Before Bachman's subordinate could close the door, Mrs. Collins barged past him and into the lawyer's office. She stopped abruptly at the sight of a white-haired gentleman sitting behind a large mahogany desk and reading a single page of a type-written document through a pair of wire-rim spectacles. Only when she cleared her throat did he look up over his glasses. Seeing that she had his attention, she spoke with authority.

"Mr. Bachman, I am Mrs. Lilian Collins, a freelance writer for several newspapers and magazines in this county, and I have only now come from interviewing Mr. William McQuigg, a vice-president of the Exchange National Bank across the street. He has informed me that you represent a client who claims to be the heir of one Charles J. Donelson who died two weeks ago under some rather mysterious circumstances and who left a large sum of money on deposit at the Exchange National Bank. Am I correct thus far, Mr. Bachman?"

The attorney looked beyond Lilian at his assistant. "You can go back to your desk, Ralph. I'll deal with this lady."

"Yes, sir." The young man closed the door behind him.

Bachman waved at a straight-back chair in front of his desk. "Won't you please have a seat, Mrs. Collins?"

"Thank you, sir." She sat, opened her purse, and took out her pad and pencil. "Now about this client of yours."

The lawyer held up both hands. "First, Mrs. Collins, tell me what your interest is in my client."

"As I said before, Mr. Bachman, I am a freelance writer for several newspapers and magazines in this county. I read a most intriguing story in *The Los Angeles Times* two days back with the headline, 'Mystic Death Cycle of Three Complete.' It was mostly an interview with the general manager of the Hotel Alexandria in Los Angeles who spoke about death, accidents, and other unusual events coming in cycles of three in hotels and other such places. My curiosity was piqued. Therefore, I began doing research into past issues of *The Times* to see if there might be other such so-called cycles of three. That is when I came across the article about the death of Mr. Charles J. Donelson. How he died raised my curiosity, but more than his cause of death, I was very curious about the fact that the police found bank deposit slips totaling nearly four thousand dollars in his apartment. This took me to the Exchange National Bank where I interviewed Mr. Martin McQuigg, the bank's third vice-president. Mr. McQuigg was quite open with me concerning Mr. Donelson's account with the bank. He told me about your request to have all the funds in Mr. Donelson's account handed over to you on behalf of your client." She held up her hand to halt any interruption he was about to make. "Yes, he told me what you said about your client wishing to remain anonymous, and he told me about his refusal to give you those funds without a signed court order from a local judge. Since more than a week has gone by since you visited with Mr. McQuigg, I have come to two possible conclusions. Either you have been unable to find a judge willing to grant you the judgement you seek on behalf of your client or your client is still insistent on remaining anonymous, which is why you cannot find a judge who is willing to grant your request. Thus, my presence in your office. I am hoping you will tell me which of my two possible conclusions is the correct one."

Bachman hesitated to respond, drooping his head for a second, then raising it again and looking Lilian straight in her eyes. "Actually, Mrs. Collins, it's both. My client won't agree to revealing her name, and I can't—"

She interrupted him. "Did you say *her* name, Mr. Bachman?"

Again, the lawyer hesitated to respond as he realized his error. He paled, then leaned forward, resting his left cheek on his left hand with his left elbow on the desk. "I'm getting too old for this profession, Mrs. Collins. I should have retired years ago. But it's what I've been doing for almost fifty years now. All that time except for the year I served in the Union Army during the War of the Rebellion. I was a corporal in Company E of the one hundredth and thirty-fifth regiment of Pennsylvania Volunteers. I was captured at the Battle of Chancellorsville in the Spring of eighteen and sixty-three. I was part of a prisoner exchange in August and was mustered out soon after because my fellow prisoners and I took an oath not to fight against the Rebs any more after that. That was the condition of our being released. I went home to Michigan and took up the law again. After my son Georgie died, my first wife divorced me, and I moved back to New York, where I was born. Lots of family there. I remarried and had a good practice there until my second wife died a few years back. That's when I decided to move out here. I received my license to practice here last summer, and now here I am talking with you about one of the few clients I've had so far. I'm so old in this business that I made that simple little mistake of referring to my client as *her*, and you caught it. Yes, Mrs. Collins, I did say *her*. My client is a woman, and she claims to be related to the late Charles Donelson."

"She *claims* to be related to the late Mr. Donelson. That sounds like you doubt her veracity, Mr. Bachman."

"There you have me again, Mrs. Collins. Yes, I do doubt that she is related to the deceased. Why, you may ask, madam? Because Mr. Donelson was a native of Sweden, and the lady in question spoke near perfect American English. In fact, I would say she spoke without any accent at all. Nothing like a New Englander or a Southerner or even an Englishman or any other European."

"Since you are revealing all this information to me, Mr. Bachman, why do you continue to keep her name to yourself?"

"Very simple, Mrs. Collins. I took an oath, a confidentiality oath to protect my client's interests until released by her death or by her giving me a release from that obligation. Until one or the other happens, I am bound to secrecy of her name. And since she will not permit me to reveal her name to any third party, I can tell you nothing more about her except that she claims to live in Pasadena. I also have my doubts about that being true in that she has not made herself known to the local police department."

"How do you know that sir?"

"One of the first things a lawyer does when he sets up practice in a new town is call on the local city and county attorneys and the judges. The second thing he does is call on the local sheriff's office and the chief of police for the city. Al Austin is chief of police here in Long Beach. As soon as my client retained me, I called Al and asked him if anyone had come to the station to ask about the dispensation of the deceased possessions and bank funds. No one had at that time. Then I asked Al to notify me the minute someone did come in to make a claim on Mr. Donelson's estate. That's when he told me his office had made the Pasadena police aware of Mr. Donelson's demise and had asked them to notify any possible relatives of the deceased living in their city. Al said he would keep me informed about anything concerning the late Mr. Donelson. To date, he's heard nothing, and neither have I."

Lilian pursed her lips. "Hm-m. I have come to the conclusion, Mr. Bachman, that you can tell me nothing more about this mystery client of yours."

"I am afraid you are quite correct, Mrs. Collins. I wish I could be of more assistance to you, but if you leave your name and telephone number with young Ralph out there, I will contact you when … and if … anything changes on this end."

"Thank you, Mr. Bachman. You have been more than gracious to me, sir. I will reciprocate by advising you of any progress I may make on the very curious death of Mr. Donelson." She stood up. "Good day to you, sir."

"Good day, Mrs. Collins."

She stopped at the door, turned stiffly to face the lawyer, then a smile curved her lips. "There is one more thing, Mr. Bachman. Could you possibly give me a description of your client?"

The attorney's lips pinched together, his eyebrows followed suit, and a deep sigh came last. "I would really like to do that for you, Mrs. Collins, but once again, I have to invoke attorney-client privilege."

"Of course, but I had to ask. Good day, sir."

Lilian returned to the street and quickly apprised Johnny Fowler of her positive meeting with George L. Bachman, Attorney-at-Law. She concluded her lengthy monologue by advising him of their next destination. "The Chicago Restaurant is in the next block of East First Street. We will be meeting Mr. William J. Gardiner there."

"Who's he, Miz Collins?"

"Mr. Gardiner is the first cashier of the Exchange National Bank."

"Didn't you get to talk to him when you were in the bank?"

"Not exactly, Johnny, which is why he escorted me to your taxi. He wanted to ask me to meet him at this restaurant down the street. And he specifically told me he wanted you to attend our meeting as well."

A big Texas grin spread over Fowler's face. "He did? Now ain't that something? Finally, I get to listen in on one of the question-and-answer deals Miss Maisy is always doing."

"Miss Maisy? Oh, yes, you mean Miss Malone, correct?"

"Yes, ma'am. Right you are."

"Mr. Gardiner said he would meet us at twelve-thirty. Do you have the time, Johnny?"

As he dug his hand into his shirt pocket to retrieve his silver pocket watch, he winked at Lilian. "I sure do, ma'am." He flipped the lid. "It's three minutes past noon."

"Very good, Johnny. Let us be on our way. We can have lunch while we wait for Mr. Gardiner."

Much to his surprise, Fowler found a parking space on the same side of the street as the Chicago Restaurant and only two doors down from the eatery. He escorted Lilian inside. "There's a table with four chairs, Mrs. Collins. Should we take that one?"

"Yes."

The counter stools were all occupied by men in work clothes, most of them shipyard workers. Many of the tables seated ladies in street wear who were accompanied by gentlemen in suits. Only a few of the diners paid any attention to the new arrivals.

Fowler pulled out a chair for Mrs. Collins, then he politely waited for her to sit. "Thank you, Johnny."

"You're welcome, ma'am." He walked around the table, pulled out the chair opposite her. He sat and scooted closer to the table.

"Please remove your hat, Johnny."

Fowler's face blanched with fright, then paled as he snatched his navy-blue cotton cabbie cap from his head and placed it on his lap. "Beg pardon, ma'am. I'm not so accustomed to eating in a restaurant with a lady."

A touch of guilt tilted Lilian's head to the right a few degrees. "My apology to you, Johnny. I am so accustomed to giving directions to my son that I forgot myself for the moment."

"Aw, that's okay, Miz Collins." A friendly smile curled his lips.

"For a second there, I thought I was back home in Texas and my dear, sweet mother was making me mind my manners."

Lilian smiled sweetly. "I will accept your remark as a compliment, Johnny. It's not often someone tells me I remind them of their mother, even if in the slightest way. So, thank you."

"You're quite welcome, ma'am."

"I noticed today's menu was written on a blackboard on the wall behind the counter. Did you see it as well?"

"Yes, ma'am, I did. That ham and Swiss cheese on rye looks like a good meal to me. And that Coca-Cola sign must mean they serve that here as well. I wonder if they keep it cold here."

Just then, a middle-aged woman wearing a white apron over a dark blue cotton dress stepped up to their table. "Good afternoon, folks. My name is Regina. I don't recall ever seeing you in here before."

Lilian spoke up. "Yes, you are quite right, madam. This is our first visit to this lovely establishment."

"Well, thank you for the compliment, ma'am. My husband and I take pride in our little restaurant here. And I hope you like our food, too. We don't serve anything fancy. Only what you see on the board behind the counter."

"The choices seem more than adequate, madam. My driver would like a ham and Swiss cheese sandwich on rye. And he would also like a cold bottle of Coca-Cola. You do have them on ice, don't you?"

"Not exactly. If you want a cold Coca-Cola, I can bring you a glass with ice in it. Will that do?"

Fowler nodded. "You bet, ma'am."

Regina looked back at Lilian. "And what can I get for you?"

"The egg salad sandwich on white is to my liking. With a glass of cold milk."

"One ham and Swiss on rye with a bottle of Coca-Cola and one egg salad sandwich with a glass of cold milk." She winked at Johnny. "Coming right up, folks."

Regina left them and went to the window to the kitchen to order their food.

The cabbie focused on Lilian again. "I usually bring my lunch with me from home. So, this is sort of a treat for me."

She smiled at him. "And dining with you, Johnny, is … sort of a treat for me as well. Being with you in this place makes me feel … a bit younger. I will have to thank Miss Malone for arranging for you to be my driver today. That is, if I ever get to meet her."

"Oh, I'm sure you will, ma'am. Miss Malone is one of a kind, sharp as a tack. I'm sure she'll get this case solved in no time."

Just then, Regina reappeared with two plates in one hand, a bottle of Coca-Cola under her right arm, and a glass of cold milk and a glass of ice in the other hand. Very adroitly, she placed the two glasses on the table, then with her now free hand, she placed the plates with their sandwiches on the table in from of the right customers. Last, she took the bottle of Coca-Cola with its Hutchinson cap from under her arm. "Would you like me to open it, young man?"

Johnny smiled at her. "No, ma'am, I can do it." He held out his hand, and she gave him the soft drink. "Thank you, ma'am." He put his right index finger in the ring of the stopper, twisted it to loosen the rubber plug, then pulled. And just like that the bottle was open. He picked up his glass with ice and poured his drink.

Regina then moved the glass of milk close to Lilian's plate. "Can I get you folks anything else?"

Mrs. Collins smiled politely at Regina. "No, thank you. I'm certain this will be enough for now."

"Well, let me know if you want dessert. We've got fresh apple pie, banana cream pie, and peach cobbler. But you better make up your minds quick before all them dock workers at the counter buy it all up."

"We'll think about it, madam."

"Suit yourself." And with that she left them alone.

Lilian and Johnny ate in silence, while at the same time keeping track of the time and observing the other customers and Regina as she moved about the other people at tables. None of their fellow diners seemed interesting to them or interested in them.

Then William Gardiner entered the eatery at 12:28. He stood just inside the doorway looking around the restaurant until he spotted Mrs. Collins and Fowler. Before he could move toward them, Regina saw him and quickly approached him.

"Well, Mr. Gardiner, haven't seen you in here for a few days. Nice to see you. Got a stool at the far end with your name on it."

"Thank you, Mrs. Reynolds. But I see some folks I know sitting at a table. I think I'll ask them if I might join them."

"Suit yourself, Mr. Gardiner." She watched him walk to Lilian and Johnny and stop at their table, then returned to waiting on other tables for the moment.

Lilian looked up at the bank cashier. "Right on time, Mr. Gardiner. Glad to see you are so punctual."

"I'm a banker, Mrs. Collins. I am trained to be punctual."

"Yes, of course, sir. This young man is my driver, Mr. Fowler."

Gardiner nodded at Johnny. "Nice to meet you, sir."

"Likewise, Mr. Gardiner. Won't you sit with us?"

"Thank you, I will." He chose the chair that faced the counter and placed his back to the big window and the street outside. "My presence here with you folks shouldn't draw attention to anyone, especially since what I have to tell you needs to be confidential."

Regina came to their table again. "So, are these the folks you saw here and wanted to join, Mr. Gardiner?"

"Yes, they are, Mrs. Reynolds. This is Mrs. Collins and her driver, Mr. Fowler."

"We've met. Can I get you the usual Friday special, Mr. Gardiner?"

"Yes, that would be nice."

Regina nodded. "Tuna fish salad on rye, black coffee, and a slice of apple pie coming right up." She turned to Lilian. "Can I get you any dessert, Mrs. Collins?"

"None for me, thank you, but I can see by the look on his face that my driver would like something." She smiled at Fowler. "Go ahead and order whatever you like, Johnny."

"Thank you, ma'am." His eyes twinkled with a sheepish grin at Regina. "That peach cobbler sure does sound good, ma'am."

She winked back at him. "I figured you for a good ol' southern boy. Georgia?"

"No, ma'am. Texas."

"Of course. One slice of peach cobbler coming right up." She left them in a rush.

As soon as Regina was out of earshot, Lilian turned to Gardiner. "So, tell us about this woman you mentioned earlier."

Gardiner nodded toward Regina. "That's her. Regina Reynolds. Her husband Andrus owns this place. He's the cook. He also sells real estate on weekends and evenings. He says once he starts making enough money in real estate that he's selling this restaurant and doing his real estate business full time."

Lilian queried. "What does this have to do with Mr. Donelson?"

"Charlie Donelson ate his lunch here regularly. He was a carpenter at the shipyard, you know."

Johnny jumped in. "So, what's the connection, Mr. Gardiner?"

Gardiner faced Fowler. "The connection, young man, is Charlie and Andrus came here from Sweden."

"So, then Regina is Swedish?"

The banker laughed. "Certainly not, Johnny. She's from Iowa." He jostled Fowler's arm. "Couldn't you tell from the way she talked?"

The cabbie blushed. "Well, she did sound like a Yankee, I guess."

"Regina and Andrus met in Nebraska and got married there before coming out here when she heard her cousin had married an immigrant from Germany or someplace like that in Europe."

A thought crossed Fowler's mind. "Now ain't that interesting?"

Gardiner smiled cleverly. "It is, isn't it? But there's more. Regina told me once that Andrus has relatives who live in Pasadena and who come down here on occasion and who he and Regina visit on occasion. And guess who joined them when they got together here or there?"

"Charlie Donelson?"

The cashier smiled at Lilian. "Your driver's pretty bright after all."

Just then, Regina returned with Gardiner's lunch and Johnny's dessert. "Here you go, gentlemen." She placed the dishes on the table. "I'll be right back with your coffee, Mr. Gardiner."

"Thank you, Mrs. Reynolds."

Lilian had a question. "You call her Mrs. Reynolds. That does not sound like a Swedish name to me."

"It's not. Andrus changed his Swedish name … Reinhold … to Reynolds … when he came here to America. His real estate name is Andrew Reynolds, not Andrus. He works very hard on his accent as well. As he puts it, he doesn't want any potential buyers to think he's some kind of Swedish numbskull. You can't be too careful in the real estate business, you know."

"Do you think the Long Beach police know all this?"

Gardiner glanced around the diner, then back at Mrs. Collins. "Do you see any cops in here?"

"No, sir."

"There you have it. The police in this town get most of their tips in the businesses they patronize. I have yet to see one of them step one single foot into this establishment."

Lilian finished her milk. "This is all quite interesting, Mr. Gardiner. Is there more?"

"No, that's about it." He picked up half of his tuna fish sandwich, took a bite, and chewed, while looking at the satisfaction on her face. He swallowed. "I hope this information has been worth the price of lunch to you, Mrs. Collins."

Although surprised by his implied greedy request, she maintained her composure. "Yes, Mr. Gardiner, it is." Then she countered. "But there's no need for you to pay for *our meals*, sir. I can do that much."

Fowler nearly choked on his cobbler.

"There is one more thing I would like to ask you, Mr. Gardiner."

The banker stopped in mid-chew. "Oh?"

"The woman who claimed to be a relative of Mr. Donelson, did she come into the bank to claim the money in his account?"

"No, she did not. Only Mr. Bachman, her lawyer, came in to speak with Mr. McQuigg about closing Mr. Donelson's account."

Lilian frowned. "I was afraid you might say that."

Gardiner swallowed the bite of sandwich and washed it down with a mouthful of coffee. He wiped his mouth with a napkin. "However, I can tell you about seeing a woman with Mr. Donelson just prior to his untimely demise. He was coming out of this very same establishment when a woman came up to him and took him by the arm. I was just crossing the street on my way here, so I couldn't hear her speak. But I did get the impression she was trying to help him walk toward his home."

"Did you see her face?"

The banker shook his head. "No, I was too far away." He smiled. "But I did notice her clothing. She was wearing a cape and a round hat with a curled brim, and it appeared to be made of straw. Both the cape and hat were dark blue in color, and her dress was white. That's all I can recall about the woman. Is it enough to help you?"

Lilian tilted her head to the right. "Enough, Mr. Gardiner? It's too early to tell. But it is better than nothing."

Later that afternoon Johnny Fowler delivered Mrs. Collins to *The Los Angeles Times* Building at 1st and Broadway in the heart of the city. She hoped to arrive there in time to catch Walt Ballard in the newsroom before he left for home for the day. The freelancer succeeded in her quest. More than excited, she sat down on a chair beside his desk.

"Mr. Ballard, you are not going to believe all that we learned today during our visit to Long Beach."

Nervously, Ballard quickly scanned the area around them before responding to her. He leaned close to her and spoke very softly. "Quietly, Mrs. Collins. No one is supposed to know what we're doing."

"Oh, yes, of course. Perhaps we should go down to the morgue where we can have more privacy."

"Good idea."

They left together and hoped none of the other people in the room payed them any attention. Silently, they descended the stairs to the newspaper's archives. Once there, Ballard ascertained that they were alone.

"Okay, Mrs. Collins, let's have it."

She removed her notepad from her purse and started to review as much as she could from reading her notes, making certain to embellish wherever and whenever she felt necessary. As she neared the end, she felt the need to stress the importance of her conversation with Mr. and Mrs. Reynolds after lunchtime at The Chicago.

"When I asked them my first question, which was why they had not gone to the police or the bank to tell them about their relationship with Charles Donelson, they said quite adamantly that they did not wish to be involved with either of them because they were concerned the police and the people at the bank might think they had something to do with Mr. Donelson's death and that would lead to their names appearing in the newspapers, which would be bad for their business at the restaurant and Mr. Reynolds's real estate business. I assured them that none of our conversation would find its way into any of my articles until everything concerning the death of Mr. Donelson was officially and completely concluded by the police and the bank. Then I asked them for the names and addresses of their friends in Pasadena, but they demurred on that question as well. They said they did not wish to involve their friends there as well. When I asked them why, they said they feared their connection to them might come back on them and their business in Long Beach." She shrugged. "I suppose now we will have to find these people in Pasadena on our own. Do you have any ideas on how we can do that, Mr. Ballard?"

"Not really. How about you?"

"I suppose we will have to start searching for any Swedish people living in Pasadena."

"And how do we go about doing that, Mrs. Collins?"

"Pasadena has a city directory, does it not?"

"Yes, I believe it does. We have one right here in our archives, I think, right along with city directories from all over the county. I'm not sure where we keep those, but I'm sure I can find out pretty darned quick. Let me ask Mrs. Lane. I'll be right back."

Mrs. Collins waited patiently for Ballard's return, and true to his word, he returned in less than five minutes with a copy of the latest city directory for Pasadena.

"Here we go. What name do we start with? Reynolds?"

"No, I think we should start with his Swedish name Reinhold."

"Okay. Reinhold it is." He flipped through the pages. "Here we are, page three-fourteen." He ran his right index finger down the list of names of residents. "Reed, Reeder, Reeme, Reep, Rees, Reese, Reeve, Reeves, Reffell, Regan, Reichardt, Reid, Reidy, Reigard, Reigelman, Reighard, Reineman." Then he went to the next page. "Reinhart, Reining, Reinis, Reinneg, Reisner, Reiter, Reitz, Reitzell, Reliable ... That's definitely not it. Nope, no Reinhold."

"Maybe it's spelled R-i-*E*-n-h-o-l-d."

"Let me check." He turned the page. "Nope. Nothing close to that either."

"How about R-i-n-e?"

Ballard checked. "Nope. Nothing like that."

"R-y-n-e?"

He turned to page 329. "Sorry, nothing like that here."

"How about trying Reynolds?"

"I suppose it won't hurt to look." He flipped back to page 316. "Oh, boy, we've got a lot of people named Reynolds here. Must be two, three dozen or more." He counted them. "I was right, thirty-six."

"There must be a way of tracking down Swedish people in a town the size of Pasadena."

Ballard shrugged, then slapped the directory. "Say! I've got an idea. Swedish people are mostly Lutherans, aren't they? So, how about checking out the churches?"

Lilian patted him on the shoulder. "Now that, Mr. Ballard, is one crackerjack idea."

"Let me see what we can find in the index." He flipped back to the front of the book. "Here it is. Page six. That's Roman numeral six." He turned to it and ran his finger down the list of churches. "Nothing on page six." He moved the digit to the next page. "I see German this and that. This Presbyterian church and that Methodist. There's even one for the Japanese on here. There's a Quaker meeting house, too." He went down lower. "Oh, wait! Here we go! Swedish Methodist Church, Reverend G.E. Kallstedt, pastor, southeast corner Summit Avenue and Villa. Then there's the Swedish Lutheran Church Reverend B.O. Berg, pastor, East Orange Grove between North Raymond and North Fair Oaks." He chuckled. "The printer misspelled Swedish for the Lutheran Church. He spelled it S-w-e-*R*-i-s-h instead of S-w-e-*D*-i-s-h." He closed the directory. "I'm too tuckered out to go anywhere this evening, Mrs. Collins. How about you?"

"Same here, Mr. Ballard. What have you got in mind?"

"Well, I'm going to call Maisy when I get home and see if we can borrow Johnny Fowler again tomorrow to take us over to Pasadena where we can have a chat with those two pastors. Are you up for that?"

"Count me in, Mr. Ballard."

As soon as he left Mrs. Collins at *The Times* building, Johnny Ballard drove three miles out to the Keystone Studio in Edendale, hoping to get there in time to meet Maisy before she hopped on the Red Car for the ride home. The traffic in the downtown area of the city was thick but moving in the right direction, most of it toward the outskirts of town. He took 1st Street west to Alvarado, turned right, followed Alvarado to Effie and left on Effie for one block to Allessandro, another right, then up the hill a half block to the main entrance to Mack Sennett's comedy factory. After making a U-turn a hundred feet or so beyond the main gate, Fowler parked his Studebaker twenty feet from the entrance, checked the time on his pocket watch, and sighed for arriving with ten minutes to spare. He climbed out of the taxi and stretched before walking to the gate to wait for Maisy to exit the lot. His only hope was she hadn't left early and he had missed her.

Al Moore, the head guard at the property's main entrance, saw the cabbie standing on the sidewalk in front of the gate and recognized him. "You're Miss Malone's taxi driver, aren't you?"

"Sure am."

"Is she expecting you?"

"I don't think so."

"What's your name again, fella?"

"Johnny Fowler."

Moore held up his hand and gestured for Johnny to stay put. "I'm going to call up to the Tower and find out when Miss Malone will be done photographing for the day. Just hang on, okay?"

"I'll be right here."

The guard went into his booth, picked up the telephone, and made the call to the producer's office at the top of the Tower.

Milo Cole answered. "Mr. Sennett's office."

"Mr. Cole, this is Al Moore. I've got Miss Malone's cabbie waiting for her down here. He says she's not expecting him. I just thought I'd call up and see if you know when she'll be done filming today."

"She's already done filming and in the makeup department getting her face cleaned. Did Johnny say why he was here?"

"No, sir, he didn't. Do you want me to ask him?"

"No, Al, that won't be necessary. I'll get word to Maisy that he's here, and she can take it from there."

"Okay, Mr. Cole. Anything you say."

They finished the call, and Moore went back to speak to Johnny. "Mr. Cole said he'd get word to Miss Malone that you're waiting out here for her. He said she's already done filming and was probably in the makeup department getting her face wiped clean. I'd say she'll be here anytime now." Moore turned and peered over his left shoulder. "Here comes the stampede now." He looked back, then up the hill to his left. "Here comes the Red Car right on time, too. Those folks that live in the city will be getting aboard. Folks who live within a mile of here will just head on down the hill. You best stand back so's you don't get run over."

Fowler nodded. "Thanks for the warning." He moved back to his cab and leaned against the right front fender to watch the studio's employees' stream through the gate and into the street to meet the Red Car. Seeing so many people coming out surprised him. He waggled his head at the thought because it had never crossed his mind that it took so many people to make a simple thing as a moving picture. As soon as the exodus ended, he returned to the gate.

"How many people work here, sir?"

Moore lifted his hat and scratched his head. "I couldn't tell you an exact figure, Mr. Fowler, but just this past Monday I counted over fifty going in that morning. I tried to count them coming out that same afternoon, but they were moving much faster than they had been in the morning. So, I don't know for certain. If Mr. Cole comes out soon, you can ask him. He knows about all there is to know about what goes on around here."

Johnny gave the guard a salute. "Thanks. I'll do that." He went back to his car, leaned on the fender again, and put his hands in his trouser pockets. Only two minutes ticked by before his wait ended.

Maisy, Mabel, Roscoe, Minta, and Milo came through gate like a gaggle of geese, all five of them chattering and laughing at the same time. Then Minta spotted Johnny as he stood up straight and took two steps in their direction.

"Hey, look! Johnny Fowler's here."

All of them stopped their blather and came to a halt to look at the cabbie. Being the de facto leader of the group, Maisy smiled sweetly at Fowler. "Johnny, I thought you were driving that writer to Long Beach today. What's her name?"

He nodded. "Mrs. Lilian Collins."

"Yes, her. Didn't you, do it?"

"I sure did, and you're not going to believe what she learned down there. Let me drive you folks' home, and I'll tell you all about it."

Mabel replied first. "For the price of riding on the Red Car, you can count me in."

Milo chimed in next. "Me, too."

Minta agreed next. "Count us in."

Maisy shrugged. "That's four M's and an R, Johnny. And we're all ears. Get your dimes out, folks."

The five passengers squeezed into the Studebaker with Fowler. The Arbuckles in the rear seat with Minta on Roscoe's lap and Mabel beside them. Milo sat in the front passenger seat with Maisy sideways on his lap. Johnny took his place behind the steering wheel.

"Everybody comfy?"

Again, Mabel took the lead. "Okay back here."

Maisy followed. "Okay in front, too." She looked Cole in the eyes. "As long as Milo keeps his hands together."

Minta hugged Roscoe. "Do you hear that, Babe? No foolishness back here as well."

"Yes, Sweetheart."

She kissed his cheek and whispered in his ear. "You'll have to wait until we get home."

Fowler started the car and headed the taxi south along Allesandro Street to Effie, made a left, drove one block to Alvarado, then right on Alvarado. As soon as he completed the turn, Maisy opened up at him. "All right, Fowler. You've got us on pins and needles here, so let's hear about you and Mrs. Collins and your trip down to Long Beach today."

"Well, for starters, I think you're going to like Mrs. Collins. She's a Yankee, but she's a lot like you in an older lady way."

"I'm not sure I know how to take that *in an older lady way* crack."

"When you meet her, you'll see that it's compliment. She's smart like you, and she talks real fancy like you do, too. You'll see. I already told her how much she's like you and that she's going to like you, too."

"You know, Johnny. You shouldn't raise a person's expectations like that."

Fowler busted out laughing.

"What's so funny, Texas?"

"Mrs. Collins said nearly the same thing when I told her how she was going to like you."

Maisy waggled her head and looked at Mabel in the back seat. "How about them apples, Normand? Another me."

The movie star groaned. "Good lord almighty! You found your long-lost mother. I'm not sure the world's ready for two of you at once, Malone."

"Well, we'll see about that once she and I meet." She turned back to Johnny. "Okay, Fowler, get on with it. How did the day go?"

"Mrs. Collins and I got to know each other a bit on the way down to Long Beach."

"That's nice, Johnny, but tell us what she learned in Long Beach."

"Okay." He took a deep breath to show his exasperation with her, but he held back the sassy words going through his head. "First, I took her to the Exchange National Bank, where she talked to Mr. McQuigg. He's one of the vice-presidents there. He told her what he could about Mr. Donelson, the man who died a few weeks back ... down there in

Long Beach … under rather mysterious circumstances. That's how Mrs. Collins put it. *Mysterious circumstances.* Anyway, Mr. McQuigg wouldn't tell Mrs. Collins a whole lot about Mr. Donelson's account at the bank, only that he had enough money in the bank to live on it for a whole year and then some. And he told her about this lawyer named Mr. Bachman who had a client who wanted the money in Mr. Donelson's account. The banker said he told this lawyer he needed proof of who his client is and a court order signed by a judge before he could hand over the money. That lawyer said his client didn't want her name made public, so he couldn't get a judge to release the money to the client. The lawyer didn't come right out and say his client was a woman when he talked to the banker. He let that slip when he talked with Mrs. Collins."

"She got that out of the lawyer?"

"Uh-huh, she did."

"I'm starting to like this lady already. Go on."

"Well, that was all she got out of Mr. Bachman, but on her way out of the bank to go see him, she was followed by the head cashier of the bank, a Mr. Gardiner. He told Mrs. Collins something real quick about a woman coming into the bank and asking questions about the late Mr. Donelson and his bank account. He told Mrs. Collins for her and me to meet him at a restaurant down the street for lunch. We went there, and he showed up right on time. He told Mrs. Collins and me how Mr. Donelson was from Sweden and that the people who owned the restaurant where we were eating were also from Sweden. Well, the husband was from Sweden. The wife was from Iowa. Anyway, they were friends with Mr. Donelson and knew him pretty good. We stayed there at the restaurant until the lunch crowd had gone just so we could talk to the folks who owned the place. They wouldn't tell us nothing unless we promised not to tell anybody about them knowing the dead man and some other folks who live in Pasadena who also come from Sweden."

Arbuckle leaned forward. "So, what has all this got to do with the three deaths at the Hotel Alexandria?"

Maisy answered for Johnny. "Good question, Roscoe. Remember how I asked Walt Ballard to dig into the newspaper files and see if he could find any other deaths like the three at the Alexandria. Well, Walt got Mrs. Collins to help do the looking and they found two deaths that happened only a few days before those at the Alexandria. Walt told me he was going to get Mrs. Collins to go down to Long Beach and see what she could find out about the one down there. Today, he went to Tom White's funeral along with Eddie and Bill."

By this time, they reached 1st Street, where Fowler turned the taxi left. "I thought I'd take Mr. and Mrs. Arbuckle home first."

Minta took a turn at leaning forward. "That's fine, Johnny, but we're not getting out of this car until you're done spilling the beans about what you and Mrs. Collins found out today."

Mabel brushed her shoulder against the Arbuckles. "I think he is done, Minta. Aren't you, Johnny?"

"Yes, Miss Normand, I am."

"How about you, Malone? You done yet for today?"

Maisy shrugged. "Probably. I can't think of anything else about this case until I get more facts. I'm hoping Eddie and Bill can come up with something tomorrow." She shook her head. "I wish we didn't have to work tomorrow, even if it is only a half day."

Minta sighed. "Me, too."

Roscoe groaned. "Me three."

Milo punctuated the others. "Me four."

While unlocking the door to her apartment, Maisy could hear her telephone ringing inside. "Oh, don't stop until I can get in there!" The key did its job. She opened the door and raced to the telephone on the end table. With one hand on the receiver and the other on a candlestick, she jerked it up to her ear and mouth. "Hello!"

"Miss Malone, I've got Mr. Walter Ballard on the line for you. Do you want me to put him through?"

A bit breathless, she replied. "Yes, yes."

"Go ahead, sir."

"Maisy, are you okay?"

"I only now got home, Walt. When I heard the phone ringing, I charged in here to answer it. So, what did you think of Mrs. Collins's trip to Long Beach today?"

"Great. She worked out just like I thought she would."

Now breathing normally Maisy sounded steadier. "Yes, I know. Johnny Fowler drove us all home from the studio."

"All of you?"

"Yes. Mabel, Milo, the Arbuckles, and me. He told us all about the interviews Mrs. Collins got today. Pretty good information. Now all we have to do is try to locate some of Mr. Donelson's friends and relatives in Pasadena."

Ballard chuckled. "We're ahead of you there, Maisy. Lilian and I looked through the Pasadena city directory when she returned here this afternoon. When we didn't find anyone named Donelson, we looked at other possible spellings. No luck there either. Then we looked up Reynolds."

"Reynolds?"

"Didn't Johnny tell you about the Reynolds couple?"

"I'm guessing Reynolds is the name of the couple that owns the restaurant where they had lunch."

The reporter chuckled again. "Good guess, Maisy. Mr. Reynolds is from Sweden, and he and Mrs. Reynolds were friends with Donelson. We're supposed to keep that a secret until this whole business about Donelson's death is done."

"Mum's the word with us, Walt."

"I knew you'd say something like that." He took a breath. "Well, as I was saying, Lilian and I were looking through the Pasadena city directory when we came up with the idea to look for Swedish businesses, and then we thought about Swedish churches. We found two. And tomorrow, she and I are going over to Pasadena to pay visits to their pastors. That's why we were wondering if we could borrow your cabbie tomorrow morning."

"I think I can arrange that. Where do you want him to pick you up? At *The Times* building again?"

The newsman turned serious. "I need to work at the station until ten, so I'd like him to pick me up there. He can get Lilian at the paper at nine-thirty. Is that all right?"

"I'll call him and tell him the plan. We film folk are required to work until one o'clock. If you get done in Pasadena before then, call the studio and talk to Milo. I'm thinking we might all get together for an early dinner at the Alexandria. Say five o'clock?"

"I'm all for it. Do I bring Lilian?"

Maisy's voice became firm. "Bring Lilian. Is she married?"

Surprised by the question, Ballard burped a laugh. "You know, I don't know. I know she has a son. Why do you ask about a husband?"

"I only thought she might like a night out with her husband, if she has one. And she can bring her son, too, if she wants to."

"But why all three?"

"The people at the Alexandria won't get suspicious of the rest of us being there, if we have her husband and son there."

"Good idea, Maisy. Can I bring my wife?"

Maisy giggled. "I didn't know you're married, Walt."

"From the hours I keep at the station and the newspaper, I'm not so sure my wife knows we're married."

Another chuckle from Maisy. "Then bring her, Walt. I'm certain she'll enjoy dining with us at the Alexandria."

"Okay, but do you mind if I ask who's paying for it?"

Maisy hesitated. "Will that be a problem, Walt?"

"Reporters don't make Alexandria kind of money, Maisy?"

"I've heard that, Walt." She paused. "I've got an idea."

"Yeah?"

Maisy giggled again. "I know you're a police reporter, Walt, but do you think you could write a little puff piece about our newest star at the studio?"

"If it means I can bring my Peggy, then I'll write a puff piece about this new star at your studio that will make him sound like he's a gift from God."

Detectives Ed Browning and Bill Ingram reported for duty at the Central Police Station in downtown Los Angeles right on time Saturday morning. Browning's wife Nealy came in with them. They waved to Walt Ballard who was sitting with his usual newspaper friends, Dusty Rhoades of the *Record* and Mack Finch of the *Express*. The trio of police reporters had been on their bench just inside the desk sergeant's domain since four that morning, but only Ballard looked like he'd been there longer since he missed his usual amount of sleep time the night before.

Rhoades leaned close to Finch. "Have you noticed that old Walt here has been getting real chummy with Browning and Ingram lately?"

"Now that you mention it, I think you're right." Finch bumped his elbow against Ballard. "Say, Walt, what's the deal with you and those two detectives? You getting some inside dope from them that we're not hearing about?"

Rhoades crooked his neck and looked around Finch. "Yeah, Walt. Spill the beans. What's going on with you and Browning and Ingram? You catching an exclusive from them or something?"

"Okay, I'll tell you, but you must promise me you'll both keep it quiet. No spreading it around, you hear? Or I don't tell you nothing."

Finch raised his hand. "I swear, Walt. Not a word out of me."

Rhoades chimed in. "Me, too, Walt. Mum's the word, pal."

"Okay then, but if I find out that either one of you spreads a word of this around your papers or any other rags in town or even any of the rags around the county, then you'll never get another lead from me ever again, you hear?"

His two cohorts shook their heads and simultaneously said the same five words. "You can trust us, Walt."

"All right then." He leaned close to them. "The cops are pretty sure they know who bumped off Tom White last Saturday night, and they've got a plan to get those Japanese thugs who did it. And there won't be a trial for any of them. You get my drift, boys?"

Rhoades shuddered. "Holy cow, Walt! Are you telling the truth?"

"Would I make up a story like that?"

Finch shrugged. "Well, you might."

The *Record* reporter nudged him. "Come on, Mack. You know old Walt better than that. He don't work for Hearst, you know."

Finch nodded. "Yeah, I see your point. Sorry, Walt."

Ballard leaned back. "Okay then. Not a word, boys. Not a word."

Together, Finch and Rhoades swore. "Not a word, Walt. Not a word."

Ballard leaned back against the wall, folded his arms, and closed his eyes. "Wake me if anything comes up, will you, boys?"

Nealy Browning went down to the Central Police Station basement, where Nellie Sharpe was waiting for her. "Good morning, Nealy."

"Good morning to you, Nellie."

"Are you ready to go to work?"

Nealy smiled. "As ready and as eager as I'll ever be."

As the two women walked toward the records room, Nellie's curiosity struck her. "Have you heard the latest on the investigation?"

"I haven't heard anything since Edward spoke with Maisy the other night. I suppose he told you all about that yesterday."

"Yes, we did get a chance to talk a bit after Tom White's funeral. Then I came to work early this morning and had a chance to talk to Walt Ballard about how he and Mrs. Collins fared yesterday. It seems Mrs. Collins is a regular sleuth in her own right."

Nellie continued her review of what she had learned from Ballard as they reached the records room. Uncertain about who might be inside, she broke off the telling when they reached the door, and they entered the room quietly. A quick look around the place indicated nobody was there ahead of them. "The coast is clear." Miss Sharpe inside first, and as soon as Nealy crossed the threshold, Nellie closed the door behind them. She reviewed the information Walt Ballard had told her, speaking as if she were reading shorthand notes. "So, there you have it, Nealy."

"You know, Nellie, every time someone in our group looks into something, I get more and more convinced that someone murdered that girl at the Alexandria the other night."

Sharpe nodded. "It does seem like that, doesn't it?"

"I'm really quite anxious to hear what Edward and Bill find out today when they go to the Hotel Travers. Edward said he suspects there must be something irregular about that man trying to hang himself with his suspenders from the head of his bed. How does someone do that?"

"Not just that, how does someone take the time to write a suicide note and include another one for the police and a third with a request to leave all his personal belongings to the chambermaid? That really sounds fishy to me."

"Well, let's see if there have been any other fishy deaths at hotels in the county in the past year."

Nealy and Nellie had been going through the old case files for almost half an hour when Detectives Browning and Ingram interrupted them.

Mrs. Browning smiled at her husband. "Checking up on me so soon, Dear?"

"Not really, Darling. Bill and I just want to take a look at the Claudius Peters file, so we don't repeat anything the initial detective on the case had learned."

Miss Sharpe held up a folder. "I thought you might want to look at it, Eddie, so I pulled it first thing this morning. Here you go."

Browning accepted the file and opened it so that Ingram could see it over his shoulder. "Your previous partner, Frank Beaumont, covered this case, Bill."

"Yes, I see that. You can bet he was really brief with his report. He always was when I worked with him."

"You're right about Frank's brevity. There's only two pages here. He wrote he interviewed the chambermaid who found Peters hanging by his neck from the headboard post in his room. She took him down by cutting his suspenders, which were wrapped around his neck. Then he dropped unconscious to the floor. He was still breathing, so she went for help. The chambermaid's name is Mrs. Minnie Lightfreit." Browning glanced at Ingram. "Can you believe that name?"

"Sounds like it's made up."

"My thought exactly. But you never know about names. So many immigrants from non-English speaking countries Americanize their names. Lightfreit looks like it was only half Americanized." The senior detective peered into the distance. "You know, Bill, I'll bet you a shiny new penny she's no longer employed at the Hotel Travers."

"No bet, Ed. I was thinking the very same thing."

Browning returned his focus to the report. "It goes on to say that a Dr. G.E. Brown was the first to attend Peters. It doesn't say if the doctor attended him at the hotel or at the Receiving Hospital. We need to find that out for ourselves. It goes on to say Peters left several letters instructing the coroner who to notify about his death. Then there was another letter where Peters said he wanted the chambermaid to have all of his belongings. Rather generous of the man, don't you think? Makes me wonder what else she did for him besides turn down his bed at night."

"I get to ask that question, Ed."

"Says here the hotel manager's name is Daniel Conklin. What do you say we go have a nice talk with him?"

"I'm with you all the way, partner."

"And after that, we can pay a visit to this Dr. Brown."

The Hotel Travers was located a block west of the Southern Pacific Railroad's Arcade Depot on the northwest corner of 5th Street and Crocker Street. Like nearly all the hotels in Los Angeles, the first floor consisted of shops and offices as well as the hotel's lobby. Offices for doctors, lawyers, accountants, and brokers of all kinds occupied the second floor. Guest rooms filled the top two levels of the building.

Instead of walking the six blocks to the Travers, Browning and Ingram hopped on a Red Car that took them right up to the front entrance of their destination. Once inside they walked directly to the registration desk where a man in a blue suit and wearing wire-rimmed glasses smiled at them.

"Good morning, gentlemen. Welcome to the Hotel Travers. Are looking for a room?"

Each detective pulled on the left lapel of his coat to show the man his badge. Then Ingram took a notepad and pencil from an inside pocket of his coat.

Browning smiled back at the clerk. "I'm Detective Sergeant Ed Browning, and this is Detective Sergeant Bill Ingram. Are you Daniel Conklin?"

"No, sir, I'm Arthur Martinet. Besides manning the front desk, I'm also the hotel's manager. Daniel is my assistant manager."

Ingram quizzed him. "How do you spell Martinay, sir?"

"That's M-A-R-T-I-N-E-T. It's French. My ancestors settled in Louisiana shortly after New Orleans was founded in seventeen-eighteen. I am the first of my family to remove here to California."

Browning spoke again. "That's very interesting, Mr. Martinet, but we're not here to talk about your ancestors." He scanned the lobby before turning back to the manager. "Is there some other place where we can speak in private?"

"Certainly, Detective. Just give me a moment to get my assistant to man the desk, and then we can go into my office in the back and speak in private."

Martinet opened a door next to the pigeon-hole message box, stuck his head inside, and spoke to his assistant manager. "Daniel, would you please come out here and mind the desk?" Conklin joined Martinet behind the counter. "These gentlemen are police detectives, and they want to speak with me in private."

Browning's curiosity prodded his brain. "Mr. Conklin, we were led to believe you are the manager here."

Conklin pursed his lower lip. "Whatever gave you that idea, sir?"

"Your name is in a report another detective filed when he was investigating the suicide of one of your guests, a Mr. Claudius Peters."

"Oh, that. I was the acting manager at the time. Mr. Martinet was away on a trip back to Louisiana to visit his family, and he left me in charge of the hotel."

Browning nodded. "Then you're just the man we want to speak with."

Martinet chimed in. "Yes, he is, Detective. No one knows the particulars of that tragedy better than Daniel. I must admit that I was quite horrified to learn of poor Mr. Peters' death when I returned from New Orleans. I'm certainly glad I wasn't here, but I most certainly do have to give Daniel plenty of accolades for how he handled the entire incident." He patted Conklin on the shoulder. "Take the detectives into my office, Daniel, and answer all their questions with as much detail as you can."

"Yes, sir, Mr. Martinet." Conklin went around the end of the counter. "Right this way, gentlemen."

Browning and Ingram followed the assistant manager around the corner and down the hall to Martinet's office. He opened the door for them to enter ahead of him. The clerk pointed to the two straight-back chairs facing a large desk and a cushioned chair. "Please be seated, gentlemen."

They sat, while Conklin went around the desk and sat down in Martinet's chair. He leaned on the desk with his hands folded in front of him. "I must tell you, detectives, that I thought that whole chilling business with Mr. Peters had been concluded by the coroner when he declared Mr. Peters died from nephritis, and the man's body was shipped back to Chicago for burial. I assume some new information concerning his death has been revealed. Am I right?"

Browning nodded again. "You are quite right, Mr. Conklin. In fact, several questions have been raised about the death of Mr. Peters. We know the coroner declared he died from nephritis, but we believe that ailment was precipitated by him being unconscious from the time he was found hanging in his room in this hotel."

"I don't understand, sir."

"Allow me to explain."

"Please do."

Browning heaved a deep sigh before proceeding. "When Mr. Peters hung himself, he nearly died on his bed. Is that correct?"

"Yes, it is."

"Well, it's more than likely Mr. Peters quit breathing while he was hanging there, and after not breathing for a short time, the brain begins to die from a lack of oxygen. Because he lived for three more days after his attempted suicide, his brain continued to deteriorate, and his other organs began to decline as well and eventually they shut down. His kidneys most likely were the first to go, and that was probably why the coroner chose nephritis as the cause of death."

Conklin nodded. "Yes, now I understand."

"When your chambermaid found him, he was probably no longer breathing, but when she cut him down, jostling him around probably started him breathing again."

"That makes sense."

Browning smiled at the assistant manager. "So, tell us about your chambermaid, a Mrs. Minnie Lightfreit. The newspapers said she went into Mr. Peters' room to clean it and found him hanging by his suspenders."

"Yes, that's right. She cut him down, then came running down the stairs yelling as loud as she could that Mr. Peters had hung himself and was hardly breathing. I immediately told Mr. Everson to call for a doctor."

Ingram interjected a question. "Who is Mr. Everson?"

"He's the second assistant manager after me. I told him to call for a doctor, and he called the Receiving Hospital. They sent Dr. Brown and two orderlies over here right away. Dr. Brown examined Mr. Peters and said he had to get him to the hospital immediately. They put him on a stretcher and took him down to an ambulance parked in front of the hotel. That was the last time I saw Mr. Peters."

Browning returned to the conversation. "What else can you tell us about the chambermaid who found Mr. Peters? Does she live here in the hotel?"

Conklin paused to gather his thoughts. "Well, there's not much to tell, really. We hired her a week before Mr. Peters hung himself. She only worked half days during the week. She was good at her job. I can say that much for her. Very meticulous at getting each of her rooms spotless every day. She was always very cheerful, too. She hummed and sang songs from her native country when she was mopping the floors in the halls."

Surprise struck Browning. "Her native country? What country would that be, Mr. Conklin?"

"I can't say for certain. When she sang the words on occasion, it sounded like German. You know, a lot of *ein*-this, a *der*-that, a *die*-there, and a *das*-something here and there. So, I figured she was German."

"Is she working today? We'd like to talk to her."

The clerk snickered. "Good luck with that. Minnie up and quit right after Mr. Peters died in the hospital. She said she was certain she saw his ghost in the hall the next morning. Scared the living daylights out of her. She let out a scream and came running down the stairs, pointing behind her and screaming bloody murder that she saw his ghost in the hall outside his room."

"When exactly did this happen?"

Conklin peered up at the ceiling for a few seconds to get his thoughts in order before answering. Satisfied with his deliberations, he nodded and focused on the senior detective. "Well, Mr. Peters died on the second of the month. That was a Sunday, and she saw his ghost the next morning on Monday. She walked out right then and there, and we haven't seen hide nor hair of her since then. She didn't even come back to collect her wages from the previous week."

Ingram and Browning exchanged looks that said what they were both thinking, but neither man divulged anything to Conklin. "Do you have an address of where she lives?"

The interviewee grinned. "Sure, but you'll have to get it from Mr. Martinet. He keeps a journal on all our employees."

"One last thing, Mr. Conklin. *The Times* ran a short item about Mr. Peters the day before he died. A local lawyer named Kuegeman stated Mr. Peters was a well-known lawyer back in Chicago. Did you know this about him?"

Conklin pursed his lips, then shook his head slowly. "Nope, sorry. Not until I read the same item in the newspaper."

Browning turned to his partner. "You have anything you want to ask Mr. Conklin, Bill?"

Ingram's head bobbled. "No, I think you've covered it all."

Conklin raised his right hand. "I've got a question for you officers, if you don't mind."

The detectives exchanged minor shrugs. Then Browning looked back at the assistant manager. "No, go ahead and ask your question or questions, if you have more than one."

"When Mr. Peters tried to take his own life, besides calling the hospital for a doctor, I told Jeff to call the police. Every death outside of a hospital should be reported to the police. Am I right?"

Browning nodded. "Right you are, sir."

Ingram stopped writing and focused on Conklin. "Who is Jeff?"

"Oh, sorry. Jeff is Mr. Everson's first name."

"Thank you."

"Well, the police sent over a detective to investigate Mr. Peters' attempted suicide."

Ingram responded. "Yes, we know. Detective Sergeant Frank Beaumont is his name."

"Yes, that was his name."

Browning grinned at Conklin. "And you want to know why we're here now asking the same questions Detective Beaumont probably asked you, right?"

Conklin pointed at Browning. "Hey, you're sharp. That's exactly what I was going to ask you."

"Well, we're just following up on this case to make sure all the I's are dotted and all the T's are crossed. Just trying to be thorough."

Conklin's head bobbled a bit. "Then why haven't you asked me about Mr. Peters' effects? Detective Beaumont did."

Browning looked at Ingram. "Can you see the egg on my face?"

"Can you see the egg on mine?"

The senior detective turned back to Conklin. "I'm sorry, sir. That is an oversight on our part. So, tell us about Mr. Peters' effects. The newspapers stated he left them to your chambermaid."

"That's what the one letter he left said for us to do. After the doctor and orderlies took Mr. Peters away and we had some time to calm down, Minnie and I, that is, she and I went through his room and gathered up everything of his that was there. The only things of any value were a gold pocket watch, a few pairs of gold and silver cufflinks, a diamond tie pin, a ruby tie pin, and an emerald tie pin. We found his wallet on the dresser drawers. It only had six one-dollar bills in it. There was also two dollars and twenty-two cents in change on the dresser. Minnie kept the valuables and the money, and we donated all of his clothes to the Salvation Army. Of course, we didn't do any of that until Dr. Brown called us on Saturday evening to tell us that Mr. Peters was on his deathbed. I gave Minnie the valuables when she came into the hotel to work on Monday morning, and I had Jeff call the Salvation Army and ask them to come pick up his clothes."

"And shortly after that, Mrs. Lightfreit saw the ghost and quit her job here, right?"

Conklin tilted his head. "You make that sound like ... there was something suspicious ... going on with Minnie."

Browning shrugged. "Do I? Maybe you're right, Mr. Conklin. We'll just have to find out for certain, won't we?"

Fear darkened Conklin's aspect. "Yes, I suppose so."

"Come on, Bill. Let's go speak to Mr. Martinet again and see if has the chambermaid's address."

Conklin held up his hand again. "Oh, wait, Detective Browning. There's one more thing about Mr. Peters' belongings."

"And what's that?"

"His Bible. Minnie didn't want it, and neither did the Salvation Army. We still have it here. What do you think we should do with it?"

Browning and Ingram looked at each other, shrugged, then turned back to Conklin. The senior partner spoke again. "Maybe you could donate it to a church."

"I don't know what church would want it, Detective Browning."

"And why is it that, Mr. Conklin?"

"It's written in a foreign language."

"And what language is that, Mr. Conklin?"

The clerk appeared vague. "I couldn't say for certain, but since Mr. Peters was Swedish, I would have to guess it's written in Swedish."

Both detectives flinched with surprise. Then Ingram asked the obvious question. "How do you know he was Swedish, Mr. Conklin?"

"He asked me if there was a Swedish church in Los Angeles, so I assumed he was Swedish."

Browning jumped into the conversation again. "And what did you tell him about Swedish churches?"

"I told him I didn't know if there is one in Los Angeles, but he could look in the City Directory and see if there might be one listed there."

The detectives focused on each other and spoke simultaneously. "And that's exactly what we're going to do. Could we have that Bible, Mr. Conklin?"

Per Maisy's request, Johnny Fowler drove Walt Ballard and Lilian Collins to Pasadena that Saturday morning. The two journalists planned to interview Reverend Gustave E. Kallstedt at the Swedish Methodist Church first, and if need be, they would pay a visit to Reverend B.O. Berg at the Swedish Lutheran Church. As Luck would have it, they found Reverend Kallstedt inside the church, rehearsing his sermon for the next day's service, speaking the words in his ancestral tongue.

Seeing his visitors enter the sanctuary, Kallstedt, a tall, thin man with graying hair, and pale skin, ceased his Swedish language oratory in mid-sentence and acknowledged them in English tinged by a definite Scandinavian accent. "May I help you folks?"

Ballard replied. "We're sorry to interrupt you, Reverend."

Kallstedt stepped down from the pulpit. "There's no need for you to apologize, sir. I am Reverend Gustave Kallstedt. This is my church." He chuckled. "You caught me in the middle of rehearsing my sermon for tomorrow. So, what brings you good people here this morning?"

"My name is Walter Ballard."

"And I am Mrs. Lilian Collins."

The clergyman smiled warmly. "Mr. Ballard and Mrs. Collins? Are you two looking for a church for marriage?"

Ballard snickered. "Oh, no, Reverend. We're both from *The Los Angeles Times*."

Lilian spoke up. "That's not quite correct, Reverend Kallstedt. Mr. Ballard works for *The Times*, while I am a freelance writer who is often published by *The Times* as well as other newspapers and magazines in this county and some surrounding counties. We've come here to ask you about a gentleman who passed away a few weeks ago."

"Oh?"

Ballard jumped in. "Yes, Reverend. His name was Donelson. He lived in Long Beach, and he was a ship carpenter down there. We were wondering if—"

The clergyman raised his hand to interrupt the reporter. "You were wondering if I knew Charles." He paused. "Yes, I did. He was one of my congregation. I presided at his funeral." He looked at Lilian before shifting his view to Ballard. "You both seem quite surprised by my admission."

The journalist tilted his head to the right. "Well, I know I am." He looked at his associate. "How about you, Lilian?"

"Yes, I am surprised as well."

"Before I answer any of your questions about Charles, would you mind telling me why you are asking about him? I hope it's not some sort of morbid curiosity on your part."

Ballard shook his head. "Oh, no, Reverend. It's nothing like that."

Mrs. Collins confirmed the reporter's statement. "I can assure you, Reverend Kallstedt, that our only interest in Mr. Donelson is whether he had any relatives or friends living in this city. You see, we are very suspicious about the manner of his death."

"The manner of his death? He died from a stroke, didn't he?"

The reporter leaned in. "We know that's what the coroner said, but we have reason to believe there might have been some foul play to his death."

Kallstedt gasped. "Foul play?"

Lilian spoke. "Yes, Reverend. Foul play. You see, yesterday I was in Long Beach making inquiries about Mr. Donelson's finances with his bank. I was told he did have a considerable sum of funds in his account, but more importantly, I learned from a lawyer that he had a client who wished to have that money. He wouldn't reveal the client's name, but he did say she may be a relative of Mr. Donelson and is living here in Pasadena. Then I spoke with Mr. and Mrs. Reynolds who own The Chicago restaurant in Long Beach."

"I know Andrus and Regina. They often come to worship here. They are good people, although Regina is a Lutheran. Andrus is a very steadfast and devout Methodist. I suspect that they sometimes attend the Lutheran church on East Orange Grove."

Ballard asked the next question. "And what about Mr. Donelson? Did he attend your church all the time? Or did he play hooky with the Reynolds people on occasion?"

"No, Charles was here nearly every Sunday morning. Even when Andrus and Regina were not." Kallstedt searched their faces to see if they believed him. When he saw doubt in both, he had to corroborate his statement. "Of course, they have already told you this, haven't they, Mrs. Collins?"

She shook her head. "No, Reverend, I am afraid they said nothing about attending your church or the Lutheran church."

Ballard explained. "I'm sorry, Reverend, but we had to find your church in the Pasadena City Directory."

"I see."

Lilian steered their conversation back on topic. "As I said before, Reverend, we are interested only in finding any relatives or friends Mr. Donelson may have had here in Pasadena."

Kallstedt shifted his gaze back and forth twice between his two visitors before responding. "I am not so certain that I can do that. As a pastor, I am prohibited from giving out private information about the members of my flock."

Ballard protested. "But Mr. Donelson is dead. Doesn't that relieve you from that obligation?"

"Yes, it does relieve me from withholding anything about Charlie Donelson, but his death does not mean I can reveal anything about the other members of my flock. I am pledged to protect their privacy as long as they are members of this church."

Walt and Lilian focused on each other; both of their faces forlorn with exasperation.

Kallstedt recognized their dismay. "I am very sorry that I am unable to help you folks."

Mrs. Collins refused to surrender. "Reverend, there must be some minor detail about Mr. Donelson that does not involve any of your other church members."

A sudden recollection flickered in Kallstedt's eyes. "Now that you say that I just now recall a woman who came to worship with him on the Sunday before he died. I do not recall her name, but Charlie did say it when he introduced her to me as they were leaving the church that morning." He raised his right index finger to his lips and tapped them lightly, while looking skyward before speaking again. "I do recall that she aided him in walking as they went down the church steps." Again, he shifted his view to his visitors, this time with a small smile. "Does that help?"

Ballard nearly choked with excitement. "Do you remember what this woman looked like, Reverend? Was she tall? Was she thin? What colors were her eyes and hair?"

Kallstedt grimaced as he considered answering the reporter. "Not really. Nothing specific like that. Only that she was nearing middle age. I remember a few streaks of gray in her brown hair, and her face appeared to be puffy around her eyes. But I do not recall the color of her eyes. Charlie bade me a good day as they left the church, but she only gave me a nod of her head. No smile. Only a nod. That is how I recall the gray streaks in her brown hair. What little I saw of her hair, I mean. Like your hair, Mrs. Collins. Just around your ears. Does that help you, Mr. Ballard?" Before the reporter could respond, the pastor recalled something else. "Oh, wait! I remember now that she was tall; almost as tall as Charlie. She wore a dark blue hat with a narrow brim, and the brim only brushed against the top of his shoulder. And now I remember her eyes. They were blue. Yes, definitely blue. And she wore a long dark blue coat."

Ballard and Mrs. Collins remained silent for a few seconds, both of them hoping Kallstedt would remember some additional details. When he said nothing more about the woman who accompanied Donelson to church that last Sunday in February, they nodded at each other before *The Times* reporter turned back to the clergyman.

"You've been every helpful, Reverend. We certainly appreciate all you've told us." He looked at Lilian. "Do you have anything else you'd like to ask the reverend, Mrs. Collins?"

She shook her head. "Not at this time, Mr. Ballard."

Ballard extended his right hand to Kallstedt. "Thank you for your time, Reverend."

The pastor accepted the handshake. "You are quite welcome, Mr. Ballard. I wish I could have given you more information about Charlie, but as I said before, I must keep everything I know about my flock confidential."

The two men released their grips.

"We understand completely, Reverend." He turned to Lilian. "I guess that does it, Mrs. Collins. Shall we go?"

"Yes." She faced Kallstedt. "You've been very helpful, Reverend."

"Allow me to show you out."

Mrs. Collins smiled politely. "That won't be necessary, sir. Again, thank you."

Ballard nodded at Kallstedt one last time, then took Lilian by her left elbow and started for the door.

Surprise tweaked Johnny Fowler's face when he saw Walt and Lilian coming out of the church. Leaning against the right front fender of his vehicle, he waited until they reached the taxi before speaking to them. "That was quick."

Ballard groaned. "The reverend wasn't very talkative."

Mrs. Collins put a shine on the reporter's remark. "However, he did impart some important information to us."

Fowler's brow rolled up his forehead. "Oh?"

Walt opened the rear passenger door. "Let's talk about it on the way back to Los Angeles." He waved at the back seat, inviting Lilian to enter the Studebaker.

"Thank you, Walt."

Ballard closed the door behind her. Then he and Fowler walked around the cab to the driver's side; the reporter around the rear and the driver around the front. They opened their respective doors, climbed inside, and closed the doors behind them simultaneously.

The cabbie spoke first. "So, you want to go back to Los Angeles now? I thought we were going to that other Swedish church first."

Lilian answered him. "Reverend Kallstedt made it quite clear that Mr. Donelson was a Methodist and not a Lutheran. So, I am certain Walt will agree with me that visiting the other church would be a waste of our time."

Ballard nodded. "I agree with you, Lilian. I think you need to go back to Long Beach and have another talk with those restaurant folks. Maybe they can give you some more information about Donelson's friends here in Pasadena or tell you something about that woman who was with him the last time he went to church here."

"You know, Walt, those were my exact thoughts as well. What do you think, Johnny? Would you like to drive me down to Long Beach again?"

"I'd be delighted to, Miss Lilian. When do you want to go?"

"As soon as we drop Walt at *The Times* building."

Ballard flinched. "Now wait a minute here. If you go down there today, I want to go with you. We're in this together, you know."

"You are more than welcome to come along, Walt. Do you agree, Johnny?"

Fowler tilted his head to the right. "The more the merrier, I always say. But before we go, I'd better call Maisy at the studio first to see if it's okay with her for me to drive you down to Long Beach again today. I don't think she'll have a problem with it, but I want to make certain she doesn't."

When the trio of assistant sleuths returned to Los Angeles, Johnny Fowler stopped at the first pay telephone booth they saw. Ballard offered him a nickel to make the call on the latest convenience in communication. The driver smiled politely. "That's all right, Walt. I'll pay for it. Be right back." The cabbie left the Studebaker and hurried to the telephone booth to place the call. He stepped inside and lifted the receiver from the switch hook, then he rattled the hook rapidly three times with two fingers and waited to be answered.

A nasal, female voice responded. "Operator."

"Hello, Central. Get me the Keystone Film Company in Edendale please. The number is E-two-five-three-two."

"E-two-five-three-two. One moment please."

Fowler waited for several seconds before he heard Milo Cole's voice on the other end. "Keystone Motion Pictures."

The operator's flat voice responded. "One moment please. Caller, please deposit one nickel in the slot."

The cabbie followed her instruction and deftly dropped the Liberty five-cent piece in the coin slot.

Hearing the ding of the pay telephone, the operator spoke again. "Thank you, sir. Go ahead with your call."

"Milo, this is Johnny Fowler."

"Oh, hello, Johnny. What prompts you to call the studio?"

"I need to speak to Maisy."

"Of course, you do. How silly of me to ask? Well, you're in luck, pal. She just finished work for the day, and she's downstairs right now. Hold on, and I'll get her up here for you."

Fowler waited patiently until he heard Maisy's voice on the other end. "Hello, Johnny. How'd it go this morning in Pasadena? Did Walt and Mrs. Collins learn anything new?"

"Not all that much, Maisy, but what they did learn might be very important to the case. It seems this Donelson fellow attended church at the Swedish Methodist Church in Pasadena, and the last time he was there he had a woman with him that Walt and Lilian think might be a nurse or some kind of caretaker because Reverend Kallstedt said she was helping him walk when they came out of the church after services were over."

"That is interesting, Johnny. The newspaper article did report Mr. Donelson was under the care of a couple of doctors down there in Long Beach. So, is this why you called?"

"No, Maisy. I called because Walt and Lilian want to go back to Long Beach right now to speak with the folks who own that restaurant where we ate lunch yesterday. Lilian thinks they might know a little something about this woman who was with Mr. Donelson at the church the Sunday before he died. And then Walt said they should pay a visit to those two doctors you just mentioned and see what they can tell them about Mr. Donelson's condition and possibly something about the woman who was with him."

"That sounds like an excellent idea, Johnny."

"I agree wholeheartedly, Maisy, but they want me to drive them down there right away. That's why I called. Is it okay with you for me to take them to Long Beach this afternoon?"

"What you really want to know is … will I pay for it?"

"Well …"

A snort of laughter escaped Maisy's mouth. "Never mind the cost, Johnny. You know I'm good for it."

"That thought never crossed my mind."

"I know it didn't, my friend, but I do appreciate you asking first. You go ahead and drive Walt and Mrs. Collins to Long Beach. Tell them lunch is on me as well, and I'll see the three of you at the Alexandria for supper this evening."

"Thank you, Maisy. Good-bye."

"Good-bye."

Fowler replaced the receiver on the switch hook, left the telephone booth, and returned to his car. "She said for us to go ahead and go down to Long Beach and lunch is on her as well."

Lilian had to ask. "Can she afford that?"

Ballard chuckled. "She's in the moving picture business, Lilian. All those people are rolling in dough, don't you know?"

She tilted her head to the right. "I suppose all those nickels and dimes we pay to see their movies do add up."

The reporter burped another laugh. "It's the California Gold Rush all over again, Lilian. Only this time, the gold is celluloid film, and the stampede might last forever."

Fowler drove them straight to The Chicago with the hope Andrew and Regina hadn't closed up for the day yet. Luck and little traffic on the road smiled on them. The restaurant was still serving customers when Johnny parked his Studebaker across the street from the eatery.

Regina recognized Lilian and Johnny the second they entered the place. "Back again, folks? Our food is pretty good, but I didn't know it was good enough to bring you down here from Los Angeles two days in a row." She shifted her eyes to Ballard. "Who's this with you? Mr. Collins?"

Lilian blushed at the thought of Ballard being mistaken for her husband. "Good afternoon, Regina. This gentleman with us today is Mr. Walter Ballard, a reporter for *The Times*." She turned to Ballard and at the same time waved her right hand toward their hostess. "Walt, this is the charming lady I told you about on the way here. Mrs. Regina Reynolds."

"How do you do, Mrs. Reynolds?"

The waitress gave Walt the once-over, then smiled politely at him. "Well, grab a table, folks, and Andrus and I will be with you as soon as the last paying customer leaves."

Ballard returned a bigger smile. "We came to have lunch first, Mrs. Reynolds. Then we can talk after the place clears out."

A twinkle danced in Regina's sapphire blue eyes. "The menu is on the wall behind the counter, Mr. Ballard. As soon as you folks are ready to order, give me a wave and I'll be right with you. Okay?" She looked over Ballard's shoulder. "Nice to see you again, Texas."

Johnny tipped his hat. "Ma'am."

Regina went about her business, while the trio found an empty table near the far end of the restaurant. A few minutes after they seated themselves and decided on their choices for lunch, the hostess came to their table, pad in one hand and pencil in the other. "Okay, folks, what can I get for you today?"

Lilian spoke first. "The Reuben sandwich looks good to me, and I'll have a glass of milk with it."

"Very good choice, Mrs. Collins. Andy cut off all the fat before slicing it for sandwiches. Would you like some sauerkraut on it? Andy makes it himself, so you won't find any better outside of Germany."

"That does sound appetizing, Regina. Do I get mustard with it?"

"I'll bring you a bottle so you can put as much as you want on your sandwich."

"Thank you."

"And how about you, Mr. Driver? What'll you have today?"

"Same as yesterday, Mrs. Reynolds. Ham and Swiss cheese on rye bread and a Coca-Cola with a glass of ice."

Regina smiled at him. "I kinda thought you would. I had it already written on my pad." She showed him the order book. "See?"

Fowler read the order. "By golly, you do have it written there. Are you some sort of mind reader, Mrs. Reynolds?"

She shook her head. "No, Johnny. I know my customers, is all. You look like a repeater to me."

Ballard smiled up at Regina. "So, tell me, Mrs. Reynolds, what do I look like to you?"

"You look like a roast beef sandwich, Mr. Ballard. On white bread with lots of mayonnaise and a slice of tomato."

The reporter had to laugh. "Well, give the lady a Kewpie doll. That's right on the nose, madam."

"Coffee, Mr. Ballard?"

"With cream and sugar."

"I'll bring the cream and sugar to the table, and you can use as much as you like."

"Thank you, Mrs. Reynolds."

Regina left them again.

The freelancer tapped Ballard on his left arm. "Now, do you see why I believe we can trust these people to tell us the truth?"

"I certainly do, Lilian. I get the feeling this woman has a mind like a steel trap."

"Exactly."

A minute after the last previous customer paid his tab and exited the restaurant, Regina locked the front door, and her husband appeared from the kitchen. They walked to the table next to the one shared by Maisy Malone's cadre of assistant amateur gumshoes and sat down. Andrew Reynolds focused on the reporter.

"My wife tells me you are from *The Times* in Los Angeles, Mr. Ballard."

"Yes, sir, that's correct. I am a police reporter for *The Times*."

"Police reporter? What kind of reporting is that?"

"Mostly, I spend my shift at the main police station downtown. I'm there from four in the morning to ten in the morning to see who gets arrested and who brings them in to be booked and for what crime they might have committed. On some occasions, someone very important in the city gets arrested and brought into the station. So, I write down all the details, and when my shift at the station is over, I go back to my desk at *The Times* and write a story about it, which is then printed in the paper the next morning. I don't get a lot of the real juicy stories to report, but what I do get, I report more accurately than my competitors do."

Reynolds nodded. "I see. So, how do you come to be working with Mrs. Collins and her driver on this business about how our late friend Charlie Donelson died?"

"Well, Mr. Reynolds, it's a little complicated, but I'll do my best to tell you straight about why we're here talking to you and Mrs. Reynolds about the death of Charles Donelson. Let me start by saying Johnny here is not *our* driver. He works with Miss Maisy Malone who's the boss on this investigation."

"Did you say … *Miss* … Maisy Malone?"

"Yes, I did. Maisy is a motion picture actress. On the side from her day job, she and her friend Mabel Normand investigate murders that seem to baffle the police."

Regina gasped. "Did you say Mabel Normand?"

"I did."

"Not the Mabel Normand in all those funny films at the motion picture shows?"

Ballard nodded. "That's her. She and Maisy have solved five or six murders for the police that I know of. This time Maisy is working this investigation with the help of two police detectives, the wife of one of the detectives, a woman who works for the police at the main station, and the three of us."

Fowler butted in. "Don't forget Mr. Cole, Walt, and the couple who also work with Miss Normand and Miss Malone. Mr. Arbuckle and his wife Miss Durfee."

"Yes, of course, Johnny."

Lilian spoke up. "That makes an even dozen in our snooping group, Andrew."

Ballard continued. "You see, Mr. Reynolds, we're not just looking into the death of Mr. Donelson. There are at least four other deaths we are looking into."

Both husband and wife gulped at each other, then gazed back at the reporter. They spoke simultaneously. "Four … others?"

"Yes, that's right. Four others. All of them died suspiciously and in their hotel rooms."

Regina blurted. "But Charlie lived in an apartment building, not a hotel."

"Yes, but he died under rather suspicious circumstances."

Andrew squinted at Ballard. "How do you mean suspicious? The newspapers here said he died from a stroke. How is that suspicious?"

Lilian stepped in. "If that was all there was about his death, then we would not be here talking to you nice people. There's the matter of someone trying to get Mr. Donelson's money from his bank account for beginners."

Ballard jumped in again. "And now we've learned he had a strange woman with him the last time he attended church in Pasadena."

Andrew posed the next question. "When was that, Mr. Ballard?"

"The Sunday before he died."

Regina and her husband eyed each other very quizzically but said nothing.

Lilian's intuition flashed into action. "You know about this woman who was with him that Sunday, don't you?"

Andrew aimed a stern stare at Lilian. "Do you recall the promise you made to us yesterday, Mrs. Collins?"

A bit bewildered Ballard focused on her now. "What promise was that, Lilian?"

She tightened her jaw for a second and tilted her head backward before speaking. "I promised—"

Fowler interrupted. "*We* promised them together, Miss Lilian."

A bee buzzed in Ballard's brain. "I don't care if the man in the moon made the promise with either of you. Just tell me what it was you promised these people."

A bolt of excitement lit up Lilian's eyes. "*We* promised these good people that their names and the name of this restaurant would not be revealed in *The Times*."

The reporter's anger burst from deep inside him. "How could you promise that? Neither one of you works for *The Times*. So, how could you do that?"

The Texas in Johnny Fowler came to the fore. "Now you just hold on there, Mr. Ballard. You've got no call to take that tone with Miss Lilian. She's a lady, and you're beginning to sound like a bluetick hound who's lost the scent of the scoundrel the law is chasing through the Buffalo Bayou back home in Harris County, Texas."

Lilian held up her hands in front of her would-be knight-errant. "It's all right, Johnny. Walt has a every right to be a little miffed at me for not telling him about the promise we made to these good people yesterday."

"A little miffed, Miss Lilian? He's being downright rude to you, and I won't stand for it. I've got a notion to go to the Studebaker and fetch my Colt's and—"

Seeing Ballard suddenly pale, Lilian leaned toward Fowler and put her left hand on his chest. "Johnny, calm down! You're scaring Walt with talk like that."

"It ain't talk, Miss Lilian. I mean every word of it. If he don't make you an apology right quick—"

The reporter knew a cue when he heard one. "I'm very sorry, Mrs. Collins. I meant no disrespect. I …" Further words failed him.

A short silence shrouded the restaurant until Andrew patted the table where he and Regina sat. "So, Mr. Ballard, what's it going to be? Are you going to keep the promise they made us yesterday? Or do we clam up about Charlie and show you the door out of here?"

Ballard furrowed his brow, gritted his teeth, and pursed his lips for a moment before answering Reynolds. "Well, I guess I have no choice. Between you and this gun-toting Texan, if I say no, our investigation into these deaths could come to an incomplete end and Johnny here puts a bullet in me and somebody else writes my epitaph that I was gunned down while searching for the story of the year. Or I say yes, and Johnny decides not to shoot me, and you tell us the one missing piece to this murder puzzle we're working on and I get to write half of the story of the year for *The Times*." He tapped the four fingers of his left hand on his tightly closed lips, stopped, then slumped his shoulders. "Okay, Mr. Reynolds, I promise that your names and the name of your restaurant never find their way into a story in *The Times* written be me."

Andrew growled. "Written by you or anybody else at *The Times* or any other newspaper in Los Angeles County."

Walt sighed. "That, too. Unless, of course, what you tell us today is that one shred of evidence that leads us to solving these murders. Then we can ask you to allow us to mention you in the story as the heroes who gave us that clue. How about that idea?"

Andrew and Regina exchanged that look again. Then both focused on Ballard. "No, not even then."

Walt shrugged. "Okay, we'll have it your way."

The husband groused. "In writing, if you please, Mr. Ballard?"

Without a moment of hesitation, the reporter reached inside his coat and pulled out a pencil and notepad.

Regina stopped Ballard from writing. "Hold on, Mr. Ballard. No pencil. I'll get you a pen and ink from the office in back."

"Of course, you will."

Roscoe Arbuckle and his wife Minta Durfee spent most of their Saturday afternoon at the Hotel Alexandria. They started by speaking with Preston Lewis at the registration desk.

The chief clerk smiled at the couple as they stepped up to the desk. "Good afternoon, Mr. Arbuckle. How may I help you today?"

"You recognize me?"

"Oh, yes, sir. I've seen you many times on the stage over the last few years. My name is Preston Lewis. I am the senior desk clerk here at the Hotel Alexandria."

"Pleased to meet you, Mr. Lewis. This is my wife, Minta Durfee. That's her stage name."

"Charmed, I'm sure, Mrs. Arbuckle."

"Mr. Lewis, we've had the pleasure of dining here the last few days, but we really haven't seen much of the hotel. I mean, we've seen the main lobby and the banquet room on the second floor and the main restaurant on the first floor, but we've been told there is so much more to see."

"You were told correctly, Mr. Arbuckle. The Alexandria does have much more to see. Would you like a guided tour, sir? I can arrange it for you folks in a moment's notice."

Arbuckle's face shone with glee. He turned to his wife. "Did you hear that, Dear? A guided tour. Isn't that wonderful?"

"It certainly is, Babe."

Roscoe turned back to desk clerk. "How soon can you arrange it, Mr. Lewis?"

Minta elbowed her husband. "Didn't you hear Mr. Lewis say he could arrange a tour in a moment's notice?"

"Oh, yes, that's right. You did say that didn't you, Mr. Lewis?"

Lewis smiled cordially. "Yes, sir, I did." He banged the bell on the counter with the palm of his left hand.

In seconds, a fellow of little stature, apparently in his early twenties, and wearing a hotel uniform, jumped up from the bellboys' bench and walked swiftly to the front desk. "Yes, sir, Mr. Lewis?"

"Mr. Arbuckle, this is Harry Posner, one of our elite bellhops. He's been with us since the hotel opened in nineteen-oh-six. Harry, these people are Mr. and Mrs. Roscoe Arbuckle. They would like a tour of the hotel. I'd like you to show them everything they want to see, and when you're done, please escort them to the main restaurant and tell Mr. Reikel that I said their dinner is courtesy of the hotel."

"Yes, sir, Mr. Lewis." The bellboy turned to the couple. "Shall we start with the lower level, Mr. Arbuckle?"

"What's on the lower level, dear fellow?"

A twinkle in his blue eyes accompanied Harry's smile. "I don't want to spoil the surprise, Mr. Arbuckle. I'm positive you and Mrs. Arbuckle will be delighted when you see what lies below."

Minta squeezed Roscoe's arm. "Let's go see what's down there, Babe. If it's anything like the lobby, then it should be a real treat."

Arbuckle waved his right hand. "Lead on, Harry."

The bellhop led the Arbuckles to a gray and black marble stairway that still gleamed from its initial polishing right after it was installed. They descended the steps gradually as they admired the beauty of the textured damask gold floral designs on rossa corsa red wallpaper. At the lower-level landing, they turned left into a corridor sixteen feet wide and twice as long with a floor made of the same marble as the stairway and equally burnished.

Roscoe leaned closer to Minta to speak softly in her ear. "Ain't this something, Dear? I thought the big dining room upstairs was classy, but this must really be some joint we're going to if the stairs and hall look so grand."

Harry twisted his head a few degrees to the left and spoke over his shoulder. "You ain't seen nothing yet, Mr. Arbuckle. Wait'll you get a load of what's right through these doors." The youth waved toward a pair of carved walnut doors with stained glass windows with alternating Asian elephants and Bengal tigers. He reached for their shiny brass door handles and pulled the doors open wide. "Welcome to the Indian Grill, folks." He stepped back to allow the Arbuckles to enter the restaurant.

The couple stopped two feet inside and allowed their eyes to feast on the dining room before them. With their mouths agape, they slowly scanned the luxurious chamber before them.

"Roscoe, I think we've died and gone to heaven."

"No, I don't think that's it, Dear. I think, somehow, we're in a dream and we've been magically transported to that palace in India. You know. The Tadge Macball."

"You mean the Taj Mahal, Babe."

Roscoe flushed a little. "Oh, yeah, that's the place."

Harry moved close behind them and leaned forward. "Now you know why this place is called the Indian Grill. Everything in here looks like it came from India. The carpet, the pillars, the stained-glass panels in the ceiling, the tables and chairs, the bar, and even the beams in the ceiling. The beams are made of teak wood, which was imported from India. Do you see those funny-looking designs in the carpet? Those are called swastikas. All the religions in India use those. They can be either right or left swastikas, depending on whether you're a Buddhist or a Hindu or some other weird religion they have over there."

Minta faced the bellhop. "How do you know all this, Harry?"

He grinned. "I read books when I ain't chasing around the hotel on some errand, like this one I'm doing with you nice folks."

"But why aren't there any customers here, Harry?"

"The Indian Grill doesn't open for business until five o'clock, Mrs. Arbuckle, but things don't really start jumping until after six. Motion picture folks like you are starting to come here a lot. Especially on Saturday nights."

"Yes, we've heard that about this hotel."

Posner winked at her. "Classiest hotel in the city, Mrs. Arbuckle. It might be the classiest in the whole West."

Roscoe suddenly recalled the real reason why he and his wife had come to the Alexandria that Saturday afternoon. "You must know a lot about the hotel, Harry."

"More than most of the help here. That's why Mr. Lewis picked me to show you around."

Minta edged herself into this new line of conversation. "I'll bet you know all the history of this hotel, don't you, Harry?"

"You bet I do. I've only been on the job here since the hotel opened back in oh-six. I was one of the first fellows hired here. There's only nine of us bellboys left from the original fourteen. Two got fired, one quit, and the other two fellows were promoted to assistant clerks when the annex was opened three years ago."

Minta pushed forward with her prodding of Posner. "I'll bet you hear a lot of things, too, don't you?"

Harry grinned with pride. "How'd you guess, Mrs. Arbuckle?"

"Well, you do seem to be quite a bright young man. It only goes to show when you talk about this place and the people who work here."

"Not just the people who work here, Mrs. Arbuckle. But most of the people who are guests here as well."

"Oh, really? Like who? Anybody famous?"

Posner grinned with pride. "Sure. How about President William Howard Taft himself?"

"President Taft? Did he stay here when he was campaigning last year?"

"President Taft stayed here two years ago."

A personal question popped into Roscoe's mind. "Did you get to meet President Taft, Harry?"

Disappointment saddened Posner's face. "No, I didn't. His people said I was too young to vote, so the President wasn't interested in shaking my hand. I tried to tell them I would be twenty-one before the election, but they just ignored me."

Minta patted his shoulder. "That is too bad, Harry."

Roscoe threw in his own moral support for the young man. "I think that's scandalous, Harry."

"Oh, I wouldn't go that far, Mr. Arbuckle, but let me tell you what is scandalous around here." He scanned the area around them to see if anyone might be within listening distance. Not seeing anyone, he bent forward to be closer to the couple and whispered. "Remember what I said about motion picture folks starting to make the Alexandria their regular place to dine on Saturday nights?"

"Yes?"

"Well, the first motion picture people to stay here were some folks from the American Biograph Company who came here back in January nineteen-ten. Their whole party consisted of thirty-five folks. Mostly actors. A few directors and some cameramen. They all checked into the Hollenbeck at first, then a bunch of them moved down here to the Alexandria. From Monday through Saturday, they were up and out of here before daylight. Then we wouldn't see them again until after dark except on Saturdays when they would straggle in here from the studio up in Edendale all afternoon. By sundown, they would all be here, and within an hour, all of them would be in one dining room or another. After eating, they would all retire to one barroom or another for a few hours before heading upstairs." The bellhop leaned forward and lowered his voice. "I'm not one to tell tales out of school, Mr.

Arbuckle, but I saw a lot of those folks going into rooms not their own, if you know what I mean."

Roscoe's head bobbed. "Yes, I know what you mean, Harry."

"One of the most accommodating gents in that group was one of the directors. Good tipper. Most Saturday nights he'd order a bottle of champagne and two glasses sent up to his room. I delivered it most of the time. Don't know who the other glass was for. Didn't ask either. I can only assume it was for one of the actresses who came out here from New York. Either that or some local girl wanting to get a job with their company. Mr. Whitmore made it perfectly clear to all the help that none of us were ever to speak a word about such things. That's why I'm not telling you folks his name."

Minta nodded. "A very sound policy, Harry."

"For sure, Mrs. Arbuckle. For sure."

Roscoe's expression turned quite serious. "I remember something in the newspapers about the famous lawyer and his detective staying here during the trial of those men who set off the bomb that blew up *The Times* building a few years back. Do you know anything about that, Harry?"

"Do I know anything about that? Does the sun rise in the east and set in the west every day? You're talking to the one man who knows more about that episode in the hotel's short history than anybody, and that includes Mr. Whitmore himself."

Minta jumped in again. "Do tell, Harry! I'm all ears." She nudged Roscoe with her left elbow. "You are, too, aren't you, Babe?"

"You bet! Go ahead, Harry. Spill the beans."

"Well, okay. Do you people know about the bombing of *The Times* building a couple of years back?"

Minta answered him. "Oh, yes, the bombing of *The Times* building where all those newspaper people were killed. What a terrible thing that was."

Harry nodded. "Yes, Mrs. Arbuckle, it was. Well, once the bomber was caught and brought up on charges, the famous trial lawyer Mr. Clarence Darrow came here to Los Angeles to defend the men who did the dirty deed. But before that, the police department here hired that so-called American Sherlock Holmes, Mr. William J. Burns, to come here and sniff around until the culprits, the McNamara brothers, were arrested and brought to trial." Posner laughed. "Mr. Burns and the defense lawyer Mr. Darrow both stayed here in the hotel while the trial was underway. At the same time, that motion picture director Mr.

D.W. Griffith was staying here. The three of them knew each other back in New York. Well, Mr. Griffith was sitting in the lobby reading his newspaper when Mr. Burns spotted him and called out to him. Mr. Griffith got up and headed off to meet Mr. Burns when at that very moment Mr. Darrow came charging through the lobby on his way to a bar. The three of them nearly ran into each other. For a second, all of us bellhops sitting on the bench thought a fist fight might break out between Mr. Burns and Mr. Darrow with Mr. Griffith as the referee. We were greatly disappointed. The three gentlemen greeted each other with awkward smiles and polite pleasantries, then quickly headed off in three directions at once. We were all pulling for Mr. Burns if there had been a fight because he often sat with us on the bench and told us some of his thrilling experiences as a private detective, giving us some of the details and clues he had concerning his latest cases, especially his investigation into the bombing of *The Times* building. Then he'd ask us for our opinions and slants on the case, and we'd tell him our thoughts and hunches and the gossip we heard around the hotel from guests and other people who work here. He took it all very seriously. I'd be willing to bet we helped him catch those murdering McNamara brothers."

Minta patted his left arm. "That's very interesting, Harry. I'd make a bet right along with you that you and your fellow bellboys were very helpful to Mr. Burns in catching the McNamaras."

Posner leaned closer to her. "I'm sure if he was still around here, Mr. Burns would be looking into something that happened earlier this week right here in the Alexandria. One of our guests died in her sleep. She was very sick when she came here, so our doctor, Dr. Newmark, he pronounced her dead and said the cause of her death was some weird condition she had. Before the day was through, people were already saying she was murdered."

The two actors feigned total shock and awe. Together they gasped one word. "No!"

"Oh, yes. Murder. Can you believe it? Murder? Here in this hotel? What a scandal that would be, if word ever got out."

Minta and Roscoe exchanged worrisome looks, but neither spoke a syllable.

Maisy and her sleuthing group gathered that evening in the lobby of the Hotel Alexandria, all of them abuzz with the facts they had learned earlier that day. She and Milo arrived next to last. Instantly, she scanned the new faces in the group, starting with the woman she had heard so much about but had yet to meet her face-to-face.

The actress held out her right hand in greeting. "You must be Mrs. Collins. I'm so glad to meet you."

Lilian returned the gesture. "Likewise, Miss Malone."

"Please call me Maisy. I just know we're going to be good friends Mrs. Collins."

"Then let's start off by you calling me Lilian."

They released the grip. "And who are these two handsome men with you, Lilian?"

"This is my husband Lew and our son Herbie."

Maisy shook hands with the father and then the son. "I'm glad to meet both of you gentlemen. Please call me Maisy."

Lew leaned a little toward their hostess. "I'm in real estate, Maisy, and Herbie is in college at Los Angeles State Normal School."

She shook hands with the son. "I know the school well, Herbie. I visit the Central Library near your college regularly. I'm surprised I haven't seen you strolling along the sidewalks at one time or another."

"I spend most of my time at school in the classrooms. But now that we've met, I believe I'll have to look out for you when I'm out and about in that area."

"You do that, Herbie, and should we meet perhaps we can get a cup of coffee somewhere and discuss your favorite subject. I'm quite fond of history. How about you?"

Young Collins flinched. "Oh, yes, ma'am. I'm also quite fond of history of all kinds. I hope teach history after I graduate."

"I'm sure you will, Herbie." Maisy turned to greet yet another pair of newcomers. "And who might these nice people be?" She held up her right hand to delay Lilian from speaking. "No! Don't tell me. Let me guess. These are the people from that restaurant in Long Beach. Am I right?"

Lilian threw up her hands. "Yes, Maisy, you are quite right. These folks are Mr. Andrew Reynolds and his charming wife Regina. They own the Chicago Restaurant down in Long Beach. They were good friends of Mr. Charles Donelson, one of the deceased people whose deaths we are investigating."

Maisy reached out to Andrew. "I'm glad you folks could join us, Mr. Reynolds. I understand you're from Sweden."

"Yes, I am, but my family came here to America before I learned to walk. Regina and I married seventeen years ago, and we moved here to California just a few years ago and bought our restaurant."

"Well, I'm very happy to meet both of you." She shook Regina's hand. "Especially you, Mrs. Reynolds. Do you come from Sweden as well?"

"No, I'm from Iowa, but I was raised mostly in Benton Township, Scott County, Missouri. It's bordered by the Mississippi River."

"I'm from the Choctaw Nation. That's now part of Oklahoma. My folks came from Kentucky by way of Arkansas."

Lilian nodded. "I suppose the motion picture business drew you out here to California."

"Actually, I was doing an act in Vaudeville in Chicago when Mr. Sennett and Miss Normand saw me and offered me a job at their new studio here in Los Angeles. I'd never been to California before, so I accepted. I've been out here for six months now."

Again, Lilian's head bobbed as she indicated Milo Cole. "And who is this handsome young man in attendance with you?"

Maisy flushed mildly with embarrassment. "Oh, forgive me, Lilian. This gentleman is Mr. Milo Cole, my good friend and escort for this evening. He's also involved in our investigation."

"Are you with the police, Mr. Cole?"

"No, Mrs. Collins, I am not. I work at the same motion picture studio as Maisy."

"Are you an actor?"

Milo hesitated to answer her question, but after swallowing hard, he managed to blurt out a response. "Well, acting is only part of what I do there, Mrs. Collins. My primary job is working for Mr. Sennett."

"So, `you're something of an errand boy then?"

Maisy dove into the exchange. "Milo does a lot more at Keystone than that, Lilian. He manages the office when Mr. Sennett is out filming away from the studio. That is, he manages the office when he's not working as Mr. Sennett's assistant director of a film. He also works in front of the camera on occasion. Milo's been in more than forty films."

Lilian nodded again. "Your name, Mr. Cole. Your first name, Milo. I find it to be rather interesting. Are you named for anyone in your ancestry?"

Milo frowned. "No, I'm not. Milo is my stage name, but Cole is my real family name."

"So, what is your real birth name?"

"I'd rather not say."

"And why not, Mr. Cole? Is it something shameful?"

"Well, it's rather odd, to be truthful, Mrs. Collins."

"Really? How odd, Mr. Cole?"

"If you heard it, you would know, Mrs. Collins."

Maisy re-entered the conversation. "You know, Milo, you're the first person I met out here in California, and I don't even know your real name. I'd like to hear it, too."

Milo glared at Maisy. "You are the last person I want to know my real first name, Miss Malone."

Maisy studied his eyes for a few seconds. "Come to think of it, Mr. Cole, about the only I know about you from before we met is your name. No, wait that's not true. I know your family lives in Connecticut. You said so the other day when we were all here."

"Yes, that's true. They do live in Connecticut now."

Lilian pressed him again. "Is that where you were born, Mr. Cole?"

"No, I was born in Pennsylvania."

"Pennsylvania. Isn't that interesting?"

Maisy interrupted. "Yes, isn't it, Lilian? Now I know three things about Milo, but I don't know anything about these other ladies." She indicated the wives of Johnny Fowler and Bill Ingram and held out her hand to the older of them. "How do you do, Mrs. Ingram?"

The detective's wife returned the gesture. "Please call me Ruth, Miss Malone. Bill has told me so much about you that I feel I already know you."

"Well, I hope it was all good."

"Oh, it was, it was."

"Then Bill can stay for dessert, Ruth." The two women laughed at the jest. "And please call me Maisy, if you will."

"Glad to, Maisy."

The actress faced the younger woman now. "And you have to be Johnny's better half, Mrs. Fowler." She offered the same greeting. "He doesn't talk much about you, but I've chalked that off to him being born and bred a Texan."

"Ain't that the truth, Miss Malone."

Maisy shook her head. "Now don't go on that way. You simply must call me Maisy, and I'll call you Marie, if you're good with that."

"I'm better than good with it, Maisy. I'm delighted."

Malone stepped back twice. "For those of you who have never met my two good friends here, this tall hunk of man is our new star at Keystone Studio, Mr. Roscoe Arbuckle, and with him is his personal leading lady, Mrs. Arbuckle who is known by her adoring public as Miss Minta Durfee."

The big man flashed his legendary heartfelt smile. "We're certainly glad to meet all of you good people. Since Maisy insists on being totally informal this evening, you must all call us Roscoe and Minta. After all, we're in this together, aren't we?"

Johnny Fowler puffed up his chest. "Right you are, Roscoe."

Remembering her manners, Maisy pointed to the Brownings. "Do forgive my lack of manners and allow me to introduce two of LA's finest. This handsome gentleman is Detective Sergeant Ed Browning of the Los Angeles Police Department, and beside him is his charming lady and much better half Mrs. Nealy Browning."

The couple nodded politely to those people new to the group.

"And this equally handsome fellow standing beside his better half is Detective Browning's partner Detective Sergeant Bill Ingram. Take a bow, Bill."

Without a word of reprisal, Ingram did as commanded.

With her left hand, Maisy took the right hand of the next person to be introduced and drew her closer. "And this pretty lady is my good friend Nellie Sharpe. Nellie works for the Los Angeles Police Department as a stenographer. Without her keeping a written record for us as we try to solve these dastardly crimes, I'm not sure how we'd succeed in bringing the villains to justice. Am I right, Eddie?"

Browning turned serious. "Right you are, Maisy. All of us officers consider Nellie to be a vital part of our jobs to keep crime at bay in our fair city. I speak for the whole department. Right, Bill?"

At just that moment, a smiling couple, both attired for a night out in the big city, entered the Alexandria's lobby, spied the posse of sleuths, and walked directly to the gathering.

Maisy saw them first. "Please, everyone, for those of you who have never met these lovely people, I'd like you to meet Venice Police Detective Vince DeDonatis and his charming wife Susie."

Together, they greeted the earlier arrivals with slight bows. Then Vince took charge as usual. "We're glad to meet all you folks. Since we're a little tardy to the party, I think we should hold off on any introductions until we're all seated at our tables."

Ed Browning had to tease DeDonatis with a gentle jest. "Just like a Venice cop. Late to the scene of a crime and first to take charge."

The beach city officer returned to the ribbing. "That's what I like about you boys from the big city. You recognize your betters on sight and get out of the way as soon as you do."

A round of light laughter lit up the group.

Maisy turned to the lone man in the crowd not accompanied by a female companion. "And this crusty looking gentleman is the only real snoop among us. For those of you who don't already know him, this is Mr. Walter Ballard, police reporter for *The Los Angeles Times*. Take a bow, Walt."

Smiling his usual friendly grin, Ballard raised his right hand and waved at everybody. "Nice to meet the rest of you folks."

Then, much to everybody's surprise, Mabel Normand and Mack Sennett suddenly appeared in the lobby and headed slowly toward the small crowd. Initially, the Keystone Studio boss grinned with delight. Then he turned sour. Sennett leaned closer to Mabel and whispered in a low growl. "I expected Roscoe and Minta, the two detectives, and Maisy's chauffeur. But all these other people? Who the hell are they? And who invited them?"

His star attraction nuzzled up to him and whispered. "Don't worry about it, Nappy. I'll split the tab with you."

Mack reversed his emotional gears and another smile blossomed on his face. "What the hell? Why not?" Turning up his vocal volume a couple notches, he waved to the group. "Good evening, everybody. It's great to see so many new faces along with those few who make their good living off me. But let's not go into that now. It's everybody's free time as well as Mabel's and mine. So, let's make a night of it, shall we? Some great food, a little wine, maybe dance the night away later on." He raised his left index finger. "And maybe Maisy can entertain us all by solving this case you all have been working on these past few days.

What do say to that, *Detective* Malone? You up for a night on my buck?"

"That's what I like about you, Mack. You're always so upbeat, no matter the time or the place or who you're with."

Mabel leaned forward and squinted at her best friend. "Have you been drinking already, Maise? This is Mack Sennett you're talking about. 'So upbeat?' Apparently, you—"

"Apparently, you didn't hear the sarcasm in my voice, Mabes."

"Oh, is that what that was? Now I get it." She squeezed Sennett's arm. "Didn't I warn you this might not be the place for you to be this evening?"

Sennett pursed his lips. "Yes, you did, Sweetheart. But I'm here now, and I'm not leaving until I get my money's worth."

Maisy stiffened. "Your money's worth? I thought—"

Mabel interrupted. "So did I, Maise. But he bought his way into this party. He even got us a banquet room upstairs. So how could I say no to him?"

"Yes, how could you?" Maisy sighed. "Well, we're all here, so let's go, folks. Dinners on the king of comedy, Mr. Mack Sennett."

Just as he had done when the LA Police Department footed the bill for Maisy's investigators' lunch, the Alexandria's manager Mr. Samuel J. Whitmore arranged for the motion picture folks and their friends to dine in privacy with their own serving staff, which was comprised of the same waiters who had worked their previous visit, including the head of food service himself, Mr. Joseph Reikel. Whitmore possessed pure genius when it came to pleasing the hotel's clientele.

As soon as everybody had placed their meal orders, Maisy called the meeting to order. "All day I've been wondering what all of you have learned that will help us solve this murder … or murders. Eddie, how about you going first?"

"Glad to. Bill and I started the day by checking into the Station and going down to the records department to see if Nealy and Nellie had found anything new yet. I'll let them reveal what they learned from their research today. Believe me, you will all be quite surprised when you hear what they will be telling us.

"From the Station, Bill and I paid a visit to the Travers Hotel to interview the desk clerk and anybody else who might know something about the death of Mr. Claudius Peters. The first person we spoke with was Mr. Arthur Martinet, the hotel's manager. For those of you who are taking notes, his last name is spelled M-A-R-T-I-N-E-T. He came here from Louisiana. His ancestors were French. His assistant, Mr. Daniel Conklin, told us Mr. Martinet was away on a trip to visit his relatives back in Louisiana at the time of Mr. Peters' demise. Martinet confirmed that, and then allowed us to use his office to interview his assistant.

"So, we could speak in private, Mr. Conklin took us into the manager's office, and we interviewed him there. After reviewing how Claudius Peters apparently died, we questioned him about Minnie Lightfreit, the chambermaid who had found the man's body."

Before Browning could continue, Maisy interrupted him. "Excuse me, Eddie, but I have a question for you and Bill."

"Sure, Maisy. Go ahead and ask."

"Did you ask Mr. Conklin about the position of the bed when he entered the dead man's room?"

Sudden alarm drained the color from the faces of Browning and Ingram. They stared at each other with complete contrition for several seconds. Finally, the senior detective looked back at Maisy and slowly answered her question. "I'm so embarrassed to say this, but ... it never occurred ... to either of us ... to ask that question."

Nealy jumped into the conversation. "Maisy? Nellie and I read the report written by Detective Frank Beaumont who was the initial officer on the case. He didn't write anything about the position of the bed."

Nellie spoke up now. "That's right, Maisy. Not a word about the position of the bed. The only thing he mentioned was Mr. Peters' chambermaid ... Mrs. Lightfreit ... found him tied to the bedstead by his suspenders."

Maisy turned to the stenographer. "That's all he wrote."

"That's all he wrote."

Walt Ballard leaned forward. "I read the original story about Peters trying to hang himself in *The Times* the day after it happened. It stated ... let me think a second to see if I can recall the exact words in the paper." Closed his eyes and pinched his face into a grimace. "I think it said, '... she found him hanging by his suspenders, fastened around his neck, from the head of his bed.' Then she cut the suspenders and he fell to the floor unconscious. Then she went for help because he was still breathing." He opened his eyes. "That last part was all my words, not the article's."

Maisy nodded and glanced around the table at all the questioning expressions. She smiled politely. "Doesn't anyone here think it's odd that Mr. Peters tried to *hang* himself from the head of his bed? Even if it was a brass bed with a high headboard …"

Lilian Collins interjected her conclusion. "Mr. Peters couldn't have possibly hung himself from the head of the bed, not unless he was four feet tall or shorter."

Maisy focused on Lilian. "Therefore …?"

Browning broke into the conversation again. "Therefore, the bed had to be standing up for him to hang himself from the head of the bed." He took a deep breath. "Therefore, if the bed wasn't standing up, someone had to …" He stared at Maisy. "Therefore, someone had to help him hang himself … or-r-r … he was murdered."

A grin spread over Maisy's face as she extended her right arm and pointed the index finger at the detective. "Right you are, Eddie!"

Browning relaxed. "Now it all makes sense. Right, Bill?"

"Yes, it does, Ed." Ingram focused on Maisy. "After we finished questioning Mr. Conklin, we got the chambermaid's address from his boss, Mr. Martinet and went to pay her a visit. That didn't work out so well because the address we were given turned out to be a vacant lot on the southwest corner of Fifth and Olive."

Another smile curled the corners of Maisy's lips. "Fifth and Olive? Isn't that across the street from Central Park?"

Browning replied. "Yes, it is. So, what are you getting at, Maisy?"

She shrugged. "Well, I was only thinking about how close Central Park is to this very hotel we're dining in right now."

All the others gasped, except for Browning. "Bill and I were thinking we'd been lied to by the manager of the Hotel Travers, so we called him to verify the address he'd given us. He repeated it to me, and it was the exact same address."

Maisy nodded. "Then what did you tell him?"

"Nothing."

"And what did the manager say when you asked him to verify the address?"

"He asked why I wanted it again."

"Then what did you tell him?"

Browning frowned at Maisy. "I said we just wanted to be sure we had the right address before we started knocking on her door."

"And he bought that?"

The detective's eyes squinted at the actress. "He must have bought it because he said, 'If there's anything else you need from me or my staff, we're at your disposal.' Satisfied with that, Bill and I talked about what we should do next."

Maisy nodded. "And what did you do next?"

"Bill came up with an idea that made a lot of sense to me. He said we should look up the doctor who treated Mr. Peters at the nearby receiving hospital. Dr. G.E. Brown. We talked about it for a bit and passed on that idea. Then Bill said maybe we should pay a visit to the mortuary where Mr. Peters was sent after he died. Neither one of us could remember if Frank Beaumont had put that information in his report, so we called the station and asked Nellie to check on it for us."

Maisy turned to the stenographer. "And what did you find, Nell?"

Sharpe smiled. "Nobody has called me Nell since I was in high school. Kind of brings back memories."

The actress tilted her head forward and looked over her eyebrows. "Detective Beaumont's report?"

"Oh, yes, of course. Well, there was nothing in it about where Mr. Peters' body was taken from the County Hospital, so I called over to the hospital and asked if they had a record of where his body taken for funeral services. They checked and told me Mr. Peters' remains were picked up by Sutch's Funeral Parlor at eight-forty-two South Figueroa after the coroner signed the death certificate that afternoon."

Maisy's expression turned grim as she focused on Browning again. "Didn't you and Bill pay a visit to Sutch's Funeral Parlor earlier in the week?"

Browning nodded. "Yes, we did, so there was no trouble going back there this morning."

"Did you learn anything from Mr. Sutch this time around?"

The detective grinned like Lewis Carroll's Cheshire cat. "Yes, we did, Miss Malone. Mr. Sutch was a literal fountain of information about Mr. Peters' death."

"I can't wait to hear this."

"Oh, you're going to like it, Maisy. Like I told you the other day, Mr. Sutch is a very thorough mortician. He brought out his notes and read them to us. Bill copied every word he said. Go ahead, Bill. Read what you copied from Mr. Sutch."

Ingram cleared his throat. "Uh-huh! Name of deceased: Claudius Peters. Age: sixty. Occupation: Lawyer. Residence: Chicago, Illinois. Date of death: March third, nineteen-thirteen. Cause of death: Suicide by hanging self. Notable marks on body: One: Contusion on throat. Two: Scratches on front of neck. Three: Slight swelling on back of head. Other notable marks: None. Reason for contusion on throat: Hanging by the neck. Reason for scratches on neck: Most likely self-inflicted while hanging. Proof: Skin under deceased's fingernails. Reason for swelling on back of head: Falling on floor when suspenders cut."

Browning took the lead again. "At that point, Mr. Sutch closed his notebook and looked me straight in the eye. He said without flinching, 'This man didn't hang himself. He was murdered. Somebody else wrapped those suspenders around his neck and choked him nearly to death, then he … or she … let go when the killer thought Mr. Peters was dead. That's how I figured he got that bruise on the back of his head. That blow to his head probably knocked him out. Then the killer ran off when he saw Mr. Peters was still breathing.' Boy, were we shocked to hear him say that!"

Maisy nodded. "So, Mr. Sutch thinks the chambermaid murdered Mr. Peters?"

"No, he doesn't. He said he read the article in the newspaper about Mr. Peters' attempted suicide and how the chambermaid came into his room and found him with the suspenders around his neck but still breathing. Then he said that the chambermaid cutting the suspenders and going for help was perfectly plausible."

Maisy nodded. "Plausible? Possibly. But not very likely."

"How's that, Maisy?"

"Did Mr. Sutch measure Mr. Peters for his height? And weigh him as well?"

Incredulity struck Browning. "What does his height and weight have to do with anything?"

"Maybe a lot. Maybe nothing. So did Mr. Sutch—"

A touch of irritation reddened Browning's face. "I don't know if he measured or weighed the body." He glared at his partner. "Did he say anything to you about doing either of those things, Bill?"

"Not a word, Ed."

"How about in his notes? Did you see anything there about the dead man's height and weight?"

"It might have been there, Ed, but I didn't see it, even if it was there."

Browning focused on Maisy again. "So, what does his height and weight have to do with anything?"

"Think back to the bed, Eddie."

The two detectives squinted at each other.

Lilian Collins huffed before speaking. "Oh, please, gentlemen. The bed! Maisy is telling us, if Mr. Peters tried to hang *himself,* he had to be strong enough to stand the bed upright, tie the suspenders onto the rail of the head, stood on a chair, and kicked it away in order to take his own life."

Maisy slapped the table. "Right you are, Lilian. Either he tried to kill himself that way or someone else tried to kill him by strangling him with his suspenders." She paused to watch everyone's reaction to her theory. then aimed another question at the detectives. "Did you gents get a description of the chambermaid from the hotel clerks?"

Again, the partners squinted at each other.

Lilian had one word for them. "Unbelievable!"

Ingram looked back at Maisy. "I'll go back to the Travers first thing tomorrow and get a description of the chambermaid."

Browning spoke softly. "I'll go with you, Bill."

"No, Ed, that won't be necessary. Only one of us should go."

"Are you sure?"

"Positive."

Maisy rapped the knuckles of her right hand on the table. "Okay, folks, let's move on. Lilian, what did you and Walt learn when you went back to Long Beach today?"

Lilian sat up straighter. "As you already know, Maisy, as evidenced by the presence of Mr. and Mrs. Reynolds, Walt, Johnny, and I had a very productive day, starting with our visit to the Swedish Methodist Church in Pasadena where we spoke with the Reverend Gustave Kallstedt. He was rather reluctant to reveal anything about Mr. Charles Donelson, the ship carpenter who *allegedly* died from a stroke at his home in Long Beach a few weeks back. The only thing he would tell us initially was Mr. Donelson was a regular member of his church. When we asked him if Mr. Donelson had any relatives in his congregation, he remained reticent about that, too. Then he told us something that until now … now that we have learned about the chambermaid and her very possible connection to Mr. Peters' death … Reverend Kallstedt told us about a woman who accompanied Mr. Donelson the last time he attended the reverend's church."

Maisy jerked erect in her chair. "A woman? Did the reverend know her name?"

Lilian tilted her head back and hesitated for a moment so all the others could see the conceit in her face. "No, Maisy, I am quite sorry to say we did not get her name." She smiled at Ballard. "Walt, would you please tell everyone what we did get from Reverend Kallstedt?"

Pure delight sparkled in Ballard's eyes. "Proud to, Lilian." He looked at Browning. "Reverend Kallstedt gave us a description of the mystery woman who accompanied Mr. Donelson to church the Sunday before he died."

A round of gasps flooded the room.

Ballard continued. "Reverend Kallstedt said she had gray streaks in her brown hair around her ears. Then he said she was much shorter than Mr. Donelson. She had blue eyes. She was wearing a dark blue hat with a narrow brim and a long dark blue coat."

"Is that all? Nothing about her face? Her nose? Chin? The color of her skin? Her possible weight? Was she thin? Obese? Plump?"

"No, nothing else."

Lilian waved her right hand toward Andrew and Regina. "Johnny drove Walt and me back to The Chicago Restaurant in Long Beach to pay another visit to Mr. and Mrs. Reynolds again. As they had been the day before, they were very helpful to us, which is why we asked them to join us here this evening. We felt it would be better, if you heard everything, they told us this afternoon directly from them."

Maisy nodded. "I'm really glad you did, Lilian. It's always best to hear from eyewitnesses firsthand instead of receiving information that's passed down the line, even if it comes from people as astute as you and Walt and Johnny." She turned her gaze onto the restaurant couple. "Go ahead, folks, and tell us what you know about Mr. Donelson. I'm certain that you're just as eager to get to the cause of his death as all of us are."

Regina cleared her throat. "First of all, Andrus and I would like to thank you for having us to dinner with all you motion picture people." She focused on Mabel and Mack. "Especially you, Miss Normand, and you, too, Mr. Sennett. Andrus and I really enjoy your comedies. We go to see them at the Bijou Theatre whenever one of your films is playing there. They are so very funny, Mr. Sennett."

The movie producer blushed at the compliment. "Thank you, Mrs. Reynolds. You've very kind."

Regina shifted her view to Mabel. "And you, Miss Normand, are such a delightful actress. You make us laugh right out loud."

Always polite to her public, if not so much to the people who had to endure her occasional obscenities and scathing sarcasm on the set or in the privacy of the business offices at the studio, Mabel smiled so very politely and blinked her eyes repeatedly as she acknowledged the flattery. "Thank you, Regina. It does me good to hear you say that."

Maisy rolled her eyes and softly replied. "Oh, brother, Mabes."

Then she purposely cleared her throat to get everyone's attention. "Yes, thank you, Regina. Now what was it you were about to tell us concerning Mr. Donelson."

Regina blushed. "Yes, of course, Miss Malone … uh, Maisy. As I was about to say, Andrus and I were rather surprised to see Lilian and Johnny back in our restaurant the very next day after their first visit. And we were delighted to meet Walt as well. Andrus and I were just as surprised that they had more questions for us. We knew that we hadn't told them everything we knew about Charlie Donelson. Not that we held back anything intentionally. We only told them the day before what they asked us to tell them. When they asked us about going with Charlie to church in Pasadena, we told them we had gone there with him on occasion, not every Sunday, only on the first Sunday of every month for Communion and on holidays like Christmas and Easter. When Charlie started being sick, his doctor had a nurse come by his apartment to look in on him to see how he was doing. We never met her or even saw her. Charlie would only mention her once in a while. He said her name is Olga Renius, and she's Swedish. Like me, she's second generation, which means her parents came over here before they started having any children. She was born in Kansas, and her whole family came here to California about five years ago. She works for Dr. Perce and Dr. Newton. Their office is at eleven Pine Avenue. Dr. Newton lives there in rooms above their offices. He can tell you all you want to know about Olga Renius."

Maisy focused on Lilian again. "Are you thinking this nurse is the mystery woman that Reverend Kallstedt saw with Mr. Donelson?"

Regina seemed surprised. "It does seem that way, don't you think?"

Mabel spoke up. "It certainly looks like she's the one to me, too."

Maisy nodded and peered at Regina again. "Do you know where this Olga Renius lives?"

"No, I'm sorry I don't, but you might be able to get it from either of the doctors who employ her."

"Dr. Perce and Dr. Newton?"

"Yes."

Ed Browning interrupted the exchange between Maisy and Regina. "Pardon me, ladies, but Dr. Perce and Dr. Newton? Aren't they the two doctors who reported the cause of Charles Donelson's death?"

Lilian answered his question. "That's what it said in the newspaper article that I found in the morgue at *The Times*. They reported to the

Long Beach police that Mr. Donelson 'died either from starvation with suicidal intent' or from a cerebral hemorrhage. They also said the poor man was 'slightly mentally unbalanced' and was starving himself either with suicidal intent or because he had insufficient means to buy enough food to maintain his health."

Andrus Reynolds spoke for the first time. "We read that same story in the *Telegram* three days after poor Charlie passed away. I can tell you this much. Charlie wasn't starving to death. That same day he died he was in our restaurant eating lunch just like he did nearly every workday … Monday through Saturday. He ordered the same thing he ordered every day. Sandwich, soup, and pie. If Charlie was starving to death, he sure did hide it good. Ain't that right, Regina?"

His wife replied grimly. "Yes, Andy, you're right." She focused on Maisy. "If Charlie was dying from starvation, then the cause had to be something besides starvation. I know the story said Charlie might have died from a cerebral hemorrhage that was caused by starvation, but that can't be either because we know Charlie wasn't starving to death. He must have died from something else. But what?"

Lilian offered a suggestion. "Perhaps we can discover the identity of Mr. Bachman's mysterious client and see how she fits into all this."

Maisy nodded. "I was thinking the very same thing, Lilian. But before we look further into that, I think we need to have a chat with one of those doctors who pronounced Mr. Donelson dead and offered their opinion on his cause of death. In the meantime, let's hear what Roscoe and Minta learned today during their tour of this magnificent hotel. Who's first? Mr. Arbuckle or Mrs.?"

Minta nudged her husband. "You go ahead, Babe. I'll jump in if and when you need me to add my two cents worth."

Nervously, Roscoe smiled at his wife. "Well, okay, Dearest, if you think I should."

She sighed. "Yes, Babe, I think you should. You're the bigshot in this marriage. Now go ahead. Spill!"

He glanced around the table. "Minta's only fooling, folks. Without her, I wouldn't be here."

Mabel piped in. "And here you are, Mr. Arbuckle. So, get on with it, will you? *Please?*"

Sennett nudged his leading female star and spoke softly to her. "Let him alone, Mabel. We aren't on a set at the studio now, so there's no need to chide him."

The actress grimaced and sighed in Arbuckle's direction. "Mack's right, Roscoe. I was a little off base, and—"

The only other person who could chastise Mabel and get away with it was her best friend Maisy. "A little off base, Mabes? How about out in left field?"

Mabel's face reddened with anger as her eyes threw darts at Maisy. In the next second, she gained control of her temper and turned ever so sweetly in Arbuckle's direction. "Maisy's right, Roscoe. I'm sorry to have been so rude." Before he could reply, she dipped her head in his wife's direction. "And I'm sorry I was rude to you, Minta. It's Nappy's fault for pouring wine in my glass all evening. I'm a little tipsy, dear."

Sennett cleared his throat as he tugged at the knot in his dark blue tie. "That's enough, Normand." He looked at the Arbuckles. "Go ahead, Roscoe. I'm really feeling involved here now. Malone's sleuthing doesn't usually intrigue me but listening to all you folks who are working with her has really piqued my curiosity. So, let's hear what you and Minta learned today." He grinned. "I'm all ears, Big Fella."

A rosy bloom colored Roscoe's puffed out cheeks as he nodded at the studio's boss. "Well, we had quite a day, Minta and me. We met with the desk clerk, Mr. Lewis, as soon as we entered the hotel, and he assigned a bellhop, a young man named Harry Posner, he was to give us a tour of the place. And what a tour it was. Minta and I had no idea how elegant this hotel is. You wouldn't believe it until you see it all for yourselves."

Minta nudged Roscoe. "Enough already, Babe. Tell them all that stuff Harry told us. That's what they want to hear. Not the glamour of this place. Only what goes on here."

Roscoe's head bobbled. "Yes, you're so right, Dear. As always." He turned to face Maisy. "This bellboy Harry Posner was a real talker, a first-class chatterbox. I would have never guessed he would tell us so much as he showed us around the hotel. He started by telling us about some of the celebrities who have stayed here at the Alexandria. The first was none other than President Taft. He followed that with a tale about the famous lawyer Clarence Darrow and the American Sherlock Holmes, Mr. William J. Burns, bumping into Mr. D.W. Griffith up in the main lobby. It was quite comical in the telling."

Minta interjected the next part of their report. "Then without even being asked, Harry got down to the very exact reason we were here at the hotel. He told us if Mr. Burns had been in the hotel this past week, he would have figured out that someone most likely had murdered Marjorie Sullivan in her sleep."

Nearly everybody at the table gasped at the mention of murder. All except Maisy and Mabel. They had worked too closely on four previous homicide cases to be surprised by such shocking revelations as the Arbuckles had just now revealed.

Calmly, Mabel asked the couple a simple question. "And what did this bellboy tell you about the other two deaths in this hotel only three weeks ago?"

Minta responded. "Pretty much the same thing. Both the old lady and the old gentleman were also most likely murdered in their sleep."

Roscoe reiterated his wife's report. "That's right. Harry said they were both more than likely murdered in their sleep."

Minta added another tidbit. "All the bellhops were whispering that as long as the clerks and Mr. Whitmore the manager weren't around."

Totally unruffled by the Arbuckles' news, Maisy had to ask them a single question. "Did the bellboy tell you *why* he and his fellow bellboys thought Mr. Clarke and Mrs. Lee were murdered in their sleep?"

Roscoe and Minta exchanged looks, then turned to Maisy. The husband spoke first. "Yes, he did."

The wife followed. "He said they were both robbed."

"And how did they know this?"

Roscoe responded. "Harry said he and another bellboy were told to pack up Mr. Clarke's belongings after his body was removed by the men from the mortuary. When they did, they found nothing of value in Mr. Clarke's room. No watch, no jewelry, no money. They immediately reported this to Mr. Whitmore."

"And what did Mr. Whitmore say about it?"

Minta answered. "He told them not to tell any of the other people who worked in the hotel about the missing items and money. He then told them his reason for doing this."

"Let me guess. He told them he didn't want anyone to know Mr. Clarke had been murdered and robbed in the Alexandria because that would be bad for business."

Surprise raised Roscoe's and Minta's eyebrows up their foreheads and dropped their jaws at the same time.

Maisy spoke again before either spouse could say another word. "Let me make another guess here. Mrs. Lee's room was found to be in the same condition as Mr. Clarke's after her body was removed by the undertakers. Nothing of value was left behind, right?" Before either one of the Arbuckles could reply, Maisy answered her own question. "Mrs. Lee's room was attended by two chambermaids who reported the same thing to Mr. Whitmore as did the two bellboys, right?"

A cacophony of chatter filled the banquet hall as all but two of the diners expressed his or her thoughts about Maisy's sudden synopsis of events surrounding the strange deaths of Mrs. America L. Lee and Mr. George W. Clarke. The pair were Mabel, who knew Maisy better than anyone there and Ed Browning because he had a very serious question for the Arbuckles.

"Roscoe, did Harry the bellboy say anything about Miss Sullivan's room after her body was removed by the morticians?"

Minta snickered. "I asked him the same question, Detective."

"And what did he say?"

Roscoe answered. "He just shrugged and said he didn't know why her room wasn't robbed."

"That's strange, don't you think, Bill?"

"Sounds strange to me, too."

Maisy giggled. "You cops are all the same. I've yet to meet one who can put two and two together and come up with the right answer. Never fails."

Browning glared at the only woman he respected and admired almost as much as his own wife Nealy. "Okay, Miss Smarty Pants. Tell us all what we're missing here?"

Maisy chuckled some more as she turned to the detective's mate. "I'll bet you know what it is, don't you, Neally?"

"I believe I do, Maisy." She looked her husband straight in his eyes. "Sometimes, my love, you are dumber than a bag of hammers." She giggled with Maisy. "The answer is right in front of your nose, Edward. Three murders and you can't figure out why."

Detective Ed Browning appeared in incredulous at the suggestion his wife and Maisy were making. "So, Miss Malone, you're saying Mr. Whitmore has something to do with these murders just because he has some silly superstition about bad things happening in threes? And you expect me to believe that?"

Maisy shook her head. "Yes, Eddie, I do. For now, at least. We still don't have all the facts about the other two murders, now do we?"

"I don't think either one of those deaths has a thing to do with the three here in the Alexandria. I don't see the connection."

The actress scanned the faces of the other diners. "What do all of you think?" She fixed her gaze on one important person. "Lilian, you led the investigation into Mr. Donelson's death. What do you think? Do you think he was murdered, and his death just might be connected to the other four?"

"I believe it's quite possible that he was murdered. But do I think his death is connected to the deaths here at the Alexandria? We don't have any real proof of that just yet, do we?"

Browning threw up his hands. "See what I mean? There's no connection between the three here and the one at the Travers and the one in Long Beach."

Mabel spoke up. "Those two happened at nearly the same time as the first two in this hotel. Even I can see that much, Eddie."

The detective shook his head. "Mere coincidence, Mabel."

A polite smile spread over Maisy's face. "When I was traveling in Europe last year, I read *The Hound of the Baskervilles* by Arthur Conan Doyle. In the story, Sherlock Holmes says, 'People say there's no such thing as coincidence. What dull lives they must lead.' Sir Arthur doesn't believe a whole lot in God, but he does believe in the supernatural … somewhat. Although he puts those words in Sherlock's mouth, he does not share them with his fictional detective. I read in a newspaper that he said, 'Two things happening in close proximity to each other could be a coincidence, three doing so is an act of the supernatural.' Two deaths in the middle of the night in the same hotel could very well be a coincidence. But three? Or four? Or five? All by natural causes. All by people alone in their rooms. No, Eddie, we're not investigating the deaths of five people who just happened to pass over all alone within the range of three weeks in hotels. I believe our killer might be a crazed maniac who if we don't catch him … or her … very soon then he or she will kill again."

Sennett spoke first. "Being an outsider here, I don't have a tainted opinion. So, from all I'm hearing, I have to agree with Maisy. There's way too much similarity in these deaths. Four deaths in the middle of the night. The fifth, a man found alone in his apartment in the evening who could have died the night before. Four of the deceased persons were robbed, while the fifth may have been murdered just to round out a superstition about evil coming in threes." He aimed his most serious expression at Maisy. "You know, Maisy, when you solved that murder of one of my actors last Fall, I thought it was a fluke. I felt the same way when you figured out who murdered that Japanese fisherman. I had no hand in you solving those murders in February and earlier this month, so I can't say much about them. But these murders? I can't see how you're going to do it, but really glad I'm here tonight to see you in action from the first row again. So, what are you going to do next?"

"Well, if Johnny has nothing better to do tomorrow, then I think I'll have him drive me … and anybody else who wants to volunteer to go with me … down to Long Beach and see if we can't find one of those doctors who had Charles Donelson as a patient and see if we can get the address of that nurse Olga Renius. And if we get it, we'll go look her up and see if she's willing to tell us what she knows about Mr. Donelson." She looked at Fowler. "What do you say, Johnny? Another trip down to Long Beach tomorrow?"

"I'd be proud to, Maisy."

"Good." She scanned the room. "Who wants to go with Johnny and me to Long Beach tomorrow?"

Lilian responded first. "What time would you be going, Maisy?"

"I'd say we can meet out front of my place at nine o'clock."

The freelancer heaved a sigh of disappointment. "That lets me out. I'll be in church from nine-thirty until eleven, depending on how long the pastor sermonizes the congregation with his usual brimstone and damnation."

"Okay, Lilian's out. Who else?"

Mabel shook her head. "Count me out, too, Maise. I sleep in on Sundays, as you well know."

"Yes, I do." Maisy shifted her gaze to Browning. "How about you and Nealy coming along?"

"Sorry, Maisy. Long Beach, like Pasadena," he tilted his head in the direction of his partner, "is out of our jurisdiction. We'd have to check in first with the Long Beach police to make sure they're okay with us working in their territory, and I'm pretty sure they'd object to us snooping around their little bailiwick."

"Of course." She turned to Milo who only looked sideways at her. "Let me guess, handsome. Golfing tomorrow?"

Sennett spoke for his assistant. "We've got a tee time at ten-oh-six, Maisy. So, we're both out."

"I didn't think you'd be going anyway, Mack." She patted Milo's arm. "But it's nice of you to speak up for dopey Quee here."

The hurt in Cole's eyes expressed his reaction to the insult.

Sennett had a question. "What's that mean? Quee? What is that?"

Maisy replied wryly. "You need to read more, Mack. There was a new Broadway play back in November titled *Snow White and the Seven Dwarfs*. Do you know the story?"

"Everybody knows the story of *Snow White and the Seven Dwarfs*. What about it?"

"Well, the playwright gave the dwarfs names, and he named the youngest—"

Cole interrupted. "Quee. She calls me that in private."

Reality struck Maisy. "You know, Milo dear, until this very minute I had no idea you knew anything about Quee."

Sennett barked. "So, what about this name? What does it mean?"

Sadness dulled Maisy's eyes. "It means odd or unusual."

Mabel burst out laughing. "So, Milo is a dumb oddity? What the heck, Maise! We all know that. But he's an *adorable* dumb oddity. Why do you think Mack keeps him around? The same reason he keeps you around. You're an adorable *brainy* oddity. The two of you are so weird, each in your own way. Where do you think all of us who write the plots for our films get our ideas for them? From watching and listening to the two of you. You're both totally off the wall sometimes, and we love you for it. Both of you."

The studio boss grinned. "She's right, Maisy. The two of you are so absolutely adorable, and we love you for it."

The man who had barely spoken a word all evening, Venice Police Detective Sergeant Vince DeDonatis, groaned with impatience. "Can we get back to the point here?"

Everybody except Walt Ballard shifted his or her eyes to the detective from the beach city. The reporter remained focused on Maisy. "Yes, let's get back to the point here. If no one else can go with you tomorrow, Maisy, then I'll go with you. Having a newspaper man along just might get this Dr. Newton to open up and tell us what we need to hear from him."

Maisy shook her head. "Sorry, Walt. I thought about asking you to go along, but then it occurred to me that having a reporter there might intimidate the doctor more than it will encourage him to speak out."

Ballard frowned. "Okay, I see your point. I guess I'll just spend another dull Sunday at home ... all by my lonesome."

Browning, who knew the reporter quite well, shook his head once quite slowly. "Really, Walt? All by your lonesome? Dusty Rhoades told me you've been sparking a secretary at *The Times*, a widow lady he said. I'm surprised you didn't bring her with you this evening."

"I would have, if I'd known Mr. Sennett and Miss Normand were going to be here." Ballard smiled at the Keystone stars. "Helen just loves your comedies, Mr. Sennett. Especially the ones Miss Normand is in. Seeing your films makes her forget the loss of her husband who was killed in a streetcar accident three years ago."

Sennett nodded. "Well, I'm glad we can put a little joy in her life, Mr. Ballard." He turned back to Maisy. "If you're thinking of taking Mabel with you, forget it. We already have plans for tomorrow."

Maisy rolled her eyes. "No, Mack, I wasn't thinking of dragging her with me tomorrow." She focused on Roscoe and Minta. "How about the two of you coming along with me to Long Beach? Your presence with me should impress Dr. Newton enough to get the address of his nurse from him. And when we find her, she should take one look at you, Roscoe, and then talk to us. What do you say, Minta?"

Arbuckle and his wife fixed their eyes on each other and grinned as wide as they could. Minta leaned into Roscoe's arm. "What do you say, Babe? Should we go to Long Beach with Maisy tomorrow?"

"Sounds like fun, Dear."

The couple turned to their friend, and Minta spoke for them. "Just tells us where and when to meet you in the morning, Maisy, and we'll be ready and raring to go."

Once the meeting concluded, Mack and Mabel invited everyone to join them to listen to the orchestra and dance in the Rose Ballroom on the Mezzanine level of the hotel. To their surprise, nearly everyone in the group accepted the invitation, with the sole exception being Lew Collins who begged off because the cigarette smoke was making his breathing somewhat difficult.

Surprisingly, young Herbie Collins stayed with his mother. His teenage hormones had raced into high gear at the rare prospect of experiencing a late night out with notables Mack Sennett, Mabel Normand, Roscoe Arbuckle, and Maisy Malone; not that she fit into the same category of fame as her friends but because of her rising notoriety as an amateur detective.

Herbie's adolescent infatuation for the rising motion picture starlet and the sleuth imprisoned him in a romantic quandary. Should he ask his mother to secure chairs at the same table as Mack and Mabel? Or should he ask her to squeeze them into seats at a table with Maisy and Milo? Before he could press her to act on either request, the sight of Roscoe and Minta taking seats with Sennett and Normand crushed his first option. Then the curtain rang down on his alternative play as Maisy and Milo joined Ed and Nealy Browning at the table closest to the studio boss. Foiled, Herbie and his mother followed Andrew and Regina Reynolds to the third table, but the Fowlers beat them to it. Vince and Susie DeDonatis sat with the Ingrams at table number four, leaving mother and son to join Nellie Sharpe and Walt Ballard at the final option.

Always generous at gatherings like this one, Sennett opened their merrymaking by ordering a magnum of French champagne for each table. Once all the corks popped and the glasses filled, he stood up, glass in handheld high, and waited a moment for everybody to follow his lead. As soon as they did, the master of comedy offered a toast.

"Here's to all of you good people who are helping Maisy solve yet another murder … or in this case, murders … and thus saving the Los Angeles Police Department the trouble of having solve it … or them all by themselves. So, drink up and enjoy because this is the last round and only round on me. Cheers, good people!"

Everyone laughed mildly, then clinked his or her glass with those of the other three people at each table. They sipped the bubbly, smiled, and replaced their glasses on their table. Seeing Sennett sit again, the group of merrymakers raised a joyful cacophony of polite chatter, only to be drowned out by the orchestra striking up its first tune of the evening, a rag-time classic and still a favorite after nearly two decades, *A Hot Time in the Old Town Tonight.*

Sennett stood again, faced Mabel, gave her a polite bow, followed by a twinkle of an eye and a charming smile. He extended his left hand to her. "Care to dance, my dear?"

"I thought you'd ask me sooner or later." She drained the last of the champagne in her glass, accepted his hand, and stood. "*Claspless Waltz* first?"

"Of course." He led her onto the dance floor, and as soon as the band finished the first line of the first verse, they began to glide around each other in surprisingly graceful moves.

Several other revelers joined them. In their own party, Roscoe and Minta scurried onto the floor, as did Maisy and Milo, the Brownings, the Ingrams, the Fowlers, and Vince and Susie DeDonatis. Once the opening verse concluded and the orchestra leader waved his baton to speed up the tempo for the chorus, all the dancers shifted to doing the faster steps of *The Turkey Trot.* When the second verse began, everyone returned to the slower pace of *The Claspless Waltz.* At the conclusion of the music, all the dancers applauded the band for several seconds as the conductor bowed graciously. Then as soon as the merrymakers ceased their clapping, the director raised his wand to his musicians, then snapped it at them to begin the unique intoxicating syncopation of the latest dance tune, *The Bunny Hug Rag.* In the next instant, everyone on the floor jolted into motion, setting the theme for the remainder of the night. Dance, dance, dance! Followed by the occasional pause to regenerate the senses with another sip of wine, a swig of beer, or a shot of something much harder.

Such gaiety did not infect everyone in the ballroom. Andrus and Regina Reynolds considered themselves to be too advanced in age to partake in the newer, faster, livelier dance moves; but they did waltz when the band showed its versatility by playing something by Strauss, Chopin, Tchaikovsky, or Debussy. Walt Ballard asked Nellie Sharpe if she would care to dance, and she accepted, leaving only Lilian Collins and her son sitting at their table.

"I know you would like to dance, Herbie, but with your asthma, I think you should avoid these new dances that require such faster steps. Even *The Claspless Waltz* is too risky for you. And those other rag-time dances would certainly be too dangerous for you. All that wiggling!" She clucked her tongue. "A waltz or the two-step would be much more suitable for you. Of course, you wouldn't want to dance with me. A lady closer to your age would be more appropriate. Someone like Miss Sharpe or Miss Malone would be more suitable for you."

"I saw a girl about my age when we first came in, Mother. She was standing by the curtain a few tables away, and she was wearing a white dress. She smiled at me. So, I smiled back at her. But then my attention was drawn to Miss Normand. After we found our table, I looked for that girl again, but I didn't see her anywhere."

"I haven't seen any girl in a white dress, Son. What did she look like?"

Herbie grinned. "She had strawberry blonde hair, and her skin was nearly as white as her dress. I hope I see her again."

Lilian patted his hand. "If she's still here, Son, I'm certain you will see her again."

"If you say so, Mother." He scanned the room once more until he saw Mabel. "What about Miss Normand, Mother? She's close to my age."

"Yes, I know she is, but I don't believe she's the waltzing type. Just look at her. She wiggles faster than everybody out there."

Herbie grinned. "Yes, she does, doesn't she?"

Lilian frowned. "Just watching her might take your breath away, Son. Better you keep your eyes elsewhere."

The college boy moped. "Yes, Mother."

After playing four tunes, the band leader halted playing and turned to the audience. "Ladies and gentlemen, this next song is a melody for the two-step. We play it tonight to honor two very distinguished guests. They came out here to California last winter to make short films for the Biograph Company of New York. We believe this is the first motion picture comedy to feature an honest to goodness airplane. Of course, you all know by now that I am talking about the motion picture *A Dash Through The Clouds,* starring Miss Mabel Normand and directed by the king of comedy Mr. Mack Sennett. Miss Normand, Mr. Sennett, would you please stand up and take a bow?"

Maisy and Milo started the applause for Mack and Mabel as they rose from their chairs and acknowledged the audience with short nods, waves, and cordial smiles.

As soon as the ovation subsided and the pair from Keystone Studio sat down again, the band leader spoke once more. "This tune is for you, Miss Normand, for having the courage to go up in that airplane with the late Phil Parmalee. And for you, Mr. Sennett, because you had the nerve to make her do it."

Laughter broke out all around, and the conductor turned around again to face his musicians. "Let's do it, boys!" He raised his baton, and the band struck up *Come Josephine in My Flying Machine*.

Herbie Collins leaned over to Nellie Sharpe. "Would you care to dance with me, Miss Sharpe?"

Being the gentle person that she was in situations such as this, she smiled sweetly. "I'd love to, Mr. Collins." She stood.

Herbie remained seated for a few seconds, then rose slowly from his chair somewhat stunned by her formality. No one to this minute in all his years since infancy had ever addressed him in such a respectful custom. And to have those words spoken to him by a lady older than he was? How wonderful for him! Or so he felt.

The couple stepped into the crowd. "Two-step, Miss Sharpe?"

"Two-step, Mr. Collins, but only if you call me Nellie. I'm not that much older than you are. And may I call you Herbie?"

"Why sure, Miss ... I mean, Nellie."

She grinned, and they danced.

Lilian had kept her eye on Herbie ever since he asked Nellie to dance with him. She leaned toward Walt Ballard. "I suggested he ask her to dance with him as soon as the band played a tune with a slower rhythm than the other modern dances. A waltz or a two-step meter. My Herbie has asthma, you know."

Ballard expressed concern with the pinching of his brow. "No, I didn't know, Lilian. Is it very bad for him?"

"His father has it as well. My husband Lew's condition is the sole reason we removed to Arizona from the Midwest. Of course, Herbie inherited it from his father, which is why we removed to Los Angeles. We were made to understand the weather in this part of California was much more suitable for people with their condition. Herbie has been doing better with his asthma since we moved here, but my Lew has not done as well so far. Even so, I worry about Herbie. As much as he wants to play sports, I have forbidden him to do so. Dancing to the slower rhythm tunes is the only compromise I agreed to make with him. So far, he has kept his word to me. No wiggle dances!"

"Not even one, Lilian?"

"Not even one!"

"Well, you're his mother, but what do you think he'll do once he leaves the nest?"

Lilian frowned. "That's what worries me most, Walt. I can only pray that he'll remember his promise to me and keep it."

Ballard nodded toward Herbie and Nellie. "Looks to me like they are enjoying themselves quite a bit doing the slower dances. Just look at them out there."

"Don't fret about that, Walt. I'm keeping my eyes on them. The second he shows any signs of his asthma attacking him I'll be the first person to come to his aid. You can bet on that much."

Meanwhile, as Mack and Mabel and the Arbuckles sat out this more leisurely dance, Joe Reikel, the Alexandria's assistant food service manager, approached the two moguls from Keystone with two women behind him: one near Joe's age and the other much younger. "Mr. Sennett, Miss Normand, may I introduce to you my wife Anna and my niece Elisabet? Anna is from Iowa. We met in Kansas City, and we were married in Omaha where her family lived at the time. Elisabet is from Austria. We call her Lisa. She came to America with my late brother Franz's widow Katerina in nineteen-oh-two. She passed away seven years ago in Kansas City. Lisa has been with us ever since."

Mabel remained seated, but Mack knew his manners quite well. He stood, held out his right to Anna Reikel, bowed kissed her hand, and straightened up. "*Enchantée, Madame Reikel.*" He faced Lisa with a polite smile. "*Enchantée, Madameoisel.* It's a pleasure to meet both of you."

Mrs. Reikel smiled back at him. "The pleasure is certainly all ours, Mr. Sennett. Meeting such important people as you and Miss Normand is certainly a thrill for Lisa and me."

Sennett tilted his head to the right. "That's very kind of you to say, Mrs. Reikel."

"Oh, please call me Anna."

"Only if you call me Mack." He turned to Reikel's niece. "The same goes for you, Lisa. Please call me Mack."

Lisa smiled politely again. "Thank you, Mack. It's my honor."

"You're welcome, Lisa." Sennett focused on Reikel again. "What brings you to the ballroom this evening, Joe?"

"I told my wife and niece that you and Miss Normand and Mr. Arbuckle were here, and they begged me to bring them here to meet all three of you."

"Well, I'm glad you did, Joe. Why don't you find three more chairs and join us?"

Reikel nodded. "Thank you, Mr. Sennett. I'll be right back."

The Keystone boss smiled at Mrs. Reikel. "Please be seated in my chair, Anna."

Roscoe stood up. "And you can take mine, Miss Reikel."

Anna smiled at Sennett. "Thank you, Mack." She turned to her niece. "Go ahead and sit, Lisa."

The young woman smiled nervously at Roscoe. "Thank you, sir."

Once the two women were seated, Sennett turned his full focus on Mrs. Reikel. "So, Anna, I take it you and Joe live here in the hotel."

"Yes, we do. And Lisa lives with us. She is learning to be a nurse."

"Is that right?"

"Yes, she assists me when I have to care for a guest in the hotel or when I assist Dr. Newmark in his practice. This summer she will become a student nurse at one of the public hospitals here in the city."

Mabel giggled. "Hoping to snag a doctor for a husband, Lisa?"

With a stern face, Anna answered for her teenage niece. "That is not Lisa's intention, Miss Normand. She wants to help the infirm and the sick like I do. Romance is not on her mind at this age. Is that not so, Lisa?"

A touch sad the girl responded. "Yes, Aunt Anna."

Minta joined the conversation. "Which hospital will Lisa be doing her studies, Anna?"

"The Clara Barton Hospital on South Olive Street. It's only two blocks from the hotel, so she can walk there and back every day. Our good Dr. Newmark wrote a very nice letter recommending Lisa to do her training there. They don't just take anyone to be a student nurse, you know."

Minta nodded. "Yes, I've heard it's a very prestigious hospital when it comes to training new nurses."

"Only the best for our Lisa."

Lilian Collins leaned closer to Walt Ballard. "Do you know those two women who just sat down at Mr. Sennett's table?"

Ballard looked along the line of tables to focus on the newcomers. "Sorry, Lilian, but I don't know them. But since Mr. Reikel is sitting with them, I would assume they are his wife and daughter, based on the fact that one appears to be in his age range and the other appears to be in Herbie's age range."

"I came to the same conclusion."

Nellie Sharpe spoke. "I believe you're both correct. When I came here with Detective Browning and Detective Ingram the morning that we were sent here to investigate the death of the Sullivan girl, I saw them with Dr. Newmark in the hall outside Mr. Whitmore's office. I couldn't hear what they were saying, but from the looks on their faces, I must guess Dr. Newmark was rebuking them for something they did or didn't do. Now that I think about it, he was speaking German to them. Since Mr. Reikel is Austrian, I would assume they understood every word he said to them."

Lilian nodded. "I see. Yes, Walt, I must agree that they could be mother and daughter, but there doesn't seem to be too much of a family resemblance. Perhaps they are not related at all. What do you think, Herbie?"

"I haven't given them much thought, Mother. I've been looking for that girl in the white dress. But since you asked, I'd have to agree with you that they are unlikely to be related. Other than being the same gender, I can't see any resemblance at all."

Nellie interjected a thought. "Looking around the ballroom, it looks like the younger woman is the only other person here close to your age, Herbie. That is, besides Maisy and Mabel."

"I suppose you're right, Nellie."

"So why don't you ask her to dance?"

Herbie blushed. "How do I do that? She and I are total strangers."

"So how are you going to meet her, if you don't ask her?"

He shrugged. "I don't know."

Lilian pressed the issue. "Nellie is right, Herbie. Just go up to her and ask her if she would care to dance. What do have to lose? The worst she can do is say no."

"Your mother has a point there, Herbie."

The mother slid her chair back. "Come on, Herbert Collins. I'll go with you."

Shock blanched Herbie's face. "No, Mother! How would that make me look?"

"Then get up and go over there and ask her to dance."

Ballard chuckled. "Go ahead, Herbie. Your mother is right. What have you got to lose? Just go on over there, introduce yourself, and ask her to dance with you. If she says no, then you're left with two options. You can simply walk away and come back here with your tail between your legs. Or you can smile at her, bow slightly, and say something like, 'Perhaps later then.' The worst she can say then is something like, 'I don't think so or I don't dance.' So again, I say, what have you got to lose? At the very least, you'll still have your dignity."

Lilian squeezed her son's right upper arm. "Walt is right, Herbie. You have nothing to lose by asking. So, go ahead and go over there."

The younger Collins searched the faces of his mother, Walt, and Nellie. Each had the same expression. Encouragement. He heaved a sigh, slid his chair away from the table, and rose to his feet. "All right, I'll go. But what if she rejects me?"

Nellie patted his left forearm. "Then that will be her loss, Herbert. I've danced with you. I know. She will never know what she missed."

Ballard smiled warmly at him. "Go ahead, Herbie. Show her you're a man."

Lilian's son straightened up a few inches taller and nodded. "All right, I'll go." Casually, he turned and walked away.

Through glassy eyes, Mabel saw Herbie Collins approaching her table. She nudged Mack. "Methinks I see a young Galahad approaching yon fair young maiden. Would there be romance in the air?" She giggled.

Sennett spoke softly to his star actress. "Behave yourself, Mabel. These people don't know you like I do."

"Oh, don't be such a fuddy-duddy, Nappy."

He lowered his tone another octave. "You heard me, kiddo. Now zip your lips."

"Oh, all right, Nappy. You win this round."

Herbie Collins stepped up to the table and aimed his attention at Lisa Reikel. "Good evening, Miss. I am Herbert Collins. I saw you come in, and immediately, I wondered if you care to dance with me?" He waved his right hand in the direction of the orchestra. "The band is playing a waltz. A tune by Strauss, I believe. *Stimmen des Frühlings?*"

"*Du sprichst Deutsch, mein Herr?*" (You speak German, sir?)

"*Nun, ein bisschen.*" (Well, a little.)

Lisa stood up from her chair. "Enough, I am certain, Mr. Collins." She turned to her uncle. "*Mit deiner Erlaubnis, Onkel Josef?*" (With your permission, Uncle Joseph?)

"*Ja, natürlich, Lisa.*" (Yes, of course, Lisa.)

She held out her left hand to Herbie. "Shall we, Mr. Collins?"

He took her hand with his right. "Please call me Herbie."

"And you may call me Lisa."

He led her onto the dance floor.

Anna turned to Sennett. "Such a charming young man! Do you know him, Mr. Sennett?"

"I can't say that I do. I've only met him and his mother for the first time this evening at dinner."

"And his mother is part of your party here?"

170

"Yes, that's her four tables down." He turned to the Arbuckles. "She works with you and Maisy, doesn't she, Minta?"

"Yes, that's Lilian Collins, his mother. She's part of our group. She's a freelance writer for *The Times* and other newspapers in the county. That's Walt Ballard, a police reporter for *The Times*, sitting with her and Miss Nellie Sharpe, a stenographer for the Los Angeles Police Department. Other than that, I don't know much more about her except that she seems to be very well educated. Maisy seems to be very impressed by her."

Sennett snorted. "Well, if Maisy is impressed by her, then she must be something special."

Anna shifted her attention to Sennett again. "That name ... Maisy. You have mentioned it twice now, Mr. Sennett. Is she part of your party as well?"

Mabel nudged Mack to keep him from answering, while slurring her own response. "No, she's only here because she's my best friend, and I don't go out on the town without her."

Sennett elbowed Mabel away from him. "Actually, Maisy is one of my actresses at Keystone."

"Really? An actress?"

"Yes, and a writer and an assistant director. She's very versatile, our Maisy. I would let her crank the camera some, if she was a little taller." He laughed at his own jest.

Mabel feigned disbelief. "Is that why you won't let me crank the camera? Because I'm too short."

Sennett put his arm around Mabel. "Trust me, dear heart, you're needed much more in front of the camera than behind it."

"If that's so, I want more money."

"Keep making hits for me, and you'll get it."

"When?"

He squeezed her tight to his ribcage. "Soon enough, dear. Soon enough."

"Okay. That's good enough for now."

The orchestra finished playing *Voices of Spring*, but before anyone could leave the dance floor, they struck up another Strauss waltz, *On the Beautiful Blue Danube*.

"Do you know this one, Herbie?"

"Anyone who can waltz knows *An der schönen blauen Donau*."

Lisa smiled much wider than before. "Then, shall we?"

Herbie smiled back at her. "We shall."

The couple glided around the ballroom for more than a minute before Lisa broke their silence. "Where did you learn to speak German, Herbie?"

"When I was ten years old, we lived in Phoenix, Arizona. I took a hike one day up to the mountains north of town, and I met this old prospector named Adolph Ruth. He mistook me for his son Erwin and called to me in German. At first, I was afraid of him because I didn't know him. Then he laughed and said in English that he thought I was his son. Then he asked me if I was lost. I told him I wasn't lost. Then he asked why I was up there in the mountains. Was I prospecting for gold? I told him I was only on a hike to help build up my lungs because I have asthma. I explained to him that is a lung disease. He said the word was the same in German, only with a minor difference in the way it's pronounced."

"Yes, I know. It is *AST-ma auf Deutsch*."

"Yes, that's what he said. Anyway, he told me a few other words in German, and I became interested in learning more from him. I saw him several times that winter, and each time he taught me more words and phrases in German." Then Herbie thought to impress Lisa with his knowledge of languages. "Back in Phoenix, we had a Mexican housekeeper named Mary Mendoza. She taught me how to speak some Spanish. My mother taught me some French, and I learned Latin from my fifth-grade teacher Miss McKee while attending Central School in Phoenix."

"You can speak all those languages, Herbie?"

"I wouldn't say I can speak all of them, but I know enough of each one to stay out of trouble if I ever go to Mexico, Spain, France, or Germany."

"Or Austria, where I was born."

Herbie smiled. "Yes, Austria. I suppose I can add that country to my list of languages."

"Yes, and perhaps I can teach you more German."

"Yes, I'd like that."

Just then, the music stopped. The young couple remained on the dance floor, neither of them wishing to return to their respective tables and the two rather overbearing women who had been watching every step they took on the dance floor.

Lisa peered deep into Herbie's eyes and saw the same desire in them as in hers. "I could stay right here forever, Herbie, as long as you stay with me."

"I was thinking the same thing, Lisa."

Just then, the orchestra struck up Irving Berlin's *Alexander's Ragtime Band*. Lisa clapped her hands. "Oh, wonderful!"

Herbie chuckled. "Don't you mean, *Wunderbar?*"

"*Ja, wunderbar!*"

"Can you do *The Grizzly Bear?*"

She giggled. "Lead the way, Twinkle Toes!"

Lilian had been watching her son and the pretty girl dance to the two waltzes, but when the ragtime tune started up, she expected them to leave the floor and return to her table where Herbie would thank her and return to his table. Much to her chagrin, the couple remained on the floor and began doing the steps to a far faster frolic. Her eyelids widened with worry, and her mouth gaped greater than it ever had before in her life. She slapped her hand flatly on the table.

"What in God's name are they doing? Herbie can't move that fast after dancing so long already. He'll lose his breath and maybe have an asthma attack. I'd better go stop them. Right now!" Sliding her chair backward, she started to rise slowly with the hope her son would realize the danger approaching him and cease his merriment with the young lady. "He must stop!" She came erect, fear frightening her more.

Too late! Herbie's grin suddenly vanished. Why? He saw the girl in the white dress again. Only this time, no smile brightened her eyes and lit up her face. Instead, a dark shadow covered her cheeks as she shook her head at him. Seeing her this way drove a dagger into his soul, and he gasped for air, realizing his malady was on the verge of striking him to his knees.

Lisa saw the distress in her partner's eyes and his face changing from pink to an ashen blue. "Herbie, what's wrong?"

He tried to speak to her but could only wheeze as he exhaled and then sought so desperately to breathe in the air of the ballroom, much of it tainted with cigar and cigarette smoke.

Suddenly, Lisa saw that he wasn't looking at her but at someone else. She turned and looked behind her. When she saw the girl in the white dress, a hysterical scream erupted through her twisted lips

Lilian jumped from her chair, knocking it to the askew behind her. She ran onto the dance floor and weaved her way through the crowd of merrymakers to reach her son before he could fall to his knees on the hardwood and possibly bang his head and cause himself a severe cranial injury; all the time screaming. "No, God, no!"

Herbie fell forward, both hands reaching out to prevent him from crashing face first into the floor. He nearly failed, only striking the surface with the right side of his face.

Dancers around Lisa and Herbie saw him collapse and heard her shriek with frightful terror. They ceased dancing and quickly parted to form a circle around the couple.

Lilian forced her way through the onlookers. "Herbie!" She dropped onto her knees beside him. "Oh, baby, breathe!" She grabbed his shoulders to turn him on his side and then on his back.

Seeing the sudden cessation of movement by the dancers, the band director signaled his musicians to halt playing their instruments. He turned to inspect the crowd for signs of the disturbance. All of the band members stood up to do the same.

Seemingly from out of the fog of humanity, Anna Reikel appeared and dropped to her knees beside Lilian. "What's wrong with him?"

"He has asthma."

"Asthma?"

"Yes."

"I am a nurse. Let me tend to him." Anna looked up at the crowd. "Someone send for the hotel doctor. Dr. Newmark." When no one moved, anger colored her face. "*Jetzt, Dummköpfe!*" (Now, dummies!)

The Alexandria's vice-president and general manager
Samuel Whitmore received an emergency call in his suite
from the front desk within four minutes of Herbie Collins
experiencing his asthma attack in the Rose Ballroom. "Has
Dr. Newmark been summoned yet?"

Desk clerk Preston Lewis answered quickly. "I called him first, Mr.
Whitmore. I was told by Joe Reikel that Mrs. Reikel is already in the
ballroom attending the stricken man, sir."

"Good! Maybe she can keep him alive until Newmark gets there.
Good work, Preston. If anyone calls and asks for me, tell them I'm in
the Rose Ballroom attending an emergency. I just hope this fellow
makes it. The last thing we need around here is another death in less
than a month. Oh, and another thing. Inform the bellboys about what's
going on up there and to keep it hush-hush for the time being. Got it?"

"Yes, sir. I'll do that immediately, sir."

"Oh, and one more thing. Call for an ambulance just in case one's
needed by Newmark. And find out if the stricken man is a guest here.
If he is, inform Newmark. If he's not and Newmark says the man can't
be sent to a hospital, find a room for the man. Understood?"

"Perfectly, sir."

"Okay. If anyone asks for me, tell them I'm attending to a special
guest and see if you can handle whatever it is they need. Understood?"

"Yes, sir."

Whitmore replaced the receiver on its cradle, donned his suit coat,
and dashed out of his suite for the Rose Ballroom.

Dr. Newmark rushed down the stairwell steps, medical bag in one hand
and a loaded epinephrine syringe in the other. He had already been
informed by Preston Lewis that the patient in the Rose Ballroom had
suffered an asthma attack and was being attended by the hotel's night
nurse Anna Reikel. Even so, he had every reason to hurry. When he

reached the Mezzanine floor, Frank Roderus, the ballroom manager, threw open the double doors to allow Newmark instant access to the dance hall. Seeing the mass of humanity before him, the physician shouted with anger. *"Aus dem weg!"* When no one moved, he realized he had spoken in his native tongue. "Out of my way! Now!"

Quickly, the crowd parted to let him pass.

Newmark recognized Anna Reikel sitting astride the fallen young man's thighs, holding his wrists, and lifting and lowering his arms alternately, each like a force rod on a water pump, trying desperately to maintain the function of his lungs just long enough to keep him alive until the hotel's physician arrived on the scene. The woman kneeling at the man's head he didn't know, but he saw that she was assisting his nurse by cradling the victim's head and tilting it backwards to keep his airway open as much as possible. Someone—probably his nurse—had known enough to loosen the man's tie and collar and unbutton the top three buttons of his shirt.

Arriving on the scene, the doctor determined instantly that the patient was unconscious but still alive. He released his bag beside Herbie and dropped to his knees next to the patient. "You've done well, Mrs. Reikel. He's still getting good air." He held up the syringe and winked at her. "Let's give him more, eh?" Newmark looked at Lilian. "Are you a nurse, madam?"

"No, I'm his mother."

"Your name, madam?"

"Lilian Collins. This is my son Herbie."

The doctor nodded at Herbie's clothing. "Then I take it you knew what to do when he has these attacks."

"Yes, but Mrs. Reikel took charge. And quite well, I might add."

"She knows emergency care in these cases." He held the syringe in front of Lilian. "I would like to give your son a shot of epinephrine to help his lungs work better and bring this attack to an end. If I can have your permission to do so, I mean."

"Yes, doctor, please do."

"Thank you. Now will you hold his shirt open wider. I want to give him the injection in his trapezius muscle. The medicine will get to his lungs and diaphragm sooner that way and make them resume their natural function more quickly."

"You do whatever you must, doctor, to keep my son alive."

Newmark smiled at Lilian. "Thank you, madam." He pulled the cork from the tip of the needle. "Open his collar more please."

Lilian spread the material as far as she could to expose Herbie's neck and shoulder, while Anna continued to pump his arms, although not as quickly as before.

Newmark smiled at his nurse. "You can stop now, Anna, while I give him the injection." He looked back at Lilian, smiled, winked, and nodded. "Here we go." He administered the injection into the trapezius muscle, then removed the needle. "Now we wait. If Herbie responds well to the medicine, then he should begin breathing much easier in a minute or two. A few minutes more and he should be conscious again. When he does come around again, Mrs. Collins, I suggest we keep him in one of our medical suites here in the hotel. Just for the night … to make certain his lungs are functioning properly again." Newmark smiled. "There will be no charge, Mrs. Collins. Medical services are an amenity of the Hotel Alexandria in cases like this."

"Really?"

The doctor nodded.

"Can I stay with him?"

"Not in the same room, but you can stay in the room next to his, if you like."

"Yes, that would be fine."

Newmark peered down at Herbie. "Ah, yes! His chest is rising and falling almost normally already. He will soon be awake, and then we can get a stretcher in here and take him to his room."

Tears welled in Lilian's eyes. "Oh, thank you, doctor. How can I ever repay you?"

"It is my job to keep people alive and well, Mrs. Collins. I do my best." He looked at Mrs. Reikel. "Don't we, Anna?"

The nurse smiled. "We most certainly do, *Herr Doktor.*"

During all the excitement surrounding Herbie and Lisa, the remainder of Maisy's group had gathered around Mack and Mabel's table. Joining them were Sam Whitmore and Harry Posner.

After observing the hotel's medical people working with their patient, Whitmore spoke to his most reliable bellhop. "Harry, I want you to go downstairs and get two of your biggest fellows and take them to Dr. Newmark's office and get a stretcher for his patient."

Posner saluted his boss with two fingers to his right forehead. "Of course, sir. I'll be back in the wink of a cat's eye."

Whitmore focused on Sennett. "Everyone on our staff is totally reliable in situations such as this one."

"I'm sure they are, Sam. But until your bellboy returns with the stretcher, maybe a couple of my people could lend a hand to your people."

"Yes, you're right, Mack. Who did you have in mind?"

Sennett looked at the two men he had in mind. "Roscoe, Milo, why don't you boys go see if you can help Dr. Newmark?"

Arbuckle pushed himself away from the table. "Sure thing, Mack."

Milo replied in kind. "Sure, Boss." Roscoe and Milo walked onto the dance floor with the bigger man leading the way. Because most of the dancers had crowded around the patient and the people tending to him, Arbuckle barked a command. "Okay, folks, let us through!"

Nearly everyone turned to see who gave the order. Upon seeing the large man marching their way, they all did as told and stepped away to make an aisle for Roscoe and Milo. As they passed through the onlookers, Arbuckle and Cole both thanked them for their courtesy, and several of them whispered Roscoe's name and pointed at him.

Having heard Arbuckle's firm directive above the light chatter of the spectators and seeing their instant obedience, Dr. Newmark aimed his view at the newly formed lane and saw Roscoe and Milo coming toward him. "*Sehr gut.* Help is here." He stood up and immediately recognized the movie actor. "Mr. Arbuckle, right?"

"Yes, sir." Roscoe took a step sideways. "And this is Mr. Cole. Our boss, Mr. Sennett, sent us to see if you need any help with your patient."

"That is very kind of Mr. Sennett. Yes, I do need your help." He nodded toward Herbie who was still lying on the floor with his head cradled in his mother's lap. "This young man has just had an asthma attack, and I would like to move him to one of the banquet rooms over there." He pointed his right index finger in the direction of the south wall. "Their doors are hidden by those very long drapes."

Roscoe smiled. "Sure thing, Doctor." He turned to Cole. "You and the doctor lead the way, Milo. I'll bring this young fellow right behind you." Lilian appeared surprised. "Can you carry Herbie all by yourself, Roscoe?"

Arbuckle chuckled. "Sure, I can, Mrs. Collins. How much does he way? A hundred and twenty-five pounds or so?"

She smiled at him quite nervously. "That's pretty close. A hundred and twenty-nine."

Roscoe winked at her. "Piece of cake, ma'am." He knelt down beside Herbie. "I'm going to raise you up a little, Herbie, and when I do, I want you to put your arms around my neck and hold on tight while I pick you up. Okay?"

"Sure thing, Mr. Arbuckle."

The comedy actor put his left arm under Herbie's shoulders and lifted him a half foot off the floor. "You can call me Roscoe."

Herbie followed orders and put his arms around Arbuckle's neck.

"That's right. Now up we go." The big fellow stood up easily with his right arm under Herbie's knees and his left under his armpits. "My father named me after Senator Roscoe Conkling because I was a fat baby and because he hated the senator. But my mother loved me right up until the day she died."

Milo and Dr. Newmark did their parts and led the way toward the banquet rooms. Lilian, Lisa, and Anna followed behind Arbuckle and Herbie.

Everybody else in the Rose Ballroom spontaneously applauded as the tiny parade passed through them until they reached one of the curtains hiding a banquet room entrance. Dr. Newmark pushed aside a single drape and opened the door, while Milo held the curtain allowing the others to enter the private chamber. The doctor switched on the lights inside as the applause faded away. Milo released the drape and followed the others into the banquet room, closing the door behind him.

Arbuckle stopped behind Newmark. "Where do you want me to put him, Doctor?"

The physician stepped up to his patient. "Let's see how you are doing, Herbie, before I decided on whether to put you on a table or on a chair. Okay?"

"Whatever you say, Doctor."

The doctor smiled at Lilian. "Right there. That's a good sign, Mrs. Collins. He spoke."

Newmark removed his stethoscope from his medical bag. With both hands, he spread the binaural tubes and inserted the ear tips into his ears. He placed the bell against Herbie's chest and listened to his heart for several seconds. "Sounds a little fast, but that is most likely because of the epinephrine. Now let me listen to your lungs. Inhale as deeply as you can, young man, then exhale slowly." He placed the instrument's bell against the patient's right chest, while Herbie took a long, slow, deep breath, and then let it out even slower. "Good. Now the other side." Doctor and patient repeated the process. "Again good." Newmark removed the instrument. "You can sit him on a chair, Roscoe, if I may call you so."

"I'd be honored, Doctor." Arbuckle set Herbie on a banquet chair. "There you go, young man."

Lilian took the chair to her son's left, and Lisa took the one to his right. Arbuckle, Cole, Newmark, and Anna remained standing and facing Herbie.

Milo turned to the physician. "Dr. Newmark, Mr. Whitmore sent one of his bellboys to get two other bellboys to bring a stretcher up here for Herbie."

Just then, Whitmore entered the banquet room. "How's your patient doing, Philip?"

Newmark smiled at the hotel's general manager. "He appears to be coming out of his attack just fine, Mr. Whitmore."

"Very good, very good." He looked at the nurse. "I see you wasted no time in getting here, Anna."

She nodded slightly at him. "My niece and I were already here, Mr. Whitmore." She indicated Lisa with a short wave of her right hand. "She was dancing with Mr. Collins when he was stricken by the asthma. His mother and I were the first to attend to him."

Whitmore turned to Lilian. "I take it you are his mother?"

"Yes, sir, I am."

"I'm so sorry this happened to your son, madam, but I can assure you that he is in good hands with Dr. Newmark and Mrs. Reikel." He turned to the physician. "What is your prognosis, Philip?"

"If it is all right with you, Mr. Whitmore, I would like to keep this young man here in the hotel for further observation through the night. Asthma is a very serious condition that can attack its victim at any time without warning. I am certain Mrs. Collins is aware of this as well. If possible, I would like your permission to arrange for them to be guests here in a suite for the night. Anna and Lisa can care for him as well."

Whitmore's head bobbed with affirmation. "If that's what you think is best for him, Philip, then I'll see to it immediately. Of course, with your permission, Mrs. Collins."

She stiffened and folded her hands at her waist. "Your gesture is certainly noted and appreciated, Mr. Whitmore, but the cost of a suite in this luxurious establishment is far—"

The general manager chuckled lightly and waved both of his hands at Lilian. "Oh, no, Mrs. Collins, there will be no charge for the suite or for breakfast in the morning or for Dr. Newmark's services and those of his nurses, if you were anticipating that as well. This is the Hotel Alexandria, Mrs. Collins. It's a medical emergency such as this very one that precipitates the very presence of a physician and nurses to be on duty here around the clock. You and your son may stay here for as long as Dr. Newmark deems it necessary and you will be most welcome to partake in all our hospitality for the duration ... again, all at no charge to either of you."

Tears rolled down Lilian's cheeks. "I don't know what to say."

Whitmore took her right hand with both of his. "You don't have to say anything, Mrs. Collins. This is the Hotel Alexandria. We are here to serve the needs of all our guests, whether they are occupants for one night or residents who live here or customers of our many shops and restaurants. We view our patrons as if they are family and treat them as such. People like you and your son. We make all the amenities we offer here at the Alexandria available to all our visitors, including the medical services that your son is now receiving. We are a community within a community."

Lilian's tears had ceased. "Thank you so much, Mr. Whitmore."

"Think nothing of it, Mrs. Collins. We are here to serve, and I hope and pray your son recovers very quickly and lives a long and prosperous life."

Just then, two stout bellhops entered the banquet room with a stretcher. Right behind them came Harry Posner. "Hold up, boys. Let me see what Mr. Whitmore wants us to do now." Posner approached his boss. "We brought the stretcher, Mr. Whitmore. What do you want us to do with it?"

The general manager turned to Dr. Newmark. "What do you say, Philip? Should the boys carry Mr. Collins up to a suite on the stretcher? Or can he walk?"

"I would prefer him to be carried, Mr. Whitmore. Walking all that way might bring on another attack from his asthma, and that could be much more ... disastrous ... than the initial ... episode." Newmark became more assertive. "Yes, by all means. Have them take him there on the stretcher."

"Yes, of course, Philip." Whitmore turned to Posner. "Harry, do you know which suites are presently available for Mrs. Collins and her son?"

Posner rubbed his chin with his right hand as he pondered exactly what to say and how to say it. He huffed a breath, then looked his boss straight in the eye. "Well, sir, offhand, the only one I can think of is … five-ten, sir."

Whitmore winced, frowned, glanced at Newmark, then looked back at the bellhop. "Five-ten, eh?"

Posner grimaced, then nodded. "Yes, sir. Five-ten."

"Are you certain that's the only suite available, Harry?"

With his face filled with regret, Posner squeezed out his reply. "Yes, sir, I am." Then another thought burst into his mind and brought on a modest smile. "I'm sorry, Mr. Whitmore. I just remembered something very important."

"What's that, Harry?"

"I've been working here since the hotel opened in oh-six … just like you've been here, sir, and I sometimes forget about the new wing. There could be a suite available over there, sir."

Whitmore snickered. "You know, Harry, I sometimes do the same thing. So, why don't you go into the kitchen and call the front desk and ask Mr. Lewis if we have a suite available in the new wing?" He turned to Newmark again. "Is that all right with you, Philip? If we wait here a bit longer before we move Mr. Collins?"

"That will be perfectly fine with me, Sam."

Lilian heard the entire conversation between the general manager and his subordinates. The last few exchanges between Whitmore and Posner struck her as odd at best. A flock of thoughts, like a murder of crows, fluttered through her mind.

Why did Mr. Whitmore ask the bellboy to check with the front desk about another suite being available in the hotel's new wing? Why did he react so strangely when the bellboy said the room number of the available suite? Why did he ask Dr. Newmark for his approval about moving my Herbie? Is there something wrong with suite five-ten? Something's going on here, but what? I need to talk to Miss Malone! And as soon as possible!

Harry Posner reported back to Sam Whitmore who had been waiting impatiently in the banquet room with Lilian Collins and her son Herbie, Dr. Philip Newmark and his nurse Anna Reikel, Lisa Reikel, Roscoe Arbuckle, Milo Cole, and two bellhops, Mal Sisson and Bobby Peck, who were not exactly eager to carry the doctor's patient to a possible available suite in the new wing.

Peck leaned closer to Sisson to whisper. "I got a nickel that says Harry brings back word that there's one suite available in the new wing and it's at the far end of the building."

Mal leaned back. "You're on."

Bobby groaned. "Let me guess. You think five-ten in the old wing is the only suite available, don't you?"

Sisson snorted. "Of course, I do, and when we get up there, keep an eye out for the ghost of that girl who died there the other night."

Peck grunted. "Aw, come on, Mal. You don't believe in ghosts, do you, buddy?"

"Word has it, Bobby, that she was murdered."

"Sure, I heard that, too. But come on, Mal, Doc Newmark says she died from some disease like tuberculosis."

Sisson shrugged. "Yeah, I heard that, too. Maybe she did die of some disease, and just maybe she was murdered."

"That is the question, isn't it, Mal? I guess we'll never know the answer to that one, will we?"

"Hey, cheese it. Harry's coming out of the kitchen."

Whitmore smiled at Mrs. Collins. "Ah, good! Here comes Harry now … with good news, I hope."

Newmark shook his head. "From the look on his face, I have to say the news is not good. No, definitely not good."

Lilian frowned as she nodded. "Yes, I do have to agree with you, Doctor. He does look quite disappointed."

Herbie offered his opinion. "I don't see what all the fuss is about. I'm feeling much better now. I can't see why we can't go back to the ballroom and enjoy the rest of the evening with the others."

Lisa squeezed Herbie's shoulder. "You really should listen to the doctor, Herbie. He's an excellent physician. If he says you need to stay the night here in the hotel, then you must listen to him."

Young Collins gave Lisa a sweet smile. "Well, if you say so, Lisa."

She returned the expression in kind. "I do."

Posner came straight across the room and stopped face-to-face in front of Whitmore. "I'm sorry to tell you this, sir. Mr. Lewis said the only suite available tonight in the entire hotel is five-ten. He said there's a few adjoining rooms available in the new wing, but there's none in the old wing, sir."

Whitmore nodded at the bellboy. "Thank you, Harry." He turned to Newmark. "Well, there you have it, Philip. It's either suite five-ten in the old wing or two adjoining rooms in the new wing. You're the doctor. It's your call."

"Five-ten has three bedrooms. One for my patient. One for his mother. And the third for my nurse." He turned to Mrs. Reikel. "You will stay with Herbie and his mother for the night, won't you, Anna?"

"Of course, Doctor."

"Then it's settled. Let's get Herbie on the stretcher and get him up to suite five-ten."

Herbie shook his head. "The stretcher is unnecessary. I'm certain I can walk to the elevator from here."

Newmark shook his head. "No, my boy, you shouldn't do any such thing."

"But I feel fine, Doctor."

"That's the epinephrine doing its job, Herbie. It will begin to wear off soon, and you'll begin to feel tired and want to go to bed. So, no more argument, young man." He turned to Posner. "Harry, get your men over here and get Herbie on the stretcher while we can do it with total ease."

Posner turned to Peck and Sisson. "Come on, boys. We're going up to five-ten."

As the two bellhops bent down to pick up the stretcher, Peck just had to grin at his partner. "You owe me a nickel, Mal."

Sisson groused. "The bet's off … if we see a ghost up there … and that's anywhere up there." They straightened up with the stretcher between them, Peck in front and Sisson in the rear. Bobby glanced over his left shoulder and winked at Mal. "Double or nothing, then? A dime if there's no ghost up there?"

Sisson leaned forward a foot and whispered. "Sure thing, pal. A dime it is."

Whitmore focused on Posner. "Harry, I want you to go down to the laundry and get a pair of pajamas from the guest wardrobe closet for Herbie and a nightgown for Mrs. Collins. Take Lisa with you. I'm sure she'll be better at picking out the right sizes for both of them."

"Yes, sir, Mr. Whitmore." Posner turned to Lisa. "Miss Reikel, if you please?"

Lisa turned to her aunt, her eyes pleading with her to intervene.

Anna's expression appeared carved in stone. "Lisa, you do as Mr. Whitmore says. Go with Mr. Posner and pick out some pajamas for Mr. Collins and a nice nightgown for his mother. We will see you in suite five-ten."

Although quite reluctant to go with Posner, Lisa conceded. "As you wish, Mr. Whitmore."

The hotel boss turned to Sisson and Peck. "Okay, boys, let's get Mr. Collins onto the stretcher and take him to the elevator."

Both nodded. Peck replied. "Yes, sir, Mr. Whitmore."

Lilian turned to Arbuckle and Cole. "Would you two gentlemen express my gratitude to Mr. Sennett for the lovely dinner and for paying for our entry into the ballroom?"

Roscoe answered her. "Certainly, Mrs. Collins."

"And would you ask Miss Malone to come up to the suite before she leaves the hotel tonight? I'd like to have a word with her."

Milo nodded. "I'll tell her, Mrs. Collins."

"Thank you, both."

Sisson and Peck had Herbie on the stretcher and ready to go.

Whitmore forced a smile. "All right then. Let's be off. Follow me, everyone."

Newmark frowned. "Yes, do lead the way, Sam. Anna and I will follow the stretcher with Mrs. Collins so we can keep an eye on him."

Whitmore's procession had two ways to go to the elevator. One through the kitchen, and the second through the ballroom. The general manager chose the latter. When Roscoe Arbuckle opened the banquet room door, strains of the *Matrimony Rag* greeted the group. They were halfway to the ballroom's exit when the bandleader noticed them and instantly halted the music. In his next breath, he began applauding the young man on the stretcher. His orchestra set their instruments aside and followed his example. All the dancers did likewise. Then the people still seated at their tables stood up and joined in with their applause.

Realizing he was the object of their ovation, Herbie raised himself onto his right elbow and waved to the crowd with his left hand, thanking them for their polite acknowledgement and letting them know he had survived the attack and was already on the road to recovery. His response promptly set off a round of cheers from most of the men and some of the women in the ballroom; a cheer that continued until he disappeared through the doorway.

Herbie smiled at his mother walking alongside the stretcher. "Can you believe that Mother? All that applause? And just for me?"

Lilian reached out with her left hand and patted him on his right shoulder. "They're all just as happy as I am that you're all right, Dear."

Arbuckle and Cole waited several seconds before exiting the banquet room. A good twenty-five feet behind the main group they walked even slower along the row of tables until they reached Maisy's party of investigators still gathered around Mabel and Mack's table.

After waiting for the applause and cheers to subside, Sennett asked Milo the single question buzzing in everyone's brain. "Is the boy going to be all right?"

Cole nodded. "Dr. Newmark seems to think so, but as a matter of caution, Mr. Whitmore and he decided to take Herbie and Mrs. Collins up to a suite on the fifth floor where the doctor and Mrs. Reikel can keep an eye on him for the night. Herbie has asthma, and apparently, all that dancing set off an attack."

The comedy king's head bobbled cheerfully. "That's good to hear, Milo. That he's all right, I mean." Sennett scanned the group around him. "Did you all hear that? Herbie's going to be okay, but the doctor and his nurse are going to look after him through the night. We can all relax now and go back to enjoying the evening."

Joe Reikel approached the party's host. "Thank you for allowing me to introduce my wife and niece to you and your friends, Mr. Sennett, but now I think I should go upstairs and see how they are doing with Dr. Newmark's patient." He bowed to Mabel. "Thank you as well, Miss Normand." He glanced at all the others. "Have a pleasant remainder of your evening, everyone. It was an honor meeting all of you. Please come back again to the Hotel Alexandria and ask for me, and I will see to it that you all will receive the best service and the best food we have to offer."

The entire group spoke some form of appreciation to Reikel for his courteous remarks and polite invitation to them. Sennett capped off their expressions of gratitude with an extension of his hand, a strong grip, and a few semiserious words. "Say, Joe, does this mean we can eat for free next time I bring a crowd with me?"

Reikel understood Mack's little joke. Even so, he made a counteroffer. "Your friends can eat for free, Mack, but you must leave a nice gratuity for all of them. *Ja?*"

Sennett laughed out loud. "*Oui-oui, monsieur!* It's a deal, Joe. See you next time."

Reikel grinned. "Yes, next time." He headed for the exit.

Mack heaved a sigh. "Back to having fun, everybody. The night is still young, and the party is just getting started."

Mabel tugged Sennett's sleeve. "How about another round of that champagne, Nappy? I'm still thirsty."

"Not for you, my dear."

She pouted. "Party pooper!"

"Do I look like John D. Rockefeller?"

"No, you look more like Ebenezer Scrooge."

"Behave, Mabel, or I'll call a cab for you right now."

She slapped the table. "Oh, all right. You win this time, but we'll just see about later, Mr. Bigshot."

Sennett smiled. "Yes, we will, won't we?"

As soon as they returned to their table with the Brownings, Milo leaned close to Mabel so he could be heard over the band and the prattle of the dancers prancing around the ballroom. "Mrs. Collins asked me to tell you she would like to speak to you before you leave tonight."

"Really?"

He nodded.

"Did she say why?"

He shook his head. "No. She just said she wanted to talk to you. I assumed it has something to do with our investigation, but I can't say for sure."

"Okay. I guess I'll have to talk to her before we leave tonight." A new thought came to her. "Maybe I should go up there right away and see what she wants. For all I know, she could be one of those early-to-bed-early-to-rise sorts. She and Herbie both." She paused for a second. "Hey, Milo. Didn't you say they were going up to a suite on the fifth floor?"

"Yes, I did. Suite five-ten in this wing of the hotel."

Ed Browning straightened in his chair. "Did you say suite five-ten, Milo?"

Cole looked at Browning, quite surprised that he had heard him talking to Maisy. "Yes, that's right. Five-ten. Why?"

"Are you certain that was the number?"

"Yes, I'm sure."

The detective focused on Maisy. "That's the very same suite the Sullivan family stayed in."

Maisy appeared jolted. "Are you certain, Eddie?"

He nodded. "Bill, Nellie, and I were up there the very morning of Marjorie Sullivan's death. Suite five-ten. I'm positive about that."

Milo shook his head. "You know something. When Mr. Whitmore and Dr. Newmark were talking about a suite for Herbie and Mrs. Collins, both of them seemed a little stressed out when the bellboy told them the only suite available was five-ten. I didn't think much about it at the time, but now that you're saying that's the same suite where the Sullivan girl died, then it's no wonder Mr. Whitmore and the doctor were a little shaken up about it."

Maisy's eyes searched Browning's. "Well, Eddie, do you think Mr. Whitmore and Dr. Newmark are a little more than superstitious about tragedies coming in threes?"

"That struck you, too, Maisy?"

"Like a bolt of lightning, Detective."

Browning nodded. "I think I should go up there with you, Maisy. I'd like to hear what Mrs. Collins has to say to you."

"I was thinking the same thing. Should we bring Bill with us?"

Eddie shook his head. "All three of us going up there together might arouse more suspicion about our motive. No, I think we should tell Bill what's up and leave it at that."

Nealy Browning interrupted. "I've got a better idea, Edward. Why don't I go up there with Maisy? No one will suspect two ladies leaving the party. But two snoops like you and Maisy suddenly sneaking away? Everybody will know for certain something is up."

Maisy giggled. "Nealy dear, I think your husband is starting to rub off on you."

Suite 510 in the Hotel Alexandria's first wing consisted of a foyer, a drawing room, two lavatories, and three bedrooms, two of equal size with a single bed in each and the third with a double bed meant to accommodate the parents of any family that should stay there. The drawing room was furnished lavishly with two damask settees, two matching armchairs, a sofa, and a mahogany writing desk. A crystal chandelier provided the primary lighting, and a pair of short lamps adorned the desk. A Persian carpet covered ninety percent of the floor. The trio of bedrooms each had a door to the main room and were joined together by a door on each side of the middle room. The bathrooms were conveniently situated at each side of the row of bedrooms. Walk-in closets were located on each side of the foyer.

Sam Whitmore explained all this to Lilian and Herbie once they were inside the suite. "Herbie, yours will be the middle bedroom, the master bedroom. I think you will be quite comfortable in there. Mrs. Collins, yours will be the bedroom to the left. It's one of the two singles. Mrs. Reikel will have the remaining bedroom. Room service begins serving at six o'clock and is available until nine o'clock in the evening. As I said downstairs, there will be no charges for the rooms, the service, and the food and drinks, if you should want for anything. You are welcome to stay for as long as Dr. Newmark deems it necessary for Herbie's health. Mr. Posner will be here with your bedclothes quite soon, and Lisa will turn down your beds. She will also be staying the night with her aunt, and she will be available to both of you as your personal chambermaid. I assume some or all of the people who are in your party will be coming up to visit at some time this evening. You are more than welcome to entertain them, if you so please. If any of them would ask for any refreshments or late-night food, those will also be brought up to you without charge. Is there anything more I can do for you, Mrs. Collins? Or for you, Herbie?"

Lilian smiled politely. "Did I hear you correctly, Mr. Whitmore, when you said Lisa will be our chambermaid?"

"Yes, you did. Lisa is on our housekeeping staff. She also works with her aunt in Dr. Newmark's clinic. She's learning to be a nurse and will be starting regular classes soon at Clara Barton Hospital. Is there a problem with that, Mrs. Collins?"

"Oh, no, sir. From what I could tell by watching her dance with my Herbie, she appeared to be a very charming young lady."

"She certainly is, Mrs. Collins." He paused. "Now is there anything else I can do for you and your son?"

"Well, there is one more thing. I would like a pitcher of ice water, if I may?"

"Certainly. Is that all?"

"That's enough for me."

Whitmore turned to Herbie who was sitting on a settee. "How about you, young man? Is there anything you would like from us?"

"Well, sir, downstairs in the ballroom I was drinking a Coca-Cola over ice before my asthma attack spoiled the evening. Would it be possible for me to get another over ice in a glass? And maybe one for Lisa as well?"

The hotel boss smiled. "Normally, our rules forbid our employees from fraternizing with our guests, but I believe we can bend the rules a little, considering the circumstances. I'll have two Coca-Colas, two glasses, and a bucket of ice sent up right away."

"Thank you, sir."

Lilian stretched out her hand to their host. "Yes, thank you, Mr. Whitmore. You've been more than generous, sir."

"Think nothing of it, Mrs. Collins. I hope young Herbie will have a restful night and be right as rain in the morning."

"Again, thank you, Mr. Whitmore. I can't wait to sing your praises and those of this magnificent hotel in my next article for the papers."

Surprise blossomed over the general manager's face. "Article? For the papers?"

"Yes, sir. I am a freelance writer here in Los Angeles. I will write about this night and this hotel and, of course, you and your staff. You've all been so very wonderful to us. It's the least I can do to repay you for your generous hospitality to my son and to me."

"I'm flattered, Mrs. Collins, but that's really not necessary."

"Before I send it to the papers, I'll bring it by your office for you to read. Maybe then you'll change your mind."

"That's deal, Mrs. Collins. Now, if you will excuse me, I'll go see about the refreshments you and Herbie requested." He bowed slightly.

Lilian did a half-curtsy in return. "Of course, sir."

As he entered the hallway, Whitmore spotted Maisy and Nealy exiting the elevator. Instantly, he recognized Maisy but not the woman with her.

Seeing Whitmore coming toward, the girl from Oklahoma put on a country smile and whispered out of the corner of her mouth. "That's the hotel's boss. He's a real talker, so be ready to greet him."

"Sure thing, Maisy."

Whitmore's face suddenly sparkled with false charm. "Why, Miss Malone, how nice to see you!" He stopped five feet in of front the two women. "I am so sorry we didn't get a chance to chat downstairs." He focused on Nealy. "And who is this with you, if I may ask?"

"This is my good friend, Mrs. Nealy Browning. I believe, sir, you are acquainted with her husband, Los Angeles Police Department Detective Sergeant Edward Browning?"

"Yes, of course." He held out his hand to Nealy. "How do you do, Mrs. Browning? I am so sorry our meeting for the first time has come on such a stressful evening."

She accepted his slight handshake. "Think nothing of it, sir."

Whitmore smiled broadly. "Do I detect the sweet melody of the South in your voice, madam?"

"Why, yes, you do, sir. My husband and I are both from Georgia. And where are you from, sir?"

"I hail from West Virginia, Mrs. Browning. Your husband and I met just this past week when he and a second detective came by the hotel to investigate the misfortunate death of that poor Sullivan girl." He lowered his head a bit reverently. "That sweet girl. She and her mother and sister had just arrived here from Seattle, hoping our drier air would be more beneficial to her condition than that damp climate in the Northwest. Sadly, it was not."

Maisy's head bobbed. "Yes, I read about it in *The Times.*"

Nealy followed Maisy's lead. "I also read about it in *The Times.*"

"Yes, *The Times* writer did a very good job of covering the story." He smiled again. "So, what brings you up to the fifth floor, ladies?"

Maisy answered him. "Mrs. Collins is a friend of mine, and we came up to give her some moral support and to see how her son Herbie is doing."

"How very thoughtful of you, Miss Malone! I'm sure Mrs. Collins will be delighted to see you both." He smiled. "Now if you will please excuse me, ladies, I have some other matters concerning young Mr. Collins to tend to. He wants a Coca-Cola for himself and another for Miss Lisa Reikel, one of our chambermaids, who was dancing with him when he was stricken by his asthma attack." He took one step to leave, then halted. "Oh, yes. In case you don't know where Mrs. Collins and her son are located, they are just down the hall in suite five-ten."

Maisy replied. "Thank you, Mr. Whitmore."

The women watched Whitmore walk off toward the elevator. Before he had gone too far, they turned around and started forward to their destination. When they came to it, Maisy knocked on the door. In mere seconds, it opened and there stood Anna Reikel looking grim for a few heartbeats before she broke into a forced smile.

"Ah, ladies, how may I help you?"

Maisy took command of the moment. "You're Mrs. Reikel, right?"

"Yes, I am."

"We haven't been properly introduced, Mrs. Reikel. I'm Maisy Malone, and this lady is my dear friend Mrs. Nealy Browning."

"How do you do, ladies? It's nice to meet you both. Now what can I do for you?"

"Mrs. Browning and I have been delegated by our friends in the ballroom to see Mrs. Collins and ask her how her son is doing and to see if she needs anything. So, may we please see her?"

Anna hesitated for a moment. "Why don't you ladies' step into the foyer, while I go tell Mrs. Collins you are here?"

"Thank you, Mrs. Reikel."

Floor length drapes covered the doorway between the foyer and the drawing room. Anna parted the curtains and stepped into the drawing room.

A few minutes later Lilian passed through the drapes into the foyer. "Thank you both for coming."

Maisy smiled at Lilian. "What are friends for, if not to be close to you when you're in need of emotional support? How is Herbie?"

"Herbie is recovering nicely, thank you." Lilian moved very close to Maisy to whisper. "I'm quite suspicious of this doctor and the hotel manager. Why don't we go out into the hall and talk where there are fewer ears to listen?"

Maisy adopted the same tone as Lilian. "Sure, we can do that."

Lilian led them into the hall. As soon as the three of them were outside the suite, she motioned to a settee between two rooms on the opposite side of the hallway. "Let's go sit over there where we can talk more privately."

Maisy sat in the middle at an angle to Lilian's right with Nealy even more angled behind the actress. "Milo said you wanted to speak to me about something, but he didn't say what it was about."

Lilian nodded. "I did that on purpose, Maisy, just in case someone other than he and Roscoe were in earshot."

"That was good thinking, Lilian. Eavesdropping seems to be the best service in this hotel."

"My thoughts exactly."

Maisy nodded in agreement. "So, what did you want to talk to me about."

"The suite number ... five-ten."

"What about it?"

Lilian leaned closer to Maisy. "Well, when Mr. Whitmore asked the bellboy ... I believe his name is Harry Posner ... when Mr. Whitmore asked Mr. Posner about an available suite for Herbie and me to spend the night, the bellboy told him the only one he knew of was five-ten. When Mr. Whitmore heard that, he seemed a bit upset. Then Mr. Whitmore told that to Dr. Newmark, and the doctor looked just as upset as the manager. That's when Mr. Whitmore told Mr. Posner to go into the kitchen and call down to the front desk and ask the clerk to check and see if there might be a suite available in the new wing. When Mr. Posner returned a few minutes later, he told Mr. Whitmore that five-ten was the only available suite in the entire hotel. Then the manager repeated that bit of information to the doctor, and both of them appeared to be quite upset all over again.

"I didn't ask either one of them anything about the suite number, but I'm positive there's something wrong with those rooms. I'm not sure what it is, but after seeing the looks on their faces, I'm more than a little apprehensive about staying the night there."

Nealy Browning touched Maisy's left forearm. "Excuse me please for sticking my nose in here, but I believe I have an idea why those two gentlemen might be a little uneasy about that particular suite."

"I'm all ears, Nealy."

"Well, I believe Edward told me suite five-ten is where Mrs. Sullivan and her daughters were staying when the younger daughter passed away this past Wednesday morning."

"You know what, Nealy? You're absolutely right about that, now that you mention it."

Lilian appeared shocked. "Good Lord Almighty, ladies! Are you telling me suite five-ten is the very scene of one of the murders we're investigating?"

Maisy nodded. "That's exactly what we're saying, Lilian." Then she backed off. "Well, maybe not exactly. We still don't have any proof that any of the three deaths here these past three weeks are murders. We're still looking for some definite proof that one or two or all three deaths were murders. So far, all we have to go on is a hunch that there is foul play involved here."

Lilian's astonishment disappeared. "A hunch? Whose hunch?"

Nealy turned glum. "My husband's. When he and his partner were here investigating the death of Miss Sullivan, he said he had a feeling that something was amiss with her death. Even more so when his chief told him and his partner, they could cease their investigating her death. Since he couldn't go on—"

Maisy interrupted. "He called me and asked for my help. Eddie is a good detective, Lilian. You can bank on that. If he says he has a hunch about anything, he's right more often than not. So, he asked me to put together our little gang of snoops to see if there was anything to his hunch. I don't think I have to tell you there's more going on in this hotel than just some classy rooms, good food, and a nice place to dance. In fact, it's my notion that we're going to wrap up this investigation sometime in the next twenty-four hours."

Nealy tilted her head to the right. "The next twenty-four hours?"

"Yep! Just as soon as I can ask your husband for one more favor."

Most of Maisy's sleuthing group gathered in the hotel's lobby to wait for her to join them. Those absent were Lilian Collins who was making herself at home in suite 510, her son Herbie who was resting quietly in his room in the suite, LAPD Detective Sergeant Ed Browning and his wife Nealy who were meeting with Maisy on the Mezzanine, and Mabel Normand who had remained in the Rose Ballroom with her boss and date for the evening, Mack Sennett. Although not part of this bunch, Andrus and Regina Reynolds had joined them, both curious about what Maisy had in store for them as well as her investigators.

Among those growing impatient, Marie Fowler leaned close to her husband and whispered from the corner of her mouth. "What's going on here, Johnny? Is Maisy coming back soon? I want to get home to the children. It's getting late, and I don't want to pay the neighbor girl any more than I have to. We already owe six bits, and we'll owe her near a dollar if we leave here in the next twenty minutes."

Fowler tilted himself in his wife's direction. "All I know, Darlin', is Maisy asked for us to meet her here, while she has a private word or two with Detective Browning and his wife."

"Is this how she always works on these investigations?"

"Darlin', I ain't sure Maisy Malone has any one set way of doing anything. She's an Okie, remember?"

"Oh, yes, I forgot that for the moment?"

"Wait here, Darlin', while I go have a word with Milo. Maybe he knows what's going on."

Cole sat on an emerald green velvet cushion chair near one of the Egyptian brown marble columns, his legs crossed and left foot dangling. He wiggled the extremity nervously as he saw Fowler coming in his direction.

The cabbie stopped a few feet short of his target. "Excuse me, Milo, but have you got any idea what's going on here? With Miss

Malone and the Brownings, I mean. My wife's getting a bit edgy about all this. Of course, this is her first-time meeting Miss Malone, so it's only natural for her to be a bit worried, I guess."

Cole sighed. "You know, Johnny, I met Maisy the day she stepped off the train from Chicago last September. She was a mystery to me then, and nothing has changed with her since. So, pardner, I guess I'm in the dark as much as you are." He sat up straight. "Maisy is Maisy, and there's not a darn thing we can do about that."

"If you say so, pard. I guess you know her better than anybody."

Cole shook his head. "No, Johnny, I don't. I might know her better than any other man around here, but the real expert on Maisy Malone is Mabel Normand. If you've got any questions about Maisy, you can go back up to the ballroom and ask her, if she's still sober enough to talk, that is."

"No, I think I'll pass on that. I've had Miss Normand riding in the back seat of my Studebaker enough times to know she's got a sharp tongue and a foul mouth to go with it. No, sir, I want no part of that woman when she's been throwing down more wine than most of the men I know who drink nothing but beer." He paused. "Why does she drink so much, Milo?"

"That's a question I can answer for you, Johnny. She's drinks so she can get out of bed the next morning and get to the studio on time to keep her spot as Mr. Sennett's leading lady."

"I don't follow you, Milo."

"Have you seen any of her films, Johnny?"

Fowler grinned. "The wife and I have seen 'purtnear' all of them. Why?"

"Then you've seen her do all those pratfalls and other stunts."

"Well, I guess we have. What about them?"

Cole shook his head. "Man-o-man, Johnny, don't you have any idea how much those hurt?"

"They hurt?"

"Yes, Johnny, they hurt. And she takes that pain home with her every night of the working week. So, to get to sleep at night, she drinks heavier than a lot of men I know."

"For real, Milo?"

Before Cole could answer, Maisy appeared at the top of the Mezzanine stairway. "Here Maisy comes now, Johnny. Why don't you ask her? She can tell you better than I can. She puts Mabel to bed more nights than I'd like to count. So, ask her."

Fowler shook his head. "No, thanks. I'll take your word for it."

One-by-one, the others in the group shifted their eyes to Maisy as she descended the stairs behind Ed Browning leading the way and his wife Nealy two steps after her husband.

Cole looked back at Fowler who was still gawking at Maisy. "Don't stare at her too long, Johnny, or your wife might get jealous."

"Good idea, pal." With that, the cabbie hurried back to his better half. "I can't wait to hear what Maisy has to say now."

Marie snarled. "I'd rather you'd ask her if we can leave now. I'm paying that babysitter by the hour, you know."

"Just hold your horses, Darlin'. I'm sure Maisy's taking all that into account, and we'll be on our way home in no time at all."

"We'd better or—"

Johnny glared fiercely at his wife and gave her a low growl. "I done told you, woman, hold your horses."

Marie blanched at his assertion of authority and replied in the soft tone she usually reserved for her babies. "Okay, I will."

Guilt twisted Johnny's lips, but he withheld any further remarks.

As soon as they reached the lobby floor, Maisy hurried past the Brownings and rushed straight to the Fowlers. "Marie, I'm so sorry I kept you and Johnny waiting so long."

Marie smiled with all the gentility she could muster. "Oh, don't you fret none, Miss Malone. Johnny's told me all about how you go about these investigations of yours. I know you can't sniff out the killer any faster than a warm-nosed hound can tree a 'coon. Takes time and a good amount of patience. So, there's no need to apologize."

Maisy took two quick steps straight ahead and embraced Marie with both arms for two heartbeats before holding her at arm's length. "Johnny said you were a real darling, Marie. A true Texas lady."

Fowler's wife smiled back at Maisy. "Well, he might have been a little long on the exaggeration side of that description of me, Miss Malone."

A bigger grin spread over Maisy's face. "Now didn't I tell you to call me Maisy? How are we going to be friends if you keep calling me Miss Malone?"

Marie let her head bobble with reticence. "Well, okay then. Maisy it is from here on out."

"Good." Maisy shifted to Fowler. "Johnny, why don't you go ahead and take Marie home? I can get another taxi to take me home tonight. I won't need you until tomorrow morning around nine o'clock, if you don't mind." She turned back to his wife. "If that's all right with you, Marie. You won't mind if I borrow Johnny again for most of the day, will you?"

"No, of course not, Maisy. I'm sure our preacher won't mind too much if we miss a prayer meeting once in a while. So, you go ahead and take him for the day. Me and the young'uns will get along just fine until you send him home."

Maisy reverted to her ancestral ways. "That's mighty fine, Marie. I promise he'll still be in topnotch shape when I do."

"I'm sure he will, Maisy."

A twinkle in her eyes was Maisy's way of reassuring Marie. Seeing that she was comforted, the actress turned back to Fowler. "Go on now, Johnny, and get this lady of yours home to her children."

"Yes, ma'am." He turned to his wife. "Come on, Darlin'. We can't keep that babysitter waiting all night long."

Marie rolled her eyes and let him take her by the arm and led her out of the hotel. Along the way, she asked her husband. "Now how do you suppose she knew I was a bit on the ornery side just before she came down those stairs?"

"Woman's intuition, I suppose, Darlin'. What else could it be?"

The couple stepped outside. "Woman's intuition? Now ain't that a wonder?"

"Get in the cab, Marie, and let that go. Okay?"

"If you say so, Johnny."

By this time, Ed and Nealy Browning had gathered all the rest of their group into a semi-circle of the same chairs that Cole had been using. All sat still as Maisy approached them and came to a halt in the gap where everybody could see and hear her.

"I know it's been a long evening and night for all of us and not a thing like we all expected it would be. First off, Lilian sends her regrets that her son Herbie had such a serious asthma attack that precipitated the extension of our presence here. But once you hear all I have to tell you, I'm sure you'll agree there is a silver lining to be found in this dark cloud shadowing over our pleasant evening."

Browning offered his support. "Just wait until Maisy spells out her plan for tonight. You'll see."

Nealy nudged him with her left elbow. "It's not all that much of a plan for tonight, Edward. It's more for tomorrow."

Maisy chuckled. "Well, I'm glad you like it so much, Eddie." The humor faded away. "Seriously, folks, I do have a plan for the night and for tomorrow that involves all of us in one capacity or another. It's my intention that we wrap up this case before the sun sets tomorrow. So, listen please, and if you have any questions, go right ahead and ask. I'll do my best to answer them." She paused to scan the faces around her. Seeing complete focus on her, she continued. "Okay, then, let's get to it."

She took a deep breath and aimed her attention at Detective Vince DeDonatis and his wife. "First off, I know it's a long drive back to Venice for you and Susie, so I took the liberty of getting you a room a few doors down the hall from where Lilian and Herbie are staying. Don't worry about the bill, Vince. I arranged it with Mr. Whitmore, the hotel's general manager. It's on the house."

DeDonatis shook his head. "You didn't have to do that, Maisy. Venice isn't that far away from here."

"There's more to it than that, Vince. Mr. Whitmore doesn't know you're a police detective, and I'd like you to be close to Lilian and her son just in case something goes awry during the night."

All but the Brownings winced at the last part of her remark. Only Vince muttered something. "What do you mean—?"

Maisy held up her left hand to stop him. "I'll get to that in just a second." She focused on Andrus and Regina Reynolds next. "Long Beach isn't exactly around the corner from here either, so I've arranged it with Mr. Whitmore for you folks to spend the night here as well. Then Johnny Fowler and I will take you home in the morning."

Regina leaned forward. "Why are you coming with us, Maisy?"

"I'm hoping one of you will go with me in search of the doctor and the nurse who cared for Mr. Donelson. I have a few questions for them. Are you and your husband willing to help me with that?"

Andrus answered for them. "We'd be very delighted to help you, Maisy."

"Good. At the same time, Detective Browning and hopefully his partner Detective Ingram will be paying another visit to the Travers Hotel to see if anyone there can provide them with a good physical description of the chambermaid Minnie Lightfreit who seems to have disappeared since she quit her job at the Travers. Eddie and Bill have a hunch that she might actually be a nurse named Minerva Lightfoot. It's a real stretch, but every idea needs to be checked out." She smiled at Ingram. "How about it, Bill? Are you willing to work on Sunday?"

"Count me in. I want to find the underlying cause of all this just as much as Ed does."

"Good." Maisy shifted her attention to the Arbuckles next. "I've got parts in this for you and Minta, too, Roscoe."

The couple's faces bloomed with delight. They reacted equally and together. "Really? For us?"

"Yes, both of you. Minta, you're going to replace Lilian in her room, and Roscoe, you're going to replace Herbie in his."

Minta spoke for both of them. "Why are we doing that, Maisy?"

Ed Browning grinned and answered for her. "She already told us, Minta. The two of you will be posing as Mrs. Collins and her son just in case something goes awry during the night."

All the others appeared slightly perplexed. All but Bill Ingram. "I get it. You think someone might try something tonight … in Herbie's room or … maybe his mother's, right?"

Nealy jumped in. "Or both, Bill."

"Both? Really?"

Maisy responded. "We can't be too careful, Bill."

"Okay, I can see that. But how are you going to pull off switching Roscoe and Minta with Herbie and Mrs. Collins?"

The leader of the pack smiled coyly at the Arbuckles. "Didn't you two make a new friend here earlier today?"

Quizzical expressions warped their faces as their eyes met for a mere heartbeat. Then the answer occurred to them simultaneously. "Harry!" They fixed their twinkling orbs on Maisy again.

"That's right, folks. Harry Posner. He has keys to everything in the hotel. He says he can get you two into Lilian's and Herbie's rooms and then out again without anyone else knowing about it." She smirked. "He says he's a regular Houdini … in reverse, and I believe him."

Laughter circled the group.

All except Bill Ingram. "Let me get this straight, Maisy, if you don't mind."

"I don't mind at all, Bill. I said to ask questions if you have any. So, go right ahead and ask."

Ingram bobbed his head. "Okay, I will." He took a deep breath. "So, we're going to all this trouble to protect Herbie and Mrs. Collins from being murdered in the middle of the night by some … American … version … of Jack the Ripper. Is that right, Maisy?"

"Not quite, but close."

"Close? What do you mean by that? Close, I mean."

Maisy tilted her head toward Ed Browning. "You tell him, Eddie, and see if he gets it."

"Bill, she means we're not looking for a Jack the Ripper replica. He used a knife or scalpel to murder his victims. We're looking for one or more persons who smother their victims."

"One or more persons?"

Maisy nodded. "That's right, Bill. Just like Burke and Hare."

"Who?"

The Brownings snickered again.

Ingram frowned. "What's the gag, Ed?"

"No gag, Bill. It's just too long a story to tell right now."

"Oh, I can't wait to hear this one."

Maisy spoke again. "And you will, Detective, but for now, Nealy and Ruth need to go home for the night, and you and Eddie need to go with Roscoe and Minta to replace Lilian and Herbie in their rooms in suite five-ten."

Walt Ballard held up his right hand. "And what am I supposed to do while all this is going on?"

Cole jumped in. "Yeah! And what about me?"

Maisy smiled. "Walt, you go home and *try* to get a good night's sleep. You'll be the first person we'll call if anything happens here tonight." She turned to Milo. "And you, sweetheart, are going to take me back up to the Rose Ballroom where we're going to dance the night away with Mabel and Mack."

The night passed peacefully. Almost.

Herbie Collins and Lisa Reikel visited in his room with two chaperones: Herbie's mother and Lisa's aunt. The two young people enjoyed the Coca-Colas Harry Posner brought them, but the presence of the two adults sitting quietly across the room in a pair of brown American Morocco leather armchairs stunted their conversation, limiting them from sharing more about each other than they wished to reveal.

As for Herbie's mother, only she and Nealy Browning knew anything about the plan Maisy was concocting to protect her and her son. When the actress told her about the scheme, Lilian had to ask Maisy point blank if she bore any suspicion that Mrs. Reikel might be a suspect in their case, and if Anna was involved, then what about her husband and her niece, could one or both of them be involved as well?

"For the moment, Lilian, I haven't got a single clue about who to suspect in the murders that happened in this hotel. For that matter, I don't know whether one person, two, or even three could be involved here. Then there's the other two deaths to consider. The one you and Walt looked into and the one Eddie and Bill looked into. We're not even sure yet that either of those two men were murdered. Mr. Peters could have hung himself, and Mr. Donelson could very well have died from a stroke. We simply don't know for sure until we find the two mystery women who were strangely connected to them.

"The same goes for the three people who died in this hotel over the past few weeks." Maisy shrugged. "Is Mrs. Reikel a suspect? She could be, but I can't say so without any solid evidence that she's part or parcel to these deaths. The same goes for her niece. She could be, and so could Dr. Newmark, Mr. Whitmore, and Mr. Reikel. Any one of them had the opportunity to murder three people in this hotel. They could have done it alone or in collusion with one or two or even all five of the others. I'm also very curious about Harry Posner the bellhop. He seems to be on our side in this, but is he really working with us or is he a spy for the others, especially his boss Sam Whitmore?"

Mrs. Browning nodded. "One murder would be so much easier to solve than two, three, four, or five."

Maisy shook her. "Ain't that the truth?" She returned her focus to Mrs. Collins. "You tell me, Lilian. What are your thoughts on what we've learned so far?"

"I'm as baffled as you are, Maisy. Like you, I don't think we have enough evidence to point the finger at anyone in particular. For all we know at this point, there could be multiple people involved with these deaths. And if there are, then are they connected with each other or are they separate killers and the murders unrelated."

"Which is exactly why I'm trying to cover all the bases, Lilian. The list of suspects in my head is already more than half a dozen. And then there's the unusual deaths of five people, each one under suspicious circumstances ... in less than three weeks ... in two hotels and one apartment house. Are they connected?" Maisy shrugged again. "I'm not sure of anything right now. Nothing except that I don't want to put you and Herbie in jeopardy. His asthma attack was so very fortuitous that I almost think you planned it for me."

Lilian snorted. "That thought never crossed my mind. Even if you had produced it as part of your plan to smoke out the killer or killers of these dead people, then the mother in me would have nixed it right away. Asthma attacks can be fatal, you know."

"Yes, I do know, which is why I was so worried about Herbie as soon as it happened. But like I said already, his attack came at the exact right moment we needed to help draw out the killer or killers of these sadly misfortunate victims."

Maisy and Nealy Browning then met with Harry Posner in the hall outside suite 510 immediately after he delivered the soft drinks to Herbie and Lisa. As usual, Maisy took command of their encounter.

"Mr. Posner, it's my understanding that you know every nook and cranny of this hotel. Is that true?"

Harry tilted his head to the right side as he peered at Maisy. "Who told you that, Miss Malone?"

"Two of our mutual friends told me that, Mr. Posner. Roscoe and Minta Arbuckle."

Posner straightened up and smiled. "Is that what they said? That we're friends?"

Maisy returned the beaming look. "Yes, they did. They told me you took them on the tour of the hotel earlier today and that you were highly informative."

A bigger grin spread over his face. "They did, eh?"

She chortled. "*They did.*" Then she settled back into her normal voice. "I was very impressed by what they had to say about you and your knowledge of the hotel." She paused to let that stroke his ego a bit. "They even told me how you know all the secrets of this place, including some secret hallways that only the help use sometimes to get into some of the rooms when the occupants are away, or they rooms are empty."

Posner frowned. "They weren't supposed to tell you that. That's privileged information, Miss Malone."

"I'm sorry, Mr. Posner. They didn't tell me any such thing. I was only guessing."

"Guessing?"

"Yes, Mr. Posner. I used to be in Vaudeville, and I stayed in a lot of hotels back east and in Europe. Many of the places where I stayed had some kind of secret hallways or stairways or both that the help used to deliver food and drinks to the lodgers. Usually, they came out in the linen closet and then into the hall. Is that how they work here?"

"Yes, Miss Malone. Each wing of the hotel has a service elevator that we use to deliver various items to the guest rooms. We use them in order to avoid crowding the guests' elevators."

"I noticed the fire escapes on the Fifth Street side of the hotel. Are they placed outside rooms?"

"No, they aren't. To get to them, people have to go through the linen closets."

"I see." She paused a breath before asking another question. "So, if I wanted to sneak into my room without anyone seeing me, then I could use the service elevator to get to the linen closet on my floor and go through it to the hall of my room. Is that correct?"

"Yes, Miss."

"And that's the only way I could sneak into my room?"

Posner hesitated a second before answering. "Into your *room*, yes."

"How about if I was staying in a suite?"

Harry frowned. "Same thing, Miss."

"But what if I wanted to make certain no one else saw me, then how would I go about it?"

"That's entirely different, Miss Malone."

"Different in what way?"

The bellhop seemed to shrink as he considered whether to tell her anything more. After a few seconds, he surrendered. "The suites are located next to the linen closets, and each one has a secret door into the master bedroom. The guests can't see the door because it's part of the wall, and it can only be opened from the linen closet. The whole point of it is get the guest out of the suite if the fire and smoke are in the hall." He paused for a breath. "If you've stayed in any really fancy hotels, Miss Malone, then you should know that the more important guests receive special services. Protecting them in case of a fire is an extremely high priority in this hotel."

"And so is their privacy, I would assume."

Posner nodded. "Yes, Miss."

"Well, sir, I would like to get two of my friends quietly out of suite five-ten and two more of my friends into it at the same time. I believe you know Mr. and Mrs. Arbuckle."

Harry smiled for the first time during their conversation. "Indeed, I do, Miss Malone. You work with them at Keystone Studio, don't you?"

Maisy gave him a precocious smile in return. "Indeed, I do, sir."

"And you want me to sneak the two of them into suite five-ten and get Mrs. Collins and her son out the same way, right?"

"Exactly, Mr. Posner. Can you do it?"

"Can I do it? Miss Malone, does the sun rise in the east?"

Shortly after midnight Harry Posner led Roscoe and Minta Arbuckle to the service elevator in the main kitchen. "Here we go, folks. We're going straight up to the west linen closet on the fifth floor. We'll go through the door to the fire escape hall to the first room where Mrs. Collins should be waiting for us. We'll go into her room, then she'll open the door to her son's room. Her son will come into her room, and Roscoe, you'll go into his. Here's some pajamas for you." Posner handed the garment to Arbuckle. "I hope they fit. They're the largest size we have." Posner stopped the elevator on the fifth floor. "Let me warn you that these walls aren't the thickest. It's best that we whisper now, if anyone has to talk. Okay?"

The Arbuckles looked at each other, then they confirmed their understanding with simultaneous nods.

Posner bobbed his head in return. "Good. Now let's go. Quietly as possible." He opened the elevator door and held it open for the couple.

They stepped as softly as they could into the linen closet that was well illuminated by two ceiling light fixtures. Both looked to their left to see the city lights through the fire escape window. Joining them, Harry smiled and whispered. "Some sight, isn't it? Los Angeles. It keeps getting bigger every day, and the lights at night keep getting brighter and brighter. I go up on the roof whenever I have a break. It just amazes me how fast this city is growing." He chuckled. "First, it was oil that started all this expansion. Now, it's people like you folks." He noted their quizzical expressions. "You know, motion picture people." His grin grew. "Every day every single passenger train that arrives in our three depots brings more and more people who are looking for jobs in motion pictures. Actors, actresses, producers, directors, writers, camera operators, film editors, carpenters, electricians. You name a job in motion pictures, and I'll bet at least a hundred people a day come here looking for work at any one of our fifty-some studios around this city of ours. They come here to the Alexandria looking for work until they can get a position in motion pictures. Yessiree Bob! Los Angeles is a regular boomtown thanks to folks like you."

Minta frowned. "Well, Harry, if it's all right with you, it's folks like us who want to get on with our little masquerade tonight."

A forlorn expression suddenly shaded Posner's face. He drooped with a sigh. "Okay. Let's go. The door to Mrs. Collins' room is right over here between the towels and the sheets."

The Arbuckles followed Posner to the hidden door. Once there, he tapped on it twice, lightly with the knuckle of his middle finger, and then waited for a similar response. Several seconds passed before the return signal was heard. He lifted a latch and pushed the door easily.

"Mrs. Collins?"

"Yes."

Posner pushed the door open wide enough for him to go through it into a very dark room. "It's me, Mrs. Collins. Harry Posner. I've got Mr. and Mrs. Arbuckle with me. I can barely see you. Are you okay?"

"I'm fine, Mr. Posner. I'll turn on a lamp."

"No, don't do that."

"It's okay. I put a pillowcase over it. I tested it. It won't make the room too bright." She turned the lamp's on-off switch. "See? It's not too bright in here, but it's better than total darkness."

Posner grinned. "Very clever of you, Mrs. Collins."

Lilian made eye contact with Roscoe. "Herbie is all set to go, Mr. Arbuckle. I left the connecting door a little ajar in order to keep any noise from being heard in the room beyond his. I hope that was a good idea as well."

Roscoe smiled. "Maisy said you were a smart lady, Mrs. Collins. She was right."

"Thank you, Mr. Arbuckle. Now let's get my son out of his room and get you in it."

Minta grabbed her husband's arm. "Good night, Babe. Don't sleep too tight. I wouldn't want anything to happen to you in your sleep."

Roscoe bent over and kissed his wife. "Without you beside me, I doubt that I'll sleep at all. I'll see you in the morning when Herbie and his mother come back to change places with us again." He turned back to Lilian. "Okay, Mrs. Collins, let's go."

She led him to the connecting door and pushed it open. "Herbie?"

His voice came out of the dark. "Right here, Mother." He rose from his bed and crossed the room to Lilian and Roscoe. "Sleep well, Mr. Arbuckle. I'll see you again in the morning."

"Same to you, Herbie." Roscoe peered at Lilian. "Give me just one moment, Mrs. Collins, while I put a pillowcase over a lamp like you did and turn it on. It wouldn't do to have me stumble around in the dark, now would it?"

"No, it wouldn't."

As soon as he placed the pillowcase over an identical lamp in her room and turned it on, Roscoe waved at Lilian and Harry with a big smile as they left the room. He turned to Herbie who seemed to have something on his mind. Before he could say anything, he scrunched up his shoulders with a shake. "It's rather warm in here, don't you think?"

Herbie grinned. "That's funny, Mr. Arbuckle. I thought it was a bit warm when I first came in here, but once Lisa came in it cooled off all of a sudden. Then it warmed up again after she left. There must be a draft coming from somewhere in here. It will probably cool off again after we leave." He chuckled. "Well, don't let the bedbugs bite, sir." He winked. "And don't be frightened by the ghost."

Roscoe stiffened. "What ghost?"

Another laugh came out of Herbie. "Don't know, sir? This is the room where that girl from Seattle died the other night. Lisa told me all about it."

"She did?"

"Yes, she did. I asked her why she screamed down in the ballroom when I had my asthma attack, and she said she screamed because she thought she had seen the ghost of the girl who died in this room the other night. Of course, I joked about it, but she seemed to be quite serious about it."

"I'd be serious about it, too, if I saw a ghost." Arbuckle paused a second. "Have you told anyone else about this?"

"No, just you. Why do you ask?"

Roscoe frowned. "Well, you might want to keep it to yourself. Not everybody believes in those sorts of things."

Herbie nodded. "I see what you mean."

The actor patted the student on the soldier. "Well, Herbie, I'll see you in the morning."

Lilian stuck her head through the doorway. "Herbie, come on. We have to go."

"Yes, Mother."

All three waved back at him as each of them passed through the connecting doorway.

Posner quietly closed the door behind them. Then he pointed to the open secret door across the room. "That's the way out. Lady first. Then you Herbie. I'll be right behind you." As they walked across the room, he turned to Minta. "I'll see you and Mr. Arbuckle at first light, Mrs. Arbuckle. Sleep well. I'm sure there won't be anyone to disturb you until I wake you with the same signal I made with Mrs. Collins."

"I don't think I'll sleep much at all knowing something bad could happen to my Roscoe."

"Don't worry about it, Mrs. Arbuckle. I'm sure nothing bad will happen tonight. You can sleep on that."

Roscoe Arbuckle fell asleep almost as fast as he would have had he been at home with his wife. Not so Minta. She tossed and turned the whole night long with worry. More than once she thought she heard someone entering the bedroom occupied by her husband. Each time she thought she heard someone or something in Roscoe's room she slipped out of her bed and tiptoed to the connecting door to listen with her ear pressed against it. On one occasion, she thought for sure that she heard the connecting door between the middle boudoir and Anna Reikel's room open and close. She waited a few minutes but only heard the all too familiar buzzing hiss of Roscoe's snoring. Her edgy vigilance continued right up until Harry Posner tapped on the secret door to the linen room at the crack of dawn. Relieved, she did likewise on her side.

The panel opened slowly, revealing the bellman, Lilian Collins, and Herbie Collins; the mother and son dressed in nightclothes and holding the same garments they had worn the night before.

Minta sighed and whispered. "Boy, am I glad to see you, Harry."

Posner stepped into the room. "Long night, Mrs. Arbuckle?"

"Too long."

Lilian followed Harry. "Good morning, Mrs. Arbuckle. Did you sleep at all?"

"Not a wink."

"I'm so sorry. I didn't get much rest either."

Herbie came after his mother. "I had good rest. It must have been from all that dancing." He smiled at the memory. "Miss Reikel was an excellent partner."

The bellhop crossed the room to the connecting door to Roscoe's bedchamber. He leaned close to it and listened for any sound coming from within. Of course, only the steady wheezing of Roscoe's labored breathing penetrated the wooden door. Posner waved to Herbie to join him. When the young fellow came close, Harry motioned for him to give an ear to the rhythmic resonance of Roscoe's robust respiration.

Herbie listened for a few seconds, then backed away. "Golly, Mr. Posner, is that Mr. Arbuckle? He sounds like a steam engine."

"He does, doesn't he?" Harry opened the door. "Come on, kid. Let's wake him up and get you in bed again. Maybe you can get a little shut eye before Dr. Newmark comes to see you how you're doing this morning."

Collins followed Posner to bed.

The bellman stopped short of the sleeping actor and turned his head to whisper over his shoulder to Herbie. "It's a good thing not to wake him too suddenly. He's a big man. Who knows how he'll react?" Then Posner leaned over the actor's head just enough so his softly spoken words could be heard. "Time to rise and shine, Mr. Arbuckle."

Roscoe rolled over onto his left side and muttered an incoherent protest.

Harry reached out with his right hand and tapped the sleeping man on his right shoulder. "Mr. Arbuckle, it's time for you to get up and get out of here."

"It's too early, Dear. Let me sleep another hour or so."

"Mr. Arbuckle, it's me … Harry Posner … the bellhop. You have to get up, sir."

Roscoe flipped over onto his right side again and opened his eyes. "Oh, yeah, Harry." He looked over Posner's shoulder. "Hello, Herbie."

Collins smiled. "Good morning, sir."

"Wow!" Arbuckle rubbed his eyes with both fists. "I see you have your pajamas on."

"Yes, sir."

"I guess I'd better get up and get out of here before that nurse comes in here again." Roscoe slid out of bed, shaking his head. "I can't believe how well I slept all night."

Astonishment straightened Posner's back. He gulped. "Mrs. Reikel came in here during the night?"

"Twice, I think. Once for sure. She came in, came over to the bed for a quick peek at me, and then left. If that door between this room and hers hadn't creaked so loud, I would have never heard her. She hardly made any more noise than a cat on the prowl. I covered my head with the blanket when I heard her come in, so I don't know if she knew it was me or not. It was so dark in here; I hope she didn't see my face." He grinned. "I did catch a glimpse of her nightgown. It was so white that it kind of glowed in the dark." He chuckled. "Well, okay, Herbie. The bed's all yours."

Hotel general manager Samuel Whitmore called Dr. Philip Newmark at 7:15 that morning. "Well, Philip, how is your patient this morning?"

"I do not know yet, Sam. I called up there first thing when I woke up and spoke with Mrs. Reikel. I asked her how Mr. Collins was doing, and all she said was he was doing fine when she looked in on him."

"And when was that?"

"She said it was almost three o'clock."

"And she didn't look in on him after that?"

"She didn't say."

"Then you better get up there right away and see how he is. I'll meet you there to see for myself."

"Of course, Sam. I won't go into see him until you get there."

Whitmore thought about Newmark's words. "No, don't wait for me. Go see him as soon as you get there, and I'll wait in the drawing room until you're done examining him."

"Yes, of course. I will see you upstairs in five-ten."

Holding his instrument bag in his left hand and down to his knee, Newmark knocked on the door to suite 510, and Mrs. Reikel answered it. "Good morning, Dr. Newmark." She opened the door wide for him.

"Good morning, Mrs. Reikel. Has our patient stirred yet?"

"I thought I heard him talking in his sleep just before sunrise, but other than that, I have heard nothing since."

"Talking in his sleep? That is a good sign." He entered the suite.

The nurse closed the door behind him, her face smirking much like Lewis Carroll's Cheshire Cat. When the good doctor turned to face her, she altered her look to a moderately malevolent mien initially, then to one less loathsome. "Yes, Doctor, a good sign." She swept past him to the door to Herbie's room. Taking the doorknob in her left hand, she knocked twice on the door with her right. "Mr. Collins, are you awake, sir?" She leaned closer to the door, turning her head to the left to listen for any sounds from within. Not hearing any, she turned the knob and opened the door a few inches. "Mr. Collins, are you awake, sir?" This time she heard the bedding being shifted. "Mr. Collins?"

"Yes, Mrs. Reikel, I'm awake."

The sound of Herbie's voice surprised the nurse, forcing her to stiffen slightly and widen her eyes. She pushed the door open a few more inches to peek through the opening. "Dr. Newmark is here to see you, Mr. Collins."

"Oh, sure. Come right in."

Anna pushed the door open all the way and stepped aside for the physician to enter ahead of her.

Newmark entered the room with a smile. "Good morning, Herbie. I hope you slept well." He walked to the bed, stopping a few feet away.

"I did sleep well, sir. Thank you for asking."

"And how do you feel?"

Herbie smiled at him. "Much better, sir."

"And how is your breathing this morning?"

"So far, my breathing is quite the usual for me."

Newmark nodded. "I am so glad to hear you say so, young man. Now please sit up on the edge of the bed. I want to examine you." As Herbie did as the doctor ordered, Newmark placed his medical valise on the night table, opened it, and removed his stethoscope. "Open your nightshirt please. I want to listen to your lungs and your heart."

Herbie followed the instruction without hesitation, being very well accustomed to this routine. He spread the garment wide and held it in place to give the doctor full access to his chest.

The physician donned the instrument, then rubbed the chest-piece on the breast of his suit coat to warm it before placing it against Herbie's skin. He smiled at the lad. "Warming it thusly makes the procedure more comfortable for the patient." He proceeded with the simple examination. "Remain still please." He applied the chest-piece and listened for the beating of Herbie's heart for several seconds. Then he repeated the test at three other spots on Herbie's chest. "Good, good. Now lean forward some."

Herbie knew exactly what to do, bending his torso fifteen degrees frontward.

Newmark placed the chest-piece beside the patient's left scapula. "Now take a deep breath please."

Turning his head away from the doctor's face, Herbie inhaled as deeply as he could through his nose, then released the air through his mouth.

Newmark listened. "Good." He moved the chest-piece down the end of the scapula. "Another deep breath please."

Herbie followed the instruction perfectly, and the doctor voiced his satisfaction again before repeating the same tests on the right side of Herbie's back and expressing his pleasure over the result again.

The physician straightened up and removed his stethoscope. He grinned broadly at Herbie. "I am happy to tell you, young man, that your heart sounds to be in perfect condition and I did not hear a single wheeze from either of your lungs."

"That's great, Dr. Newmark."

The doctor patted Herbie's right shoulder with his left hand and winked. Then he turned to Mrs. Reikel. "Anna, go see if Mrs. Collins is awake yet, and if she is, then ask her to join us in the drawing room." He turned back to Herbie. "You may get dressed now, while I go meet with your mother so I can tell her the good news as well. I will see you in the drawing room in a few minutes, *ja?*"

"*Javold, Herr Doktor!*"

Newmark chuckled. "Lisa told me you spoke a little German."

Young Collins held up his right thumb and index finger and held them an inch apart. "About this much, sir."

The man chuckled again. "You are a smart boy. Now get dressed and I will see you in the drawing room." He replaced the stethoscope in his medical bag, closed it, grabbed it by the handle, and exited the room. In the drawing room, he saw Sam Whitmore pacing the floor. "Oh, yes, Sam. I was so eager to see my patient that—"

Whitmore ceased walking back and forth, then glared at Newmark. "That you forgot to wait for me before going in to see young Herbie."

"Yes, that is correct."

The hotel boss grimaced. "Well, I can't blame you. If he was my patient, I probably would have done the same thing. So, how is he?"

Before Newmark could answer, Lilian Collins burst into the parlor ahead of Anna Reikel. "How is my Herbie? Your nurse wouldn't tell me anything. So, how is he?"

The physician smiled broadly. "I am pleased to tell you Herbie is awake and feeling quite well, Mrs. Collins. I see no reason at all for him to remain any longer. You may take him home as soon as he dresses."

Whitmore raised his right hand. "Not so fast, Philip. The young man hasn't had his breakfast yet. For that matter, neither have you, Mrs. Collins. You can order room service and dine right here, or if you wish, you can go down and have breakfast at any of our restaurants that serve breakfast. The choice is yours. Or your son's."

Simultaneously, someone knocked on the suite's door and Herbie opened the door to his room.

Mrs. Reikel answered the rapping and found her niece standing in the hall. "Ah, Lisa, you are just in time. Come in. Mr. Collins has only now come from his room. He is quite well this morning."

"*Nein danke da bin ich mir sicher.*"

Too eager to learn how the charade in suite 510 had gone, Maisy left her bed early and called Johnny Fowler to come for her and drive her to the Alexandria. She entered the hotel just as Harry Posner and the Arbuckles exited the service elevator. With fire in her feet, she scurried to the main elevator. She saw the tricky trio traipsing through the lobby toward her. They spotted her and sped up their steps. She backed away and turned to meet them. Seeing that each of them wore a grin from ear to ear, she surmised all had gone well during the night. A smile of her own greeted them as they stopped a few feet from her and formed to a tight half-circle with Roscoe in the center, Minta to his left, and the bellman to his right, each of them short of breath.

"It went well, right?" Maisy shifted her eyes from one to the next and back again until they focused on Roscoe. "Someone sneaked into your room and tried to kill you, right?"

Arbuckle shook his head.

"Well, what did happen?"

"Not much."

Posner answered. "Very simple, Miss Malone." He drew in a deep breath, then continued. "Last night, I got Minta into her room, then I got Roscoe into his." He inhaled again. "And then I got Mrs. Collins and her son out." One more gulp of air. "Then this morning, I got them switched back again." A big smile curled up the corners of his face, wrinkling his cheeks.

With her breath under control now, Minta colored Posner's report with a touch of her own. "I was extremely nervous the whole time, Maisy. I barely slept a wink; I was so worried about Babe. He's not a very light sleeper, you know. He snores a lot, but I'm quite used to it. Every time he stopped tooting during the night, I jumped out of bed to go listen at the door between our rooms to make certain he was okay and no one was in there with him trying to do him no good."

Roscoe embraced his wife with his left arm. "Do you see why I love her so much? She really cares for me."

Maisy wiggled her head with a touch of doubt. "Sure, Roscoe, I get it. She loves you." The girl from Oklahoma shrugged. "Who wouldn't love you, you big lug?"

Posner had his breath back. "Now what do we do, Miss Malone?"

She searched their faces for a second. "I think the three of you should go get some breakfast, while I go up to suite five-ten and see how Lilian and Herbie are doing."

As she exited the elevator on the fifth floor of the original wing of the hotel and turned toward her destination, Maisy caught a glimpse of Lisa Reikel standing in front of the door to suite 510. A single thought struck her mind. Hurry to get to Lisa before she entered the room. She took three quick steps, then stopped as the young woman moved forward, speaking in German as she did. To her dismay, Maisy failed to hear Lisa's words clearly. She slowed her pace and continued to 510, arriving there as Anna Reikel nearly had the door closed. The nurse held it open but not very wide.

"Oh, hello, Miss Malone." She forced a polite smile. "What brings you here so early this morning?"

Maisy returned the friendly greeting. "Good morning to you, too, Mrs. Reikel. I came to see my friends, Mrs. Collins and her son Herbie. I hope they are both doing well."

"Yes, they are both doing quite well, thank you."

"That's good news. May I see them?"

"Please step into the foyer, and I will speak with Mrs. Collins."

"Thank you."

The nurse opened the door wider to allow Maisy to enter. Once the actress moved past her and stood aside in the foyer, Anna closed the door behind her. "Please wait here, Miss Malone."

"Of course."

Mrs. Reikel edged past Maisy to the drawing room doors, opened them only enough for her to enter the parlor, then closed them behind her.

Another thought came to Maisy. *I do believe she doesn't want me to see what's going on in there.* Then she heard muffled talking from the drawing room. First female voices. *Probably Mrs. Reikel and Lilian Collins.* Then a man's voice. *Southern drawl. Must be Mr. Whitmore.* She scored on both accounts.

The drawing room doors opened again, revealing the hotel's boss. "Miss Malone, how do you do? We've never been formally introduced, but I've heard much about you. I am Samuel Whitmore, vice-president, and general manager of the Hotel Alexandria. How nice to see you this morning! Please do come in and join us. Have you had breakfast yet? I was just about to call down to room service and order for all of us. You are most welcome to join us, if you like."

Stunned for a mere second, Maisy stepped into the parlor, her face glowing with real joy. She called up her own family's version of a *below the Mason-Dixon Line* drawl and sweetened it with the thickest dark brown molasses her vocal cords spread on her words. "Why, thank you, sir! I would be most delighted to join you'all for breakfast." She stepped forward a few paces. "Did I hear your name correctly, sir? Was it Mr. Samuel *Whitmore?*" She put extra emphasis on his surname.

"Why, yes, that is correct, Miss Malone. Samuel J. Whitmore from Berkley County, West Virginia."

Maisy pressed the tip of her right index finger to her right cheek and rolled her eyes toward the ceiling for a second before aiming her gaze back on Whitmore. "Berkley County, *West* Virginia, sir?"

Whitmore smiled, a bit puzzled. "Why, yes. *West* Virginia."

"Is the seat of Berkley County a town named Martinsburg?"

"Why, yes, it is. I was born and raised not too far from there. Does that town hold some sort of meaning for you, Miss Malone?"

"Why, yes, it does, Mr. Whitmore. Three years back when I was an entertainer in Vaudeville our troupe happened to play a theater right in Martinsburg. It was called ... now let me think." She squinted her eyes, then snapped her fingers. "The name was Kilmer's China Hall. Yes, I do believe that the name of the theatre where we played the last week of March nineteen-ten and the first two days of April. I recall it perfectly because the theatre caught fire in the early hours of April third. Our troupe was quartered in the Hotel Berkley above the Citizens National Bank. When the fire alarm sounded, we all rushed to the street to see the blaze. While standing on a sidewalk not too far away, I happened to speak to a gentleman who asked me if I was one of the entertainers in the troupe then in town. I replied that I was, and he said he had seen our show twice that week. Finally, he said he was salesman in a local dry goods store and his name was John … Ashby … Whitmore."

The hotel general manager's neck stiffened with astonishment. "My goodness gracious, Miss Malone! That is my younger brother you met that night."

Maisy broke out the best, biggest, brightest, beguiling stage smile that she could muster for the occasion. "No, foolin', Mr. Whitmore? Now don't that beat all?"

"It certainly does, Miss Malone."

"I guess the world is getting smaller every day now, what with Mr. Bell's invention of the telephone and now *Signore Marconi's* invention of the wireless telegraph and then his invention of the radio. I was aboard *Titanic* last year and watched a man send a wire from the ship to a place on shore in Cherbourg, France. I don't know Morse code, but I think he was contacting the police there to be waiting for me on the dock. You see, I was a stowaway on *Titanic*. Lucky for me, I was discovered on the ship before the start of the next leg of the voyage to New York. I might have been one of those poor unfortunate souls who went down with *Titanic*, instead of being here talking to you, Mr. Whitmore."

The general manager's head bobbed. "So, you were aboard that God-forsaken ship?"

"Only long enough to see how elegant it was from stem to stern. Even so, it's still sad all those folks perished because an iceberg struck it so close to the end of its first and only voyage."

"And now here you are in my hotel, and we are so glad to have you, Miss Malone, even if you aren't a guest here. Now if you will excuse me, I must call the kitchen and order breakfast for all of you good people."

Maisy watched him walk away to make the call in Mrs. Reikel's room, then as soon as he was out of sight, she turned her attention to Mrs. Collins who had been waiting patiently on the settee for her to finish her chat with Whitmore. "Good morning, Lilian." She sat down with the freelance writer.

"Good morning, Maisy. I didn't expect to see you here so early."

"I have other matters to tend to today, so I thought I would come by and see how Herbie is doing. Is he awake yet?"

"He's up already and quite chipper this morning. Lisa Reikel is in his room with him right now."

Maisy nodded and glanced around the drawing room. "I don't see Mrs. Reikel. Is she here?"

"She's in the other room over there." Lilian pointed toward the closed door. "She's giving her report on Herbie to Dr. Newmark. He's in there with her."

"Is that why the door is closed?"

"Yes, I suppose it is."

Maisy bobbed her head. "I see." She paused for a second with her view aimed in the direction of the nurse's room. Then she looked back at Lilian. "Well, I was surprised to see Mr. Whitmore up here so bright and early."

"It's his hotel, isn't it?"

"Yes, it is, and that's what concerns me. The three of them in there together."

"Oh?"

Maisy chose a different tack to take. "I wish I could stay and have breakfast with you and Herbie, but Johnny Fowler is waiting for me in the lobby. He's driving me down to Long Beach to see if we can find that nurse Mr. and Mrs. Reynolds told us about. Olga Renius. Her and the doctor she works for, Dr. Oran Newton. I'm hoping they can tell us something about Mr. Donelson's death."

"I wish I were going to Long Beach with you, Maisy. Until this asthma attack of Herbie's, I was hoping you'd take me along with you." She shrugged. "But that's a moot question now, isn't it?"

"I'd love to have you along, Lilian. It would give me a chance to get to know you better. But it's just me and the Arbuckles."

"I wish I could be a little mouse in your purse, just so I could hear you two chat with that doctor and his nurse. I think I'd get a great story for one of the papers I write for."

Maisy smiled comfortingly. "I'm sure when we finally wrap up this case that you'll have a great tale to tell. You and Walt, that is."

Lilian heaved a sigh. "Yes, I know you promised him that he could write the story for *The Times,* which leaves me to write one for the rest of the county. I suppose that's better than nothing."

The actress patted the writer's right hand. "I'm pretty sure Walt will be willing to share the byline with you, Lilian."

"Do you think so?"

Maisy grinned, patted her hand, and winked at her. "He owes me, Lilian." She nodded. "He owes me."

Maisy, the Arbuckles, and Johnny Fowler arrived at the offices of Dr. Perce and Dr. Newton shortly after nine o'clock that same Sunday morning. The three movie actors approached the building, while their driver stayed with his taxi.

Of course, the clinic was closed, but a foot-square wooden sign hanging between the clear glass insert of the door and a Venetian blind covering the entire length of the transparent portion of the entrance read: *Doctor on call 24 hours a day, 7 days a week, 365 days a year. Please ring the doorbell three times if you have an emergency.*

The actress smiled at the big man. "Go ahead, Roscoe, ring the bell. I know you're just dying to do it."

Minta snickered. "It's the little boy in him, Maisy. He loves doing things like this."

With a wide, toothy grin, Arbuckle pushed the button with his right thumb and held it down for a count of two, then repeated the action twice more.

The trio waited patiently until a male voice echoed from a tube above the doorway. "What's your emergency?"

His accent sounded familiar to Maisy. *A twang of Missouri maybe?* She shouted at the tube, trying to imitate the speaker. "We need to speak with a doctor about one of your nurses."

A short pause, then came an annoyed rejoinder. "Now just how is that an emergency?"

Expecting such a response, Maisy smiled. *Definitely Missouri.* She proceeded with the truth. "She just might be in bad way with the law."

"And how is that?"

Feeling frustration fighting its way into the exchange, the amateur sleuth went for the jugular. "She just might be involved in a murder."

After a few seconds pause, the man grumbled. "This better not be some kind of a hoax, ma'am."

"I assure you, sir, it's no hoax."

After another short pause, he asked a question. "Do you know the nurse's name?"

"Olga Renius."

"Olga?"

"Yes, Olga Renius. We're told she's in your employ, sir. She is, isn't she?"

After a moment of silence, he spoke again. "I'll be down in a few minutes. Just wait there."

The sleuth turned to her friends. "I'll bet you a half-penny he's calling the police." She dug in her purse and pulled out an English bronze coin with the likeness of King George the Fifth on one side and on the other sat Britannia the national personification of Great Britain as a helmeted female warrior holding a trident and shield. "I brought a sock full of these back from England last spring. Since half-pennies are no longer minted here in the United States, I use one to bet on sure things. That and it's a great conversation starter whenever I pull it out of my purse. It's kind of a good luck piece as well. I showed it to Charles Chaplin when he was here in Los Angeles last month. He told me if I ever lost this one, then he could get me as many as I want. I didn't tell him I already had jewelry box drawer filled with them. So far, this one has done the trick for me."

At that moment, the clanging emergency bell of a police van was barreling down Pine Avenue and growing louder by the second rudely disrupting the peace and quiet of a Sunday morning.

With a touch of conceit, Maisy grinned at Roscoe. "Did I call it or did I call it?"

Concern suddenly filled Minta's face. "Do you think that's for us?"

Maisy nodded. "Probably, but we have nothing to worry about. We aren't breaking any laws." She bobbled her head. "Well, none that I know of."

The clicking of the door being unlocked interrupted their chat and put them into motion. Maisy placed herself at the peak of their triangle with Roscoe to the right and Minta to the left, each two steps back. They held their collective breaths as the door opened to reveal a man in a white physician's coat, brown trousers, and black shoes. He glared at Maisy for a heartbeat before seeing Roscoe and being taken aback, sure that he recognized the big man but couldn't quite place him just yet.

"Doctor, my name is Maisy Malone."

The medical man returned his focus on her. "Who?"

Minta answered for Maisy. "She's Maisy Malone, and I'm Minta Durfee. This big lug is my husband, Roscoe Arbuckle."

"Arbuckle? That fellow in the moving pictures?"

Roscoe smiled sweetly. "Yes, sir, that's me."

Maisy resumed control of the conversation. "We all work in the motion picture business at Keystone Studio in Edendale."

The doctor squinted at her. "Edendale? Where's that?"

Before she could answer, the police van arrived, and two officers jumped out of the front seat and scurried up to the trio of actors and the doctor. The shorter of the two made eye-contact with the doctor. "Are you Dr. Newton?"

"Yes, officer, I am."

"Are these the people causing the disturbance, sir?"

Newton eased his way between Maisy and Minta to face the two lawmen. "I must apologize to you, gentlemen. I was mistaken about the intent of these good people. They are here to inquire about one of our nurses, so your services won't be needed after all."

The stocky officer squinted at the physician. "Are you certain of that, Dr. Newton?"

"Indubitably, my good fellow."

The taller officer joined in the conversation. "Just the same, Dr, Newton, we need to get all your names for the report we'll have to make when we get back to the station. This big gent I believe I've seen somewhere before."

Newton grinned. "Of course, you have, officer. This is Mr. Roscoe Arbuckle the motion picture actor. This sweet lady is his wife, and this other young lady is Miss Maisy Malone. Both of these ladies are also in the motion picture business. They work at the Keystone Studio up in the Edendale part of Los Angeles."

The shorter officer chuckled. "Sure, that's where I recognize you folks from. You're actors in those farce comedies put out by your studio. You work with Mabel Normand and Mack Sennett, don't you?"

Maisy smiled. "Yes, officer, you're quite correct."

The taller policeman tipped his hat. "Well, it was nice meeting you folks. Hope we meet again, but under better circumstances, of course."

Roscoe offered to shake hands with him. "I hope you enjoy our movies, officer. Thank you for being on the job."

The short lawman frowned at Newton. "Next time you need us, Doc, make sure it's a real emergency before you call. Okay?"

"I'll do just that, officers. Thank you for coming."

Roscoe shook their hands. "Same from me, boys."

Minta giggled as she sidled up to Maisy. "Us, too, officers."

Maisy smiled. "Yes, us, too."

The two policemen turned to leave but hesitated when they saw Johnny Fowler leaning against his Studebaker. Shorty squinted an eye at him. "You can move along, too, bud. Nothing to see here."

Maisy jumped in as usual. "That's our driver, officers."

"Oh, all right. He can stay then."

The lawmen squeezed back into the seat of their van and left Maisy and her friends to converse with Dr. Newton.

"Now, Miss Malone, where were we? You were saying something about our nurse, Miss Renius?"

"Yes, we were, Dr. Newton, but first I believe I should tell you a little about why we're interested in Miss Renius."

"Oh, please do, but let's talk about her inside in my office. Okay?"

At the same time that Maisy and the Arbuckles were interviewing Dr. Newton, Detectives Ed Browning and Bill Ingram were paying another visit to Sutch's Funeral Parlor.

Unlike many undertakers, Wendall Sutch and his family did not live on the premises of his business. They resided at 2075 La Salle Avenue in the western neighborhood of Los Angeles. Because the Los Angeles Railway Yellow Car passed right by his home several times a day, Sutch, although being a man of means, rode the streetcar to work and back six days a week. But on pleasant weather Sundays, he and his family walked to the Congregational Church on El Molino in Pico Heights to worship their Lord and Savior.

Browning and Ingram took the Yellow Car out to the Sutch house, arriving there shortly after ten o'clock. Finding no one at home, they sat on the porch and waited patiently for the family to return from their usual church services.

More than an hour passed before Wendall Sutch, his wife, and two children came strolling down the sidewalk toward their prominent home. Mr. Sutch recognized the detectives as soon as he saw them. Not so his family. His son Arlington posed the question. "Who are those men on the veranda, Dad?"

"Those gentlemen are the two police detectives I told you about at supper the other night."

His wife Gertrude made the next inquiry. "What do you suppose they want now, Dear?"

"They probably want to ask me some more questions about the death of Mrs. Lee."

"I thought the police were through investigating her death."

"So, did I, Dear."

Browning and Ingram stood up as soon as they spotted Mr. Sutch and his family coming down the street. The senior detective nudged his partner and spoke to him out of the side of his mouth. "Let's make this as simple as we can, Bill, like Maisy said. Just the two questions and nothing more … unless he asks us something in return."

"Right, Ed."

The Sutches stopped halfway up the walkway leading from the public sidewalk to their front porch. Mr. Sutch smiled at their visitors. "Good morning, detectives. Allow me to introduce my family. This is my wife Gertrude, our daughter Eleanor, and our son Arlington."

Browning and Ingram tipped their hats to Mrs. Sutch and her two children. Eddie returned the greeting. "Good morning, Mrs. Sutch, Miss Sutch, Master Sutch. I am Detective Sergeant Edward Browning, and this is my partner Detective Sergeant William Ingram."

The mother acknowledged Browning's introduction with a polite smile and an extended right hand. "Good morning, gentlemen."

Each officer returned the gesture with a light grip of her fingers, a gentle movement of them, and a polite tipping of their hats.

The undertaker looked Browning in the eye. "Something tells me you gentlemen want to speak to me again about the late Mrs. Lee. Am I right?"

"Yes, sir, you are quite correct. If you don't mind, Mr. Sutch, this will only take a moment at most."

Sutch faced his wife. "Dear, would you please take the children inside, while I speak with these gentlemen?"

"Certainly, Dear. Come along children."

Arlington protested. "Can't I stay and listen to Dad and these cops talk about the dead lady?"

Mr. Sutch patted his son's right shoulder with his left hand. "You run along with your mother, Arlington, and I'll tell you later about our conversation."

"Aw, Dad!"

"You heard your father, Arlington."

The two policemen and Mr. Sutch watched Mrs. Sutch guide her children up the porch steps and into the house.

"Now, gentlemen, what more can I tell you this time?"

Browning cleared his throat. "Just two questions, Mr. Sutch. First, is it possible that Mrs. Lee was smothered by someone holding a hand over her mouth and pinching her nose at the same time?"

"Good question, detective. The answer is yes but smothering her in that manner would leave some sort of bruising or at least redness to the nose and around the mouth. I saw no signs of either if you recall."

"Yes, now I remember. Okay. What if someone sits on a victim's chest? Can that kill them?"

Sutch bobbed his head. "Yes, it can. Of course, like I explained to you previously, Mrs. Lee died from a cessation of breathing."

"Yes, *Pickwickian syndrome.* I remember that, too."

The undertaker peered deeply into Browning's eyes. "Is it your feeling that Mrs. Lee was murdered by someone sitting on her chest?"

Browning glanced at his partner, then faced Sutch one last time. "Thank you, Mr. Sutch. You've been very helpful again."

"I take it you're not going to answer my question."

The two detectives tipped their hats again and left without saying another word.

Having heard everything, she hoped to hear from Dr. Newton, Maisy herded her friends back into Johnny Fowler's taxi and told him to drive them as safely and as rapidly as he could back to the Hotel Alexandria in Los Angeles.

The cabbie leaned closer to the passenger beside him in the front seat of the Studebaker. "Why all the rush, Maisy?"

"I want to get back to the Alexandria in time to gather everybody for lunch."

"Everybody?"

"Yes, everybody." Maisy huffed a deep breath. "I only hope all of them got the messages I left them this morning."

Maisy delighted in seeing all of her fellow sleuths gathered together in the Hotel Alexandria's second floor Banquet Room Apollo. To her further pleasure, she saw Mack Sennett at the far end of the table, force-feeding black coffee into his primary star at Keystone Studio Mabel Normand. It wouldn't do her popularity any good if her condition caused her to blurt out something inappropriate at this little conclave.

Besides Mack and Mabel sitting at the main table, she saw Milo Cole, Ed and Nealy Browning, Bill and Ruth Ingram, Lilian and Herbie Collins, Roscoe and Minta Arbuckle, Vince and Susie DeDonatis, Walt Ballard, Johnny Fowler, and Nellie Sharpe were there, along with a squad of six uniformed LAPD officers; two guarding each exit.

A second table featured six employees of the hotel, starting with the main man himself Samuel J. Whitmore. Seated with him were the food manager Joseph Reikel and his wife nurse Anna Reikel and their niece Lisa Reikel, the hotel's primary physician Philip Newman, and the man who knew everything that went on in the most luxurious hotel west of the Mississippi River Harry Posner.

Walt Ballard sat with a group of folks that were mostly strangers to the rest of Maisy's group. They included Andrus and Regina Reynolds, Reverend Gustav Kallstedt, Wendall Sutch, Melvin Bresee, Charles Pierce, and five empty chairs, each meant for the guests who had yet to arrive for the impromptu luncheon.

Maisy stood up and tapped her water glass with a teaspoon to get everyone to cease talking and look at her. "May I have your attention please?" She continued to beat on the glass. "Please, would everyone quiet down?" This time the room went silent, and Maisy replaced her spoon on the table. "Thank you, thank you." She scanned the room. "To begin with, I'd like to thank our generous host ... Mr. Samuel Whitmore ... for extending the hospitality of this magnificent hotel to all of us. Thank you, Mr. Whitmore."

Suddenly, Mabel stood up. "Yes, thank you, Mr. Whitmore." Then she clapped her hands to show her appreciation, which encouraged everyone else to follow her example.

Being the Southern gentleman that he had groomed himself to be, Whitmore came to his feet and took a bow. Smiling with gratitude, he waved his right hand at the small crowd to acknowledge their polite show of thankfulness. After one last wave, he sat down again, as did everyone else.

Maisy resumed her introductory speech. "We're all here because a few days ago Mr. Whitmore said something to the press that caught the attention of our friends at the Los Angeles Police Department." She motioned in the direction of Ed Browning and Bill Ingram. "He was quoted in the newspapers that terrible things come in cycles of three. He was referring to the deaths in this hotel of Mrs. America Lee, Mr. George Clarke, and Miss Marjorie Sullivan. All three died in their sleep. All three were pronounced dead by Dr. Philip Newmark and the other physicians at this hotel. Of course, we all know Dr. Newmark saved the life of our friend Herbie Collins last night."

Mabel repeated her earlier gesture, rising, and applauding. "Let's hear it for Dr. Newmark." Everyone else joined in, clapping their hands, and some even cheering.

Newmark stood slowly and acknowledged the accolade in the same manner as Whitmore had. When the applause ceased, he returned to his seat.

Maisy smiled and cleared her throat. "As I was saying before that wonderful tribute for Dr. Newmark, each of the three deceased guests who passed away in this hotel earlier this month ... each one was already ill from some serious condition, disorders that could bring about their deaths at any time day or night. Strangely, all three died in the middle of the night, around the same hour of the early morning. This caused the Los Angeles Police Department to dig a little deeper into their deaths. Detectives Eddie Browning and Bill Ingram were then dispatched to this hotel to interview several people about the sad passing of Miss Marjorie Sullivan. When they finished their questioning here at the Alexandria, they returned to the Central Police Station and reported back to their captain what little they had learned." She paused for dramatic effect. "Then, lo and behold, their captain informed them that the case was closed, and they were not to investigate it any further. Now, how odd was that?" She paused again to survey the room. To her surprise, she thought she saw a vaporous form behind the group of hotel people. Her eyelids fluttered as the thought that she was seeing a ghost swooped through her mind. She wanted to gasp, but quickly suppressed the impulse by looking down and clearing her throat. Confident that she had only imagined the apparition, she forced a smile and looked up again, her view focused on Mabel, the one person in the room who knew her the best. "Well, as I was saying, when I heard about how the two detectives were thwarted in getting to the truth of Miss Sullivan's quite sudden and unexpected demise—" Again, she paused. "Well, my inquisitive nature pushed me into snooping around myself."

Mabel interrupted her friend. "She had help … from a lot of us." She waved her hand at the folks seated at the same table. "And here we are." She patted Sennett's left forearm. "Everybody except Mack here. He had his fill of Maisy and me investigating murders when he found a body on the beach back on Christmas Day. A dead Japanese fisherman. Deader than a mackerel, he was. So dead that Mack almost lost his lunch over it." She tweaked his cheek. "Isn't that right, Sweetie?"

Sennett smiled to hide his frustration with Mabel. He put his arm around her, pulled her to him, and spoke softly. "That'll do, Mabel honey. I'm sure no one wants to hear about our little adventure last winter." He kissed her on her right cheek and whispered in her ear. "Quit embarrassing yourself *and* Maisy. Or do I have to drag you out of here by your hair?"

Mabel winced, then forced a smile. "I'm sorry, folks. I'm a little bit under the weather this morning and not feeling too well."

Mack eased up on her and looked back at Maisy. "As you were saying, Miss Malone?"

Maisy smiled weakly at her boss. "I've got a better idea." She turned back to her audience. "Why don't we have some lunch before I go any further?"

Whitmore stood up. "That's a capital idea, Maisy. How about it, folks? Shall we eat?"

Roscoe slapped the table. "I could eat. So, what do say, folks? It's almost one o'clock. What's on the menu, Mr. Whitmore?"

The hotel's general manager looked at his food service manager. "How about it, Joe?"

Reikel stood up and clapped his hands as loud as he could. When a waiter appeared through the kitchen door, he signaled him with both hands. "Bring on the buffet!"

The waiter turned back to the door. "Bring on the buffet!"

A parade of more waiters then emerged from the kitchen, each carrying either a large platter or a chafing pan. The two dozen dishes contained everything that could make the mouth water: Salmon Mayonnaise, Potted Shrimps, Norwegian Anchovies, Soused Herrings, Plain & Smoked Sardines, Roast Beef, Round of Spiced Beef, Veal & Ham Pie, Virginia & Cumberland Ham, Bologna Sausage, Sliced Brawn (Jelled Pig Brains), Galantine of Chicken, Corned Ox Tongue, Lettuce, Beetroot, Tomatoes (sliced), and an assortment of cheeses: Cheshire, Stilton, Gorgonzola, Edam, Camembert, Roquefort, St. Ivel, Cheddar. To wash it all down, iced draught Munich Beer straight from a barrel that two muscular chaps brought out on a cart.

Mabel turned to Maisy. "This looks like a last meal for a party of condemned prisoners."

"You might say that Mabes. All this food you see coming in was on the luncheon menu for the first-class passengers on *Titanic* the day it struck the iceberg that sank it and fifteen hundred people died."

"Only you would know something like that, Maise. You can be such a ghoul at times."

"Ever see a cow or a hog get butchered, Mabes? Or wring the neck of a chicken?"

"That's exactly what I mean, Maise. Ghoulish things like that."

"That's life on a farm, Mabes. Where do think all that meat and poultry in a butcher's shop comes from?"

"That's not something I think about, Maise."

Sennett elbowed both women. "Will you two please shut up about all that gory stuff? You're spoiling my appetite."

Whitmore stood up. "Mack, your table first."

"Thank you, Sam."

Roscoe slid his chair away from the table and popped to his feet. "You don't have to call me to the buffet twice." He took one step before Minta grabbed the tail of his coat.

"Don't be so fast, Babe! There's plenty of food on that buffet. Save some for the rest of the folks here."

Arbuckle pouted. "Yes, Dear." He stood back and let all the other people at their table go ahead of him.

After everyone had dished the food, they wanted into their own plates and bowls and filled their glasses with chilled beer or cold milk or ice water and returned to their seats, the main door to banquet room opened, and a lone gentleman in a gray suit stepped cautiously inside ahead of two uniformed officers from the Long Beach P.D.

Maisy looked down her table for the right member of her group. "Mrs. Collins, I believe you know that man."

Lilian looked back at Maisy, then at the newcomer and the two men in blue. She smiled. "Yes, I do." She stood up and walked over to the trio of late arrivals. "Good afternoon, Mr. Gardiner. It's nice to see you again."

"Mrs. Collins? Am I in some sort of difficulty here?"

"Pish-tosh, Mr. Gardiner. You're here as my guest. Mine and our hostess Miss Malone." She focused on the policemen. "I didn't expect you two, officers. Have you eaten lunch yet?"

Both shook their heads and spoke simultaneously. "No, ma'am."

"Well, there's plenty for all. Please help yourselves, while I have Mr. Reikel order another table for you." She turned back to Gardiner. "Have you had lunch yet, Mr. Gardiner?"

"No, Mrs. Collins, I haven't. But never mind that. What am I doing here? Who are all of these people?"

"That can wait, Mr. Gardiner. Right now, you should have some lunch with us. Just help yourself and you can sit over there with our other special guests." She pointed at the table where Andrus Reynolds and his wife sat with the two undertakers and the clergyman. "I believe you know Mr. and Mrs. Reynolds. They can tell you what we're all doing here."

"I certainly hope so." The banker took a deep breath and let it out slowly. "Well, I am hungry, and that food does look delicious."

"It is. Now help yourself." With that, Lilian returned to her seat, nodding at Maisy once she sat down.

Mabel leaned close to Maisy. "Who's that?"

Maisy shrugged. "Another one of our guests of honor."

"Are you expecting more guests of honor?"

"I hope so."

"How many?"

Maisy rolled her eyes. "Maybe four."

Mabel shook her head. "I sure hope you know what you're doing."

"So do I, Mabes. So do I."

The luncheon continued as Maisy had hoped. All ate with gusto, especially Mack and Roscoe, but not so much the six people who worked at the Alexandria. All of them seemed a little nervous about the presence of Los Angeles policemen and the addition of the two Long Beach officers. The talk at their table remained rather restrained. The least loquacious being the youngest of them: Lisa Reikel

As the diners gradually finished consuming their meals, Maisy kept an eye on the main door.

Sennett took notice of her touch of anxiety. "What's troubling you, Malone?"

Before Maisy could respond, Mabel answered for her. "She's okay, Nappy. She's just worried that the rest of her guests won't show up." The Keystone star attraction nodded at the four empty chairs across the room. "I guess her case hangs on those seats being filled pretty soon or we're all leaving here with full bellies and empty expectations."

At that moment, the main entrance to the banquet room opened, and Preston Lewis, the hotel's lead desk clerk, stepped inside. He gazed around the room until he saw Sam Whitmore looking back at him. The hotel's vice-president raised his right-hand chest high and signaled Lewis to come to him with a wag of his index finger. The clerk nodded and immediately crossed the room to his boss.

"What is it, Preston?"

Lewis bent over and whispered in Whitmore's ear. "Sir, there are four people outside who say they were invited to this luncheon. Should I let them in?"

"That's not up to me, Preston. Go over and ask Miss Malone. This is her party."

"Yes, of course, sir."

Lewis straightened up, took a deep breath, and tried to look casual as he strolled across the room to Maisy's table. He approached her with a touch of anxiety. "Miss Malone? May I have a word with you?"

Maisy smiled at him. "Are you going to tell me my last four guests have finally arrived?"

The clerk flinched. "You were expecting them?"

"Yes, I was, Mr. Lewis. Please show them in."

"Yes, of course." He headed for the door.

Maisy stood up, clinking her water glass with a teaspoon again. "If I can please have everyone's attention again?"

In seconds, the room fell silent.

"I'm happy to tell you that our final four guests have arrived."

Lewis opened the door. "Please come in, gentlemen, miss." He held the door wide for them to enter. "Miss Malone is expecting you."

As the newcomers entered the room, Maisy indicated them to the diners. "To all of you who don't know these people, I'd like you to meet Mr. Daniel Conklin and Mr. Arthur Martinet, desk clerks at the Travers Hotel. And Dr. Oran Newton and Miss Olga Renius, a nurse at

Dr. Newton's clinic in Long Beach." She paused. "These good people and Mr. William Gardiner who arrived earlier with an escort of police officers from Long Beach ... they have all come here to identify Mrs. Minnie Lightfreit and Mrs. Maggie Engeltod for the Los Angeles Police Department detectives who are here to arrest one of them for the three murders committed in this hotel these past few weeks."

As expected, the entire room instantly filled with chatter by all but Ed Browning, Bill Ingram, Lilian Collins, and the six people sitting at the middle table.

Maisy looked at Browning. "Eddie, would you like to take it from here? After all, it's your case."

The detective shook his head. "No, Maisy, you tell them."

Lilian interjected her opinion. "Yes, Maisy, you should tell us. You put the whole thing together. So, go ahead and explain it to all of us."

Mabel couldn't resist. "Go ahead, Malone. Spill!"

"Okay, I will." She cleared her throat. "As I said earlier, each of the three deceased guests who passed away in this hotel earlier this month ... each one was already ill from another serious condition, disorders that could bring about their deaths at any time day or night. All three died in the middle of the night, around the same hour of the early morning. Enter the Los Angeles Police Department to dig a little deeper into their deaths. Detectives Ed Browning and Bill Ingram came to this hotel to interview several people about the passing of Miss Marjorie Sullivan, the last victim. When they finished here at this hotel, they returned to the Central Police Station to report to their captain what little they had learned. Then, their captain informed them that the case was closed and they were not to investigate it any further. This struck Detective Browning as being odd. He contacted me and asked me what I thought about Miss Sullivan's sudden demise when her sister and mother said she seemed to be getting better. That's when I started snooping into this case myself.

"I immediately started gathering people to help me. All of them are here this afternoon and sitting at this table, with the exceptions of Mack and Mabel here and Walt Ballard over there sitting with our star witnesses. That's right. Our star witnesses. Each of those good people knew a piece to this murder puzzle, but none of them knew all of it, which is why they're here ... to verify their parts for the rest of us.

"So, let's start with Mr. Sutch, Mr. Pierce, and Mr. Bresee. They're three of the best undertakers in Los Angeles. Maybe the best in the whole county. These three auspicious gentlemen each did something that they were not charged to do by the county coroner. They performed partial autopsies on the three ailing victims ... who were ... *murdered* ... in this very hotel."

Just as she expected, the room filled with gasps, although not everyone showed such shock.

Maisy noted that the four men and two women employees of the Alexandria remained unshaken by her sudden statement. Shifting back to the trio of understakers, she resumed her discourse. "Gentlemen, what were your conclusions on how Mrs. Lee, Mr. Clarke, and Miss Sullivan died? Mr. Sutch, you did the autopsy on Mrs. Lee. What was your conclusion, sir?"

Sutch stood up and faced Maisy's table first. "Mrs. Lee may have died from *Pickwickian syndrome*."

"Would you please explain what that is, Mr. Sutch?"

"Yes, of course. *Pickwickian syndrome* happens to people who are overly overweight. The medical term for it is 'obesity hypoventilation syndrome.' In more clinical terms, this condition is defined as the presence of awake alveolar hypoventilation characterized by daytime hypercapnia—"

Maisy laughed, interrupting the mortician's medical explanation.

Sutch's expression turned from medical lecture to common sense. "Is there a problem, Miss Malone?"

She nodded. "Well, just a little one, sir. I believe only a handful of people in this room know what you're talking about. In other words, would you mind putting all that in terms we common folks can absorb in our less educated brains?"

He smiled back at Maisy. "Yes, of course, Miss Malone. Basically, an obese person dies from self-suffocation due to too much carbon dioxide in the bloodstream."

"And this is how Mrs. Lee died?"

"Not quite."

"And how is *that*, Mr. Sutch?"

"I tested Mrs. Lee's blood for carbon dioxide content."

"And what were your findings, sir?"

Sutch cleared his throat. "I found her arterial $PaCO_2$ to be only half the amount necessary to bring on death."

"Meaning ... ?"

"Meaning she did not die from *Pickwickian syndrome*."

"So, what did she die from?"

Sutch hesitated, knowing he had the complete attention of every person in the room. He cleared his throat. "Ahem! It's my professional opinion that Mrs. Lee died at the hands … and body of a murderer … or murderers."

More gasps from the audience.

Maisy resumed her dialog with Mr. Sutch. "Hands and body, sir?"

"Yes, someone sat on her chest when she was in bed and possibly covered her mouth and nose with his or her hands in order to smother her, although I doubt the latter because there were no signs of her being suffocated in this manner."

Shock and awe flooded the room again.

When silence prevailed once more, Maisy added her own opinion. "In other words, she was definitely murdered."

"Precisely!"

Maisy paused for dramatic effect. "Is there historical precedent for murdering someone in this manner, sir?"

"I'm certain there is, but off the top of my head I can't recall any such cases."

"How about the Burke and Hare murders in eighteen-twenty-eight Scotland? Would you say that would be a sufficient example of such a dastardly way of committing murder?"

"Why yes! Absolutely!"

Another cacophonic round of disbelief buzzed through the room.

Maisy waited several seconds for quiet to resume. "Mr. Pierce, would you please tell us about the cause of Mr. Clarke's demise?"

Sutch sat down, and Charles Pierce stood up. "Certainly, Miss Malone. George Clarke died from a cerebral hemorrhage."

"Would you please explain that term, sir?"

"Yes, of course. A cerebral hemorrhage is commonly referred to as bleeding of the brain or a brain bleed. This condition can be caused by pulmonary hypertension."

"And that is?"

"Pulmonary hypertension is high blood pressure that affects the arteries in the lungs. Blood is pumped from the right side of the heart to the lungs, where it picks up oxygen. The oxygenated blood returns to the left side of the heart and is then pumped to the rest of the body. Pulmonary hypertension narrows the lung arteries, making it harder for blood to circulate through the lungs. Over time, this side of the heart may enlarge and become weaker, making it harder to keep up with the body's demands and lead to eventual death by a number of causes."

Maisy nodded. "And one of these was the cause for Mr. Clarke's demise, sir?"

Pierce shook his head. "No, I don't believe so."

"You don't believe so? Why not?"

"Because, Miss Malone, I didn't find any blood clots anywhere in Mr. Clarke's body. According to his physician, Dr. Newmark, Mr. Clarke was suffering from hypertension prior to his death, but it wasn't so severe yet to bring about his demise. You see, Miss Malone, it's my opinion that Mr. Clarke died from a burst artery in his brain that was caused by a deprivation of oxygen by some external force."

"Some external force? And what would that be, sir?"

Pierce hesitated to reply as he scanned the room. "It's my belief, Miss Malone, that some*one* or some-*two* persons applied the external force by covering Mr. Clarke's nose and mouth and sitting on his chest; thereby, depriving him of oxygen and increasing his blood pressure to the point that the artery in his brain burst and thus killed him. In short, Miss Malone, Mr. Clarke *was* murdered. Just like the victims of Burke and Hare in Scotland nearly a century ago."

Once again, the room filled with gasps and sudden outbursts of shock and disbelief.

And Maisy waited patiently until quiet returned before speaking to the undertaker one last time. "Thank you, Mr. Pierce. You've been very informative, sir."

"You are more than welcome, Miss Malone." Pierce sat down.

"Mr. Bresee, thank you, sir, for joining us for lunch today."

Melvin Bresee stood up slowly. "The honor is mine, Miss Malone. I'm quite pleased to be here with my colleagues and to share in this most delicious luncheon." He turned toward the hotel's vice-president and general manager. "Thank you, Mr. Whitmore, for such a bountiful buffet."

Whitmore reacted with a smile and a nod for the mortician but offered no vocal response.

Bresee faced Maisy again. "How may I be of service to you and your group, Miss Malone?"

Maisy cleared her throat to get everyone's attention. "Mr. Bresee, I understand you helped Assistant County Coroner Seager with the autopsy of Miss Marjorie Sullivan this past week. Is that correct?"

"No, Miss Malone, it is not correct."

"Then who did perform the autopsy?"

"No one, Miss Malone."

"No one?"

"No one. The girl's mother forbade it. And … since Dr. Newmark and Dr. Seager declared Miss Sullivan died from natural causes and there was no reason to suspect foul play in her death, no autopsy was performed."

"I see. So, what was the official verdict by Dr. Seager?"

Bresee glanced at Whitmore's table before answering Maisy. "Dr. Seager concluded Miss Sullivan died from pulmonary tuberculosis. In other words, natural causes."

"I see. So, what made you think differently, sir?"

A deafening silence of expectation shrouded the room as all eyes focused on the undertaker.

Bresee reached inside his coat and brought out his journal. "I have your answer right here, Miss Malone. This is my current record book. I have kept one for all the funerals I have worked since I joined my father and brother in our family's funeral parlor business fourteen years ago." He opened the book and flipped a few pages to find the entry he wished to share with the audience. "Wednesday, March nineteenth. Deceased: Miss Marjorie Sullivan. Pronounced dead by P. Newmark, M.D. Hotel Alexandria. Cause of death: Heart failure due to phthisis. Physician's notes: Mother does not want autopsy, embalming only for immediate travel to Seattle for funeral." He lowered the book. "Having attended medical school, I was rather curious about Dr. Newmark's determination of the young woman's cause of death. He wrote *phthisis*. Unaware of that ailment, I looked it up in my medical journal."

"And what did you find, Mr. Bresee?"

"I discovered phthisis is a Latin word derived from the Greek word *phthinein*, which means *to decay*. Phthisis is a disease better known as pulmonary tuberculosis."

"Pulmonary tuberculosis?"

"Yes, that's correct."

A murmur rippled through the room.

"Excuse me, Mr. Bresee, but I've always been told tuberculosis is a very infectious disease."

"It is."

Maisy tilted her head to the right, her expression quite puzzled. "I don't quite understand, Mr. Bresee. If Miss Sullivan was suffering from pulmonary tuberculosis, then why wasn't she in a hospital or, for that matter, in a sanitarium instead of a suite here at the Hotel Alexandria? I mean, her ailment was contagious, was it not?"

Appearing even more professorial, Bresee tapped his lips with his right index finger before answering. "That's a very good question, Miss Malone." He shifted his piercing eyes in the direction of the employee table. "Perhaps Dr. Newmark can answer it for you."

She raised her hand to prevent Newmark from answering. "Yes, perhaps, but not just yet, Mr. Bresee. For the moment, I'd like you to tell us what you did when you were preparing Miss Sullivan's body for the trip to Seattle."

"Yes, of course." He cleared his throat. "I don't usually question the physician who pronounces a person dead and the cause or causes of that person's demise. But in this case, like you, Miss Malone, I was very curious about Dr. Newmark pronouncing her cause of death to be by heart failure due to phthisis, which is, as I said before, pulmonary tuberculosis. I learned in medical school that if this were the case with Miss Sullivan, then her lungs should have been filled with phlegm. That word comes into our language from the French word *fleume*, which was derived from the Latin word *phlegma*, which means *clammy moisture of the body*. The Romans took it from the Greeks. Their meaning of the word was *inflammation*, which was derived from *phlegein*, which means *to burn*. In our language today, most people refer to phlegm as mucus. They would be correct in doing so, but educated people in the medical field call mucus *phlegm* because they know how to spell it."

Maisy laughed lightly at the undertaker's joke, inciting a round of laughter from most of the other people in the room.

Incensed by the general reaction to Bresee's remark, Bill Ingram jumped to his feet and pounded the table with his right fist. "What's wrong with you people? Murder is no laughing matter. This is serious business here. Five people have died under suspicious circumstances these past few weeks, and you people act like this is one of those farcical comedies Mr. Sennett churns out at his funny factory."

Ed Browning reached over and took a firm hold on Ingram's right forearm. "Easy there, Bill. No one's—"

Ingram jerked his arm from his partner's grasp. "No, Ed, I won't … I can't take it easy. We're dealing with murder here, and there's not a thing funny about that." He faced Maisy. "Why don't you get on with it, *Miss Malone*? You're the detective in charge here. So, why don't you point your finger and tell us who's the killer in this room, so we can arrest them and haul the culprit off to jail?"

Vince DeDonatis jumped angrily to his feet. "That's enough, Bill. I want to know who the killer *or* killers are as much as anyone here. But that's not enough for me. You're a detective. Don't you want to learn how she came to her conclusion about who the guilty person is *or* persons are? I know I sure as Hell do."

Another rumble of prattle filled two-thirds of the room. Only the people at Whitmore's table sat silent.

Maisy cast an eye over the diners and nodded. "Detective Ingram has a good point. This is taking longer than I had intended." Her focus returned to the undertaker. "Thank you so much for enlightening us with your language lecture, Mr. Bresee, but I must agree with Bill to some extent. So, would you please get to the crux of your findings?"

"Certainly, Miss Malone."

Ingram and DeDonatis both sat down and waited for Bresee to resume revealing the imperative piece of evidence he had found.

"As I was saying about Miss Sullivan's cause of death, she did die from heart failure, but her heart failing suddenly in the middle of the night was not precipitated by pulmonary tuberculosis. How do I know this? I inserted a flexible tube down Miss Sullivan's main bronchus and then into the left bronchus, where I used a pump to remove any and all of the phlegm I could. I repeated this process with the right bronchus. The results were less than an ounce of phlegm in total from both lungs." With a stern eye, he aimed his attention on Dr. Newmark but said nothing as the physician shifted nervously in his seat.

Having spent seven years in Vaudeville, Maisy recognized a cue when she heard one. "Are you saying that wasn't enough phlegm in her lungs to impede the beating of her heart?"

"That is exactly what I am saying, Miss Malone."

Maisy nodded, then stared directly at the hotel's physician. "What do you have to say about that, Dr. Newmark? Do you still stand by your diagnosis that Miss Sullivan died from phthisis?"

Newmark exhaled heavily and remained silent.

"Dr. Newmark, I think everyone present would like to hear your answer, sir."

Now appearing quite fearful, his reply trickled softly through his lips. "Perhaps I was too quick with it."

"Would you say that a little louder, Doctor?"

Newmark grimaced, slapped the palm of his hand on the table, and popped erect. "Yes, I was too quick with my diagnosis. Is that what you wanted me to say, Miss Malone? Yes, I made my diagnosis too quickly. I came to that conclusion because I had been treating the girl for two weeks and was very much aware of her condition and how it could be fatal at any time. When I examined her on her death bed, I simply assumed phthisis had been the cause of her heart to stop." He aimed his angry face at Bresee. "I didn't have the luxury of time to make a more thorough diagnosis like you did, sir. I'm certain that had I the time that I would have come to the same conclusion as you, sir." He turned back to Maisy. "Does that satisfy you now, Miss Malone?"

Without wasting another second, Maisy aimed her focus on the two desk clerks from the Travers Hotel. "Mr. Conklin, Mr. Martinet, my next question is for you gentlemen. Is there anyone in this room, besides Detectives Browning and Ingram, that either of you … or both of you … recognize?"

Martinet stood up. "Yes, there is, Miss Malone."

Conklin joined Martinet. "Same with me, Miss Malone."

"And who would that be, gentlemen?"

The senior clerk pointed in the direction of the table where Whitmore, Newmark, Posner, and the Reikels sat. "That young woman sitting with the older woman and the four gentlemen with them."

"Do you mean Miss Lisa Reikel?"

Martinet sneered. "Yes, her. But we knew her as Mrs. Minnie Lightfreit. She was a chambermaid at the Travers Hotel for a short time this winter."

Joe Reikel glared at his niece. "Lisa, is this true?"

Maisy answered for her. "Yes, Mr. Reikel, it's true. Your niece was working at the Travers Hotel under an assumed name. And if you had read the newspapers, then you would know that she is the very same chambermaid who found Mr. Claudius Peters hanging from the frame of his bed in his room. Isn't that right, Lisa?"

The girl hesitated before answering. "Yes, that is quite correct, Miss Malone. I did find him, the poor man. I called for help, and Mr. Conklin called for an ambulance. When I found Mr. Peters, he was hanging from the head of his bedstead."

"The head of his bedstead? Was the bed's frame standing on its end?"

"Yes, that is correct. I pulled it out, and the bed dropped back on the floor."

"Was he breathing when you found him?"

"I do not recall if he was breathing or not. He still had his necktie around his throat, choking him. By the time I could get it loose, he was already unconscious. That's when Mr. Conklin came into the room."

Maisy looked at the clerk. "Is that right, Mr. Conklin?"

Reluctantly, the clerk nodded. "Yes, that's right. I shook him very vigorously, and he started breathing again, but he didn't become conscious again. Then the ambulance attendants arrived and loaded him on a stretcher and took him to the receiving hospital. That was the last I saw of him."

Maisy nodded. "I have one more question for you, Lisa. Why did you give Mr. Martinet an assumed name instead of your real name?"

Anna Reikel stood up. "I can answer that, Miss Malone. I told her to do it."

"But why?"

Anna spoke with some authority. "Reikel is a very well-known name in the hotels of this city, Miss Malone, because nearly every hotel with a restaurant knows the best food manager in this city is my husband."

Maisy smiled. "I can believe that because I've eaten here several times now, and the food is always wonderfully delicious." She sighed. "That clears up one death. From what Detectives Browning and Ingram have told me and from what I've heard here this afternoon, I'm inclined to believe the coroner was correct. Mr. Claudius Peters did take his own life."

Ed Browning stood up and faced Lisa Reikel. "So does the Los Angeles Police Department."

"Thank you, Detective Browning." She waited for him to sit again. "That brings us to the death of Mr. Charles Donelson of Long Beach. Dr. Newton, would you please tell us about Mr. Donelson's passing?"

The physician stood up to address the group. "I was one of Mr. Donelson's doctors. My partner, Dr. Lewis Perce, could not be here with me today because he is on call at Seaside Hospital in Long Beach. However, I have brought one of our nurses with me because she was Mr. Donelson's primary home care nurse." He turned to the young woman seated next to him. "Olga, would you please rise?" As she assented to his request, Newton introduced her. "This young woman is Miss Olga Renius. Like Mr. Donelson, she is Swedish and speaks their language quite fluently."

Olga bowed her head slightly as she looked at Maisy and then the other people at her table. For the moment, she ignored Whitmore and the five other Alexandria employees at his table. She sat down again as Dr. Newton resumed his talk.

"When Mr. Donelson's health began to weaken at the beginning of the New Year, he came to our clinic to be examined. Dr. Perce and I

LARRY NAMES

discovered Mr. Donelson's blood pressure was a little high. Much more concerning to us was Mr. Donelson's heart rate was quite irregular. Dr. Perce and I read up on his ailment in the latest medical journals. The latest of these came from two doctors named Jolly and Ritchie at the Royal Infirmary in Scotland. They published their findings on *Auricular Flutter,* which is their name for this heart disease. Some physicians refer to it as irregular heartbeat, and others call it atrial fibrillation. In short, it's a disease where the heart doesn't work at a normal rhythm, causing the blood to thicken and even clot. It was one of those clots that may have killed Mr. Donelson. However, neither Dr. Perce nor I can be one hundred percent positive of this. Why? Because one of the symptoms of atrial fibrillation is an acute shortness of breath. Patients find it hard to breathe and must force themselves to breathe until their blood is properly oxygenated again and their breathing becomes normal. If the patient is unable to do this immediately upon experiencing a shortness of breath, then he will lose consciousness and, in most cases ... expire. This was Dr. Perce's immediate conclusion about Mr. Donelson when we initially examined him and pronounced him dead. Then I reminded him that Mr. Donelson could have died from a stroke. This seemed to be the easier choice for his cause of death, so that was why we chose it. We felt a blood clot in the brain was easier for the coroner to accept."

Maisy tilted her head forward. "So, what changed your mind, Dr. Newton?"

"You did, Miss Malone, when you visited me this morning at my office. I hadn't given any thought to Mr. Donelson being murdered until you told me about the three deaths this month here at this hotel and the possible murder of a guest at another hotel at the same time. It was you, Miss Malone, that got me to thinking that Mr. Donelson just might have been murdered as well. Five deaths in less than three weeks, all under suspicious circumstances? Each of them could have been by natural causes just like the coroner said. But you convinced me to look further into these cases."

"And what are your thoughts now, Dr. Newton?"

"I believe you need a motive for someone to want to murder these five people."

Instantly, Maisy leaned forward and slapped the table as hard as she could, creating a sudden reverberation that echoed throughout the room. She shook her right index finger at the physician. "Precisely, Doctor, which is why we invited the last gentleman at your table to join us here this afternoon." She smiled at the fellow in question. "Mr.

Gardiner, would you please stand up and tell us what you know about Mr. Donelson's death?"

William J. Gardiner, the first cashier at the Exchange National Bank in Long Beach, rose slowly with dignity. "I'm most delighted to do so, Miss Malone. As you said earlier, I have come here to identify the nurse who cared for Mr. Donelson in his last days. As you already know, that lady is sitting at this table, Miss Olga Renius. She did care for Mr. Donelson for the better part of two months. I know so because she accompanied him to our bank on several occasions during that time when Mr. Donelson came in to deposit his earnings at the shipyard. Then just before his death, a different woman came into the bank with Mr. Donelson. As I waited on him, I asked him about the woman. He would only say she was another nurse. When I pressed him about Miss Renius, he would only say Miss Renius was away for the day and this woman was substituting for her. Unfortunately, I didn't get a very good look at her then or when I saw her with him after he left the Chicago restaurant where I usually take my lunch. On both occasions, she had a scarf wrapped around her head and most of her face. However, I did see her eyes, eyebrows, and nose, and I noted her height and stature. She was tall like Miss Renius, but unlike Miss Renius, she was heavy set. Not plump, but certainly more muscular."

Before Gardiner could finish his statement, Lisa Reikel shrieked and pointed at the curtain covering the door to the kitchen. "*Geist! Geist!*" ("Ghost! Ghost!") Then tears burst from her eyes and ran down her cheeks. "I am so sorry, Miss Sullivan. Please believe me. I am so very sorry."

Everyone in the room looked at Lisa. Then some of them directed their focus on the curtain. All seemed puzzled; all but Maisy Malone and Herbie Collins. They saw the phantasm in front of the drapery; a young woman in a white dress pointing at the Lisa and the other people at her table.

Still quite terrified, Lisa then popped to her feet, shook her right index finger at her aunt, and shouted in German. "*Ich habe dir gesagt, dass ich mit diesem Geschäft nichts zu tun haben will. Sie haben Fräulein Sullivan ermordet, nicht mich.*" ("I told you that I didn't want to have anything to do with this business. You murdered Miss Sullivan, not me!") Still pointing at Mrs. Reikel, she turned to Maisy and declared in English. "She did it. She murdered Miss Sullivan. She wanted me to help, but I refused. I admit that I was in the room when she killed Miss Sullivan, but I did nothing to aid her. She did it. She said she was merely checking on her because Dr. Newmark had instructed her to do so. But she lied. She killed that girl. I didn't." She looked back at the fading form. "Please forgive me for not stopping her. Please!"

The hotel physician jumped to his feet. "I did no such thing. I did not give Anna any such instruction. She murdered the girl in her sleep in the same manner that those two nefarious Scotsmen murdered their victims in Scotland nearly a hundred years ago. I know that is how she did it. I am a physician, not a murderer."

Maisy sneered at Newmark. "Do you mean William Burke and his accomplice William Hare? The two men who murdered sixteen people over a period of ten months by smothering them with their hands as they sat on their chests?"

Newmark nodded once. "Yes, those evil men!"

"And how did they use their hands to smother their victims?"

"One of them would pinch off the victim's nose, while the other would put a hand over the victim's mouth."

Maisy glared at the hotel's resident physician. "And you knew this all along, Dr. Newmark?"

The doctor started to answer her question but thought better of it. Instead, he shook his head and muttered softly. "I have nothing more to say on this matter."

Maisy snorted a laugh. "You've said enough, Doctor." She focused on the hotel's general manager. "What have you got to say about these three deaths in your hotel, Mr. Whitmore?"

The boss shook his head and shrugged. "This is all news to me."

A smirk painted Maisy's expression. "Oh, really, Mr. Whitmore? Do you mean to tell me you didn't know Mrs. Lee and Mr. Clarke were *robbed* ... as well as ... *murdered?*"

"I was unaware of both ... those ..."

Walt Ballard jumped up. "Oh, come now, Mr. Whitmore. You knew perfectly well they were robbed. You paid off my newspaper to keep that fact out of the story we printed, and since I didn't see that fact printed in any other newspaper that carried the stories of Mrs. Lee and Mr. Clarke dying in your hotel, then I can assume you paid off their publishers as well. That must have cost you a pretty penny, sir."

Whitmore's head drooped. "Yes ... yes, it did. A thousand dollars each."

Maisy slapped her hand on the table again. "There's your motive, everyone. Now the question is, why was Miss Sullivan murdered?"

All the others focused on Whitmore, but he remained silent.

Ballard chortled. "I can answer that one, too, Maisy."

Attention shifted to the reporter.

"If you recall Mr. Whitmore's statement in the story in my paper ... which, by the way, I wrote ... his statement where he said ... and I quote ..." He pulled a newspaper clipping from his inside coat pocket, held it up for all to see, and read from it. "And I quote, 'This is not a superstition, but the course of events has proved it over and over again to be a psychological fact.' He went on to say, 'When I was notified this morning of the passing away of Miss Sullivan, *all of my suspense ... was at an end.*' He went on to say, 'I was able to relax and stop wondering who would be ... *the third.*' Unquote." He replaced the clipping in his coat pocket. "I believe, you Maisy, figured out that Miss Sullivan was murdered by someone in this hotel just to soothe the nerves of ... *his* ... *or her* ... boss."

A smug smile curled the corners of Maisy's lips. "Is that true, Mr. Whitmore?"

Before the general manager could respond, Joe Reikel jumped to his feet and shook his fist at his wife. "Yes, it's true. You murdered all three of those people in this hotel, and I am quite certain you had something to do with the murder of that poor man in Long Beach as well when you were working for Dr. Newton there under the name of ... *Maggie Engeltod.* Such a name! But perfect for you. Maggie ... the *Angel of Death!* You murdered Mrs. Lee and Mr. Clarke so you could steal their valuables. You didn't think I knew this? I know where you hide your money." He grinned quite mischievously. "You didn't know that did you?" He held up a handful of paper money. "See?"

Her eyes bulging, Anna shouted at him. "That money is mine!"

"No, Anna, it's not. It's mine now."

LAPD Detectives Ed Browning and Bill Ingram rose from their seats very casually and in sync. Browning smiled smugly. "And you're going to need it, Mr. Reikel. We're placing you under arrest as an accessory to the three murders Mrs. Reikel committed in our city."

"How can you do that? I didn't murder anyone."

"No, you didn't, Mr. Reikel, but you knew your wife had and you said nothing about it."

Maisy cleared her throat. "Sorry, Eddie, but I don't think you can prove that in court. The only witness you would have to him knowing she had murdered three people ... or four ... would be his wife, and the spousal privilege law of eighteen-fifty-three forbids both spouses from testifying for or against the other spouse."

Browning frowned and shook his head. "How do you know so much about the law, Maisy?"

"I read a lot."

"Okay, you got me there. But what about Lisa testifying against her aunt?"

Maisy turned to the niece. "What do you say about that, Lisa? Would you be willing to testify against your aunt?"

Still standing, Lisa shrugged. "I do not know, Miss Malone. I was only with her when she murdered Miss Sullivan in order to satisfy Mr. Whitmore's need to have a third death to make his belief that bad things happen in cycles of three."

Harry Posner jumped out of his seat. "I can testify that Mrs. Reikel and Lisa sneaked into Miss Sullivan's room the night she died."

Detective Browning aimed his eyes at Posner. "How would you do that, Mr. Posner?"

A big grin spread across the bellman's face. "I just happened to be coming out of the elevator when I saw Mrs. Reikel and Lisa going into the linen closet. I wondered what they might be up to, so I followed them." He paused for dramatic effect. "That's when I saw them opening the utility door to Mrs. Sullivan's bedroom. The mother was a sound sleeper, so she never stirred until her other daughter woke her up to tell her Miss Marjorie had died in her sleep."

Maisy played defense lawyer again. "But you didn't actually see Mrs. Reikel murder Miss Sullivan, did you?"

Posner frowned and shook his head. "No, Miss Malone. I didn't actually see her do the dirty deed, but I should think Miss Lisa did."

Browning spoke again. "Then we should arrest you, Miss Reikel."

"But I did not do anything. I did not kill anyone."

Maisy plowed in. "But you didn't do anything to stop your aunt from murdering Miss Sullivan, did you, Lisa?"

"No, but —"

Ingram threw the next punch. "Then you're as guilty of murder as she is, Miss Reikel."

Browning tossed her a life preserver. "Or you can agree to testify against your aunt and get on with your own life." He paused. "The same goes for the rest of you." He pointed at the other five people around Anna. "Testify against her, and you can all go on with your own lives."

Anna Reikel burst out laughing. "You will never get *them all* to do that. And you have no proof I killed those other people."

"And why is that Mrs. Reikel?"

"I know too much about them. They will go to the gallows with me if they do." She continued cackling.

Maisy shook her head. "No, Anna, they won't. You see, they may be a little unenlightened, but they aren't crazy … like you. They know something you don't."

The murderess replied in her native tongue. *"Ja? Und was ist das?"* ("Yes? And what is that?")

"Sie verstehen, Frau Reikel, dass Mord … nicht zum Lachen ist." Maisy scanned the room at the many questioning faces. She smiled as she saw the girl in the white dress wave farewell to her, then turn and blow a kiss to a smiling Herbie Collins who was blinking through a few final tears. Then Maisy fought off her own sobbing before translating her last remark to Anna Reikel. With a wave of her arm to the gathering, she spoke proudly to the group. "They understand, Mrs. Reikel, … that … murder is no laughing matter."

A MAISY MALONE MYSTERY
AFTERWORD

If you've enjoyed this book you might like to leave a review on Amazon. Reviews help authors like me and also help readers like you find books they'll like. REVIEW ON AMAZON US. If you live elsewhere, leave a review on your country's Amazon book page!

If you would like to know when the next Maisy book will be published, please join the Readers' Club. Copy and paste this URL.:

https://dashboard.mailerlite.com/forms/63788/58365061058528284/share to join.

And how about trying the next Maisy Malone book? What's it about? Well... In this cozy mystery, silent film actress, Maisy Malone takes on the LAPD, when Bartender Charlie Quinn is found dead in the basement holding cell at the Los Angeles Police Department's Central Station. The police were the first suspects for his death. The LA County Coroner ruled Quinn died by accident. Maisy Malone wasn't buying the coroner's verdict, so she decided to prove the real cause for Quinn's death. With the help of comedy film star Mabel Normand and star vaudeville mime Charlie Chaplin, Maisy tracked down the truth and proved Quinn's death was actually **MURDER IN THE FIRST REEL.**

Get the book here: MURDER IN THE FIRST REEL: A Maisy Malone Mystery: Names, Larry D: 9780910937849: Amazon.com: Books.

Larry Names – Wisconsin

REVIEWS

"I won this book through the Goodreads First Reads Program, and I couldn't put it down! I'd never read any of Larry Names' work before, so I wasn't quite sure of what to expect but I certainly enjoyed this fun read. Usually, I'm pretty good at guessing endings of mystery novels, but this one kept me on my toes right up until the last page. The characters are all likable. (However, Maisy's catchphrase, "Fair enough," did get on my nerves a little after hearing her say it so many times.) Part of what I enjoyed most is that many members of the book's cast were indeed real-life silent movie actors. That concept is part of what originally drew me to the novel - the inclusion of Mabel Normand and Mack Sennett - along with the setting in the early Hollywood motion picture business. Knowing what I know about the real-life Keystone studio I would love to see Maisy Malone return in another mystery featuring the already established cast and crew along with newcomers to the motion picture business such as Charlie Chaplin, Harold Lloyd, and Fatty Arbuckle. Here's to hoping!"

Kindle Reader, Amazon.com

"Maisy Malone comes to Hollywood to become an actress in the moving picture industry in 1912. From the moment I read her dialogue I could see and hear Mae West in my mind's eye. When you meet Mabel Normand and Maisy together you see two giggling teenage girls sharing confidences.
With each character Larry Names developed you can get a vision of a bygone era. An era he richly enhanced with glimpses of the period such as the police use of the "Indian Motorcycle" or the building construction use of "Sears Catalogue Home Plans" or the extras bench where the movie extra would sit hoping to be used in what was being filmed that day.
The mystery is the quality of Agatha Christie or Sir Conan Doyle, you may remember "Maisy is Sherlock's smarter sister "Shirley". " I enjoyed this story immensely and hope that the "sleuth" Maisy will appear again to solve another mystery."

ABOUT THE AUTHOR

Larry Names has had 45 titles published to date, 28 novels, and the remainder non-fiction all dealing with sports teams or sports figures. He is a recognized authority on the Green Bay Packers, Chicago Cubs and Chicago White Sox. He resides in central Wisconsin with his wife Peg on a family farm that has been in his wife's family since 1854. They have a son, Torry and a daughter, Tegan.

Larry has four children from his first marriage: daughter Sigrid, an author in her own rite; son Paul; daughter Kristin, an award-winning screenwriter; and daughter Sonje. He also has 17 grandchildren and two great-grandchildren.

The author was born in Mishawaka, Indiana and has lived in nine different states during his life and went to 11 schools growing up and three colleges after serving his country in the Navy. He is an avid researcher, genealogist, and traveler.

For more information about Larry Names and his books, go to
www.larrynames.com

"Like" Larry Names on his Facebook Fan page at:
https://www.facebook.com/LarryNames/

Larry is available for interviews, book signings, book talks, etc. Please contact him through the website.

LARRY NAMES
Book List
NON-FICTION
LAMBEAU YEARS, THE, PART ONE, **THE HISTORY OF THE**
GREEN BAY PACKERS, VOL. 1
LAMBEAU YEARS, THE, PART TWO, **THE HISTORY OF THE**
GREEN BAY PACKERS, VOL. 2
LAMBEAU YEARS THE, PART THREE, **THE HISTORY OF THE**
GREEN BAY PACKERS, VOL. 3
SHAMEFUL YEARS. THE, **THE HISTORY OF THE GREEN BAY**
PACKERS, VOL. 4
LOMBARDI'S DESTINY, PART ONE, **THE HISTORY OF THE**
GREEN BAY PACKERS, VOL. 5
BURY MY HEART AT WRIGLEY FIELD: THE HISTORY OF THE
CHICAGO CUBS
-WHEN THE CUBS WERE THE WHITE STOCKINGS, PART ONE
GREEN BAY PACKERS FACTS & TRIVIA, 1ST EDITION
GREEN BAY PACKERS FACTS & TRIVIA, 2ND EDITION
GREEN BAY PACKERS FACTS & TRIVIA, 3RD EDITION
GREEN BAY PACKERS FACTS & TRIVIA, 4TH EDITION
CHICAGO WHITE SOX FACTS & TRIVIA
OUT AT HOME BY MILT PAPPAS, WAYNE MAUSSER AND LARRY
NAMES
HOME PLATE BY STEVE TROUT, DAVE CAMPBELL, AND LARRY
NAMES
DEAR PETE: THE LIFE OF PETE ROSE

FICTION
SHAMAN'S SECRET, THE
LEGEND OF EAGLE CLAW, THE
BOSE
BOOMTOWN
COWBOY CONSPIRACY
PROSPECTING FOR MURDER
TWICE DEAD
THE OSWALD REFLECTION
IRONCLADS: MAN-OF-WAR
IRONCLADS: TIDES-OF-WAR
TEGAN O'MALLEY – THE TRAVELER IN TIME
TEGAN O'MALLEY – STOWAWAY ON TITANIC
A TWO REEL MURDER – STARRING MACK SENNETT & MABEL
NORMAND – A MAISY MALONE MYSTERY
MURDER ON RATTLESNAKE ISLAND – STARRING MACK
SENNETT & MABEL NORMAND – A MAISY MALONE MYSTERY

With others
HUNTER'S ORANGE

PK FACTOR, THE
As Bryce Harte/Larry Names
CREED #1: CREED/A TEXAS CREED
CREED #2: WANTED/TEXAS PAYBACK
CREED #3: POWDERKEG/TEXAS POWDERKEG
CREED #4: CREED'S WAR/KENTUCKY PRIDE
CREED #5: MISSOURI GUNS
CREED #6: TEXAN'S HONOR
CREED #7: BETRAYED/TEXAS FREEDOM
CREED #8: COLORADO PREY
CREED #9: CHEYENNE JUSTICE
CREED #10: ARKANSAS RAIDERS
CREED #11: BOSTON MOUNTAIN RENEGADES
AUDIOBOOKS
CREED #1: SLATER CREED, THE
CREED #2: TEXAS PAYBACK
CREED #3: POWDERKEG
CREED #4: KENTUCKY PRIDE
CREED #5: MISSOURI GUNS
CREED #6: TEXAN'S HONOR
CREED #7: TEXAS FREEDOM
CREED #8: COLORADO PREY
CREED #9: CHEYENNE JUSTICE
CREED #10: ARKANSAS RAIDERS
CREED #11: BOSTON MOUNTAIN RENEGADES
IRONCLADS: THE TIDES OF WAR
A TWO REEL MURDER – STARRING MACK SENNETT & MABEL
NORMAND – A MAISY MALONE MYSTERY
OSWALD REFLECTION, THE
PROSPECTING FOR MURDER
SHAMAN'S SECRET, THE
BOSE
BOOMTOWN

KINDLE EDITIONS
THE OSWALD REFLECTION
BURY MY HEART AT WRIGLEY FIELD: THE HISTORY OF THE
CHICAGO CUBS
-WHEN THE CUBS WERE THE WHITE STOCKINGS, PART ONE
PROSPECTING FOR MURDER
A TWO REEL MURDER–STARRING MACK SENNETT & MABEL
NORMAND – A MAISY MALONE MYSTERY
TEGAN O'MALLEY – THE TRAVELER IN TIME
TEGAN O'MALLEY – STOWAWAY ON TITANIC
IRONCLADS: TIDES OF WAR
CREED #1: A TEXAS CREED
CREED #2: TEXAS PAYBACK

CREED #3: TEXAS POWDERKEG

CREED #4: KENTUCKY PRIDE

CREED #5: MISSOURI GUNS

CREED #6: TEXAN'S HONOR

CREED #7: TEXAS FREEDOM

CREED #8: COLORADO PREY

CREED #9: CHEYENNE JUSTICE

CREED #10: ARKANSAS RAIDERS

CREED #11: BOSTON MOUNTAIN RENAGES

LAMBEAU YEARS, THE, PART ONE, THE HISTORY OF THE GREEN BAY PACKERS, VOL. 1

LAMBEAU YEARS, THE, PART TWO, THE HISTORY OF THE GREEN BAY PACKERS, VOL. 2

LAMBEAU YEARS THE, PART THREE, THE HISTORY OF THE GREEN BAY PACKERS, VOL. 3

SHAMEFUL YEARS. THE, THE HISTORY OF THE GREEN BAY PACKERS, VOL. 4

LOMBARDI'S DESTINY, PART ONE, THE HISTORY OF THE GREEN BAY PACKERS, VOL. 5

COMING SOON!

LOMBARDI'S DESTINY, PART TWO, THE HISTORY OF THE GREEN BAY PACKERS, VOL. 6

www.ingramcontent.com/pod-product-compliance
Lightning Source LLC
Chambersburg PA
BHW071142170626
809CB00002B/738